# Killing The Elite

*Anonymous*

Books by Anonymous –

The Book With No Name
The Eye of the Moon
The Devil's Graveyard
The Book of Death
The Red Mohawk
Sanchez: A Christmas Carol
The Plot to Kill the Pope
The Day It Rained Blood
The Greatest Trick the Devil Ever Pulled
Showdown With the Devil
Killing the Elite

*And on the eighth day God said, "I hope there will be billionaires."*
*Then he laughed, for he had created sarcasm.*

Anonymous

**One**

<u>Part One – The Coat</u>

Rueben Donaldson's earpiece buzzed. It was a safe bet Martin Rossman's had buzzed too. The two men were standing guard outside their boss's hotel room in matching grey suits, dark sunglasses, earpieces, and guns holstered snug against ribcages. Both men had years of military training behind them. Donaldson, early forties, had wiry brown hair and weathered skin from his time serving overseas. Rossman, mid-thirties, was slimmer, tanned, bald. In response to the buzz, the two men shared a concerned look.

That high-pitched buzz meant it was time for action. Proper, serious action. Donaldson's heart pounded. He'd waited a long time for a moment like this.

"Help!"

That one word sealed the deal. This wasn't fake. The voice came through loud and clear in Donaldson's ear, and no doubt Rossman's too.

Donaldson whipped a keycard from his pocket and sliced it through the reader on the door. He held the handle, ready to jerk it open the moment it unlocked. Red light became green. Door unlocked. In they charged, guns drawn.

The sight that greeted the bodyguards as they entered the room was far from what either of them expected. There was no intruder. The president of the United States was standing alone in the lounge of his penthouse in a black bathrobe with gold trims. His gown was open, revealing a pair of white boxers. He was frantically tying it together.

'There's someone in here!' he said, panic etched into his face.

Rossman charged off to search the other rooms in the suite, his gun leading the way.

*Find the threat.*

Donaldson scanned the lounge, corner to corner, floor to ceiling. He kept his gun pointed at the floor, ready to lift and fire as soon as he saw the intruder. Rossman shouted "Clear," from the first room, then the second. Still no sign of the uninvited guest.

Was the president losing his mind? It was possible. The guy was fucking old, and he did ramble a bit, plus without his camera-makeup on he looked like the living dead, even on a good day.

'Where is he, Mister President?' Donaldson asked, his eyes still searching the lounge. Rossman was in the bathroom now.

'I can't see him,' the president replied. 'But he's here. I know he is.'

Donaldson really wanted to say, "What?" but feared it would sound disrespectful. Something more tactful was required. 'In this room?' he asked.

'Shut the place down!' the president bleated. 'You can't let him escape.'

THUD!

Donaldson heard it and spun around. No one there. He'd felt something though. A mild breeze like someone rushing past him towards the entrance.

'What the fuck was that?' he said, inadvertently verbalising his thoughts.

'It's him,' said the president. 'He got out! He's in the hallway. Get him!'

Donaldson rushed through the open door back into the hallway. There was nothing straight ahead except for a door to the fire exit. He turned to his right and pointed his gun down the hallway. No one there. One-eighty-degree turn. No one that way either.

Martin Rossman joined Donaldson in the hallway and did the same bloody thing, pointing his gun at nothing while swivelling around. But then the president finally did the decent thing.

'HE'S INVISIBLE!' he shouted. 'GO GET HIM!'

In any normal situation Donaldson and Rossman would be throwing looks at each other, "knowing looks" that said, "*he's fucking lost it*". But this was the president. Etiquette decreed that he be cut some slack.

'You take the stairs,' said Rossman. 'I got the elevator.'

Without another word, or any kind of debate, Rossman charged off down the hallway towards the elevators. Donaldson sprinted over to the fire door, burst through it into a cold, grey stairwell and began his descent. Chasing an invisible man. Forget the weird stuff in the past, this was fucking stupid.

The initial excitement of hearing the buzz in his earpiece had faded. This was a nonsensical, wild goose chase, with no fucking goose. Shit, maybe it was a training drill, or the president playing a practical joke. Problem was, the president had no idea how to play a practical joke. Not a good one anyway.

Donaldson reached the bottom of the first flight of stairs and stopped on the landing. That's when he heard it. The pounding of feet on the stairs below.

But there was no one there. No one visible anyway. Just an empty stairwell. What the fuck?

'MOTHERFUCKER!' Donaldson yelled at the stairwell. 'I'm coming to get you!'

He backed up his brave war-cry by pointing his gun down at nothing in particular. They never taught this at the academy. How to shoot an invisible man. Donaldson took aim anyway.

BANG!

Just a warning shot. He couldn't fire too many. He'd probably woken up the whole hotel just with that one shot.

*Keep chasing.*

He bounded down the steps two at a time, his feet on autopilot. It was hard to hear the other person's footsteps beneath the sound of his own. With any luck he'd catch up with the invisible bastard. It was possible. There was no guarantee that the invisible person was young and fit. He or she could be old and slow. But what if they were armed? How the fuck do you know if an invisible person is carrying a weapon? Does the weapon become invisible too? *Fucking academy.* This needed to be added to the curriculum. Donaldson concluded that the person had to be unarmed. And naked? Possibly naked. Fuck it. How the fuck should a bodyguard know the answers to any of this shit?

After running down six flights of stairs, he stopped again on a landing and cocked his ear. The other person's feet were still going. In fact, the fucker seemed to have put some distance between himself and Donaldson. Like, maybe three floors. Bastard.

'FREEZE!' Donaldson yelled.

Ignored. Sonofabitch! Second warning shot coming up.

BANG!

Ricochet off a banister.

Fuck. Duck!

No more warning shots. Donaldson started running again. Bloody stairwell and its stupid ricocheting. Who designed this fucking thing anyway? Stairwells were stupid.

He slowed down a little as he came closer to the bottom of the stairs. He'd made his way down eighteen floors. Eighteen fucking floors.

And then a breakthrough.

The emergency fire door on the ground floor rattled. The invisible fucker couldn't get it open. The silver handle that stretched across the width of the door was wobbling as the invisible person pounded on it in an attempt to open it.

Donaldson rounded the stairs on the second floor. He was close. 'FREEZE! OR I'LL SHOOT!'

CRACK!

The fucking emergency door flew open. It was dark outside but a small shaft of light from a streetlamp filtered into the stairwell, along with a cool breeze.

'Fuck!'

Donaldson heard that for sure. It was a man's voice. An invisible man just said, "fuck". But why?

'Shit!'

Fuck and shit. This guy had some vocabulary. Not dissimilar to Donaldson's inner monologue.

But then in a microsecond the situation changed. The intruder was there, in the doorway. Visible. Just for a second. A blur dressed in red. And then he was gone again. Into the night. Running. Running but still visible.

Donaldson rounded the last landing and hurried down the final steps so fast he could have joined the Riverdance troupe. The fire door was open. Stuck underneath it on the floor was a translucent coat with black and white lines fuzzing through it like the lines on an old home video recording. Donaldson was struggling for breath but he staggered over to the door, gun pointed, ready to shoot. He stepped out into a back alley. Nothing that way. One-eighty-degree turn. Skinny guy. Red tracksuit. Big black van.

'FREEZE!'

Ignored. The skinny guy dived into the van via a side door.

BANG!

Damn! Missed him. Hit the side of the van.

Screeching tyres.

Four more shots fired. Hit nothing. Not even a fucking tyre.

*"Why did I shout FREEZE? I'm not Keanu Reeves. This isn't Speed. Or Point Break. You fuckwit!"*

Despondent, Donaldson bent over to catch his breath. The translucent coat. It was under his feet. He reached down and picked it up. It felt like nothing he'd ever touched before. It was like stroking a thousand wet bees. And it was long, like a bathrobe. What the fuck was it?

He tucked his gun back into its holster inside his jacket. The gunfire had definitely woken a few people up. That was confirmed when a fire alarm sounded. A moment later Martin Rossman burst through a door from the lobby and joined Donaldson in the stairwell. Elevator shmelevator. Running was quicker.

'Did you get him?' Rossman asked.

Donaldson shook his head. 'No,' he said, holding up the coat. 'But I got this.'

'What the fuck is that?'
'I think it's an invisible coat.'

## Two

'I don't know what to make of it,' said Rueben Donaldson. 'I'm guessing when you put it on, it makes you invisible?'

The president held the coat in his hand. He shook his head. 'Invisible coats. I hope this isn't the Russians.' He looked up at Donaldson. 'I don't suppose by any chance you got the guy's phone?'

It was an odd question to ask, but Donaldson did what he always did when the president asked him a question. He answered it truthfully and without judgement. 'No, sir. I was lucky to get the coat. I think he got it stuck under the fire door. He left it and jumped into a van that was waiting for him.'

'Fuck. I think that piece-of-shit was filming me. Or he was about to.'

The president walked over to the sofa in the middle of the penthouse suite's lounge and slumped down into it. He was still wearing his bathrobe, and still having trouble keeping it tied together. After rearranging it and fidgeting around to get comfortable, he picked up a remote and switched the television on. He was greeted by a black screen, which he promptly ditched in favour of a news channel.

'Why would you think he was filming you?' Donaldson asked.

The president muted the television so he could watch the scrolling bar at the bottom which had all the breaking news updates. 'I was about to get into the shower. Then I heard this clattering sound, like someone dropping something. I looked down and saw this fucking phone on the floor. But when I reached for it, it disappeared. I know it sounds crazy, but I heard a man say, *"shit"*. That's when I realised I was dealing with someone invisible. I want this guy found. I don't know how long he was watching me for, or worse, how long he was filming me for. But I want him dead.' The president finished his rant and took a deep breath. 'Did you get a license plate for the escape vehicle?' he added.

Donaldson tapped the side of his head. 'Stored right here, sir.'

'Good, write it down somewhere.' The president clicked his fingers at Martin Rossman, who was standing behind Donaldson. 'Go find me Navan Douglas, right now.'

'Yes sir.'

Rossman left the hotel room and closed the door behind him. The president slumped back in the sofa and stared at the invisible robe he was holding in his hand. 'This is so bad,' he groaned.

'Anything else you'd like me to do, sir?' Donaldson asked.

'No. You can go back to your post. Keep quiet about this, of course. Not a word to anyone. *Anyone.*'

'Yes, sir.'

'You've done well, Rueben, thanks.'

'Yes sir, Mister President.'

As soon as Donaldson left the room, the president unmuted the TV. The reporter in the news studio broke the news that there had been gunshots heard at the hotel the president was staying in. Fucking hell. Never a quiet moment.

Barely a minute passed before there was a knock at the door, followed by the Attorney General, Navan Douglas opening it and marching in. Douglas was a tall, broad-shouldered man in his mid-fifties, with short white hair and big round spectacles that made his eyes look like marbles. He was positively youthful-looking compared to the crusty seventy-three-year-old fart who had summoned him.

'You okay, sir?' Douglas asked the old fart.

The president nodded.

'Rossman says an invisible coat. Is that right?"

The president held up the offending item.

'Holy fucknuts. Is that what I think it is?'

'I believe so. I don't know how the hell they got their hands on it, but we need to bury it somewhere.'

Douglas approached the president's sofa and reached out for the invisible coat. His boss handed it to him and turned back to watch the television.

'It feels strange, doesn't it?' said Douglas, running his hand up and down the material.

'Yeah,' the president replied with a sigh. 'We're going to need to put out a statement about the gunfire. Can you cook something up?'

'It's already done, sir,' said Douglas, still marvelling at the fibre of the coat. 'I don't believe it. We need to know who had this and where they found it.'

'You think?'

Douglas ignored the sarcasm as if he were oblivious to it. 'This is the motherfucking Coat of No Colours,' he said, announcing it like he was in an R-rated Indiana Jones movie.

'Yep.'

'Have we got any clues as to who the fuck had it?'

The president reached over to a coffee table by his sofa and picked up a glass of orange juice that had lost its youth. 'Donaldson got the license plate of the escape vehicle,' he said, taking a sip of the drink. 'That's our only lead.'

'And this guy was filming you?'

'Trying to. I don't know how much he got.'

'And what were you doing?'

The president looked across at him. 'I was watching TV.'

Douglas checked his watch. 'Right, of course. What shall we do with this coat then?'

'Bury it. Do I have to say everything twice? Make it disappear. Somewhere where no one will ever find it.'

'Hold on a second, sir. This is a big find. Maybe we could do some analysis on it? You know, see how it was made. Make some more?'

The president almost spat out some of the shitty orange juice. 'Absolutely not,' he said, placing the glass back down on the coffee table. 'Can you imagine what would happen if that coat, or any invisible coat for that matter, fell into the wrong hands? I mean look what just happened today!'

'It'd be a really useful weapon though.'

The president stood up and gave Douglas his best *serious* look. 'Exactly. And who could you trust with it? Think about it. You give it to your most trusted assassin. Then you never see him again. We've got to bury it, just like Roosevelt did when he found it. But we've got to do it better.'

'Destroy it then?'

'It *can't* be destroyed. My thoughts are, we bury it in the White House vault with the staff of Moses.'

Douglas pulled a face like he was sucking thick milkshake through a straw. 'Is it wise to have them both in the same place?'

The president pulled on his chin. 'Fuck. Oh God, I hate when you're right. Where else?'

'I'm thinking Bratwurst. General Calhoon's people have been guarding that place for years, and so far we've had no incidents.'

'Bratwurst. What else have we got there?'

'Religious artefacts. If we can place this in an uncrackable safe and take it down to Bratwurst, my feeling is it'll be buried forever. Or for our lifetimes at least.'

'Bratwurst eh?' said the president, mulling over the suggestion. 'That place is so top secret I'd forgotten it even existed until you just mentioned it. I like it. Do it.'

'Yes sir, I'll get a safe for it, then I'll have Calhoon and her people take me down there. If I like what I see, I'll bury it there.'

'Okay, great. Anything else we need to be thinking about right now?'

'There is one thing, Mister President.'

'Go on.'

'Donaldson and Rossman. They've seen the coat. They know it exists.'

The president ran his fingers through the wispy white hair on his head. 'They've gotta go. I don't want to see either of their faces again. See to it.'

'Yes, sir. I'll call Calhoon and tell her I'm coming to see her with two of your bodyguards, and that I'd like them taken care of. She has good people for that.'

The president baulked at the suggestion. 'Not those Dead Hunter people?'

'*Fuck no*, sir. She's got plenty of more discreet "in-house" operatives for a job like this, and Calhoon's smart enough not to ask any questions.'

'Good,' the president pointed his remote at the TV and switched it off. 'I'm going to take a shower. Oh, and don't forget, get the license plate from Donaldson before he's taken care of. Whoever the fuckers were who had this coat, they need to be dead. ASAP. All of them. And anyone else who knows about it.'

## Three

'This is my trailer,' said Diago, walking up to the nicest one in the park. It was a black and red custom job that outshone everything around it. He could tell Penny was not particularly impressed by it though.

'This is where you live? All the time?' she asked.

'Wait until you see the inside.'

Penny was timid. That's why Diago had picked her. Choosing a victim every night was entirely dependent on how he was feeling. If he was full of zest and vigour, he'd go for a big guy, someone who would put up a fight. But tonight, Diago was tired. It had been a long day, so when he'd set eyes on Penny, a shy, slightly frumpy, but not unattractive young woman, he knew she wouldn't put up much of a fight. He was a hundred percent certain she would be okay with the sex part. And once she was tired out from that, she'd be much easier to kill.

He opened the door to the trailer and stepped aside. 'Go on in,' he said with a smile. He noticed Penny blush. Excellent. Just where he wanted her. 'I promise you'll love it,' he said, as he ushered her inside and shut the door behind them.

He was right. Penny was up for fucking. He didn't even have to try any pretext. He just said, "Wanna fuck?" And that was all it took. He made passionate love to her, making good on his promise to treat her to the monster fuck of her young life. He knew she'd had a good time, after all, he was a buff, well-endowed six-feet-two dashingly handsome, cold-blooded male. He had a mane of long, shiny dark hair that most women would kill for. Chicks loved his hair.

After the amazing sex, Penny collapsed into the bed, a big smile on her face, happy with the world. For sure, this was the best time to kill someone. Diago was lying on his side next to her, eyeing up the flesh on her neck. She was babbling on about something or other, but he wasn't paying attention. He was just counting down in his head. Three-two-one—

Just as he was about to do the deed, his phone rang, breaking the moment. No matter. Penny was going to be riding the monster-fuck-high for a while. He had time. He could play with her a bit before he killed her. He reached over to the bedside table. (That's how awesome his trailer was. He had a fucking bedside table. A good one too. Real veneer.) He snatched his phone from the table and checked to see who was calling. The number was unknown. He answered it anyway.

'Hello.'

'It's me,' came the reply.

Diago recognised the voice. 'What do you want?'

'I've got something for you. Something big.'

'Like what?'

'Meet me outside.'

'Outside? Outside where?'

'Would ya just walk out of your fucking trailer, for fuckssake?'

'Ugh. Hold on.'

Diago leaned over and kissed Penny on the forehead. 'I'll be back in a tick,' he said.

Penny smiled, she giggled a bit too. Understandable really. She didn't know she was going to be brutally murdered in a minute.

Diago pulled on a pair of purple pants and stumbled out of his trailer into the cool night air. There was a full moon in the sky. It was peaceful too. The cold, damp grass licked the sweat off his webbed feet as he walked away from the trailer into the darkness.

'Over here!' a voice whispered.

Diago trudged over to where the voice had come from. There was no one there. Weird.

'Can you see me?'

Diago sighed. This was fucking tiresome. 'No. Where are you?'

'Exactly.'

'This isn't funny.'

And then, just like that, a man appeared right in front of him. Right out of thin air. Diago jumped back.

'How the fuck did you do that?' he asked.

The man standing before him was wearing a strange see-through coat with black and white fuzzy lines on it that looked like they might be moving. The man in the coat was Navan Douglas, the Attorney General, and a special advisor to the president. He had a big grin on his face, which was unusual for a man who was normally so serious. 'Pretty neat, huh?' Douglas said.

'What is going on with that coat?'

Douglas pulled his arms out of the strange hooded coat. He was wearing grey pants and a black shirt underneath it. As soon as the coat was off, he held it out for Diago to get a better look at it.

Diago reached out and touched it. 'I don't believe it!' he said eventually. 'Is that what I think it is?'

'It most surely is.'

'The Coat of No Colours?'

'Yup.'

'The coat Jacob gave to Benjamin?'

'Yup.'

'Where the fuck did you find it?'

Douglas looked around, checking to make sure no one was in hearing distance before answering the question. 'Last week someone wearing this coat tried to kill the president.'

'Nooooo way!'

'Uh huh. The guy got away, but one of the president's bodyguards snagged the coat.'

'That's mental. Why are you bringing it here?'

'I want you to have it.'

*Jackpot!* Diago could have kissed Douglas. 'Really?' he said, praying it wasn't a joke.

'Yes. The president asked me to bury it away where no one would ever find it. I've just come from a trip to Bratwurst with General Alexis Calhoon. She thinks we buried it there, but in fact we buried an empty safe. I kept the coat because I want you and your people to take a look at it.'

'Take a look at it? What for?'

'I want you to work out what it's made of. And then make some more.'

A grin broke out on Diago's face. 'Can I try it on?'

Douglas let Diago take the coat. 'Go nuts. It only makes you invisible when you pull the hood up. Just do it for ten seconds. Then I want to see you again.'

'Done.'

Diago slipped his arms into the sleeves of the coat. It was comfy, and it fitted like it was made for him. He pulled the hood up. Boom. Invisible. Brilliant. 'Holy fuckbeans. This is incredible. What a find!'

'Okay, take it off again,' said Douglas.

Diago marvelled at his invisibleness for a few more seconds before lowering the hood and becoming visible again. 'I'll show this to Athena and Yoga,' he said. 'They'll have an idea what to do with it.'

'Good. I want regular updates on your progress. Understood?'

'You got it.'

'And don't go using it yet. If word gets out that there's an invisible person running around, the president will know I lied to him.'

'Sure, I promise. Out of interest. If we do manage to make more of these, we can keep some, right?'

'You and your people can have one each.'

'One each?'

'Yeah. For vampires like you, an invisible coat will enable you to go out in daylight. A real treat, especially since Santa Mondega became so inhospitable to you and your kind. I know you're angry that the world leaders haven't found a new safe haven for you yet, so I thought

I'd do my bit by giving you this. But in return, I want a hundred more of them. When this president is dead, I was thinking the next president will be much more in tune with my suggestion that we use invisible coats in modern warfare.'

Diago snickered. 'You've got a twisted mind, Navan. I like it.'

'Good. Look, I gotta go. I don't want anyone seeing me round here. Keep in touch.'

'Yes, sir.'

Navan Douglas left the trailer park and headed to the nearest airport, no doubt feeling pleased with himself. His plan to create more invisible coats would be a game-changer in international warfare.

Unfortunately for Navan Douglas, Diago had other plans. First of all, he made himself invisible again, then returned to his trailer, where he tortured Penny for a few minutes, tearing pieces of skin off her body, while she screamed in terror because she had no idea what was happening. When the torture began to bore him, he lowered the hood on his invisible coat, revealing himself to her. Then he sank his vampire fangs into her neck and drank her blood before dragging her body outside with the intention of feeding her to the lions later. With that small chore done, Diago used his phone to send a message to the residents of the other nearby trailers, requesting that they attend an important meeting at midnight.

When the witching hour arrived, Diago, the ringmaster of the aptly titled "Diago's Travelling Circus", headed for the Big Top in his new coat. Every other vampire from the circus was already there, waiting in the circus ring. Acrobats, clowns, trapeze artists, knife-throwers, human cannonball midgets, all of them were present and eager to hear what the boss had to say.

In his invisible state, Diago walked into the centre of the ring unnoticed, before lowering the hood on his coat. It drew gasps from those that saw him suddenly appear as if from nothing. Everyone gathered around to hear what he had to say.

'My friends, I have great news,' Diago announced.

'What are you wearing?' asked one of the midgets.

'Don't ruin the moment,' Diago replied. 'Just shut up and listen. This unusual item of clothing I am wearing is the infamous Coat of No Colours, gifted to Benjamin by his father, Jacob.'

There were gasps from the audience. To prove he wasn't bullshitting, Diago pulled up the hood, vanishing before their eyes once again.

More gasps.

He lowered the hood again, reappearing for the benefit of the others. 'Friends, we vampires have suffered much in recent times,' he said. 'With no city of our own to live in, we have been hunted down by Scratch's people, treated like second-class citizens by the elite. But now we have this coat, new avenues are open to us. Our challenge is to find a way to replicate this coat, create many more like it, then the world will become ours. Daylight will no longer hinder our movements. With coats like this one, we can walk among humans in daylight.'

'Where did you get it?' one of the acrobats called out.

Diago smirked. 'Navan Douglas, the Attorney General just gifted this to us without the president's knowledge. I assured him we would create more for him, but by the time he finds out we've double-crossed him, all of the world's leaders will be dead. Vampires will become the new elite!'

The crowd erupted into cheers. Working in a circus sucked. Ruling the world would be much more fun.

# Four

***"Here lies Ruth Palmer, a fine woman who opened up Coldworm
Abbey to homeless people and those in need.
An angel to the people of the local community, and a devoted mother.
Rest In Peace"***

An unshaven, dark-haired man in his late thirties was standing over the gravestone, staring at it. His name was JD, aka the Bourbon Kid. The woman buried in the grave was Beth Lansbury. Ruth Palmer was an alias Beth had used to avoid being detected by the Devil. It hadn't worked. The Devil had found her. He'd laid an elaborate trap that ended with Beth stuck in the nineteenth century. Well, the Devil was now dead, killed by JD. It hadn't brought Beth back though. It would never bring her back. On either side of Beth's grave were the headstones for her children, Emma and Vincent. *JD's children.* His entire family was buried in the grounds of Coldworm Abbey.

Dark clouds permanently hovered over the graveyard, emptying rain onto anyone who visited. JD kept the hood of his long black coat pulled up over his head. It kept the rain off, but it did nothing to stop the constant pitter-patter sound.

Visiting Beth's grave was something he did once a month, depending on how busy work was. He had been staring at the gravestones for five minutes, trying to remember the faces of the people buried beneath them, when he was interrupted by a call on his cell-phone. He reached into his pocket and checked the display.

ALEXIS.

General Alexis Calhoon was one of the few people JD took calls from. He lifted the phone to his ear. 'Hey, what's up?' he asked.

'Hi, JD,' Calhoon's voice came through loud and clear over the rain. 'How's things?'

'Same as ever.'

'I've got a job for you, if you're interested?'

'I'm not.'

'I figured you'd say that, but I couldn't *not* call you about this one because it pays very well.'

JD's curiosity got the better of him. 'Go on.'

'It's not from me, and I can't vouch for the person who wants to hire you. He's rich and has friends in high places, so he was able to get a meeting with me. I can't say I really took to him, but I heard him out anyway. And like I said, the money is good on this one, so I thought I'd tell you about it, in case you wanted to take it on.'

'How much?'

'Fifty thousand dollars for a week's work.'

'I'm listening.'

'The man who wants to hire you is Antonio Rodriguez. And, erm, it's a strange request.'

'Aren't they all?'

'I guess so. He wants you to drive his daughter to school for a week.'

'You're right. That's strange. Why does he want me?'

'He's been getting anonymous threats from someone who says they're going to kill his daughter, so naturally he's worried. And because he's rich, he wants to hire the best in the world to protect his little girl. He said if you don't want the money, I'm to ask Rex if he'll do it instead.'

'How old is the girl?'

'Twelve.'

'Tell him the price is a hundred grand.'

'So you'll do it?'

'Yep, one week for one hundred grand. But tell him he's got to hire Rex as well. I don't wanna have to talk to this guy's daughter for a week. Rex can do that. I'll just drive. And make sure this guy knows if he doesn't pay, I'll kill him and all of his family, and any friends he might have.'

'Okaaaaay, I'll pass that on. Can you start tomorrow?'

'That depends. Where is it?'

'He owns a big estate in San Antonio. I'll text you all the details.'

'Okay.'

JD ended the call and then made another to his friend, Jacko. Jacko, a former bluesman, was now in charge of Purgatory, a roadside bar positioned over the gateway to Hell. Purgatory had a travel portal in the men's toilets, from which Jacko could send people to any bathroom in the world. JD had recently used the portal to travel to Coldworm Abbey. And he intended to use it to travel back to Purgatory.

'Hey, man,' said Jacko, answering the call promptly. 'Are you done?'

'I'm done. I'll be at the portal in two minutes.'

'I'll have it ready.'

JD slipped his phone back into his pocket. He took one last look down at the headstone on Ruth Palmer's grave, and said what he always said.

'See you next month.'

# Five

## Part Two – The president

Sanchez hated the president. Flake, on the other hand, thought the president was a decent guy doing a difficult job. And she was excited about meeting him in a few days' time. She couldn't remember ever feeling so proud. It was the sort of thing a person would want their parents to know about. Flake's family consisted of Sanchez and a group of psychopaths known as the Dead Hunters. The Dead Hunters were drinking in the bar area downstairs. She could hear them bickering. More to the point she could hear Elvis and Rex arguing over the rules of a card game. The two guys were in their late thirties, but partied and argued like they were much younger. Elvis's girlfriend Jasmine (who *was* much younger) usually started the arguments, although her voice was absent on this occasion. The only quiet one in the group was JD, better known to the rest of the world as the Bourbon Kid. Even on a good day, he tended to sit on his own, drinking and not talking to anyone.

Flake was upstairs in the main bedroom of the Tapioca, checking her appearance in the mirror. She was wearing a knee-length grey skirt, a white polo-neck sweater and a grey blazer that matched the skirt. She had the Eye of the Moon on a chain around her neck. The magical blue stone looked odd outside the polo neck, so she tucked it inside. It didn't make much difference though. She still wasn't sure if she looked okay because this wasn't a normal look for her at all. Waitress outfits, cop outfits, jeans and a T-shirt, those were the things she was most comfortable in, even though her days as a waitress and a cop were long behind her. Sensible shoes though. Flake wasn't one for high heels, she was a sneakers or flat shoes kinda gal. Her mousy brown hair was tied up in a bun, but she wasn't sure if that was the right thing to do either. Did women wear their hair down when they met the president? Who the fuck knows? Flake's meeting with the most powerful man in the world wasn't for another few days, but she wanted to be sure she dressed appropriately.

The fashion conversation she was having in her head was interrupted by the sound of her boyfriend Sanchez somewhere nearby. He was singing, "Do they know it's Christmas?" by Band Aid. As well as getting most of the lyrics wrong, he was deliberately replacing the word *Christmas* with his favourite word *breakfast*. It was an unsubtle hint aimed at Flake, reminding her that his breakfast was late.

Sanchez strolled into the bedroom. He was wearing the same thing as usual, black pants and a stained white shirt with a black waistcoat. He looked like an older, out-of-shape Han Solo, like really out-of-shape, and a lot shorter, with black hair that was kind of thick, but also thinning out in readiness for going bald on top. He stopped singing when he saw Flake checking herself out in the mirror.

'What the fuck? Are we getting a visit from the tax man or something?' he asked.

Flake turned around to face him. 'I'm thinking of wearing this for our meeting with the president,' she said, hoping for a compliment.

'Why? Are you hoping to get a job as his secretary?' Sanchez asked.

'No, but we need to dress smart. I'm thinking we need to go shopping to get you a suit too. You can't wear that replica from the *Twins* movie.'

'Why not?'

'Well, for starters it's supposed to have been returned to Domino's party store. And secondly, it's outdated.'

Sanchez scoffed. 'Yeah, right. Outdated, my ass.'

Flake sighed. 'How do I look anyway? Do I look smart?'

Sanchez shrugged. 'I suppose so. If you were my secretary, looking like that, I'd sexually harass you, for sure.'

That was likely to be the best compliment she'd get from Sanchez. It didn't really count though, because he'd badger her for sex if she was dressed like a homeless person. 'That's very sweet of you,' Flake replied. 'I'll see what Jasmine thinks.'

'She'll tell you to lose the skirt, the jacket and the polo-neck, but you can't ask her anyway. I'm pretty sure she's not here.'

Flake sighed again. Without Jasmine, Elvis was probably her best bet. The Elvis Presley lookalike was always full of compliments. And if not him, then Rex the Hell's Angel might say something nice. He was a sweetheart most of the time.

She headed downstairs. Elvis and Rex were playing a card game at one of the round tables in the middle of the saloon. They looked like they'd been out drinking all night. Elvis was wearing a black suit with just a white vest underneath the jacket. The vest was askew and rumpled. His normally well-styled black hair was unkempt and strands of it were hanging down over his face while he checked his cards. Rex was wearing blue jeans and a black waistcoat that showed off his giant muscles. His wavy brown hair was tied up in a black bandana. The big giveaway that he'd drunk too much was the position of the eyepatch he wore over his missing eye. It was a couple of inches out of place.

But then there was JD, sitting on his own in a corner a few tables away. He was dressed all in black, and still wearing his long hooded coat even though he was indoors. He looked relatively sober and unusually approachable, which was more than could be said for the other two, who were quibbling over the rules of their (probably made up) card game. It was only eight o'clock in the morning. The Tapioca wasn't open to the public yet, but Elvis and Rex had helped themselves to some bottles of beer from the fridges behind the bar.

'Where's Jasmine?' Flake asked.

'She's not here,' Elvis replied without even looking up. He placed a card down on the table.

'Well, where is she?'

'Don't ask,' said Rex. He didn't look up either. This was a serious card game.

'If you two want any more free drinks you're going to have to tell me where she is.'

Rex glanced up. 'She's gone on a date.'

'A date?' The sentence made little sense. Jasmine and Elvis were a couple, so why the hell was Jasmine on a date? 'Who with?' Flake asked.

Elvis placed another card down on the table and swivelled around on his chair. 'Remember she had an agreement with God that he'd take her to a basketball game, or something like that?'

Flake's jaw dropped. 'She's gone on a date with God?'

'Yeah,' Elvis replied, still not noticing her new outfit. 'Any more questions?'

'I'm about to make breakfast. You guys want any?'

Rex replied for both of them. 'We've been to Dirty Marie's.'

Dirty Marie was known for her early morning breakfasts. They were for drunk people who stayed out all night. Flake saw her as a rival, an inferior rival, but a rival nonetheless. Elvis and Rex could fuck off if they thought Flake was making them another breakfast any time soon. The traitors.

'We could do with some more beers though,' Elvis said as he started dealing out the cards for a new hand of whatever shit game they were playing.

'Help yourself. You know where they are.'

No one had even bothered to comment on Flake's outfit. Ignorant fuckers. She looked over at JD. Eye contact. He even smiled. Sort of.

'Nice outfit,' he said. 'Suits you.'

'Thank you. It's for my meeting with the president on Friday. Can I get you anything? Or have you been to Filthy Marie's too?'

'Dirty Marie's,' Rex said, correcting her.

Flake ignored him and approached JD's table. 'You okay?' she asked him.

He gestured for her to lean in close like he wanted to whisper something to her that he didn't want the others to hear. She moved in and leaned her head down. He spoke softly in her ear.

'Lose the bun. You look better with your hair down, or in a ponytail.'

Flake was pleasantly taken aback. 'You think?'

'Yeah. The bun just ain't you.'

She reached back and untied the bun, then shook her hair to free it down to her shoulders. 'You didn't answer my question,' she said.

'That's much better.'

'Are you okay? You've been kinda quiet lately.'

'I'm fine.'

'You're thinking about Beth aren't you?'

JD broke off the eye contact and stared down at his glass of bourbon. 'It's not easy losing someone you thought you'd be with forever.'

'She was the luckiest woman in the world. She knew that. Don't you forget it.'

'Yeah.'

'You know, you probably don't wanna hear this, but there might be someone else out there for you.'

'It wouldn't matter if there was.'

'Why not?'

'Everyone I care about gets killed. That's my curse.'

It seemed like he was about to go into a fit of depression so Flake tried to lighten things a little by shoving him playfully on the shoulder, something only she could get away with. 'If that was true everyone here would be dead too,' she said with a smile that she hoped he would reciprocate. 'Now, I know exactly how to cheer you up. I'll make you one of my epic breakfasts. How does a fry-up sound? I've got bacon, eggs, sausages, mushrooms—'

'Thanks, but no.'

'I make the best breakfasts, you know.'

JD smiled. 'There's more to you than just a good breakfast, Flake.'

It was Flake's turn to smile, and almost blush. 'It's what I do best though. You know, you kill people, Jasmine gets naked, Elvis does his Elvis thing, Rex has his magnetic hand, Sanchez is the luckiest man alive, and me, I do the best breakfasts in the world.'

'You surely do. What's on the menu today?' he asked, probably humouring her.

'I've been working on something new for Sanchez. A special breakfast sandwich. Maybe you'd like to try it first? Take it for a test drive?'

He contemplated the offer for a moment then answered with genuine enthusiasm. 'Go on, I'll be your guinea pig. Don't fuck it up though.'

'When have I ever fucked up a breakfast?'

Sanchez came thundering down the stairs behind the bar. 'Flake, I want two extra sausages today,' he called over to her. 'And I think I'll have some beans too. My gut's a bit bloated so the beans might help shift a bit of the trapped wind.'

Flake turned away from JD. 'Okay honey,' she called back. 'But I was going to try out my new breakfast sandwich on you today.'

'I don't want a *new* breakfast,' Sanchez replied, recoiling in horror. 'Can you just do the regular please? For fuck's sake! I'm fucking starving.'

'I'll get right on it.' Flake looked back at JD. 'You still want the new sandwich?'

'You bet.'

While Flake headed to the kitchen to get started, Sanchez strolled over to the table where Rex and Elvis were playing cards.

'What game are you playing?' he asked.

'You can't play,' said Elvis.

'Why not?'

'Because we're not playing Snap,' said Rex. 'It would take too long to teach you the rules to this game.'

Before Sanchez could grumble about being left out, the door to the ladies washroom opened and Jasmine strolled out. She was wearing a pair of blue cut-off jeans and a white crop top that showed off her silky-smooth brown skin. Her long dark hair was tied back in a ponytail. Sanchez soaked it all in, counted to three in his head and then looked away. Experience had taught him that if he was still staring at Jasmine after four seconds, Flake would appear from nowhere and clout him round the ear.

'Hi guys,' Jasmine beamed. 'Ooh, cards, can I play?'

'They're not playing Snap,' Sanchez informed her.

'Why not?'

'How was your date?' Elvis asked, placing his cards down on the table to signify he'd had enough of playing.

'We watched a game of basketball in Australia,' Jasmine said. She walked up to Elvis and kissed him on the cheek. 'It was fun.'

'And?'

'And I gave him a handjob.'

Rex spat some beer out onto the table. 'You jerked off God?'

Jasmine slid down onto Elvis's knee and wrapped an arm around his shoulder. 'Yeah, that was the whole point of going. We re-enacted the scene from *Coming To America* where Patrice tries to jerk off Eddie Murphy at the basketball game. Only we properly did it, until we were asked to leave.'

'Did God look like Patrick Swayze?' Sanchez asked.

'No,' Jasmine replied, rolling her eyes. 'He looked like Eddie Murphy. Keep up.'

Elvis stroked Jasmine's hair away from her face and spoke softly in her ear. 'Is that all you did?'

She nodded. 'Yeah, Mrs God won't let him have penetrative sex with anyone, so he said a handjob was all we could do. That way he hasn't actually cheated on her.'

'Mrs God?' said Sanchez, incredulous. 'Who's Mrs God?'

Jasmine rolled her eyes again. 'Jesus's mom, you idiot.'

'I thought Mary was the mother of Jesus?' said Rex.

'Pfft,' said Jasmine. 'I suppose you think Joseph was his dad? Jesus, son of Joseph. Honestly, and you're supposed to be God's bounty hunter!'

'Is Elvis okay with this?' Sanchez asked.

After an awkward silence, Elvis replied. 'I'm fine with it.'

Jasmine kissed him on the cheek again and made him an offer. 'In the sake of fairness, I'm totally cool with you jerking someone off if you want to get even.'

'I'm not jerking anyone off,' Elvis said, dismissing the idea before anyone could make jokes.

'I was kidding,' said Jasmine. 'You can sleep with anyone you like. Only once though. Then we're even.'

Elvis weighed up the idea. 'Okay,' he said nodding. Then he called out to the kitchen. 'Yo, Flake, you up for it?'

'Dream on, loser!' came the reply from within the kitchen.

Sanchez put his hands on his hips and glared at Elvis. 'I'm right here you know,' he said.

'I know,' said Elvis. 'I was just keeping you in the loop.'

'Well, stay away from Flake,' Sanchez said in his toughest voice.

'Or what?' said Elvis.

'Or she'll kick you in the nuts.'

Rex sighed. 'Are we playing cards anymore or what?'

'Is it Snap?' Jasmine asked.

'No,' said Rex. 'It ain't Snap.'

'Fine.' Jasmine jumped up from Elvis's knee and headed back to the washroom. Rex picked up the deck of cards and started shuffling them. Before he had a chance to deal any out, a phone buzzed on the table in front of him.

'Hold on a sec,' he said, putting the cards down. 'I've gotta take this.' He answered the call. 'Hello, General, what can I do for you?'

Elvis looked up. 'Is that Calhoon?'

Rex nodded. For the next thirty seconds or so, he engaged in a discussion with Calhoon about a job she was offering him. When the call ended, he eyed JD suspiciously.

'Calhoon says you insisted on me joining you on a bodyguard job?' he said.

'Uh huh,' JD replied.

'You're lucky it pays well,' said Rex. 'Otherwise I wouldn't be going.'

# Six

Sanchez hated being kept waiting. He and Flake had been in the lobby of the Poseidon Hotel for nearly an hour. The place was huge. The carpets were red with a weird black pattern on them, like snakes crawling across the floor. There were armchairs dotted around with people sitting in them reading books. Sanchez and Flake were on a black leather sofa that backed onto a giant pillar in the middle of the room. Porters, waiters, chambermaids, concierges and management types were hurrying around like their jobs were on the line. Yet for all the scurrying around no one had thought to offer Sanchez any free snacks, which was annoying him no end. Surely these people could see he was important? He was wearing a proper suit. Not one from a party store. A proper fucking suit. Made to measure. Black pants, black jacket, white shirt, red rose in the jacket pocket. Smart new black shoes. Christ he'd even combed his hair, what was left of it. In his mind he looked a bit like Marlon Brando in the Godfather, but with better hair. Even Flake was in on the act. She was dolled up in a new grey skirt-suit with a white polo-neck sweater. Her hair was down too, which was unusual. It made her look way out of Sanchez's league.

'Who does this asshole think he is?' Sanchez grumbled. 'We've been waiting almost an hour, for fuckssake!'

'He's the president of the United States. He can make us wait as long as he likes.'

'No he can't. Another five minutes and I'm going home.'

'You are not,' Flake hissed. 'The president might not be able to make you wait here, but I sure as hell will.'

There was a steely determination in Flake's voice. Sanchez knew it well. He was going to have to stay put. Not that he was really going to go home in five minutes anyway. After all, it's not every day you get to meet the president. Sanchez had once been a president himself for half a day (president of Santa Mondega, or mayor as other people had called him at the time), so he knew how stressful the job could be, what with all the assassination attempts and stuff. He'd lost count of the number of people who tried to kill him during his brief one-day tenure.

'Look, here comes Alexis,' said Flake, elbowing Sanchez in the ribs.

General Alexis Calhoon, a powerful black woman in her fifties, strode out of an elevator and headed in their direction. She was wearing a smart black jacket and matching skirt, and she was holding a thick hardback book. She smiled at Flake as she approached.

'Good morning,' she said. 'How are you both?'

'I ate some peanuts earlier,' Sanchez replied. 'And they're messing with my guts, so can you tell us how much longer we've got to wait? I need to decide whether to go to the toilet now, or after we meet with old shit-fer-brains.'

'We're fine, thanks,' Flake added.

Calhoon sighed. 'Good. The president is ready to see you now. He's had a bit of a morning. I'm sure you've seen the news.'

'If you mean the thing about the two dead senators and the creepy one from the British government, then yes we have,' said Sanchez. 'Are their deaths connected?'

Calhoon forced half a smile. 'It's not just those three,' she said. 'A whole bunch of people have been assassinated overnight. Five of them were senators, but we're just hearing the Italian and Dutch leaders are dead too.'

'Five senators?' said Flake, ignoring the bit about the foreign leaders. 'I thought it was just Baynard and Palmer?'

'That's all CNN are reporting, but Fox just got the news about Babcock. He's been cut open from chin to balls, and that's not the worst of it.' She lowered her voice. 'Between you and me, it's looking like a coordinated terrorist attack. Politicians on all sides are being taken down, not just here, all over the world.' Calhoon caught sight of a hotel porter looking her way. 'Anyway, enough about that. The president will see you now, but obviously it's going to be a bit brief. Chances are, if you're in there for more than ten minutes, he'll get a call to say someone else is dead. This is looking like something really big.'

Sanchez grimaced. 'I hope Kevin Kline is okay.'

'I'm sure he'll be fine,' said Calhoon, graciously. 'Now, there's one other thing before we go up to see him. I've been asked by the Attorney General Navan Douglas to present you with your medals.'

'Why can't the president do it?' Sanchez asked. 'Is he too lazy?'

'No, but as I said, there's been a lot going on today.' She held up the hardback book she had been keeping by her side and flipped it open. There were no pages inside. It actually contained a thick blue felt material with four gold rings embedded in it. 'There's one for each of you,' she said. 'Elvis and Jasmine already have theirs. Douglas thought it would be nice if you two were wearing yours when you met the president.'

Sanchez reached into the box-disguised-as-a-book like he was reaching into a box of chocolates. His fingers hovered over the rings while he decided which one to take.

'That one's yours,' said Calhoon pointing at the biggest one.

Sanchez snatched the ring out and took a look at it. It was engraved with his name on one side and an American flag on the other.

'Awesome,' he said, gazing at it. He was about to impress Calhoon with his impersonation of Gollum from Lord of the Rings but his phone buzzed in his pocket, ruining the moment. He cupped the ring in one hand while fishing out his phone and checking the display with the other. It was a call from Elvis, which was certainly more appealing than listening to Calhoon. Sanchez excused himself and wandered off to a quiet area of the lobby to take the call.

Flake wanted to berate Sanchez for being rude, but Calhoon was about to give her a gold ring, so she let it slide. Calhoon picked out a ring and handed it to Flake. It was similar to Sanchez's ring, except it was smaller and had Flake's name on it. It fitted perfectly on her middle finger. It was the second best piece of jewellery Flake had ever owned, the first being the Eye of the Moon, which was on a chain around her neck, concealed behind her polo-neck sweater.

'Well deserved,' said Calhoon with a generous smile. 'I think you're ready to go see the president now.'

Flake and Calhoon waited a short while for Sanchez to finish his private phone conversation, then the three of them headed over to a bank of elevators.

'Who were you talking to?' Flake whispered to Sanchez as they waited for a lift to come down.

'It was Elvis.'

'What did he want?'

'He wanted to know the best place to hide out in Santa Mondega.'

'What for?'

'I'm not entirely sure.'

'The best place is the Tapioca, surely?' Flake suggested.

'No it's not.'

'Then it must be the tunnel underneath the Tapioca, the one that leads to the church.'

'Wrong again, Flake. It's Chinatown.'

'Chinatown? What? Who is he hiding from anyway? And what's he done now?'

Sanchez nudged Flake in the ribs. 'Elevator's here,' he said.

The discussion about Elvis and Chinatown ended as the two of them joined Calhoon in the confined space of the elevator carriage.

They were minutes away from meeting the most powerful man in the world.

## Seven

The president sighed. This was going to be one of those days. Being president sucked balls. All those plans he had for making the country and the world a better place for rich people were going to have to wait. It was obvious why no leader in history ever managed to keep all their promises. There was always some bloody disaster going on that needed to be dealt with. And then there was all the fucking meetings. Christ, the meetings pissed him off, especially the ones with the general public. Pretending to be interested in their feeble achievements made him want to cut his ears off sometimes. At least the hotel rooms were good though. Being away from the White House was the best part of the job. But even then, there was no escape from the bloody meetings. He picked up an espresso from the coffee table in front of him and threw the drink down his throat. Life without caffeine was impossible in this job.

'Who am I seeing at ten-thirty?'

'It's actually eleven-fifteen now, Mister President,' said Navan Douglas. 'But you're seeing two of the people who helped rescue Arizona a few months back, remember?'

'Arizona?'

'Your illegitimate daughter.'

'Oh, right, yes, her. And who are these people that rescued her?'

Navan Douglas patted his boss on the shoulder to show he understood how tired he was. Douglas had been with the president right from the early days when he was campaigning to be a local councillor. Back then they both had brown hair. Those days were long gone, since then they'd transitioned from brown hair through to grey and on to white. That's what politics does to you. And days like today were one of the main reasons. Thirty-six high-profile people dead in one morning. Many of them high-ranking politicians, a mix of Democrats and Republicans. These terrorists didn't discriminate, which made it all the more baffling. Leaders of other countries, and members of royal families were also showing up dead. What the fuck was going on? Terrorism? Alien invasion? Hoax? Was it a dream perhaps? Douglas had no idea and neither did the president, who was sitting in a spongey orange chair in the penthouse suite of the Poseidon Hotel looking thoroughly fucked off.

'Sanchez Garcia and Flake Munroe,' Douglas said.

'Yes, of course. And what am I talking to them about? Am I giving them anything?'

'I've already arranged for them to receive some specially engraved gold rings, sir. I had General Calhoon hand them over, so that you don't have to.'

'Oh, thank Christ for that. I don't think I could survive one more person making a joke about me proposing to them when I hand them a ring.'

'I know it's a drag, Mister President. All you need to do is make some small talk, shake hands with Miss Munroe, and if you can get away with it, try fist-bumping Mr Garcia. You won't want to shake hands with him. Hygiene issues.'

The president stood up and re-tucked his shirt into his pants. Then he loosened his tie a little. 'I don't want to shake hands with any of these fucking cunts. I swear that's the thing I do most in this job, shake hands with peasants.'

'I know, sir. Will there be anything else?'

The president licked his finger and flattened down one of his eyebrows. He looked like he'd been up all night. He'd had two hours of sleep and it was showing. 'Just send them in,' he said with a sigh. 'And if I haven't booted them out within ten minutes, knock on the door and tell me there's an emergency.'

'Yes, sir. I'll go get them now. By the way, you have some food between your teeth, sir.'

'Oh for fuckssake, not again?'

'Fraid so, Mister President.'

'Fine. I'll sort it out before they come in.'

'Very good, sir.'

Navan Douglas excused himself and headed out of the president's suite. There were two armed bodyguards standing outside the door, preventing any scum from getting in. Douglas ignored them and marched down the corridor to the elevator at the end. He was only halfway there when the shiny, gold-plated doors on the elevator parted, revealing three people inside the carriage. Douglas recognised Alexis Calhoon, but her two companions were people he'd only ever seen in photos, Sanchez Garcia and Flake Munroe. How they were a couple was a mystery. Sanchez was overweight and probably fifteen years older than Flake, who scrubbed up quite nicely, like a budget version of Lily James, who Douglas had recently seen in the movie *Baby Driver*.

Calhoon ushered Sanchez and Flake out of the elevator, but stayed inside it, knowing she wasn't invited any further.

'Good day to you both,' Douglas said, with fake enthusiasm as he approached them. 'I am Navan Douglas, the Attorney General. You must be Flake.' He took Flake's hand and shook it. 'And Sanchez,' he said, nodding at her chubby Mexican partner.

'That's correct,' said Flake with a smile. 'Nice to meet you too, sir.'

Douglas looked past them and smiled at Calhoon. 'Thank you, General, I'll take it from here.'

'Yes, sir.'

The doors closed in front of Calhoon, and the elevator took her on a ride back down to the lobby, leaving Douglas with his two new guests.

'How do you like your new gold rings?' he asked.

'They're wonderful,' said Flake.

'Bit tight,' Sanchez added. He was about to say something else, but Flake trod on his foot.

'The president is very excited to meet you both,' Douglas lied. 'I'll take you to see him now. Please come with me.'

Douglas led the unlikely couple down the corridor to the president's suite, asking polite questions about how their morning had been, and generally ignoring their responses. When the three of them arrived outside the president's room, Douglas addressed the nearest of the two bodyguards, a six-foot-two bruiser with brown skin, short black hair and a humourless look on his face.

'Alvin, these are the president's guests, Flake Munroe and Sanchez Garcia. He's expecting them.'

'Yes, sir.'

Alvin opened the door to the president's suite. Navan Douglas marched through it and waited for Flake and Sanchez to follow. Flake entered first, and marvelled at the magnificence of the place, while Sanchez strolled in behind her, pretending to be unimpressed.

'This place is amazing,' said Flake. 'It's like that place Richard Gere and Julia Roberts stayed in, in Pretty Woman.'

Sanchez looked around. 'Where's the president?' he asked. Then he sniffed the air. 'Smells like old people in here.'

Navan Douglas pointed at a shiny orange sofa. 'Why don't you take a seat over there,' he said. 'The president will be with you shortly. He's just freshening up.'

As the two guests headed for the sofa, Douglas noticed the president's television was still on, albeit without any sound. A scrolling bar on the bottom of the screen confirmed something the Attorney General already knew. The leaders of Brazil, Germany, France and Australia had all been murdered in the last hour. *What a morning.* He needed to be away from these idiots so he could make some important calls to find out what was going on.

'I'll leave you here now,' he said, excusing himself. 'Have a good meeting. Don't be nervous, the president is really looking forward to chatting with you. Hopefully, I'll see you again later.'

With that, he ducked back out of the president's suite and hurried down to the elevator. He made a call on his phone and pressed it against his ear. It rang and rang, just like it had done every other time he'd tried to call Diago that morning. The circus vampire wasn't answering.

# Eight

'Do we just wait here then?' Sanchez asked, walking around the president's suite, inspecting everything.

'I guess so,' said Flake, who was still sitting on the super-comfy, orange sofa watching the news that was scrolling across the bottom of the television.

The suite was magnificent. The reception room, which doubled as a lounge was bigger than the upstairs of the Tapioca. There were pieces of furniture that neither Sanchez nor Flake even knew the name of. Everything was coloured orange, black or red.

'What's that thing over there?' Sanchez asked, pointing at a soft rounded object.

'I think it's a pouffe.'

'A pouffe?'

'Yes, you sit on it, or just rest your feet on it, but you can also lift the top up and store things in it, I think.'

'Why's it called a pouffe?'

'How should I know?'

'Look it up on your phone.'

'You look it up.'

Sanchez walked over to one of the tall windows which had dark red curtains on either side of it. He peered down at the street below. 'Fucking hell, we're high up.'

'Ssshhh, be quiet,' said Flake. 'Stop swearing. Remember where we are.'

Sanchez turned away from the window and looked around for something else to complain about.

'Why don't you think up some interesting questions to ask him?' Flake suggested.

'Like what?' said Sanchez, folding his arms.

'Something interesting, you know, something no one else has ever asked him. You're good at that sort of thing.'

'You're right, I am,' said Sanchez, scratching his chin as he contemplated a good question to ask the most powerful man in the world.

'I think *I'll* ask him how much sleep he gets,' said Flake.

'Pah, that's a rubbish question. I bet he gets asked that all the time.'

'At least I've got a question for him.'

'So have I,' Sanchez announced. 'I'm going to ask him who he thinks would win a fight between Thunderlips the Ultimate Male, and Mumm-Ra the Ever Living.'

Flake groaned. 'What kind of question is that?'

'It's the kind no one will have asked him before. Who do you think would win that fight?'

'I don't know,' Flake said, 'Is Mumm-Ra that thing from Thundercats?'

'Yes, and Thunderlips was the wrestler in Rocky 3.'

'Then I guess it would have to be Mumm-Ra,' said Flake. 'He had superpowers, didn't he?'

Sanchez shook his head. 'Wrong! It's Thunderlips, the Ultimate Male.'

'I'm going to regret asking this,' said Flake, with a tired sigh, 'but why would Thunderlips win this fight between a fictional wrestler and a cartoon character?'

Sanchez strolled over to the pouffe and sat down on it. It was quite comfortable after all. 'Easy,' he said. 'Mumm-Ra was outwitted by a group of cats on a weekly basis. Thunderlips would never lose to a cat. Plus, if Mumm-Ra can't beat a Thundercat, what chance will he have against anything else with Thunder in its name?'

'You're stupid. If you ask the president that question, he'll know for sure that you're an idiot.'

'If he gets it wrong, he'll be the idiot.'

'Of course,' said Flake, giving up on the argument. She checked her watch. 'I wonder what he's doing?'

'Taking a dump probably,' said Sanchez. 'I bet he always drops a load before a big meeting.'

Flake patted the cushion next to her on the sofa. 'Come sit here with me,' she said. 'Otherwise it'll look like we've been arguing.'

Sanchez left the pouffe and returned to the sofa. He slumped back into it, causing Flake to bounce up a little.

'I'm fucking starving,' said Sanchez. 'We should call room service.'

'No, we shouldn't.'

'I bet the food here is amazing. I bet every food item in this place is better than anywhere else. The burgers must be incredible.'

'There's a question for you. Ask him what the food is like. Then he might offer to get you something.'

'Why wait for him?' said Sanchez, standing up again. He knew his impatience and fidgeting was beginning to really grate on Flake's nerves. Food would help. He spotted an old-fashioned phone on a small table beside the wall and strolled nonchalantly over to it. He picked it up and made a call to room service.

'Hello, this is the penthouse, do you do burgers?'

'Yes sir,' came the reply.

'Send up two cheeseburgers and two large fries please. And a diet coke.'

Flake put her head in her hands, fearing that ordering on the president's room service might be a felony or something worse.

'Do you want anything?' Sanchez asked her.

'No. Put down the phone.'

'Fine.' Sanchez hung up the call, hopeful that his order had been taken anyway. 'I don't know what you're fretting about,' he grumbled. 'It's all paid for by the taxpayer anyway.'

'Just sit down and be quiet. Last thing we need is the president coming out and finding you ordering takeaway and charging it to his room.'

Sanchez sat down next to her again and huffed. 'Where the bloody hell is he anyway?' he grumbled. 'Does he know we're waiting out here?'

Flake glowered at him. '*Shut up.*'

Sanchez managed to stay quiet for about ten seconds before his restlessness kicked in again. He stood up and looked around. 'Where's the bathroom in this place?'

Flake closed her eyes and concentrated on her breathing in order to stay calm. By the time she reopened her eyes, Sanchez was wandering around again, looking for the bathroom. There was no point in trying to calm him down. His impatience and his infatuation with everything toilet-related could not be reasoned with.

'Just don't walk in on the president while he's on the crapper!' she said as he headed to a door at the back of the room.

Sanchez waved a dismissive hand her way, then opened the door and walked through it into a private hallway. There were three doors, one on the left, one on the right and one straight ahead. He picked the one on the right and twisted the door knob. It opened into a darkened room, with just a little light glowing somewhere inside.

'Hello?' Sanchez called out. 'Anyone here?'

No answer.

No answer meant *"come on in and take a look around,"* so he did. He waited for his eyes to adjust to the dim light. This was no bathroom. It was an enormous bedroom. The dim light was coming from a door in the far corner. An en suite, no doubt. Sanchez trod carefully across the soft, red carpet, creeping past an enormous king-sized, four-poster bed.

As he approached the en suite, he got wind of a foul stink. Was it possible that the president was in there doing his daily log?

No. It wasn't.

The smell was coming from the bed.

The president was laid on his back on a gold-coloured duvet on the four-poster bed. Sanchez just hadn't noticed him before because it was dark and the bed was so ridiculously big. It was clear what had caused the foul smell too. The president had shit himself. And it wasn't anything to do with the hotel food. It was because someone had cut him open from his balls to his chin. There was blood all over his shirt and pants. The duvet was fucked too. A big patch of black blood surrounded the president, and the blood wasn't dry. This murder was fresh. Recent.

# Nine

'FLAKE! FLAKE! QUICK! GET IN HERE!' Sanchez yelled. He backed away from the president's dead body, retreating towards the door.

Flake heard his cry and within seconds she burst into the room, almost knocking Sanchez over in her haste. She flicked a switch on the wall, which shone some much needed light on the situation.

'Jesus, Sanchez! What have you done?' she asked, staring at the dead body of the president.

Sanchez grabbed her arm and put his finger over his lips, signalling for her to be quiet.

'What?' said Flake, looking around. 'Is the killer still in here? And why are you shushing me? You just yelled for me to come in here.'

'I panicked when I called for you. Then I realised the killer might still be here.'

Flake gestured around the room. 'Look,' she said. 'No one here.' She walked up to the bed and stared at the body. 'Holy shit! Who did this?' she said, grimacing at the hideous sight. 'It wasn't you, was it?'

Sanchez tutted. 'Well, *obviously* I didn't do it.'

'I can certainly believe you didn't do it on purpose,' Flake replied. 'But let's face it, your track record for accidentally killing people is almost as bad as Jasmine's.'

Sanchez scoffed. 'Didn't you run over an old lady in my ambulance once?'

Flake unclasped her necklace and placed it on the president's chest in the hope that the Eye of the Moon might bring him back to life. She pressed the big blue stone against his skin.

'What the fuck are you doing?' Sanchez asked, incredulous.

'I'm seeing if the Eye of the Moon can heal his injuries.'

'He's dead. All you're doing is putting your DNA all over the corpse.'

Flake recoiled and stepped back. 'Shit, I didn't think of that.'

'Well, he's fucked, Eye of the Moon or not, he's fucked.'

'I guess so.' Flake looked at the blood on her hands and on the Eye, then wiped them on the bedsheet next to the corpse.

'Do you think this is a set-up?' Sanchez asked, images from all kinds of rubbish crime shows racing through his head.

'A set-up?' Flake baulked, as she refastened the Eye of the Moon around her neck. 'Why would it be a set-up? You think we're being framed for this?'

'It all makes sense, doesn't it?'

'No, it doesn't. Explain.'

'Think about it, a couple of known assassins like ourselves have been invited up to the president's room on the morning he's been murdered. It's the perfect set-up. We get framed for the murder and no one questions it, especially now you've got the president's blood on your hands and you've wiped them on the duvet.'

Flake looked at the president's corpse again. What Sanchez was saying made sense for a change. After a brief pause she pulled herself together. 'Here's what we do,' she said. 'We go outside and tell the security guards the truth. We found him dead. I can explain that I tried giving him CPR. You haven't touched him have you?' She glared at Sanchez. *'Have you?'*

'What are you suggesting? That I've been fiddling with him?'

'I'm just asking.'

'Well I haven't, okay?'

'Fine, then we just go and raise the alarm.'

'Woah, woah, wait a second,' said Sanchez, not wanting to rush things. 'Let's talk this through a minute.'

'What's to talk about?'

'The set-up, remember? What if one of his own people wanted him dead, and killed him just before we got up here, so that we could take the fall for it?'

Flake sighed. 'And *who* would do that? In fact, who *could* do that? Who could get into the president's private hotel room and slice him up, then get out again without being seen?'

'The vice president.'

'That's it. You're not watching any more TV.'

'Think about it, someone who's in line to be the next president is surely the most likely candidate.'

'Again, too much TV, Sanchez. Let's just go and tell the bodyguards what's happened. The longer we're in here, the more it'll look like we were involved.'

'Then you agree, we *are* suspects?'

Flake took a slow breath before replying, 'No.'

'Hang on a minute,' said Sanchez. 'If we didn't do it, and the vice president didn't do it, then who the fuck did?'

'I don't know, that's why we have to raise the alarm. The killer could still be in the building.'

Sanchez gasped and covered his mouth. 'Maybe the president committed suicide?'

'No he didn't.'

'I think that's it,' Sanchez went on, convinced he was correct. 'I can't say I blame him either. Have you seen the state of the First Lady?'

'IT'S NOT SUICIDE!' Flake snapped. She grabbed Sanchez by his arm. 'If he killed himself, where's the knife he did it with? Did he hide it after he died? NO! BECAUSE HE DIDN'T KILL HIMSELF!'

'There's no need to be snippy.'

'Come on, we're getting out of here, NOW!'

Flake dragged Sanchez out of the bedroom, through the hallway and back into the lounge area. They were heading towards the exit door when someone outside knocked on it. It stopped Flake and Sanchez in their tracks.

'What do we do?' Sanchez whispered.

'I don't know.'

The person who knocked on the door didn't wait for permission to enter. The door knob began to turn.

'Shit!' Sanchez whispered. 'I told you. It's a set-up.'

'Shut up!'

The door opened, and an elderly lady in a smart, pale blue pant-suit walked into the room. She saw Flake and Sanchez and smiled at them. 'Hello,' she said, letting go of the door, which then swung shut by itself. Sanchez recognised the woman right away. It was the First Lady.

'Morning, your highness,' he said with a fake smile.

'Is that good-for-nothing husband of mine still in here?' the First Lady asked, with more than a hint of humour in her voice.

'He's taking a dump,' Sanchez replied. 'A big one. He'll be in there for ages.'

The First Lady laughed politely. 'Oh, don't worry about that. I've seen him doing worse things. Nothing shocks me. I'll go get him.' She moved towards the bedroom.

'NO, wait!' said Flake, holding up her hands, inadvertently showing off her blood-stained palms.

The First Lady looked horrified. 'What is—'

The old bag never finished what she was going to say. Without warning, Flake fired two bolts of blue lightning from the palms of her hands. The lightning bolts hit the First Lady in the chest, lifted her off her feet and blasted her across the room. Her legs thudded into the back of the posh sofa, causing her to bounce over it and land face-down on the floor behind it in a crucifix pose, smoke smouldering up from her back.

'Well, you've done it now,' said Sanchez, shaking his head.

'Oh gawd!' said, Flake, turning over her hands and staring into her palms, stunned by what had just happened.

'Don't point those things at yourself!' said Sanchez. 'Are you mental?'

'What just happened?' Flake asked, still bewildered.

'You fucked up the old lady. Maybe you're turning into the new Dark Lord,' said Sanchez peering over at the smoking torso of the First Lady. 'She looks pretty dead. We're definitely fucked now.'

'I didn't mean to do that though,' said Flake. 'Those laser bolts just came out of nowhere.'

'Actually they came out of your hands. I saw it.'

'That's never happened before though. I've been wearing the Eye of the Moon for months. It's never made me blast lightning at anyone before.'

'Maybe subconsciously you wanted to do it?'

Flake lowered her hands and glowered at Sanchez. 'I did *not* want to do it. It just happened.'

'At least she's not ugly anymore. She's smoking hot now.'

'That's not funny.'

'Fair enough,' said Sanchez. 'Do you still want to go out and tell the bodyguards that we had nothing to do with any of this?'

Before Flake could respond, the door to the room flew open again, and the two bodyguards from outside charged in, pistols drawn. Alvin, the big, humourless bodyguard saw the smouldering First Lady and pointed his gun at Flake and Sanchez. His buddy, a short, stocky, white dude with cropped blond hair, moved towards the smoking hot First Lady to see if she was okay.

'Where's the president?' Alvin asked, glaring at Flake.

Sanchez raised his hands in surrender. Flake attempted to do the same, but the Eye of the Moon took control of her hands again. Bolts of electricity shot out from each of her palms. Alvin was blasted in the neck, almost decapitating him. He bounced back against the wall, dropped his gun and slid down to the floor, accompanied by a toasty smell. His short, stocky partner saw what was coming, and in one perfectly oiled, well-trained move, he dived behind a cushioned chair and started shooting, blazing wildly at Flake and Sanchez. Flake fired off another laser bolt in his direction, intentionally this time. The blue electricity blew a hole through the chair, and struck the bodyguard in the chest, smashing him into a hardwood desk. He bounced off it and collapsed onto the floor, not far from the First Lady. Smoke fizzled up from his frazzled torso.

Flake sprinted over to the door and slammed it shut. 'Holy beans, Sanchez. What are we gonna do now?'

Sanchez did not reply. Flake stared at the three dead bodies. This was a disaster.

'Sanchez, I—'

The reason for Sanchez's silence became clear.

Flake went numb. He was splayed out on the sofa. Blood was gushing out of a hole in his forehead. There was a smattering of blood on the sofa behind him.

'Sanchez? Sweetie?'

The ensuing silence felt like a wicked taunt, a terrible trick. Time stopped and then immediately sped up again.

She sprinted over to him, unclasping the Eye of the Moon from her neck as she dived onto the sofa next to him. She pressed the precious blue stone against his chest. 'Come on, come on!' she whispered. The Eye's healing powers were needed now more than ever.

Nothing happened

'For fuck's sake, *come on!*' She pressed the stone against the hole in his head. Nothing.

'No, no, no, no, NO!' she said, frantic, as she pressed two fingers against Sanchez's neck, checking for a pulse.

He didn't have one.

She tried his wrist. Again, nothing.

She tried slapping him around the face, hitting him in the chest. Nothing worked.

It took her a lot longer than it should have, but eventually she realised the obvious reality of the situation.

Sanchez was gone.

# Ten

Flake's head was spinning. Sanchez, the great love of her life was dead. Shot in the head by one of the president's bodyguards. And now Flake was alone, trapped in a hotel penthouse suite with a bunch of dead bodies, one of whom was the president of the United fucking States. She had to think fast. There was only one thing that came to mind that made any sense. *Make a run for it.* She took one last look at Sanchez. He had a goofy look on his face, and blood had dribbled down into his eyes. She leaned down and kissed him on the lips for the last time.

'I love you Sanchez. I'll always love you.'

She put the necklace with Eye of the Moon on it around her neck again and considered her options. It was hard to concentrate, to think rationally, but that was the *one* thing she had to do.

Most important. How to get out of this place?

There could be other exits in the penthouse suite, but with it being the president's place, using any exit other than the front door would likely lead to setting off a fire-alarm, or bumping into more bodyguards. The best way out had to be through the front door. The men guarding it were already dead, their lifeless bodies strewn across the floor in front of her as evidence. Do it. It's the only way out.

Flake bolted for the door. Her fingers touched the door knob. She hesitated. She had no gun, just the pesky Eye of the Moon, a weapon with a fucking mind of its own. Should she grab a gun from one of the fallen bodyguards? At this point it made no difference. Fuck it. Guns are good. It's better to have one and not need it, than to need one and not have it. She scampered over to the bodyguards and relieved them of their weapons. She tucked the guns down the back of her skirt and let her jacket hang down over them, concealing them from any prying eyes.

She took one last look over at Sanchez then went for it. Through the door, out into the hallway. No one in sight. Good start. Someone must have heard the gunfire though. It was merely a matter of time before more armed guards showed up. What was the best way out? Stairs or elevator?

The elevator was at the end of the hall, a good forty metres away. Much closer to her, a door with the words "EMERGENCY STAIRS" was inviting her over to it. It made sense. If any guards came up, they would most likely come up via the elevator. Probably.

Fuck it. Stairs it is.

Flake barged through the door into the stairwell. The door swung shut behind her and made the kind of clicking sound that suggested it had locked itself. She walked up to the banister and peered over it to see what the downward route looked like, and if anyone was coming up. There was nothing spectacular to see, just a standard cold, grey stairwell that went down for miles. There was only one thing to do. Down we go.

Flake rounded the first corner and started the descent, the tapping of her shoes on the steps echoing all around the stairwell. She was halfway down the first flight when something really hit her. Hard. Sanchez was dead. She'd seen it with her own two eyes. His legendary luck had finally run out. A chill came over her. She carried on running, but now there were tears rolling down her cheeks. Her nose filled up with snot. Her throat burned.

*"This is no time for self-pity,"* she told herself. Clear your mind. Focus on the stairs. Aah yes, the fucking stairs. Those fucking stairs were never-ending. Rounding one flight after another was dizzying. She was five flights down when things took an inevitable turn for the worse.

A fire alarm sounded.

*Shit!* Flake stopped running, aware of the echoing of her shoes pounding on the steps. *"They're onto me. What do I do now? Keep going? Exit the stairs onto the next floor?* Stupid though it was, Flake just wished there was someone with her to tell her what to do. But who the fuck would know what to do in this situation? It was unique. There's no rule book detailing the best way to escape from a hotel after you've murdered the First Lady and a couple of the president's bodyguards.

Then came the footsteps pounding on the stairs, several floors below her. Was it people fleeing because of the fire alarm? She peered over the banister. There was nothing to see. Nothing interesting anyway. Her heart was pumping gas. Her pores were opening up and releasing sweat. Her nose was closing up for the day. And her eyes, well they were filled with water making it fucking impossible to see much anyway. Flake needed someone to think for her.

*Her phone.* That was the answer. Why didn't she think of it sooner?

She pulled it from her jacket pocket. Who to call? JD, Elvis, Rex, Jasmine? No, none of the above. The answer was Jacko. Jacko could get her out. He was in Purgatory with a travel portal that could open up a quick escape route. She pulled his number up on her phone and made the call. It rang four times before he finally answered.

'Hello Flake. What's up?'

She tried to keep her voice to a whisper. 'Jacko. Help me! Sanchez is dead. I'm trapped in a hotel and I need to get out. People are trying to kill me. Can you get me out?'

'Sure thing. What hotel?'

'Umm, oh shit. It's the… uh, Poseidon Hotel, in Chicago.'

'The Poseidon? Is that where the president is staying?'

'Yes. But he's dead too. And I accidentally used the Eye of the Moon to kill the First Lady and a couple of bodyguards. Jacko, get me the fuck out of here. PLEASE!'

Jacko remained as chilled out as ever, completely unfazed by any of Flake's panicked rambling. 'What floor are you on?' he asked.

'I don't know. I'm in the stairwell heading down to the lobby. I'm about five flights from the top, I think. But I don't know what to do. Should I get off on the next floor, or what?'

'Is that a fire alarm I can hear?'

'Yes. They're onto me. Fuckin' hurry. This is an emergency.'

'Hold on. Just wait one second.'

'I can't wait….. Jacko!…. Jacko! Are you still there?'

Jacko did not reply. Flake looked around for a floor number on any of the walls. There was a number in red on the wall behind her. 48.

'Fuck my ass, forty-eight, really?' she muttered to herself. It was depressing to know how far from the bottom she was. 'Jacko, you there?'

Jacko's voice came through loud and clear a few seconds later. 'Okay, Flake, you've got fifty-four floors in that place. Get off on floor number forty.'

'Forty? Why forty?'

'Just get to forty. You must be close to it by now. Get there and wait for help.'

'That's it? Wait for help?'

'Flake, get moving! I'll stay on the line.'

'Fuck!'

Flake's legs were close to giving up on her, but the adrenaline was keeping her going. She scrambled over to the next flight of stairs and stumbled down them, running like a one-legged hooker chasing a non-paying client. She missed half the steps but somehow managed to stay upright. Hotel guests were starting to show up in the stairwell, unsure whether they were even supposed to be there. Flake deviated around a young couple. She came close to knocking the fuckers over too. Dithering bastards. Eventually, after what felt like ages, she arrived at a landing with the number 40 painted on the wall. She burst through the adjacent door into a long corridor with doors to apartments on both sides. Guests were milling around in the corridor, debating with each other about how best to react to the fire alarm.

As Flake looked one way and then the other, she made eye contact with a few of the hotel guests. Everyone seemed to look at her like they knew what she'd done. And then the alarm stopped blaring out, leaving a ringing echo in Flake's ears, which was soon drowned out by a woman's voice making an announcement over a tannoy system. *'Ladies and gentlemen, please return to your rooms. The fire alarm has been halted. Security will be carrying out a thorough search of the premises. This is a red alert. Please stay in your rooms. Anyone out in the corridors or stairwells will be met with hostility. Return to your rooms, immediately. Thank you.'*

Fuuuuuuck!

As the people on the floor began scurrying back into their rooms, bumping into each other in their panicked state, Flake saw two men at the end of the corridor. Men in grey suits. Big, burly men, with earpieces in. They clocked her almost immediately. One of them pointed at her and said something to his colleague. Then both men pulled out pistols and started making their way towards Flake, fighting their way through the fussing individuals in the corridor.

Flake put her phone to her ear. 'Jacko. They've found me already. What do I do? I've gotta move.'

'Where are you?'

'I'm on forty, but I've got to get off.'

'Stay where you are.'

'They're pointing guns at me. I've gotta go.'

Flake stuck the phone back in her pocket and pushed open the door to the stairwell.

THUD!

She walked straight into a fist. A big fist. From another big dude in a grey suit. The punch hit her just below the neck. It knocked her back onto the floor in the hallway of unbridled panic.

'FREEZE!'

It took a moment for Flake's head to clear. She looked up. The situation had changed considerably. There were now four men in grey suits, and they were all standing over her. Three had guns pointed at her, the other was rubbing his fist, having just hit her in the chest with it.

'ROLL ONTO YOUR FRONT!' one of the men yelled.

Flake did as she was told. As soon as she was face down, someone relieved her of the two guns that were tucked down the back of her skirt. A big hand pressed her head down against the floor. Two more hands ran up and down her legs, up her sides, over her ass. Those hands touched just about everything. Presumably they were looking for more weapons.

'You're gonna fry for this, you bitch.'

'I didn't do it,' Flake mumbled through a mouthful of drool and carpet. Her vision was becoming more hazy by the second. Everything was a blur, in every way possible.

But then the cavalry arrived. Four gunshots. Just like that. Four dead guys in grey suits. One of them, possibly the heaviest, fell onto Flake. His stubbly cheek pressed against her ear, while his deadweight corpse squeezed the life out of her.

There were screams further down the corridor. More gunfire. A shootout was underway, featuring lots of yelling, interspersed with loud bangs. It ended quickly, only to start up again a few seconds later followed by an eery silence. That lasted about three seconds. Then there were more voices yelling again. More gunfire. More silence. Boots on the floor, running. Towards Flake.

The heavy load pinning Flake to the floor was lifted off her. She breathed a sigh of relief. A hand grabbed her just above the elbow and lifted her off the floor.

Through her tear-filled eyes Flake couldn't make out the identity of her rescuer. A familiar, gravelly voice soon confirmed it though.

'Flake, can you run?' JD asked.

## Eleven

JD lowered the hood on his long black coat, revealing unshaven face. 'Come on,' he said. 'We've gotta go!'

Flake didn't have much of an idea about where to go or what to do, so JD took hold of her hand and dragged her along the corridor. Every few steps, another government agent would show up at one end of the corridor or the other. Each one was dispatched with the obligatory bullet to the head from JD's Glock 17. There wasn't time for much else. Rapid fire was the only option. After dragging Flake halfway down the corridor, he eventually stopped outside room number 4033. He let go of her and twisted the door knob. Naturally, the fucking thing was locked. In the midst of all the panic, the blaring alarm, the tannoy announcements and the gunfire, most of the hotel guests had dived back into their rooms for cover, so it was inevitable that someone had locked themselves in room 4033. Well, that person was in for a big fucking surprise.

JD pushed Flake out of the way, stepped back from the door, and pointed his gun at the lock. With almost no hesitation, he fired off two shots. A chunk of the door splintered away. He kicked it open and dragged Flake inside.

'AAAAAGH!'

The high-pitched scream came from an elderly lady who was standing inside the room, clinging to her husband. They were a smartly-dressed couple, both in their seventies, both grey-haired and both fucking petrified. The lady was wearing a black and orange patterned dress, her husband, a grey sweater with light blue golfing pants.

'Get out of my fucking way,' JD bellowed at them, while pointing his gun at the old man. 'Face that fuckin' wall!' He nodded his head in the direction of the wall opposite the bathroom. 'NOW!'

The old man twisted his wife around and the two of them faced the wall like a couple of prison inmates awaiting a body cavity search.

JD pulled Flake over to the bathroom. The door was already open. He expected to see a hole in the back wall with Jacko standing on the other side of it. But the hole wasn't there, and nor was Jacko.

'Fuck.'

Flake looked at JD, a crumb of hope in her eyes. 'Is the portal supposed to be open?' she asked.

'Yeah. Fucking Jacko. What the fuck is he doing?'

JD fumbled in his pocket for his phone.

'It's okay,' said Flake, holding up her phone. 'I've got him here.' She put her phone to her ear. 'Shit, the line's gone dead. I'll call him again.' She pressed RECALL on her phone.

'Come on, hurry up,' said JD, his impatience aimed at Jacko more so than Flake.

'It's engaged,' said Flake, panicking.

'Try again.'

While Flake attempted to call Jacko again, JD left the bathroom. The elderly couple were still facing the opposite wall like a couple of well-behaved sweethearts. But the busted door into their hotel room was open. And that meant more fucking government agents. Those fuckers were everywhere. The first two that burst into the room were dressed in plain clothes, but JD knew a fucking agent when he saw one. He blasted the first guy twice in the chest, and then hit his buddy in the leg before finishing him off with one in the face as he went down.

While he attempted to break a world record for the fastest reload of a Glock, he yelled back to Flake in the bathroom.

'Flake! Any luck?'

No reply. JD finished reloading and aimed his gun at the busted door, ready to pump two in the face of the next dumb fuck who came his way.

'JD!'

'Yeah, what?'

Flake walked out of the bathroom. 'Jacko says he can't open the portal.'

'What? Why not?'

'Apparently those two old people have seen into Purgatory. God knows about it, and he's mad as hell. No more portal until further notice.'

JD darted his eyes at Flake, hoping she was making a shit joke. She wasn't. He returned his gaze to the door, his gun ready. 'Okay,' he said eventually, while formulating a new plan in his head. 'This is gonna be somethin' else.'

'What are we gonna do?'

'We're gonna have to make a run for it. If we can make it out of the hotel, then we're gonna have to steal a car and hope for the best. I gotta be honest though, I don't rate our chances.'

Flake said something in reply but it was drowned out by JD firing two more shots at the fucked-up door. Those dumb bastards just kept on coming. The bodies were piling up in the doorway. Pretty soon the bloody exit would be blocked off.

JD reached inside his coat with his free hand and pulled out a second pistol. He jerked it towards Flake, who was still behind him. 'You've got about twenty shots in there,' he said. 'Get ready to use them. We're going to take the elevator down to the second floor, then we'll get off and use the stairs.'

Flake took the gun. 'Why the second floor?'

'Because the lobby will be carnage. Close your eyes a second.'

Flake had the good sense to do as instructed. Two more shots were fired. She reopened her eyes and was surprised to see no new dead people in the doorway. But then two gentle thuds on the other side of the room drew her eyes away from the door. JD had gunned down the old couple.

'Oh God. Why did you kill them?'

'They saw Purgatory. It had to be done if we want that portal opened again.' He placed his hand on her shoulder and looked her dead in the eye. 'You ready for this? It's gonna be mental.'

## Twelve

'You cover the rear.'

JD was blunt with his instructions. It was what the situation called for. He headed over to the busted door, leaned over a mound of dead bodies and poked his head out. It had temporarily gone quiet out in the corridor of chaos.

Flake was a metre behind him, both hands on her gun. No nerves, no trembling fingers. She'd pulled her shit together. All thoughts of Sanchez had temporarily vanished to the back of her mind. 'Let's do it,' she said.

JD stepped over the pile of bodies and checked both ways down the corridor again. Flake followed suit, almost banging her head on the door frame, so high was the pile of corpses underfoot. Whichever way JD pointed his gun, she directed hers the other way, making sure they had both directions covered. There were a lot of dead people in the hallway. Most of them were government agents. Some were civilians.

'Okay, MOVE!' said JD.

He didn't bother grabbing Flake's arm this time. He knew she'd sorted her head out. He sprinted down the hallway to a bank of six elevators at the end, and pressed a button in the wall to call one. Flake caught up with him, and turned her back on the elevators, ready to shoot the fuck out of anything that came from the other end of the corridor. A painfully long ten seconds passed before a pinging sound announced the arrival of their carriage.

JD slapped her on the arm, then headed for the elevator on the end, his gun pointed at the doors. They opened. No gunfire. Empty carriage. *Thank God.*

He ducked inside. Flake bundled in after him and covered the doors while he jabbed the button for the second floor.

The elevator doors closed and the slow descent started. JD tucked his gun inside his coat. Flake didn't ask why. It made sense. Discretion was required. She tucked hers down the back of her skirt. When the doors reopened, they needed to look harmless, forgettable.

When the doors did part on the second floor, they were greeted by a hallway identical to the one they had come from, except it wasn't decorated in corpses. The guests were inside their rooms. Perfect.

JD stepped out of the elevator, checked all avenues, then signalled for Flake to head for the emergency stairwell at the other end of the main corridor. Her heart sank. So much running. Fucking running. Never again after this. Flake was done with running.

She moved at a brisk pace, not sprinting, not drawing attention to herself, but also not going slow enough to get a kick up the ass from JD, who was close behind. It crossed her mind that running with a gun tucked down the back of her skirt was way more dangerous than running with scissors. In fact, whoever came up with the phrase about the dangers of running with scissors had clearly never run with the barrel of a gun between their butt cheeks.

Halfway down the corridor, JD fired off a couple more shots at something behind them. It startled Flake, but she never looked back. When she reached the door to the stairwell, she barged it open. The stairwell was cold. It felt colder than the last time she'd been in it, which wasn't even that long ago.

JD followed her through and kicked the door shut behind him. Flake leaned over the banister to check if anyone was on the ground floor. Two more security guards. They looked up. Both their heads exploded before Flake even heard the report from JD's gun.

And then they were running down stairs again. JD hurdled over the banister and landed on the floor below before Flake had rounded the final turn. He pushed open the fire door and took a look at what was outside, his gun concealed behind his back.

'It's all good,' he said. 'Guns away. Walk casual.'

Flake still had her gun tucked down the back of her skirt anyway, so she ignored the first order. JD took hold of her hand and they walked through the door, out into the daylight. They were in a parking lot. Hundreds of people were milling around. There was a lot of chatter, yelling and *fucking sirens*. There were also a lot of cars. They walked casually through the parking lot like a loved-up couple. No one took any notice of them, despite JD's long black coat. Most people were busy looking at their phones. Some were filming what was going on. There weren't many cops or government agents around. If the secret service really were "locking down" the building they were doing a shit job of it. Probably because JD had killed most of them.

They breezed right out of the parking lot and onto the sidewalk. Hundreds more people were gathered on the opposite side of the street, staring up at the hotel and filming it with their phones. Everyone was so busy trying to get some good footage for their social media pages, they didn't pay any attention to JD and Flake. The two of them made it across the street without anyone pointing a camera or a gun at them.

Almost.

'HEY YOU! POLICE! FREEZE!'

JD and Flake both spun around to where the woman's voice had yelled from.

BANG!

It was Flake who took the bitch down. Bullet to the throat. All in one swift movement. Pistol drawn from the back of her skirt, lifted, aimed, fired. All in a split second. Sorry cop lady. You should have stayed quiet.

It silenced the crowd of people outside the hotel for a brief, golden moment. Then everyone went shit nuts. It created enough of a diversion that JD was able to smash the window of a nearby jeep. Flake bundled into the passenger side. JD had the vehicle hot-wired before she even buckled up.

'Point your gun at anyone who looks at us,' said JD. 'And try calling Elvis or Jasmine. See where they are.'

'Got it.'

JD hit the gas and the jeep screeched out into traffic. Flake pulled up Elvis's number on her phone.

No dialling tone.

She tried Jasmine.

Same thing.

'Their phones are off!' she groaned.

JD swung the jeep around a sharp corner and onto the wrong side of the road.

'We've got company,' he said.

The sound of police sirens confirmed it.

'Fuck. I'll try Rex.'

She pulled Rex's number up on her phone and made the call. The big guy answered after four rings.

'What's up Flake?'

'Rex, thank God. Me and JD are in trouble. Where are you?'

'JD?' Rex sounded confused. 'What the fuck's he doing with you?'

'Sanchez is dead.'

There was a brief pause before Rex spoke again. 'Put me on speaker,' he said. 'I wanna speak to JD.'

Flake switched the phone onto loudspeaker. 'Done,' she said.

Rex's voice, agitated, came through loud and clear. 'Where the fuck are you? What's going on?'

JD swung the jeep around a corner and yelled at the phone. 'Rex, listen, we're being chased by the whole fucking world. They think Flake killed the president.'

'Whaaaaat?'

'No time to explain. You got a biker hideout round here anywhere?'

'Where are you?'

'Downtown, Chicago, not far from the Poseidon hotel.'

'Poseidon? Yeah, I know a place near there. It's called the Gunslingers. You could be there in ten. Just don't let the cops track you there. You lead the cops to these guys and......... well, they won't like it.'

'Where is it?'

'It's underneath a pizza place called "Another One Bites the Crust". Pull into the underground parking lot there. There's a secret entrance. I'll tell the boss man there to expect you. They'll take you in. Okay?'

'You're the best, Rex,' said Flake.

'Good luck. And I'm sorry about Sanchez. If you get any problems just call me again...... Is the president really dead?'

'Yeah,' JD replied. 'It's all over the news.'

'Shit. Speak to you later. Good luck.'

## Thirteen

Flake typed in the address of the Gunslingers club on her phone. 'I've found it,' she said. 'Just like Rex said, it's a pizza place.'

'Any idea where the entrance is?'

'Rex said it was in an underground parking lot, didn't he?' I can't see one on this map. Hopefully Rex's friends will be looking out for us.'

'They'd better be.' JD glanced in his rear-view mirror for the hundredth time. 'We've still got company,' he added.

A siren blared out behind them, confirming what JD had said. Flake looked over her shoulder. Through the rear window she saw a police car weaving through the traffic, blue and red lights flashing. A second cop car swung out of a side-road behind it and joined the chase.

'Take the wheel,' said JD, reaching into his coat for a gun. 'I'll deal with this.'

'It's okay,' said Flake, winding down her window. 'I'll handle it.' She leaned as far out of the window as she could, and waved her hand at the cop car closest to them.

ZAP!

A blue bolt of lightning shot out of Flake's hand and blasted into the front left wheel on the cop car. Big fucking explosion. The cop car's rear end rose up, overtook the front, and then the car somersaulted down the middle of the road in a ball of flames. There wasn't time for Flake to admire her handiwork because the second cop car zipped past its exploding buddy. It was gaining fast too. The jeep JD had stolen was no match for the speed of a police pursuit vehicle.

Not a problem for Flake though.

ZAP!

She was getting a taste for it. Instead of hitting a wheel, Flake's laser bolt hit the car's front grill. Fucked it up good and proper. The hood exploded into a ball of fire. The squad car skidded sideways and came to a stop. But unlike in a TV show, the cops didn't bail out. The poor fuckers were trapped inside as the car lit up into a raging inferno.

Flake wound her window back up. Her palm was hot. But it felt good. JD was looking at her.

'That's not bad,' he said.

'I've been practising.'

'No shit. I hope you're not out of ammo because there's another one up ahead.'

JD pressed a button that wound Flake's window back down again.

'Thanks,' she said. 'Keep it steady.'

'Go fuck 'em up.'

Over the course of the next ten minutes, Flake successfully took down six squad cars and one helicopter. The fun ended when the cops stopped showing up and JD steered the car off the main road just past the pizza place they were looking for. They cruised down a long ramp into an underground parking garage. It was gloomy and badly lit, with more empty spaces than cars.

'See any bikers or entrances?' JD asked.

'Over there,' Flake replied, pointing at a set of tall, wide, silver doors on the far wall. JD steered the jeep over to the doors, tyres screeching loud enough to draw the attention of any bikers who might be nearby. It worked because as they approached, the silver doors began to open, inviting them in.

JD drove the jeep through the opening into an even darker area with no lights at all. He slowed the car to a stop almost immediately. The tall doors closed behind them, and a set of lights came on above. They were in a secret section of the underground. The walls were covered in street art. There were paintings of dragons, snakes, swords, hot chicks, guys with beards, knives, guns, Don Johnson, Mickey Rourke. JD edged the jeep towards a workshop with a whole bunch of Harley Davidson motorcycles parked outside.

'I guess this is it,' said Flake. 'What now?'

JD parked a safe distance away from all the motorcycles. 'Time to go make friends.'

'Maybe I should do the talking?' Flake suggested.

JD didn't reply. The two of them left the jeep and walked up to the entrance. The sound of police sirens in the distance served as a reminder that they were far from safe.

The workshop looked like a cross between a tattoo parlour and a social club. Its frontage was covered in more artwork, but in the centre of it was a wooden door painted entirely black.

As JD and Flake approached, the door opened and a pair of middle-aged Hell's Angels dressed in blue denim and black leather stepped out. The one at the front was a short fellow with long ginger hair, bad teeth and a shaggy beard. His buddy was more like Rex, six-foot-six and built like a wrestler. He had piercing blue eyes and short, thinning brown hair.

'Hold fire, wait there,' said the ginger one, holding up his hand.

Flake stopped and put her arm across JD just in case he was thinking of ignoring the biker's order. 'We're friends of Rodeo Rex,' she called out, with a big smile.

'Yeah, we know,' said the ginger guy. 'Did anyone follow you here?'

'We *were* followed,' said Flake. 'But we took care of them.'

'You'd better,' the man replied. 'Because we don't take kindly to cops in this place, or people leading them here.'

Flake hoped with all her heart that JD wouldn't respond to the veiled threat with one of his own. Fortunately he kept quiet.

'We're just looking to lay low for a while,' Flake said, keeping up her forced smile. 'We just need to get in contact with some friends of ours, then we'll be on our way.'

The bigger guy looked at JD. 'You the Bourbon Kid?' he asked.

'Yeah. Who are you?'

'I'm Bruiser, my friend here is Axl. He's the president of our gang.'

It seemed odd that Axl, the short ginger guy, was the gang leader, but it wasn't something worth arguing about. Axl eyeballed JD, giving off an, "I'm not scared of you" vibe. JD disregarded it.

Two more bikers made their way out of the workshop. One was big, but fat and old with a bad mullet hairstyle, the other was a tall, slim, shaven-headed twenty-something with tattoos all over. They both had their eyes on JD. No one was remotely interested in Flake. It briefly crossed her mind that the Gunslingers club might be an offshoot of the Blue Oyster Club from the *Police Academy* movies.

'You're the guy who broke Rex's hand?' said Axl. 'That right?'

'That's right,' said JD.

'He forgiven you yet?'

'Ask him.'

The meeting was becoming a little less hospitable than Flake had hoped. She could see more bikers inside the workshop, looking out at what was going on. There was a mixture of bearded men and skinny, trampy-looking biker chicks, with lots of tattoos. All of them, male or female looked like they could kick some ass if needed. Flake felt like a fucking loser in her grey suit and polo-neck.

One of the biker chicks, a scrawny, pale, under-dressed skank with long dark hair that had white streaks in it, poked her head around the door and called over to the short, ginger guy. 'Hey, Axl, ain't it courteous to invite guests in for a drink?' she said, while loudly chewing some gum.

'It is,' said Axl, still eyeballing JD. After a few seconds of uncomfortable silence, Axl waved his thumb towards the workshop. 'Come on inside. Make yourselves comfortable.'

## Fourteen

From the outside, the Gunslingers club looked like a shithole. The inside was another matter. JD and Flake followed their hosts through a wide corridor into a gangster's paradise. They walked past a restaurant-sized kitchen and several private rooms with people inside, fucking. Loudly. They eventually arrived in the club's social area. The place was huge. It had no windows, but it was decorated by all kinds of neon lights. Logos for different beers and spirits lit up the walls in red, blue, green and yellow. Deep pinks and golds emanated from fitted lamps above a thirty-metre long drinks bar on the far wall, which had a hundred different branded spirit bottles stocked behind it. The room had roughly fifty tables spread evenly around. Some were big enough for group gatherings, others more suitable for couples wishing to have a private conversation. There were two pool tables in one of the darker corners. All around the walls were televisions, all tuned into a music channel that was playing "Eminence Front" by The Who. And of course, there were lots of bikers drinking, playing pool, and generally having a good time, while a few scantily dressed biker chicks grooved to the music.

Axl led Flake and JD over to a big, round table. 'What do you say we have a few drinks and you tell us why you're here?' he said, gesturing for them to sit down.

'No thanks,' said JD, pointing at a smaller table further away. 'We'll sit over there and mind our own business.'

Axl looked surprised, and more than a little offended. He exchanged a look with his giant buddy, Bruiser, then shrugged. 'Fair enough. I'll have one of the girls come over and take your order,' he said.

Flake followed JD over to the small table he had picked out. It was far enough away from everyone else to ensure no one overheard them talking. Even though Flake was concerned by JD's rudeness towards Axl and Bruiser, she was also glad she didn't have to sit with them and explain why they were there.

A biker chick in blue denim cut-offs and a pink T-shirt took their drinks order and then returned a minute later with a large bourbon for JD and a gin and tonic for Flake. All free of charge.

'This place is really nice,' said Flake.

'I don't like it,' said JD.

'Why not?'

'Too much going on. Just keep your wits about you. We're not out of the shit yet. And remember, these people could make a lot of money by turning us in. Dead or alive.'

Flake picked up her gin and tonic. It had a tall pink straw in it. She sucked on it and the level of the drink went down a few inches. It woke up her tongue and the back of her throat which were both drier than sandpaper. She let out a deep sigh. 'Boy, did I need that.'

'Hang in there,' said JD. 'You're doing good, 'cos it's been kind of a day so far, right?'

'Yeah. Yeah, it has.' The image of Sanchez with a bullet hole in his head flashed into her mind. She shook her head to be rid of it. 'How did your job with Rex go?' she asked, hoping for a response to take her mind off everything else.

'It was a fucking disaster.'

'Oh. I haven't dragged you away from it, have I?'

'No. The job is finished.' JD was engaging in conversation with her, but his eyes were constantly darting back and forth, scouring the room, looking for potential trouble. Flake took another sip of her drink and watched a small television on the wall behind the bar. Unlike all the others that were tuned into the music channel, the one behind the bar was playing live footage from a CCTV camera set up outside the pizza place on the street above them.

'When did you learn to fire the laser bolts?' JD asked, as if he'd had enough of checking out all the bikers that were hanging out in the bar area.

Flake cast her mind back to the first time the blue electricity had blasted out of her hands. 'The first time it happened I wasn't even expecting it,' she said. 'Shot the fucking First Lady. Didn't even mean to.'

'First Lady, huh? Nice.'

'If I hadn't done it, Sanchez would still be alive.'

JD reached across the table and grabbed Flake's hand. He looked into her eyes. 'It's not your fault,' he said.

'They shot him.' Flake's voice began to crack. Saying it out loud was way worse than saying it over and over in her head.

'Exactly,' said JD. '*They* shot him. You didn't. Christ, you saved his ass more times than I can remember.'

'He saved mine too. Lots of times.'

JD let go of her hand, sat back and picked up his glass of bourbon. He downed the whole lot in just a few seconds. 'We need to get out of here,' he said.

'What? Why?'

The answer to Flake's question was on the small TV behind the bar. The security camera footage showed cop cars pulling up outside the pizza place. Their hideout had been compromised.

The on-screen drama had caught the eye of quite a few of the Hell's Angels. Axl and his big goon, Bruiser, marched over to Flake and JD's table, followed by a group of their buddies. They all looked mighty pissed. Then the music stopped, and the place went quiet, aside from someone coughing somewhere in the midst of everything.

'You fucker!' said Axl, jabbing his finger in JD's direction as he arrived at the table. 'You said you weren't followed!'

JD stood up. 'We're leaving.'

Flake pushed her chair back and stood up. The chair made a screeching sound against the hardwood floor, drawing a few biker eyes away from JD and over to her.

'Sit the fuck down!' said Bruiser the giant, eyeballing both of them. He suddenly looked even bigger than before. And a heck of a lot more menacing.

Axl moved a little closer to JD, his confidence growing. 'You brought the cops here,' he said, his voice low and raspy.

'We lost the cops,' said JD. 'You know that.'

'TV says different,' said Axl, glancing up at the screen behind the bar.

'Maybe you tipped 'em off,' JD retorted. 'Thought you'd get yourself a big reward.'

Flake decided to intervene before things turned ugly. 'Is there a back way out of here?' she asked. 'We'll leave right now.'

'Shut the fuck up, lady. This is between me and your friend.'

'Listen asshole,' said JD. 'We're leaving, so back the fuck up.'

'I don't think so,' said Axl. He leaned back and spoke out of the side of his mouth to the crew behind him. '*Fellas.*'

That one word was the cue for just about every guy in the place to pull out a gun and point it at JD. Axl took a step back to make sure he was out of the way of any gunfire. His big buddy Bruiser whipped out a six-shooter with a long barrel, and pointed it at Flake's head.

'Looks like we got ourselves a big payday coming,' Axl said, maintaining solid eye contact with JD the whole time.

Flake raised her hands in surrender and waited for JD to make a call on what to do next, which he duly did.

'You definitely got something coming,' he said to Bruiser. *'Flake.'*

Flake had known exactly how the situation was going to play out from the minute JD told her, "we've gotta go." She could read his every move before he made it, unlike the Hell's Angels who had no idea what they were getting themselves into. From the moment she had raised her hands in surrender, she'd been waiting for him to say her name, because when he said her name, what he really meant was, *start shooting those fucking laser bolts out of your hands.*

## Fifteen

Flake already had her hands in the air. She subtly aimed her palms at Bruiser and Axl, the two most troublesome members of the biker gang. JD had given her the signal to blast them to pieces with her blue lightning. There was only one problem. The fucking blue bolts of electricity weren't coming out. When she'd fired them at the First Lady and the president's bodyguards earlier in the day, it had been instinctive, without any thought, or planning. But after that, she got a taste for it, and intentionally blasted the cop cars that were chasing her and JD. Shooting cars had been easy. Shooting at people, not so much. She wanted to blast the hell out of the Hell's Angels, but maybe her instincts were holding her back? After all, it would be murder, unlike shooting the cop cars and thereby causing the deaths of the cops in them, which was more likely to be considered manslaughter. Either way, no matter how hard she concentrated on shooting at the Hell's Angels gang, nothing was happening.

'Flake,' JD repeated.

'Yeah, I know. It's not working.'

'Great.'

Bruiser kept his six-shooter trained on Flake's forehead. 'Any weapons you've got, drop 'em now,' he said, throwing a glance JD's way.

'You put your guns down,' JD replied. 'Or this place is going down in flames.'

'You got three seconds,' said Bruiser. 'Or I shoot your lady in the face.'

'*Flake*,' said JD, once more in the tone that meant, *"fucking blast these fuckers"*.

Flake tried subtly thrusting her palms forward. Still no laser bolts. 'It's still not happening,' she whispered under her breath.

'Three,' said Bruiser, starting his countdown.

'Make it happen,' JD muttered through the side of his mouth.

'I'm trying.'

'Two....'

Flake tried visualising the laser blasts. Still nothing.

'One!'

JD stuck both hands inside his coat and pulled out a pair of pistols with the intention of killing everyone on his own. He needn't have bothered though because Bruiser suddenly leapt forward and ran right past him. He stumbled like someone who was tied to the back of a moving car, except it was his gun that was dragging him along. Before he lost his balance and toppled over, he let go of the gun. The gun didn't clatter onto the floor, it flew across the room, spinning over and over as it went. It eventually made a loud CLANK as it hit something at the back of the room.

'Afternoon everybody,' said a deep southern voice.

Flake breathed out for the first time in about ten seconds. She recognised the voice and looked around. Bruiser was on the floor staring at his empty hand. His gun was in the possession of Rodeo Rex, who had snatched it from him using his magnetic metal hand.

'Is this how we're treating our guests these days?' Rex asked as he walked past Bruiser to join up with Flake and JD.

'How the fuck did you get in here?' Axl asked, confusion on his face.

Rex tucked Bruiser's gun down the back of his jeans, then raised his metal hand above his head. It silenced the crowd of Hell's Angels, although that wasn't why he did it. With one quick move he swung his hand down again, pointing it at the floor. Every gun that was aimed at JD and Flake followed suit, dragging its holder's arm down with it. Flake couldn't tell if it was his magnetic hand that made the guns point to the floor, or if it was just Rex's gesture that made the bikers voluntarily lower their weapons, and she didn't care.

'Never mind how I got in here,' said Rex, answering Axl's question. 'I wanna know why you people are pointing guns at my friends?'

'It was a misunderstanding,' said Flake, hoping to take the sting out of the situation.

'They brought the cops here!' said Axl. He pointed up at the television behind the bar. It showed a fleet of armed cops preparing to storm the parking lot that led down to the Gunslingers club.

'No they didn't,' said Rex. 'Everybody put your guns away and act casual.'

'How the fuck are we supposed to act casual when we're being raided?' Axl complained.

'I don't have time to explain,' said Rex. 'I gotta speak with my friends in private for a minute.'

ZAP!

Finally, at the most inappropriate moment, Flake's palms decided to start firing lasers again. Axl took a shot to the face, which obliterated his head. One of the other guys took a blast in the chest, knocking him back into a bunch of his buddies. To add to the chaos, JD started shooting. Bikers went down in all directions like sparks from a firework. A handful escaped by diving out through the exits, and the barmaid ducked down behind the bar. When the shooting stopped, the room was filled with smoke and dead bodies. Flake and JD had wiped out most of the Gunslinger gang.

Rex shook his head. 'What the fuck did you do that for?' he asked.

'I'm sorry,' said Flake. 'I can't control it.'

JD tucked his guns back inside his coat. 'You got the portal open for us?' he asked Rex.

'Yeah. We gotta go. Quick.'

'Jacko told us the portal had been shut down.'

'Yeah, God shut it down. But Jasmine's been shot. Lucky for us, God likes her, so he gave us permission to use the portal again. But we've gotta go right now because Jasmine's gonna die if we don't get the Eye of the Moon to her in the next two minutes. So let's go.'

Rex headed over to the disabled toilets at the back of the room. JD ushered Flake on while he covered the rear, checking in case any bikers weren't really dead.

'What happened to Jasmine?' Flake asked as she followed Rex into the washroom.

'She got shot,' said Rex. 'Weren't you listening?'

'Yeah, but how did she get shot?'

'Never mind *how*. Just haul ass!'

## Sixteen

Purgatory was a drinking hole similar to the Tapioca, only with less customers on account of it being in the middle of a secluded desert known as the Devil's Graveyard. There were only two ways to get to Purgatory; via a secret turn at a crossroads in the desert, or through the travel portal in the men's toilets. Flake, Rex and JD entered via the portal after making their escape from the Gunslingers club.

Since its inception, Purgatory had been run by a man in a red suit, known by several names, such as the Man in Red, Scratch, Legba, Iblis, and more often than not, "the Devil" on account of him being the actual Devil. But since his recent murder by the Dead Hunters, the Devil had been replaced by a young black man named Jacko. When he'd been alive, Jacko had been Robert Johnson, the legendary bluesman, who'd known more about the crossroads than any other person alive. For that reason alone, he was a fitting caretaker. Jacko was standing behind the bar in his trademark black suit when Flake, Rex and JD burst in from the men's toilets.

'What took you so long?' he asked, concern all over his face.

The reason for his concern was clear for all to see. Jasmine and Elvis were on the floor by a table near the portal. Elvis was sitting upright, but Jasmine was lying across him with her head in his lap. There was blood all over her purple catsuit, and all over Elvis's hands and his light blue suit. Flake rushed over to help them, unclasping the Eye of the Moon from the chain around her neck as she ran. She dived down onto the floor next to Jasmine like a quarterback sliding for a first down. In his eagerness to help, Elvis unzipped Jasmine's catsuit down to her waist. Her whole upper body was covered in blood, and her face showed no signs of life.

'Where should I put this?' Flake asked, pressing the stone against Jasmine's chest as a starting point.

'Bit lower,' Elvis replied. 'She took quite a few bullets, mostly around her gut, I think.'

Flake spotted a gaping black hole that was oozing blood just above Jasmine's navel. She pressed the Eye against it, blocking the hole. There were other wounds near it, so every ten seconds or so, Flake pressed the magic blue stone onto another one. It didn't seem to be having much effect. And it was bringing back memories of trying the same thing on Sanchez. Bad memories.

'Am I doing this right?' she asked.

'I think so,' said Elvis. 'Remember that time you were stabbed in the neck? Sanchez pressed it against the wound and bandaged it down.'

'Do we have any bandages?' Rex asked, his question directed at Jacko.

'All out,' Jacko replied, an apologetic look on his face. 'You could try a T-shirt?'

'We need to put pressure on all the wounds,' said Flake as she watched blood dribbling out from the multitude of gunshot wounds on Jasmine's torso. 'We need more than one Eye of the Moon!'

Elvis leaned back and took off his jacket, then he ripped off his white shirt. He pulled Jasmine's arms out of her catsuit and wrapped the shirt around her torso, trying to put pressure on as many injuries as possible. There were still no signs of life.

'Oh fuck,' said Rex, tugging at his hair. 'How long does this take?'

'What happened to her?' Flake asked.

'It's a long story,' said Elvis. 'Where is Sanchez anyway? He knows how to do this.'

'He's dead,' said Flake, not wanting to elaborate any further because to speak about it would mean reliving it.

Elvis looked up at Rex, who confirmed it with a stern nod of his head.

JD left the others and headed over to the bar. He clicked his fingers at Jacko, then pretended to inject himself in the arm with an imaginary syringe. Jacko bent down behind the bar and rose back up a moment later with an empty syringe, by which time JD had already used a knife to make a deep incision in the palm of his hand, drawing out plenty of blood. He had the blood of Christ in his veins, and the stuff had emphatic healing powers. He took the syringe from Jacko and filled it with as much blood as he could, then he headed back over to the others, pushed Rex aside and crouched down next to Jasmine. He grabbed her right arm and pierced it with the needle on the syringe, injecting her with his blood.

'Will that work?' Flake asked.

'It worked on Rex once.'

'You gave me about a litre though,' Rex reminded him.

'Yeah, well there isn't time for me to squeeze out a litre.'

For ten seconds after the injection nothing much happened, but then just as everyone was beginning to fear the worst, the colour began to return to Jasmine's face. Where her body had looked cold and fragile, it began to show signs of life. She coughed and then opened her eyes a little.

'Oh, thank fuck!' said Elvis. He leant down and kissed Jasmine on the lips. 'Hang in there, baby. It's gonna be all right.' He looked at Flake and JD. 'You guys are awesome.'

Flake managed a smile. After trying and failing to save Sanchez with the Eye, it was a relief to know that Jasmine was coming back from the brink, thanks to a mix of the Eye and JD's holy blood.

'Rex, can you get her some water?' Elvis asked.

'You bet,' said Rex.

The big man headed over to the bar. Jacko already had a glass of water waiting for him. Rex took it and ran back to the others. He handed the glass to Elvis, who then carefully poured some of the water over Jasmine's lips. She opened her eyes wider, coughed again, then looked around at the others.

'You're gonna be okay,' said Flake. 'We've got you.'

In spite of her condition, Jasmine managed to speak. 'Sorry about Sanchez,' she said in a husky voice.

Flake appreciated the kind words, but rather than respond, she chose to move the Eye onto another of the bullet wounds under the shirt-bandage Elvis had tied around Jasmine's torso.

Elvis stroked Jasmine's hair. 'You know, you look like shit, sweetie,' he said.

'You too,' said Jasmine, the words coming out with a cough.

Flake glanced over at Elvis, with the intention of giving him a visual scolding for telling Jasmine she looked like shit. But she changed her mind when she spotted a patch of blood and a pair of bullet holes around his ribcage. He saw her staring and put her mind at rest.

'I'll be okay,' he said. 'Just fix Jasmine up first.'

'What a fucking day this is,' said Rex. 'Did you know the whole world thinks Flake shot the president?'

'Really?' said Elvis, looking like he thought it might be a joke. 'The president's been shot?'

'He's dead,' said Rex. 'Half the world leaders are dead. It's all over the news.'

Flake took another look at Elvis's body. His injuries were pretty serious too. One of the bullet holes was pumping blood out like a busted drinking fountain. 'I'm gonna do a couple more minutes on Jasmine, then I think you need a bit of healing up there, Elvis,' she said. 'You should at least be putting pressure on those wounds.'

'I know,' said Elvis. 'But I feel okay. I've been shot before. If you stay calm, the bleeding slows down.'

'Who shot you both?' Flake asked, hoping for a proper answer.

'We were doing a job for Alexis Calhoon,' Elvis replied. 'A mystery job, one she couldn't tell us about on the phone. We had to go to her ranch to find out about it. I wish we'd never taken the job now. It was a mess right from the start.'

There were two other figures in Purgatory that had gone unnoticed throughout the chaos. One was Eric Einstein, the crazy, ginger-haired scientist. He was sitting at a table on his own tapping away on a laptop. The other was a great big black and brown dog. The dog had been watching intently as the gang tried to save Jasmine. As soon as Flake made eye contact with the big Alsatian he trotted over and licked her face.

'Whose dog is this?' Flake asked, stroking the big mutt's head.

'He came through the portal with me and Jas,' said Elvis.

'He's been hurt,' said Flake, noticing a patch of blood on one of the dog's front legs. 'Jacko can you get me a napkin or something? Anything that looks like a bandage?' She checked the dog's collar. 'It says his name is Goober. Jacko, napkins please! And can you get him some water? He looks thirsty.'

'Yes, ma'am,' said Jacko with a sarcastic salute.

Elvis looked up at Rex. 'How did you and JD get on with the bodyguard job?'

'It was a fucking disaster,' Rex replied. He pointed to a bandana that was wrapped around his leg just above the knee. 'I got shot too.'

'Well don't just stand there,' said Elvis. 'Tell us all about it.'

## Seventeen

### Part Three - The Gangster

Rex drove his van up to the tall, arched, iron gates at the front of the Rodriguez estate. Someone must have seen him arrive because the gates opened for him, enabling him to cruise through without stopping. The estate was enormous. From the outside it had looked big, but much of it was hidden by a high wall that ran around the perimeter. Once inside the gates, Rex got a good look at a golf course that was set back from the road, with plenty of woodland all around it.

Being a proud biker, Rex wouldn't normally drive anywhere in a van. But seeing as how he was scheduled to stay at the Rodriguez estate for a week, he'd packed a whole bunch of clothes and enough weapons and ammunition to take out a small army, just in case the need arose. He parked the van, slung his sports bag over his shoulder and headed for a set of gold-rimmed wooden doors at the front of the mansion. One of the doors opened as he approached. A silver-haired lady in her mid-fifties, wearing a white dress and a red cardigan came out and greeted him with a smile and a "hello".

'Hi, I'm Rex,' he said, returning the smile.

'Lovely to meet you, sir,' the lady replied. 'I am Merris, the housekeeper. The master of the house is expecting you. Are you on your own? I was told to expect two of you. '

'A buddy of mine is coming too, but we travel separately.'

'That's fine,' said Merris. 'Would you care to follow me?'

'Yes ma'am.'

The long drive had left Rex feeling sticky and in need of a shower. He was wearing blue jeans and a black leather waistcoat, and he had a black and gold Harley Davidson bandana wrapped around his head, just to make sure everyone knew that in spite of the van, he was really a biker, and damn proud of that fact.

The inside of the mansion was flashy and just a little bit tacky. There were fancy paintings on the walls, gold trims on everything and a show-off's staircase in the middle of the entrance hall that led to more fancy shit upstairs. Rex was impressed.

He followed Merris through several corridors, all of which had shiny, white tiled flooring. Every corner had a green, leafy plant in it, and there were even more of the expensive paintings and ornaments to admire. Merris was polite enough to point out things, like where the bathrooms were, where the kitchen was, and how to get to the golf course.

Every time they passed a window, Rex saw at least one or two henchmen strolling around the grounds outside. They all seemed to be carrying guns or rifles about their person. Some were on horseback, others on foot or in golf buggies. Most of them were overweight though, or just lacking any great muscle definition. Classic henchmen, in fact.

Eventually, Merris stopped outside a set of double doors. She knocked twice before opening one of them. 'Through here,' she said, gesturing towards the open door.

'Thank you,' Rex said, giving the delightful housekeeper one last smile before he left her and entered the room.

'Have a nice day,' Merris said, closing the door behind him.

The room she had taken him to was even more impressive than everything else he'd seen so far. A set of large French doors at the back let in the light from outside and offered a great view of one of the golfing fairways. There were more paintings on the walls, more exotic plants, and even candle chandeliers hanging from the high ceiling. It was all quite marvellous. The centrepiece was a long white marble table in the middle of the room. A man was seated at the far end, eating a breakfast of fruit and pancakes.

'Come on in, Rex,' he said, his smile bright, white and faker than a twelve-dollar bill. 'I'm Mister Rodriguez, but you can call me Antonio.'

Antonio was in his fifties, well-tanned and in pretty good shape too. He was wearing a white suit with a matching shirt that had the top three buttons undone, showing off a smooth bronzed chest. His brown hair was so thick it looked like a wig but probably wasn't. He put his knife and fork down and pointed at a seat beside the table.

'Sit down,' he said. 'Care for some breakfast? I can have my chef whip something up for you.'

'No. I'm good thanks,' said Rex, dropping his sports bag to the floor. 'If it's all the same to you, I'd like to see my room. I could use a shower.'

'Of course, of course. But first, just indulge me a few minutes with you. I like to know the people who work for me.'

'Just a tip,' said Rex. 'When my friend the Bourbon Kid gets here, choose your words carefully. If you tell him that he's working for you, he might kill you.'

Antonio laughed. 'No problem,' he said, tapping his head to imply he'd been forgetful. 'I should say it like, like he's doing me a favour, yes?'

'Yeah. And you should pay him his money pretty quick too.'

'Aah yes, money,' Antonio said. 'Please, please sit. Let me explain to you what the job is.'

Rex pulled out a chair on the side of the table and sat down. Antonio reached down below the table and picked up a black leather case. He slid it across the table.

'There's fifty thousand in there.'

'The job is for a hundred.'

'That's right. Fifty up front and then ten per day when the day is done.'

'That wasn't the deal.'

Antonio's smile never faltered. 'Oh, I'm sorry,' he said. 'There has obviously been a miscommunication. Never mind. I tell you what, as a compromise, I'll give you twenty a day. That's five days' work for a hundred and fifty grand. How's that, eh?'

'I guess that'll be fine. You want me and my buddy to drive your daughter to school, is that correct?'

Antonio didn't reply. His eyes flickered at something over Rex's shoulder. The incident was over in a millisecond. But a millisecond was enough for Rex to get a sense of what was about to happen. An ambush. A rookie ambush by all accounts, but still an ambush that had to be dealt with. So Rex dealt with it. He kicked his seat back, and in one swift move he stood up and spun around to face his attacker. A fat henchmen had crept up behind him, brandishing a wooden baton. He had a sweaty, bearded face and messy brown hair, and he was wearing blue sleeveless overalls that showed off some big, but very hairy arms. He swung his baton at Rex's head. Not quick enough. Rex reached out and grabbed the goon's wrist with his metal hand, stopping the forward motion of the baton. He squeezed hard, which was all it took to end the feeble attack. The sweaty henchman dropped his weapon and fell to his knees.

'I give, I give!' he cried.

Rex released him and turned to confront Antonio. The smug billionaire was grinning from ear to ear. 'Bravo!' he said, applauding. 'Bra-fucking-vo!'

'Let me guess,' said Rex. 'That was an audition?'

Antonio continued clapping. 'It surely was,' he said. 'And you passed with flying colours. That's Ozzy, by the way.'

Rex looked down at Ozzy and offered him some advice. 'When my friend arrives later, if you try and ambush him, he'll kill you. Then he'll kill your whole family too. Capiche?'

Ozzy was too busy rubbing his injured wrist to respond. Antonio was loving it though.

'This is brilliant,' he said. 'Ozzy, after you show Rex to his room in a minute, send Nico up. I want him to try the ambush on the Bourbon Kid.'

'Yes, sir,' Ozzy said, before climbing to his feet, looking embarrassed.

Rex eyed up Antonio Rodriguez again. There wasn't much to like about him. As well as being a rich, greasy, slimebag, he was only too happy to have his henchmen killed off for a bit of amusement over breakfast. That said, the guy was paying well, so Rex sat back down.

'If that's what your henchmen are like, I can see why you need me and my buddy. By the way, this guy Nico who's going to ambush the Bourbon Kid, he's gonna end up dead, you realise that?'

Antonio laughed. 'Fuck Nico, he's a scumbag. He's got it coming.'

Ozzy, who was still loitering by the table catching his breath, agreed with his boss. 'Nico is an asshole,' he said.

Rex ignored the out-of-shape henchman and focussed on Antonio. 'Tell me, why does your daughter need me and my buddy protecting her? What are you afraid of?'

'I'm glad you asked,' said Antonio, picking up his knife and fork and resuming his breakfast. 'See, I've had a letter from someone threatening to kill me and my daughter this week.'

'Is that unusual for you?' Rex asked. 'I kinda figured there would be lots of people wanting to kill you.'

Antonio looked momentarily offended. 'Why would you think that?'

'You've got a small army of disposable henchmen here. Usually when someone has an army of henchmen it's because they've made a lot of enemies.'

Antonio speared a piece of melon on his fork and popped it into his mouth, the fork scraping against his teeth. 'That's funny,' he said with a smile. 'And true. Life's a fight. Last man standing gets rich and becomes the king. And when you're the king, you gotta pay a lot of big men to protect you from all the wannabe kings out there.'

'And which wannabe is threatening you this week?'

'I wish I knew.'

'I think you do know. That's why you've hired me and my buddy. You could save us a lot of time by just telling me who the problem character is.'

Antonio put his knife and fork down again and swallowed the last of his melon. 'Okay, here's the thing. And this is just between you and me, right?'

Rex did not respond.

'Okay, well, I think it's one of my henchmen that made the threat. That's why it's serious. I figure when they see I've hired you, whoever was planning to kidnap my little girl will realise they've made a mistake and get the fuck out of town. I'm gonna put the word around that you're here to find the person who sent the letter. That should be enough. You probably won't even have to kill anyone.'

'Can I see the letter?'

'Did I say it was a letter? Sorry, I meant it was a phone call. Someone with a voice disguiser called me and made the threat.'

'And what did they say?'

'They said that they were going to kill me and my daughter, Paige.'

'Just now you said they were going to kidnap her.'

'Well, I'm worried that they might. Either way, I want her protected. She's my only child. You and the Bourbon Kid will escort her to and from school for the next five days, then your job is done. Hopefully, any kidnappers or assassins will see the two of you and think twice about it.'

Rex mulled over what Antonio had said before choosing his next words. 'If you're lying about any of this, and JD finds out, he'll kill you and your daughter, you do know that, right?'

The confident smirk vanished from Antonio's face. 'JD?' he said. 'The Bourbon Kid is JD?'

'Yeah, but don't call him that.'

'What do I call him then?'

'Don't call him anything. In fact, be smart, say as little as possible to him. And don't make jokes. Or smirk. Or be smug. He doesn't like any of those things. And if you tell him any lies, he'll know, so get your fucking story straight before he gets here.'

'He sounds intense. Is there anything he *does* like?'

'Yeah, being left alone. Can someone show me to my room now, please?'

'Of course. When you've freshened up, feel free to go for a walk around the estate. Enjoy what it has to offer. Be here for supper at seven p.m., and I will introduce you to my daughter, Paige. You'll like her, she's a smart girl.'

Rex stood up and retrieved his sports bag. 'Remember,' he said, slinging the bag over his shoulder again. 'When JD gets here, don't be smug, don't lie, and don't act like you're the boss. You'll live longer.'

Ozzy the hopeless henchman escorted Rex to the door and gave him directions to his room. As soon as Rex headed off to find it, Ozzy returned to his boss's table.

'Hey boss,' he said to Antonio. 'Is it really true that one of the guys is threatening to kill Paige?'

'Don't be ridiculous,' said Antonio, shaking his head. 'No one here would dare hurt Paige.'

Ozzy scratched his head. 'Then why hire these new guys?'

'That's none of your business. Now go and get Nico like I asked. And not a word of this to anyone else.'

## Eighteen

After taking a shower in the rather excellent guest room that had been assigned to him, Rex went for a stroll around the grounds. The Rodriguez estate was vast, and despite all the henchmen hanging around the place checking for intruders, it was a very beautiful place too. Green fields, woodland, a pond that was almost big enough to be a lake, horses, a shooting range, the place had everything. Everything but the sunshine. The skies were grey, hinting at a possibility of bad weather to come.

Rex walked across a long and ever-so-slightly downhill stretch of grass to a woodland area. He passed by six or seven henchmen. They all ignored him, and wisely kept their distance as they patrolled the estate. Some were on horseback, others on foot.

The woodland was more Rex's kind of place. The trees were full of chirping birds, and there was plenty of wildlife on the ground. Rabbits, squirrels, badgers, foxes and a few other creatures Rex couldn't identify scurried around as he passed through.

He was deep into the woods when he saw something that looked like a wolf. It had reddish fur but with a white underbelly and a black streak down its back. It trotted up to Rex and stopped in front of him. Rex crouched down to get a closer look at the animal. A staring match appeared to be all it was interested in.

'What's your name then?' Rex asked the creature.

'Her name is Jackie,' a woman's voice replied. 'She's a jackal.'

Rex stood up and looked around for the owner of the voice. A woman strolled out from behind a row of bushes. She had long dark hair and big brown eyes. Her skin was bright and luminous, just like her smile. She was wearing skin-tight black pants, brown ankle boots and a white blouse. At a guess, Rex would have said she was in her mid-twenties.

'You must be Rodeo Rex?' she said.

'I am. And you are?'

'Selene.'

'Mrs Rodriguez?'

'That's right,' she nodded at the animal Rex had been eyeballing. 'Don't mind Jackie, she won't bite. She's well trained. She won't hurt you unless you try to hurt me. But you're not going to do that are you?' She walked up to Rex and held out her hand. 'Nice to meet you, should I call you Rex, or Rodeo Rex?'

'Rex will do fine.' He took her hand and shook it out of politeness. The skin on her hand was soft. The look in her eyes, disarming. Rex was instantly smitten. 'You out here on your own?' he asked.

'It's perfectly safe,' she said, smiling, and making good eye contact. 'And there's always a henchman within shouting distance.'

'Yeah, there's plenty of those guys, ain't there?'

'There certainly is. How are you enjoying your stay so far?'

'So far, it's been fine. My room is very impressive, like everything else I've seen.'

'Have you met Paige yet?'

'Your daughter?'

Selene's smile broadened. 'Do I look like I have a twelve-year-old daughter?'

'Sorry, I guess not.'

'Paige is Antonio's daughter from his first marriage.'

'You're the second wife?'

Selene nodded. 'We've been married since I was nineteen.' She pointed into the woods. 'The way you're headed there, it's nothing but trees. I can take you on a tour around the grounds if you like?'

'It's okay. I'll make my own way around. You like it here?'

'What's not to like?'

'I dunno, all the henchmen?'

Selene laughed. 'You know, you're not what I expected.'

'What did you expect?'

'A big, dumb, angry psychopath.'

'You're thinking of my friend, the Bourbon Kid.'

'I haven't met him yet.'

'That's probably for the best. He's not exactly a people person. Did your husband tell you why we were hired?'

'Only that you were to keep an eye on Paige.'

'Yeah, but why though? What danger is she in?'

Selene laughed. 'Paige is more a danger to herself than anything else. My guess is, Antonio wants you to stop her from running away to join the circus.'

'Excuse me?'

'There's a travelling circus in town. Paige saw the poster and wants to go. Apparently they fire midgets out of a cannon. But Antonio has forbidden her from going. You see, Paige is autistic. If she goes to a circus with all its bright lights, loud noises and scary clowns, she's liable to have a meltdown. Personally, I'd be happy to take her, but Antonio won't allow it under any circumstances.'

'I don't much care for the circus myself,' said Rex. 'Seen one too many evil clowns in my time.'

'Evil clowns?'

'Well, you know, circus folk in general,' said Rex, not wanting to elaborate on the clowns he'd met (and killed) because they were all vampires.

Selene stared at Rex's eye patch. 'It's none of my business,' she said, 'But what happened to your eye?'

'I had a run-in with some cannibals.'

There was a pause while Selene took the revelation on board. 'I'm sorry,' she said eventually. 'I shouldn't have asked.'

'It's okay. You're actually the first one.'

'To ask about your eye patch?'

'Yeah. The cannibal thing was quite recent, and no one I've met since it happened has had the guts to ask about it. Congratulations though, I've been waiting.'

Selene smiled again. Rex was beginning to melt a little inside with every smile she gave him. It was quite beguiling. Her wealthy, gangster husband was a lucky man.

'It was nice meeting you,' she said. 'I'll leave you in peace now. Have a pleasant stay.'

She made a clicking sound through the side of her mouth and began to walk back the way Rex had come from. The jackal, reacting to the clicking sound she made, leapt to its feet and joined her, walking by her side. Selene never looked back. Man, she had a great walk too. The swing of her hips was mesmerising. When she was twenty metres away, Rex called after her.

'Nothing but trees this way, you say?'

'That's right,' she replied without looking back.

After a quick spot of power-walking, Rex caught up with Selene. He strolled alongside her, with the jackal in between them. And seeing as how she'd had no problem asking him about his eye-patch, Rex asked a personal question in return.

'How did you meet Antonio?'

Selene stopped and turned to face him, flashing him another of her bright-white smiles. 'Congratulations,' she said. 'You're the first one.'

'To ask you how you met your husband?'

'First one today.'

The woman was a tease. An out and out tease. Rex liked it. A lot.

'I just can't picture the two of you meeting on a dating site or in a bar,' Rex said with a grin.

'And why not?'

'You just seem very down to earth. Not snobby or pretentious.'

'Why, thank you, I think. Does that mean you think my husband is pretentious?'

'No, but rich men often attract divas.'

'Divas? Ha!' Selene playfully slapped Rex on the arm. 'As a matter of fact, it was an arranged marriage. Does that make more sense to you?'

'You have arranged marriages down here?'

'My father was in debt to Antonio. But, they came to an agreement. In exchange for my hand in marriage, Antonio wiped out my father's debt.'

'That's very romantic.'

'It was a lot of money. My parents would have lost their home, and therefore so would I. Instead, I married the wealthiest and most powerful man in town. And I get to live here in this wonderful paradise.'

'Well, it is a paradise, a lovely place.'

The sound of horse hooves pounding on the ground was followed by the appearance of a henchman on horseback riding through the woods towards them. He was in his thirties with leathery skin. And he dressed like a cowboy, with the obligatory rifle hanging on a strap from his shoulder.

'Everything okay, Mrs Rodriguez?' he asked, throwing a wary glance at Rex.

'Yes thank you, Lucas. Everything is fine.'

'Would you like me to escort you back to the house?'

'No, that's not necessary, thank you. I have Jackie with me.'

'I'm afraid I have to insist.'

'And why is that?'

'Your new friend here, his partner just showed up. And he's killed Nico and Clyde.'

Selene looked surprised. She stared at Rex, open-mouthed.

'Yeah, that was always gonna happen,' Rex said, apologetically. 'I warned your husband, but I knew he wouldn't listen.'

'Nico had his neck broken,' said Lucas, glowering at Rex. 'And Clyde had his face caved in.'

'Not my fault,' said Rex.

The corner of Selene's mouth curled up into a wry smile. 'Nico was a waste of space,' she said.

'That may be,' said Lucas. 'But your husband wants you back at the house, now.'

Selene hesitated a moment, as if she were about to protest, but Lucas kept a steely glare aimed in her direction. A look of disappointment fluttered across her face. It was gone in an instant, replaced by a forced smile. 'Of course,' she said. She tapped Rex on his elbow. 'It was nice meeting you. Perhaps I'll see you later at dinner?'

'Maybe, yeah.'

Selene gifted Rex one last smile, then climbed onto the back of Lucas's horse. She wrapped her arms around his waist and squeezed her legs in against the sides of the sturdy brown mount. Lucas gave Rex a disingenuous smile, lowered his head and then tapped the rim of his hat. 'Good day to you, Mister.'

'Right.'

With that, Lucas turned the horse around and rode back to the house with Selene clinging to him.

Rex looked down at the jackal by his side. 'I guess it's back into the woods then?' he said. The jackal didn't reply. Instead it turned its back on Rex and fucked off into a row of bushes.

Before Rex could even tell the jackal how he felt about it snubbing him, his phone rang. It was a call from JD, which was unusual. The Bourbon Kid wasn't generally one for making calls, unless it was serious.

Rex put the phone to his ear. 'Hey man, what's up?'

'What happened there? Looked like you were doing well.'

Rex looked around. There was no sign of JD anywhere. 'Where the fuck are you?' he asked.

'I'm up on the mansion roof. Been watching you hit it off with the brunette. What went wrong?'

Rex looked back at the main building. It was almost a mile away. 'What are you talking about?' he grumbled.

'I found a sniper rifle up on the roof. Been watching you through the sighter.'

'A sniper rifle? What the fuck is a sniper rifle doing on the roof of the house?'

'I don't know, but I'm gonna find out. So, who was the brunette?'

'It was Antonio's wife, Selene.'

'Aah, is that why the henchman came and took her away? Busted you hitting on the boss's wife?'

'I wasn't hitting on her.'

'There was a lot of smiling going on.'

'Get fucked.'

'I've counted thirty-seven henchmen so far. That's a lot, don't you think?'

'Yeah,' Rex agreed. 'It is. What did you make of Antonio?'

'I don't like him. He's full of shit.'

'Yeah, I thought so too. Did he tell you his daughter Paige is autistic?'

'No.'

'Well, she is. According to Selene, we're just watching her so she doesn't run off to join the circus.'

'I don't buy that for a minute.'

'Well, tomorrow morning bright and early we're taking the girl to school.'

**Nineteen**

After an evening meal with the Rodriguez family and a couple of Antonio's henchmen, JD retired to his room for the night. The room he'd been given at the Rodriguez estate was fine indeed, but even so, he didn't trust Antonio Rodriguez, and he didn't like the look of any of the henchmen either. And there were a lot of henchmen. A fucking lot. And then there was Rex, the lovestruck fool. At dinner, Rex had spent much of the time fawning over Selene, right in front of her husband. To make matters worse, Selene seemed to like Rex too. There was no accounting for taste.

However, the dinner did give JD and Rex a chance to meet Antonio's autistic daughter, Paige. The twelve-year-old had a dreadful pudding bowl haircut. She was skinny too, like a rake. JD recognised some of her autistic traits. She said virtually nothing throughout the meal, and made barely any eye-contact with anyone either. She also divided the food on her plate into sections so none of it was touching, and her right leg bounced up and down non-stop the entire time. Despite all that, JD quite liked her. His younger brother, Casper had been autistic, so he had an understanding of the condition, which in turn meant he had a little bit of sympathy.

JD spent the night sleeping with one eye open. In the morning, he took a shower in his en suite bathroom then slipped into some casual clothes, black jeans, black vest, gun holster, black leather jacket, and a pair of black sneakers with red laces, just for a touch of colour. After concealing a few extra weapons about his person, he left his room, headed downstairs, ignored everyone he met, left the house, climbed into the big black Mercedes that was parked out front, and waited for Paige and Rex.

He was impressed with the vehicle. It had plenty of cool gadgets and the seat was comfortable. He turned on the radio, and the song "Little Red Riding Hood" by Sam the Sham and the Pharaohs came on.

A minute into the song, Rex strolled out of the house, dressed in his usual jeans and waistcoat. He headed for the driver's side and tapped on the window. JD wound it down a little so Rex could poke his head through.

'Want me to drive?' Rex asked.

'No. You're in the back with the girl.'

'Fine.'

Rex opened the back door and climbed in. Before he'd even got comfortable, Paige walked out of the house with a rucksack over her shoulder. She was in full school uniform, which consisted of a scarlet coloured jacket with a matching skirt and tie, and a white blouse. Rex leaned across the back seats and opened her door for her. She chucked her rucksack onto the seat then climbed in.

'Good morning,' she said, politely as she shut the door.

'Morning Paige,' said Rex. He leaned forward and tapped on the back of JD's seat. 'Onward please, driver,' he added, with a sly grin.

JD drove the car down to the gates at the end of the driveway. They opened automatically, and he steered the car out into the road.

'Could you change the music channel, please?' said Paige.

JD ignored her.

'What sort of music do you like?' Rex asked her.

'I like John Denver.'

'Really? What's your favourite John Denver song?'

'Take me home cunt—' Paige sneezed loudly before she could finish the song title.

'Did you hear that?' Rex asked JD. 'She wants to go home already.'

'Take Me Home Country Roads,' said Paige, wiping her nose. 'I can't stand this stuff we're listening to. Can you find a country music channel, please?'

JD switched the radio off.

'That's better, isn't it?' said Rex, smiling at Paige.

'Yes,' Paige replied, before adding. 'I like your hair.'

JD was thankful that he was in the front. Small talk with children was not his thing at all. And Paige wasn't in any position to be commenting on anyone else's hairstyle. Her fringe looked like she'd cut it herself, while drunk.

'Driver, would you like to hear a joke?' Paige asked from the back seat.

'No.'

'It's a good one.'

'I don't care.'

'It's about the pope.'

Rex intervened. 'I'd like to hear a joke,' he said, purely out of kindness. 'By the way, Paige, did you know one of my friends killed the pope?'

'No, I didn't,' said Paige. 'And that's not relevant to my joke.'

'Okay,' said Rex. 'You carry on then.'

'Well, you see, one day the pope is at a charity event.'

'That's where my friend killed him,' said Rex.

'What?'

'At a charity event. She shot him six times in the chest because she thought he was a zombie.'

JD glanced in his rear-view mirror. Paige looked agitated by Rex interrupting her. And Rex looked kinda "fucked off" because she wasn't interested in his story, which was bound to be better than her joke.

'Anyway,' Paige continued, 'the pope gets drunk at his charity event. He drinks too much wine, and he decides to drive home even though he's over the drink-drive limit. He steals a limousine from the parking lot and drives off in it. And because he's drunk he forgets to check how fast he's going. Before long, he's zooming down the highway at a hundred miles an hour in his limousine.'

'Sounds realistic,' said Rex.

'But he drives past some highway patrol officers. They see how fast the limo's going and chase after it. The limo is swerving all over the road too, so they know the driver is drunk. Eventually, after a ten mile chase, the pope pulls over. One of the cops gets out and walks up to give him a ticket while his partner waits in the car. Anyway, after about a minute, the first cop comes back and he hasn't given the limousine driver a ticket, so his partner says, "why didn't you breathalyse him or give him a speeding ticket?" and the first cop says, "I couldn't, the person in the car is super important, so I had to let him off." And his partner says, "Why? Who was it? Was it someone famous?" And the other cop replies, "I don't know, but his driver was the pope!"

There was an awkward silence at the end of the joke.

'Geddit?' said Paige. 'The cop thought the pope was chauffeuring someone else around!'

Rex laughed politely.

JD switched the radio back on. He found "Under the Bridge" by the Red Hot Chilli Peppers. Way better than listening to a twelve-year-old girl tell jokes about the pope.

'I thought you would like that joke?' said Paige. 'I looked it up last night. It's a joke about a driver, and you're driving me around. Don't you see? It's topical.'

'You gotta give her that,' said Rex, his appreciation of the joke increasing. 'You got any other jokes, Paige?'

'No. That was my only joke. I don't normally tell jokes.'

'No shit,' JD muttered.

'That's a damn shame,' said Rex, generously.

Paige tapped the back of JD's seat. 'Take a right turn up ahead,' she said, 'then pull in outside *Big Buns and Footlongs*.'

'What for?' asked JD.

'You have to stop there and pick up my lunch for me. They should give you both a breakfast sandwich too. They usually give one to Nico, my regular driver, but seeing as he's not here today, they're going to make two. One for each of you.'

'Breakfast sandwich?' said Rex.

'You both get one,' said Paige. 'They're free of charge. The owner, Alicia, is a friend of my dad's.' She pointed out of the window. 'See, it's over there, the place with the big red sign.'

JD pulled over outside the shop and killed the engine. 'I'll go,' he said to Rex. 'You stay in the back.'

'No, I should go,' said Rex. 'It'll look weird if there's no driver and I'm sitting in the back with a young girl.'

'That's what the tinted windows are for,' JD replied. He climbed out of the car and locked it so that Rex couldn't escape.

*Big Buns and Footlongs* was a sandwich shop, sandwiched between a barber shop and a hardware store. The storefront was in need of some modernisation. The windows were dirty, and the red sign above the shop had seen better days. The pavement outside was covered in gum and old milkshake stains. Inside the shop, a young boy, aged maybe twelve or thirteen was standing behind the counter. JD walked in and went straight up to the counter.

'I'm here for Paige Rodriguez's lunch, and two breakfast sandwiches.'

The serving boy was a goofy looking, dark-haired Latino wearing a white apron over a green shirt. He didn't react to the request, instead he stared open-mouthed at JD. 'You're the—.'

'That's right. I'm the new driver. Paige's lunch and two breakfast sandwiches.' JD checked the name badge on the boy's apron. His name was Kai. And he needed some encouragement to get on with his job. 'Yo, Kai, I'm on the clock here.'

Kai was clearly nervous. He'd recognised JD for sure. For a few more seconds he stared blankly at his new customer, blinking a little more than necessary. Eventually when he snapped out of it, he reached down below the counter and grabbed two brown paper bags filled with food. He placed them on the counter. 'Will that be all?' he asked.

'Yeah. How much do I owe?'

'They're already paid for.'

JD frowned. 'They are?'

'The man you're driving for, Antonio Rodriguez, he offers this store protection. In exchange, we give Paige six tubs of custard and a banana every day. And we make a sandwich for Nico, her driver.'

'Okay, a few things,' said JD. 'First of all, Nico is dead. He won't be back. Second, six tubs of custard?'

'Nico is dead?' said Kai, smiling. 'Good, he was a dick.'

Before Kai could say any more, a large, Latino lady in a blue dress walked out of a kitchen area behind him. She had shoulder-length dark hair, and an irritated look on her chubby face. 'Kai, I think you've said enough,' she said. She looked at JD. 'Mister Rodriguez will be angry if his daughter is late for school.'

JD picked up the sandwich bags. 'Thank you for the food,' he said, with a polite nod of his head. 'I'll see you tomorrow.'

'Yes. Goodbye, sir.'

JD left the sandwich shop and walked around the driver's side of the car and climbed in, setting the brown bags down on the passenger seat. Rex and Paige were playing a game that involved adding up the numbers on the license plates of passing cars. JD grabbed the bag with Paige's lunch in it and leaned over the seats so he could hand it to Rex.

'What have we got here then?' Rex asked, taking the bag and opening it. His enthusiasm waned when he saw the contents. 'Custard?'

'That's mine,' said Paige, snatching the bag from him.

'That's a lot of custard,' said Rex.

'And a banana,' said Paige.

JD turned on the radio again. "People are Strange" by the Doors mercifully drowned out the custard conversation. He hit the gas, and the journey to Paige's school resumed. When they arrived at their destination, JD parked the Mercedes right outside the school gates. He turned down the volume on the radio and looked back at Rex.

'You walking her in?' he asked.

'I dunno, am I?' Rex said, looking at Paige.

'My driver normally opens my door for me,' said Paige, looking at JD. 'That way I don't drop my lunch.'

'I got the sandwiches,' said JD, looking at Rex.

'Fine,' Rex sighed. He opened his door, climbed out and walked around to Paige's side of the car. He opened her door for her and she slid off the seat onto the sidewalk.

'Thank you, Rex,' she said, politely.

'No problem. Have a nice day at school. See you at four?'

Paige slung her rucksack over her shoulder. 'See you at four,' she said. 'Don't be late, please.'

'Yes ma'am.'

There were a group of girls at the school gates, all of similar age to Paige. They were all watching, no doubt wondering who her giant bodyguard was. Paige walked past them and through the school gates without acknowledging any of them.

Rex joined JD in the front of the car for the return journey. 'See them girls giving her shitty looks?' he said.

'Nope,' said JD swallowing some food he'd been chewing. 'Here's your sandwich.'

He held out an eight-inch sub, wrapped in red and white paper. Rex took it and unwrapped it. From the first bite he realised it was something special. The taste was heavenly. He looked over at JD who was experiencing the same thing.

'Holy shit, this is good!' Rex said during a fleeting moment where his mouth was empty.

'Yeah,' JD agreed. 'Don't tell Flake though.'

'Don't tell Sanchez!'

A street cop walked out into the road in front of the car, headed around to JD's side and tapped on the window. JD wound it down. The cop crouched down to get a look at them. He was in his fifties with a neatly trimmed grey-beard and a kind face.

'Excuse me fellas,' he said. 'You can't stop here. This is a school drop-off point.'

'Fuck off,' JD replied, before winding the window back up.

The cop tapped on the window again.

JD wound it down again. This time he grabbed the cop by his shirt and yanked him forward. The cop's face connected with the frame of the door, busting his nose. As he reached for a gun that was holstered by his hip, he felt the barrel of JD's gun press into his cheekbone.

'We're eating,' said JD. 'Understand?'

'Yeah, I understand,' the cop said. He retracted his hand from his gun and used it to catch the stream of blood that was flowing from his nose onto his beard. 'I'm sorry,' he added. 'I didn't recognise you. It won't happen again, I promise.'

'Good. Have a nice day.'

JD let go of the cop and wound the window back up again. The cop gathered himself together and fucked off to irritate someone else.

'There's a guy over there who looks a bit suspicious,' said Rex through a mouthful of food.

JD looked around. No one looked suspicious. 'Who?' he asked.

Rex took another bite of his sandwich while he pointed down the street. 'That guy. The one in the strange coat.'

JD looked at where Rex was pointing. 'What are you talking about?' he complained. There's no one there.'

Rex wiped some sauce from his mouth and looked up. 'That's weird,' he said. 'The guy was right there, like one second ago.'

'What did he look like?'

'I dunno. He just had a weird coat on. It had fuzzy black and white lines on it. You know, like he'd come out of an *Aha* video.'

JD sighed. 'Just eat your fucking sandwich.'

# Twenty

## Back in Purgatory

'Where the fuck are you going with this story?' Flake asked. 'Weren't you supposed to be telling us how you got shot?'

'I'm giving you some background,' said Rex, irritated by Flake's interruption.

Elvis and Jasmine were at the back of the room on the sofa, half asleep as they listened to Rex's tale. Flake, JD and Rex were sitting on stools at the bar. JD was puffing on a cigarette and occasionally chipping in on Rex's story. And Goober the dog was sitting at the feet of Flake, his new best friend.

'It sounds like you're telling us about some woman you've got the hots for,' Flake groaned. 'How is that relevant to you getting shot?'

Before Rex could respond, Jacko called out from behind the bar. 'Flake, you're on TV.'

The television on the wall in Purgatory was tuned to a news channel that was reporting on all the assassinated politicians. There was no sound coming from the TV, but the screen had two mugshots on it, one of Flake and one of Sanchez.

'Turn the volume up then,' said Rex.

Jacko picked up a remote and unmuted the TV. A female reporter on the side of the screen was in the middle of telling the audience what everyone in Purgatory already knew.

'Sanchez Garcia was killed by one of the president's bodyguards. His accomplice Flake Munroe escaped with the help of the infamous mass-murderer, the Bourbon Kid. Current estimates suggest they killed as many as fifty people during their audacious escape from the Poseidon hotel.'

The picture of Sanchez was replaced by one of JD. Flake looked away from the screen and stroked Goober's head. It was a good way to take her mind off the loss of Sanchez for a moment. The dog nuzzled his head against her thigh, comforting her in return.

'Jeezus,' said Rex. 'The vice president is dead too? And the speaker of the house? Who the hell is in charge of the country now?'

The newsreader answered his question. 'Our political correspondent Janice Litman believes that by the rule of succession, the Secretary of Defence, Rebecca Howe should now be the acting president. Unfortunately, Miss Howe is presently unaccounted for. Government officials believe she is in hiding, fearing for her life. If

Miss Howe is unable to take up the post for any reason, then the next in line is the Attorney General, Navan Douglas.'

'Navan Douglas,' said Flake, looking back up at the TV. 'I met him this morning. He escorted me and Sanchez to—' She broke off in mid-sentence. Saying Sanchez's name would be tough for a while yet.

Jacko muted the television again. 'Rex, why don't you carry on with your story,' he said. 'Take everyone's mind off what's going on.'

'All right,' Rex replied. 'I'll skip forward to the night before I got shot.'

## Twenty-One

It was close to midnight and Rex was in his room on the second floor of the Rodriguez estate. The room had an en suite bathroom, a large double bed, a decent sized TV on the wall, and best of all it had a minibar filled with Rex's favourite cider, Randy Panda.

Rex was lying shirtless on the bed, drinking cider and watching the Brian Bosworth movie *Stone Cold* when there was a gentle knock on his door. Gentle enough that he almost didn't hear it. He put his cider down on the bedside table and reached under his pillow for his gun. He double-checked it was loaded, then slunk over to the door. He was a little wobbly on his feet because he'd polished off five bottles of the cider. After steadying himself and taking a few breaths, he pressed the barrel of his gun against the door at the right height to shoot a henchman in the chest if necessary.

Another knock.

'Who is it?' he asked.

'It's Selene. Can I come in?'

'Hang on.'

Rex hurried back to the bed and stashed his gun, checked his reflection in the mirror, quickstepped back to the door, unlocked it and pulled it open. Selene was standing outside in a black, silk bathrobe, with matching pyjamas underneath.

'What can I do for you?' Rex asked, trying to sound nonchalant and cool.

'You could invite me in?'

'Right.' He stepped back and allowed her to enter the room. 'Isn't this a little late for a social visit?' he said, closing the door behind her.

Selene turned to face him. 'I've got a favour to ask. It's kind of forward.'

'Go on.'

'Can I sleep here tonight?'

'Seriously?'

'Yes. Seriously. My husband has a guest staying in our room with him, so I've been shunted.'

'Shunted? To *my* room? Antonio asked you to come sleep in *my* room?'

'Technically it's not your room,' said Selene, with one of her enigmatic smiles. 'You're just staying here.'

'Pedantic,' said Rex. 'But true, I suppose.' He walked over to the bed, grabbed the remote and muted the television.

'Actually, it would be better if you kept the TV on,' said Selene. 'It'll drown out our voices.'

Rex unmuted the TV. 'Is there something you wanted to talk about?' he asked. 'Because while you're here, I wanted to ask you, why is there a sniper rifle on the roof of the house?'

Selene laughed. 'That's what you want to ask me about?'

'Yeah. You're the only person I trust to give me a straight answer.'

'It's there for the coconuts.'

'Coconuts?'

Selene walked over to the bed and perched on the edge of it. 'We have coconut shooting contests from up on the roof,' she said. 'Roughly once a month. And I usually win. I can take down a coconut from a mile away.'

'That's all it's there for?'

'Rex, this is a huge estate. A sniper rifle is handy for security, you know.'

'Right. I'm sorry,' said Rex. 'Is there something I can do for you? Are you serious about sleeping here?'

'The reason I'm here,' said Selene, moving closer to Rex, 'is that when Antonio has one of his mistresses over, I have to sleep in another room.'

'He has a mistress?'

'Several. Normally I can find a spare room easily, but tonight, they all seem to be taken. We have a lot of henchmen staying here at the moment.' She smiled at him. 'So, is it okay to stay here?'

'Won't your husband be angry if he finds out?'

'Absolutely, yes. But I'm not going to tell him. Are you?'

'No.' Rex walked over to the minibar. 'Can I get you a drink?'

'I don't need one,' Selene replied, eyeing up all the empty bottles of cider on the floor. 'I'm ready for bed.'

Rex was caught off guard. He hadn't expected her to show up, let alone ask to stay the night. 'Uh, yeah, actually I think I've drunk enough too. Why don't you make yourself comfortable? I just gotta use the bathroom.'

Rex left Selene and headed into the en suite. He closed the door behind him and looked in the mirror above the sink so he could ask his reflection for some advice. Seriously, what kind of shit was this? The lady of the house, the wife of the boss, was in his room, asking to share his bed. These rich folks were fucking nuts. Come to think of it, so was *he* for letting her into his room. Elvis would know what to do in a situation like this, but Rex couldn't call him because, well, Rex wasn't eight years old. And Selene might hear.

He splashed some cold water over his face and mulled over what to do. Was she a threat? A honeytrap? Or just lonely? What the fuck did she want? Sex, most likely, but there was no way that was happening. Sleep with her and next day she'll be asking for some dangerous favour, like murdering her husband, or all of the henchmen. Rex looked at his reflection again. He had a frown on his face. He snorted a quiet laugh in response to it. His reflection was worrying way too much. All he had to do was walk back into the bedroom. That's where all the answers were. It would soon become clear what Selene wanted, and it might be nothing more than a bed for the night.

He flicked off the bathroom light and returned to the bedroom. Selene's pyjamas were on the floor outside the bathroom door. She was on the bed, naked, looking at Rex.

'I like to sleep naked. That okay with you?' she asked, her dark red lips inviting him over every time they moved.

Rex's defence was well and truly knackered. Selene had a body to die for, creamy white skin, curves in all the right places. Inviting was an understatement. She definitely wanted the sex. Whatever else she wanted would become clear later. After they finished fucking.

\*\*\*\*\*\*\*\*\*\*\*\*\*\*\*\*\*\*\*\*\*\*\*\*\*\*\*\*\*\*\*

In a security office situated in another part of the building, Lucas, the head henchman was watching the CCTV footage of everything that went on around the estate and in its corridors. He had observed Selene entering Rex's room, in her nightwear. It wasn't hard to work out what was going on inside.

## Twenty Two

### The Next Morning

'It's not Saturday is it?'

'No it ain't Saturday,' JD replied.

'Then where the fuck is she?' Rex muttered. He was sitting in the back seat of the Mercedes waiting for Paige to show up for the morning ride to school. JD was in the driver's seat, flicking through stations on the radio. He eventually settled on the song, "In the City" by Joe Walsh.

'Give her a break,' JD said, 'she's a child.'

'Yeah, and she's fucking late. Do we really have to wait?' said Rex, raising his voice to be heard over the music.

'You wanna ride to school *without* her?'

'No, of course not. But I have better things to be doing than sitting around in a car waiting for a child to show up. And since when did you become so tolerant?'

JD looked over his shoulder at Rex. 'What's the matter with you? You worried Antonio knows you fucked his wife?'

Rex went quiet for a moment. 'What makes you think I did that?'

'I'm in the next room.'

'Fuck. You heard?'

'I heard.'

'You think anyone else heard?'

'How the fuck should I know? I can't speak for the hearing levels of all the henchmen, can I? But here's the thing, if Antonio knows what you did, we're gonna have to kill him, and all of his henchmen.'

Rex grunted something under his breath and stared out of the back window at the mansion's front doors. There was still no sign of Paige. 'Something tells me we're gonna end up killing all the henchmen anyway,' he said.

'It's what they're there for.'

'Yeah, right. Hey, here she comes.'

Paige was ushered from the building by Merris, the housekeeper. Merris waved to JD and Rex, then vanished back inside. As Paige approached the car, it was clear she had been crying, and her school uniform wasn't as smart as the day before. Her shirt was untucked, her socks were down, and her hair was messy. Instead of climbing into the back with Rex she got into the front with JD. She slammed the door shut and set her rucksack down on the floor without saying a word. Then she buckled up and folded her arms. She was clearly in a major huff.

Rex leaned forward from the back seat. 'What are you doing in the front?'

Paige didn't reply. JD started the car up, and the journey to school began with Rex sitting in the back on his own, and no one speaking.

Eventually, after a minute of silence, Rex had a moan about the situation. 'I look like a fucking idiot back here. I'm not the schoolchild. What's the point in me being here if I'm just sitting in the back on my own?'

No one replied to his rant. Instead JD glanced over at Paige.

'You okay?' he asked her.

'No.'

'Why not?'

'I don't want to go to school today.'

'Because?'

Paige deliberated for a moment before deciding to spill the reasons behind her bad mood. 'Yesterday two of the girls from the year above stole my lunch.'

'Your custard?'

'Yes.'

'*All* of your custard?'

'Yes, and they didn't even eat any of them. They just stamped on all the tubs, and my banana.'

JD glanced in the rear-view mirror and made eye contact with Rex. Rex closed his eyes, knowing what was coming next.

'I can solve that problem for you,' JD said to Paige. 'I'm happy to go speak with the headmaster for you.'

'Headmistress. Mrs Lampkin.'

'When we get to school, I'll go see her.'

Paige unfolded her arms. 'Really? You promise?'

'I promise.'

'Good. Thank you. Just don't kill her. That'll get me expelled.'

'Right. No killing the headmistress. I'll keep that in mind. You could show me who the girls are who stole your lunch too, if you like.'

'I'm not sure about that,' Paige replied. She reached forward and changed the station on the radio. 'I'm not listening to any more of your rock music either,' she said, a smirk appearing on her face now that she was no longer in a mood. The first song she came across was by Nirvana. She tutted, switched to another station and found Led Zeppelin. Still unimpressed, she moved on to Radiohead, then Guns 'n' Roses. The final straw came when she happened upon, "Janie's Got a Gun" by Aerosmith. She quit fiddling with the radio and sat back, folding her arms again. It was JD's turn to smirk.

'You're so stupid,' Paige said. 'Stupid radio. Stupid songs by old men.'

'John Denver was old,' JD reminded her. 'And you like him.'

'Not anymore I don't.'

After two more songs by old men, JD pulled over outside *Big Buns and Footlongs*. Rex got out of the car, slammed the door to remind everyone he was still in a mood, then marched into the store to pick up Paige's lunch and some epic breakfast sandwiches.

'He's even grumpier than you,' said JD.

'I am not grumpy.'

'Wanna play the staring game? Whoever smiles first loses.'

Paige turned her head to look at JD. Judging by the stern look on her face, the game was on.

JD looked her in the eye. He was confident he would win because Paige didn't like eye contact at the best of times. She took the challenge seriously though, and tried several looks in an attempt to win. She started off with a solemn look. But as the corners of her mouth began to quiver she switched to a pout. JD didn't flinch. Paige's pout started to fade, slowly at first, but then it fell apart completely and she ended up with a big grin on her face. Rather than admit defeat, she reminded JD that he was stupid, then stared out of her window so he couldn't see her smile.

When Rex eventually returned with the sandwiches and Paige's lunch, the journey to school resumed.

School had already begun when they arrived. Being late meant there was no hustle and bustle of other kids arriving at the same time. No queue of cars, no stressed out parents. Just the usual parking spot right outside the school entrance.

'We're fifteen minutes late now,' said Paige, stating the obvious. 'You drove too slow.'

Rex disagreed. 'Hey, *you* were late!' he called out from the back, his mouth full of bacon, sausage, egg and all the other goodness in his sandwich.

'Look, the school gates are locked,' said Paige. 'One of you will have to ring the bell and explain that it was your fault, otherwise I'll get in trouble.'

JD killed the engine. 'I can do that,' he said, opening his door. 'It'll give me a chance to go in and see Mrs What's-her-name.'

'Lampkin,' said Paige.

'That's right, Lampkin. Ready?'

Paige opened her door, picked up her rucksack and stepped out onto the sidewalk. JD was already there to shut the door for her.

'Ready to rock 'n' roll?' he asked her.

'No, actually,' said Paige. 'I'm still waiting for Rex to hand me my lunch.'

'Right.' JD opened the back door. 'Rex, have you got—'

CRACK!

Something hit JD on the back of the head. Everything dissolved into a bright, white haze. He banged his head on the frame of the door and dropped to the ground. In the middle of the dizziness that engulfed him, he heard Paige scream his name, and something landed on the ground nearby, making a loud clank. JD couldn't react to any of it. He was on his back, gazing up at the sky. The morning sun mixed in with the artificial, bright, white haze temporarily blinded him.

'JD! HELP ME!'

Paige's voice was further away. JD twisted his head to see where she was. Spots of white floated back and forth in his field of vision. He focussed upon a blurred image of Paige. She was floating. Her feet were a metre off the ground, and she was getting smaller, her screams becoming more distant.

'JD! REX!'

A backseat door on the other side of the Mercedes opened. Rex climbed out into the road.

'HEY! STOP!' he yelled.

BANG!

'Aaargh, shit!'

THUD!

Rex fell against the side of the car.

BEEEEEEEEP!

A passing car honked its horn at him.

JD blinked a few times. His vision cleared slightly, apart from the floating white spots that weren't going anywhere. He planted his hand down on the sidewalk and pushed himself up onto his feet. Paige? Where was she?

*There.* There she was. Floating in the air again. Floating towards a set of open doors at the back of a black van. There was a burly man in the back of the van, his arms out, ready to take her in.

JD started to move, to chase after Paige, but his legs didn't get the memo from his brain. He staggered sideways. The side of the car stopped him from falling again. He pushed his weight against it and straightened up, then reached inside his jacket for a gun. Yanked one out. The old reactions were good. Vision still swimming though. He aimed his gun at the van. Paige was screaming. Panicked screams. *"Help me. JD help me!"*

THUD!

The van doors slammed shut. There were no more screams from Paige. The roar of the van's engine drowned out everything.

JD blinked some more. In one of the van's back windows, Paige's face stared back at him. Then she vanished. The van got smaller. One chance left. Shoot the tyres.

BANG!

Too slow. By the time JD fired, the van was too far away. It screeched around a corner and disappeared completely. JD's adrenaline rush subsided and he fell back onto the sidewalk. More blinking. What happened to Rex?

'Rex?' JD called out. 'You okay?'

Through his distorted, snowy vision, he saw Rex hobble onto the sidewalk in front of him.

The big Hell's Angel reached out and grabbed JD's arm. He hauled him up onto his feet and propped him up against his shoulder. They both stared at the road where the van had been. The image of Paige staring out through the van's back window flashed through JD's mind.

'That fucker shot me,' said Rex. He had blood seeping from a hole in his jeans, just above the knee. He pressed his magnetic hand against it, and hooked out a misshapen bullet, which he dropped onto the sidewalk.

JD rubbed the back of his head where he'd been hit. He had a lump the size of a golf ball growing back there. 'What the fuck just happened?' he asked. 'I never even saw anyone. Who hit me?'

'No one hit you.'

'The back of my head would disagree with you.'

'What I mean is, we've got ourselves an invisible kidnapper. You just went down with no one near you,' said Rex. 'And I got shot by a no one who wasn't there.'

'Invisible kidnapper, huh?' said JD, still wincing as he rubbed his head. 'Antonio's got some explaining to do. Did you get the plates on the van?'

'Are you kidding? I got shot, and nearly fuckin' run over.'

JD looked at his hand. It was covered in something sticky. 'What the fuck is this?' he said, trying to focus on it.

'It's custard,' Rex replied.

Paige's rucksack was beside the car, its contents scattered across the sidewalk. Books, pens, pencils, tissues, a phone, and a solitary squashed tub of pink custard were all that remained as evidence that she had been there only moments earlier. The pink custard was splattered onto the side of the car, on the sidewalk, and on JD's hand. There was also a baseball bat a little further down the sidewalk.

'I think that's what hit you in the back of the head,' said Rex, pointing at it.

JD sighed. 'You think I don't fucking know that?'

## Twenty-Three

### Back in Purgatory

'You slept with the boss's wife?' said Flake, aghast at what she was hearing from Rex. 'And then Paige was kidnapped?'

Rex frowned. 'You know, Paige being kidnapped was more shocking than me sleeping with Selene,' he pointed out.

'Did you get blamed for it all?'

'Can you keep your voice down?' said Rex. 'You'll wake the others up.'

Jasmine and Elvis were still half asleep at the back of the room. 'I can hear you,' Elvis called out, even though his eyes were closed.

Rex and Flake were sitting at the bar, with Goober by Flake's feet. JD was at a table on his own, watching the television. The news was constantly being updated by stories of more dead politicians and celebrities. There was some big shit going on in the world right now.

Jacko was behind the bar, tapping away on a laptop. 'I've got it,' he announced. 'Medicine Island.'

'Medicine Island?' JD repeated. 'Where's that?'

'Did you say Medicine Island?' Flake called out. 'That's in the Pacific ocean isn't it?'

'Correct,' said Jacko. 'It's perfect for your needs. It's really small, and more importantly it's totally uninhabited.'

Rex was perplexed. 'You're gonna send Flake to live on a desert island?'

'Not just any desert island,' Jacko replied. 'About eighty years ago the US government built a medical facility on this island. The intention was to use it to test the effects of vaccines on deadly viruses. Naturally, it all went to shit when a virus killed all the people who worked on the island.'

Flake sputtered. 'You want me to go to an island with a deadly virus?'

'It's perfectly safe now,' said Jacko. 'You'll be fine.'

JD got up from his table and took off his coat. He hung it on the back of his chair then joined Jacko behind the bar. 'If we send Flake there,' he said, looking at the screen on Jacko's laptop, 'what are the chances of anyone rocking up on shore and finding her?'

'Beyond remote,' said Jacko. 'The island is surrounded by deadly rock formations making it perilous for any ships or boats to get too close. And there's nowhere for a plane to land, realistically. A helicopter maybe. It's perfect for Flake to hide out until we prove her innocence.'

Flake was horrified. 'Are you honestly talking about sending me to a desert island to live, on my own?' she asked.

'I think the dog will go with you,' said Jacko.

JD shoved Jacko in the back, then offered Flake some reassurance. 'This'll only be temporary,' he said. 'I'll come with you, check out the island, make sure everything is okay. Once you're settled, we'll bring you food and anything else you need. The island will be a place for all of us to hang out. Jasmine will love it. She'll probably move in with you.'

'Great.'

'You got a better idea?'

Flake sighed. 'Better than living on the island of Dr Moron? I'm sad to say, no, I *don't* have a better idea. It's just not what I had planned when I got up this morning, you know?'

'I know,' said JD. 'But let's at least take a look at this place. It could be good.'

'It's ready to go,' said Jacko. 'I've directed the portal to a bathroom in the research centre on the island. Go take a look. If it's anything like the pictures I'm looking at, it'll be a paradise.'

'Are we sure this place is uninhabited though?' Flake asked.

'Only one way to find out,' said JD, making his way around the bar to join her.

'What if there's wild animals there?'

JD smiled. 'It's not Jurassic island. There won't be anything there we can't handle.'

'There'd better not be.'

Flake got up from the table and took off her suit jacket. She stuck it on the back of her chair and headed over to the portal with JD.

'Hey, hang on a minute,' said Rex. 'Don't you want to hear the rest of the story?'

'Your story can wait,' said Jacko. 'Why don't you check on Jasmine and Elvis while these two go check out the island?'

Rex sighed. 'Gimme another drink then.'

'Get it yourself,' said Jacko. 'I'm busy.' He called over to JD and Flake who were waiting by the men's toilets. 'If you like the island, I'll get Einstein to set you up with a TV, satellite dish, phone network, all that stuff, okay?'

JD pressed a button in the wall by the toilet door and it slid open. The button was a recent addition, put in place by Einstein. It was deemed more efficient than opening and closing the door by hand.

Einstein was a fan of sci-fi so the sliding door appealed to his sense of nerdiness.

When the portal door was open they saw a filthy bathroom on the other side. It had a row of shower cubicles and a few washbasins, all of which were covered in cobwebs, dust and grime.

'Looks better than jail, right?' said JD.

'Way to sell it to me,' Flake replied. 'Come on, let's do this before I change my mind.'

JD went through first, brushing away the cobwebs, although not enough to stop them from tickling Flake as she followed on behind. The temperature was much cooler than in Purgatory. The air was fresh even though the shower room they were walking through was coated in dust and filth.

'Are we going to find a bunch of skeletons in this place?' Flake asked, half expecting something to jump out at them.

'We might,' said JD. 'But you've dealt with skeletons before, haven't you? At least if we see any here, they'll actually be dead.'

They made their way through the shower room into a locker room, and then through to a cold, sterile hallway. It was like walking through an empty hospital.

'I wonder how many people lived here?' Flake asked.

'Same number who died here.'

She shoved JD in the back. 'Aren't you supposed to be cheering me up?'

He opened one of the many doors in the corridor and took a look inside. 'Sleeping quarters,' he said.

Flake peeked into the room herself. 'Are we sure this wasn't a prison?' she said, unconvinced about the comfort of the place. Sleeping quarters was certainly a more apt description than bedroom. There was a set of bunkbeds against the wall and a closet and chest of drawers. That was pretty much it.

JD closed the door. 'Let's go check out the island. It'll be more scenic.'

'It better be.'

Once they were outside, Flake was impressed by what she saw. The island was every bit as good as Jacko had claimed. It was a paradise made up of exotic trees, thick green bushes, sandy beaches, a stream and even a small waterfall that was visible on a higher part of the island. It was warm too. JD and Flake walked down to the beach and stared out at the sparkling blue ocean.

'Wow,' said Flake. 'This might actually be the best place in the world.'

'It might be,' said JD. 'Once we get you set up here I think you'll get lots of visitors. The others are gonna love this place.'

'Will you stay with me tonight?'

'Did you really think I was gonna leave you on your own?'

Flake crouched down and grabbed a fistful of sand. It was warm. She let it slip through her fingers then stood up again. 'I'd really appreciate it if you stayed. I really don't wanna be alone tonight.'

'No one would want to be alone after everything that happened today. You hungry?'

Flake shook her head. 'Not right now. I don't think I could eat anything today. My stomach is in knots. I'll tell you what though, if we can get an oven sorted and some food, I'll make you breakfast in the morning, you know, as a thank you for everything today.'

JD looked puzzled. 'Flake, I'll cook you breakfast. You deserve a break.'

'But breakfast is my thing. I cooked three a day for… for Sanchez sometimes. I don't know what else I can do to thank you.' She was tearing up again. The memories of the morning were flooding back into her mind.

JD stroked some stray hairs out of her eyes. 'You were brave to hang in there after what happened. A lot of people would have just given up and got themselves arrested, or shot.'

Flake forced half a smile. 'I'm still making you breakfast, okay?'

JD ran his hand down her arm. 'You killed Jessica the vampire queen,' he said. 'You killed Cain with the Brutus dagger, and you faced down Scratch with a fucking fire hose. You're gonna be just fine on this island.'

Flake blushed. 'Jeez, you remember all that?'

'Everyone remembers that. That's some major shit.'

Flake surprised herself by reaching forward and embracing JD in a hug. It was brief, just a couple of seconds, but it made her feel better. She stepped back and looked into his eyes. 'No one ever mentions that stuff, you know. All anyone talks about is how Jasmine killed the Pope, Jasmine killed the cast of the Planet of the Apes TV show, Jasmine was in a porno, and yeah, Jasmine looks great naked.'

'Are you jealous of Jasmine?'

'No.'

'Good, because you can do any of those things she's done.'

'I have no intention of *ever* being in a porno.'

'Me either.'

Flake slapped him playfully on the arm. 'Anyway,' she said, changing the subject. 'What happened to Paige? Did you rescue her?'

JD didn't reply. He was staring past Flake at something higher up on the island.

'What's the matter?' she asked.

'You should go back to Purgatory. See how Jasmine is.'

'Why? Is something wrong?'

'Something's up there,' JD said, staring up at the highest point of the island, 'and it's watching us.'

## Twenty-Four

Back at the Poseidon hotel

'Where the hell is the secretary of state?'

'We think he's dead too, sir.'

Navan Douglas was going crazy. The perfectly orchestrated killings of numerous world leaders and important public figures was a total clusterfuck.

He was in the lounge of the president's penthouse suite with three secret service agents. Several murders had taken place in the lounge that morning. The corpses had all been removed and taken off for autopsies, along with the body of the president, who had been assassinated in the master bedroom.

'Find Alexis Calhoon,' Douglas raged, not at anyone in particular. 'And tell her to call me immediately.'

Douglas stormed out of the room and headed to his own hotel room on the next floor down. He needed some time to himself. Time to think. Time to straighten out what the fuck was going on. When he got to his room, he sat down in a comfy chair in the lounge and tried to get things straight in his head. He knew there were all kinds of outlandish rumours circulating in the media and online. Everyone seemed to think the Russians were behind the killings. It was an obvious conclusion to arrive at because no prominent Russians had been assassinated. The Chinese president was dead, the fat fucker in charge of North Korea was dead too. Douglas chewed on his fingernails. What the fuck was going on?

He stood up and paced around his room, desperately trying to figure out what was going on all over the world. His stomach was making strange noises brought on by stress and too much caffeine. Was he somehow responsible for all this? He couldn't talk to anyone about it, about what he knew, about what'd done. He'd given a fucking invisible coat to a vampire. A fucking vampire. Diago, the fucking bastard vampire. That asshole was supposed to be on the government's side. He and his vampire crew were protected as an endangered species. In return for the government protection, they carried out jobs, assassinations etc. But now they had an invisible coat, which they were supposed to be duplicating for the government, except the government didn't know about it. Only Navan Douglas knew about it because it was his *stupid fucking idea* to arrange it behind the president's back. What on earth had possessed him to take such a risk?

To make matters worse, Diago wasn't answering his phone anymore. If the vampires really had created more invisible coats, and used them to assassinate the world leaders, then Douglas was fucked, especially if they were working with the Russians. And matters were about to get worse.

His cell phone rang. It was Alexis Calhoon. It was a call that had to be answered.

'Hello Alexis.'

'Navan. Have you heard?'

'Oh God, what now?'

'The Secretary of Defence has been found. She's dead too.'

'Oh, Christ, no.'

'That means you're up, sir. As the Attorney General, you are the new acting president. Or, you will be, if we can find anyone to swear you in. In the meantime, have you got any big calls you want to make?'

This disaster was getting worse. In his wildest dreams, Navan Douglas had fantasised about a bizarre scenario that saw him become president. He never imagined it would come true. And certainly not because of some secret deal he'd done that had gone bad. So very, very bad.

'Have you had any luck tracking down Flake Munroe or the Bourbon Kid?' he asked her.

'No sir, but as I said earlier, there's just no way they're behind all of this. It's got to be the Russians.'

Douglas's conversation with Calhoon was interrupted by the arrival of one of the secret service agents, a big black dude named Cedric. The fucker didn't even knock. He had a special high-level security keycard that opened any door in the hotel. So he used it to open Douglas's hotel room. He marched in with a stressed-out look on his face. A sure sign that this was more bad news.

'SIR!' he yelled.

Douglas lowered the phone away from his ear. 'Yes, Cedric.'

'Sir, I've just had a call on my cell from Michael Van der Lay.'

'Go on.'

'He says we have multiple ballistic missiles heading our way. The Russians have launched a full scale attack.'

The colour drained from Navan Douglas's face. 'You've gotta be fucking kidding?'

'No sir. Missiles are due to hit Chicago, Washington and Texas in approximately two minutes. It'll be up to you to decide how we respond.'

'Chicago? But we're *in* Chicago!'

'Yes, sir. Two minutes to impact.'

'Two minutes? What the fuck? How has that happened? Why am I only hearing about this now?'

Douglas already knew the answer. Everything was in disarray. There was no one around to make a decision. And apparently, the buck now stopped with him.

'You need to end that call, sir. Van der Lay needs to speak with you.'

'FUCK!' Douglas put his phone to his ear. 'Calhoon, did you hear all that?'

'Yes, sir.'

'Any suggestions?'

'It's your call, Mister President.'

Douglas ended the call, and tried to do the deep breathing exercises his psychiatrist had recommended to him a few years ago. It wasn't working. He was panicking worse than the time he slagged off the First Lady in an email and accidentally sent the email to her. He waited for his phone to ring again with a call from Michael van der Lay. Douglas was going to have to make a huge decision on that call, without even running it by anyone else. Ten seconds went by. Ten seconds closer to obliteration. He looked over at Cedric who was waiting for him to say something.

'GET OUT!' Douglas yelled at him. 'Can't you see I'm having a fucking panic attack?'

'Sir, if we're under nuclear attack and you're the acting president, then you should be out of harm's way. The president's helicopter is on the roof ready to take us to wherever you wish to go. And if I may say so sir, I think the skies might be the safest place to be right now.'

'The helicopter,' Douglas muttered to himself, his brain still frazzled.

'Yes, sir. If we leave now, we could be in the helicopter before the nukes hit. SIR!'

Douglas contemplated the suggestion. The whole fucking city was about to get wiped out by a nuclear attack. 'Good thinking, Cedric,' he said, a ray of hope glowing in his cowardly heart. 'Helicopter it is. Lead the way!'

Cedric marched over to Navan Douglas, grabbed him by his arm and pulled him out into the corridor. From there he shoved the acting president around like a convict, such was the race to get up to the roof. In the midst of it all, Douglas's mother called him. It was the one call he was happy to take. She wouldn't want him to make any big decisions.

'Hi, mom,' he said, panting heavily as he was bundled up a flight of stairs by Cedric.

'Have you seen the news?' his mother asked.

'Yes, mom. I have. Do yourself a favour and get below ground. The Russians have fired nukes at us.'

'Oh, goodness. Should I tell the neighbours?'

'If you want. Just stay on the line for a few minutes. It'll stop anyone else from calling me.'

## Twenty-Five

JD moved swiftly and silently through the thick jungle trees, making his way up the ridgeline towards the island peak. Something was up there. He'd seen it move. Medicine Island was supposed to be uninhabited. But there was some kind of Robinson Crusoe hanging around up there. Or even worse, Tom Hanks.

When JD neared the area where he had seen movement, he unsheathed his hunting knife from his hip. Whoever—or—whatever was on the island, had to be eliminated. With half the world looking for him and Flake, he had to make sure no one could give up their position.

SNAP!

The sound of breaking twigs and rustling leaves up ahead told JD that whoever was there was making a run for it. There was no need to continue creeping silently. He tucked his knife away and started running. It wasn't long before he caught a glimpse of his target through the dense, tangled vegetation. It was a man. A caveman. Long straggly brown hair, tattered brown loin cloth. No weapon of note. This guy was scared. As JD got closer, the man looked back. He had a bearded face and fear in his eyes. It was a matter of time before he was caught, and he knew it.

When the caveman was within touching distance, JD reached out and grabbed his shoulder. The other man was so weak he lost his balance, making it easy for JD to drag him down onto the ground. He flipped the caveman onto his back, and then sat on his chest. The unshaven, long-haired hippy looked terrified.

'Please don't kill me!' he begged. He had an Australian accent, which sort of ruled out the possibility of him being a caveman.

'Who are you?' JD asked, unsheathing his knife again and pressing it against the man's throat.

'No one, just a guy. Been living here for years on my own. Shipwrecked.'

JD twisted the man's head to one side and pushed his hair away from his face 'You've got gills,' he said, staring at a set of gills on the man's neck.

'Evolution. They started growing when I arrived here.'

'Bullshit.' JD looked back over his shoulder at the man's feet. 'You've got webbed feet.'

'Like I said, I've changed since I've been on the island.'

'No you haven't.'

There was desperation in the man's eyes. 'I'm a normal man like you. You don't want to hurt me. I'm harmless, see.'

'Don't lie to me. Who are you?'

The man made a sudden choking noise. He started fighting for breath like someone in the middle of being strangled to death. His chest heaved and his eyes bulged, then he exhaled and stopped breathing. His head flopped to the side, and his body went limp. He stared straight ahead at nothing, his mouth open, his body completely still.

JD rolled his eyes and let out a deep sigh. He tucked his knife back in its sheath then shifted so his knees pressed hard against the gills on both sides of the man's neck. Then he squeezed the caveman's nose, closing off his nostrils. Approximately thirty seconds passed before the caveman suddenly sucked in a huge breath of air through his mouth and stopped pretending to be dead.

'Last chance,' said JD. 'Tell me who you are, or I'll cut those gills off.'

The scraggly man groaned. 'My name is Orto.'

'How long you been here on the island?'

'Ten years.'

'How did you get here?'

'Shipwrecked, I told you already.'

'And I told you the lies don't work on me. Choose your next words carefully because the next lie will be the last.'

Orto looked bewildered. 'Who *are* you?'

'You heard of the Bourbon Kid?'

'Yes. But that's not you, *is it?*'

'It is. Now, last chance, how did you get here? And are you alone?'

'It's just me, I swear.'

'And why are you here?'

'They were going to kill me.'

'Who?'

'The elites. Who do you think?'

'Why were they going to kill you?'

'I was going to tell the world their secrets.'

JD pressed his knife down harder on Orto's throat. Hard enough to draw blood and a girly scream. 'I said no more lies.'

'I fucked something up. I slept with someone I shouldn't. It's not really a big deal.'

'Then why come here?'

'I was exiled, sent back to the seas, but I found this place and I liked it because it was uninhabited, so I stayed.'

'You swam here?'

'Yeah.'

'From where?'

'Portugal.'

'Who exiled you?'

JD's interrogation was interrupted by a shadow that passed over him and his prisoner. An enormous shadow, a shadow that kept moving, kept getting bigger and bigger. In a matter of seconds it covered the whole island, plunging it into darkness.

The look on Orto's face switched from petrified to slightly smug. 'Now you're fucked,' he said. 'I'll survive this, but you won't.'

## Twenty-Six

'Oh fuck,' said Jacko. 'This is bad.'

Rex was at the back of the lounge bar in Purgatory, checking on Elvis and Jasmine. They were still on the sofa. Elvis was half awake, Jasmine was still fast asleep with her legs across him. 'What's bad? Rex asked, looking around.

Jacko was behind the bar, pointing at the big television on the wall. 'The Russians have started nuking the whole fucking planet. Look!'

A news reporter on the TV was warning everyone to get below ground if possible. Some camera footage showed a tsunami wiping out a sports stadium in the middle of a football match.

Rex walked up to the television to get a better look at what Jacko was talking about. Footage on the screen was showing chaos everywhere.

'Is that Spain?' Rex asked, as he stared at the madness on screen.

Jacko wasn't paying any attention to him. He was frantically tapping away on a laptop.

Rex raised his voice. 'We're safe here in Purgatory, aren't we?'

'Of course we are,' Jacko replied without looking up.

The sound of someone running filtered in through the portal. It was shortly followed by the arrival of Flake, back from Medicine Island. She was panting heavily. It looked like she had something to say, but she needed to catch her breath first.

'You okay, Flake?' Rex asked her.

Before she could reply, Jacko looked up from his laptop and asked her another question. 'Where's JD?'

Flake pressed her hand against the frame of the portal door as she composed herself. 'There was someone on the island watching us,' she said eventually. 'So I've come back here while JD sorts it out.'

Jacko grabbed his head with both hands. 'Shit!' he said, wincing. 'There's a fucking tsunami heading for Medicine Island right now.'

Flake stopped breathing heavily. 'What?'

'The Russians have blasted nuclear missiles at the West. Some of the nukes have hit the ocean floor. The Pacific is blowing up into a series of mile-high waves.'

Flake didn't respond. She turned and sprinted back through the portal.

Rex glared at Jacko. 'Good one. Now look what you've done.'

Jacko ignored him. He had more important things to do than argue. He was checking satellite pictures of the Pacific on his laptop.

'She's insane,' he muttered. 'Medicine Island is about to get wiped out.' He glanced up at the portal. Then he and Rex exchanged a look. They were thinking the same thing.

'Can a tsunami get in through the portal?' Rex asked.

'Yeah it can.'

'We can't shut the portal though, not with Flake and JD out on the island!'

'We might have to!'

Elvis spoke up from his spot on the sofa. 'You can't shut it until Flake gets back.'

BOOM!

HISS!

The sounds coming through the portal woke up Jasmine. 'What was that?' she asked, echoing what everyone else was thinking.

'That's a tsunami,' said Jacko. 'I've gotta close the portal.'

'Just wait a second!' said Rex. He rushed over to the portal and poked his head through it. All he could see was the research centre's shower room on the other side of it. There was no sign of Flake, or JD. 'WHERE THE FUCK ARE THEY?' he shouted at no one in particular.

Elvis pushed Jasmine's feet off his lap and hobbled over to the portal. He squeezed past Rex and stepped into the shower room on the other side.

Jacko screamed at him. 'GET BACK IN HERE!'

'Just wait a goddamn minute,' Elvis replied. 'I'll tell you if there's any water coming.'

'Do you know how fast that water will come through here?' Jacko said, exasperation evident in his voice.

'No, how fast?' Elvis asked.

'I don't know,' Jacko replied. 'But it'll be fucking fast. Probably too fast for you to get back through the door. If you see it, you're fucked.'

'You don't know that.'

Rex stepped through the portal too, and grabbed Elvis by his upper arm, ready to yank him back through into Purgatory at the first sign of water. The medical centre, which was a gloomy place anyway, turned a shade of grey, then almost black as the giant wave outside blocked out any sunlight.

'GET BACK IN HERE!' Jacko hollered.

Rex yelled back at him. 'JUST HOLD ON A MINUTE!'

Jacko tugged at his short black hair. 'We're gonna have to close up the portal,' he groaned. 'God will go fucking mental if he finds out we allowed a bloody tsunami into Purgatory. You know there'll be sharks and whales caught up in that wave. It'll be a fucking nightmare.'

'I know what you're saying,' said Elvis. 'But if JD survives, then comes back and asks who closed up the portal, I'm telling him it was you.'

'We've got no choice,' said Jacko. 'Get back in here.'

'We've got time,' said Rex. 'The portal closes up instantly. It's not like we'll be pushing the door shut against the tide. It'll just slide shut. We can at least wait here until the water arrives. We owe Flake and JD that much.'

## Twenty-Seven

'I'll survive this, but you won't.'

JD didn't know what to make of Orto's confident claim. The whole island had gone dark, like day had switched to night in a matter of seconds. Leaves began to rustle. The air turned cold and damp. A rumbling sound far away filtered into JD's ears. And then the sound of his name.

'JD! HURRY! WHERE ARE YOU?'

It was Flake calling him. She was close by.

JD looked down at Orto. The caveman with the gills and webbed feet glanced at the knife in JD's hand. He knew what was about to happen. He cried out.

'NO!'

Too late. JD slid his knife across Orto's neck, cutting his throat. Blood spilled out all down the caveman's chest, and his cry of "NO" ended before it had a chance to become operatic.

Flake called JD's name again, from much closer than before.

'Over here,' he called back.

Flake burst through the jungle leaves and arrived at the death scene. She glanced at the dead body of Orto, but said nothing. JD stood up and wiped his blade on a big green leaf.

'WE GOTTA GO!' Flake yelled, panic written all over her face. 'A fucking tsunami's coming!'

The darkness that engulfed the island hadn't been caused by clouds. Now that JD was standing up he could see it on the horizon. A wall of ocean water a mile high was coming their way. He dropped his knife. There was no time to waste.

Flake started running back down the hill towards the research centre with JD right behind her. Running up the hill had taken a lot out of Flake. Her tank was empty and she was running on fumes. With visibility poor, she snagged her foot on a tree root and stumbled over, burning her hands on the coarse ground as she tried to break her fall. JD had no time to react. He tripped over Flake and crashed into the trunk of a tree. The impact spun him around as he fell to the ground. He was back up into a crouching position almost immediately, looking over his shoulder at Flake.

'GET ON MY BACK!' he yelled at her.

There was no time to argue, reason or debate the benefits of it. Flake scrambled to her feet and climbed onto his back. She wrapped her arms around his neck, and her legs around his waist. He was off and running immediately.

Heavy rain began to fall from above, not from the clouds, but from the crest of the big, black ocean wave that was riding high over the island. This wasn't a wave that was going to hit the shore and then crash through anything that got in its way. This bastard was so damn big it was passing right over the island, swallowing it up as it went.

When JD reached the bottom of the hill he took a turn and sprinted up the path to the medical centre. Most of the heavy rainfall was landing on Flake, who was inadvertently acting as an umbrella for JD. He raced through the front entrance of the research centre, ducking down to ensure Flake didn't hit her head against the frame of the door. Once inside the building, the sound of the tidal wave transitioned from a loud belly rumble into a very vocal lion's roar.

JD barrelled along the corridors towards the locker room. The ocean entered the building behind them and raced through every opening in pursuit of them, busting open doors, shattering windows. Flake could feel the cold air from the water creeping up on her. As they approached the locker room they saw Rex and Elvis standing beside the portal, waving them on and yelling indecipherable nonsense at them. It was impossible to hear anything over the sound of the howling winds, the breaking windows and the cascading water that was sweeping through the building.

As JD bounded into the shower area of the locker room, Rex and Elvis ducked back through the portal into Purgatory. A wall of ocean water shot down the corridor behind them. It hit Flake in the back and knocked JD's feet out from under him, separating them. The two of them were hurled forward through the portal entrance into Purgatory, submerged in water, along with a slew of bewildered fish.

Behind the bar, Jacko hit a button to close up the portal, but not before a wall of water burst through the entrance, wiping out all the tables and chairs in its path. Rex, Elvis, JD, Goober and Flake all slid across the floor of Purgatory, crashing into things. Jasmine's sofa bounced up and ejected her so she could join her friends in the new waterslide event. A wave of filthy brown sludge hurdled over the bar and smashed Jacko in the face, knocking him over too. The rushing water carried on going, streaming out through the batwing doors at the front of Purgatory on its way into the desert outside.

When the chaos died down and everyone was able to catch a breath, Rex climbed to his feet and wiped some debris from his shoulders. He was drenched in ocean water and sludge.

'You couldn't have cut it a bit finer could you?' he groaned, standing over JD, who was in a heap on the floor, covered in water and foam.

JD sat up, then climbed unsteadily to his feet. He spat out some water, wiped a few stray hairs out of his eyes, and looked around while he tried to get his breath back. Flake was laid out against the wall the by bar entrance. JD staggered over to her and grabbed her arm. She was a mess. Her clothes were soaked through and her hair was flattened and stuck to her head and face. She looked up at him, relief and exhaustion written in her eyes.

'What a fucking day this has been,' she said.

'SHARK!'

That got everyone moving again. It was Rex who had shouted out the name of the ocean's most fearsome predator.

'It's okay,' said Jacko, holding onto the bar as he pulled himself up. 'It's only the front of a shark. The portal closed on it as it was coming through.'

The front half of a shark slid past Flake and JD on its way out through the front doors with the last of the ocean water. It looked pissed off.

There were plenty of sea creatures sliding around inside Purgatory, including a rather large herring, whose tail was repeatedly slapping Jasmine around the face. Flake trudged over to help. Jasmine was on her side up against a wall, looking worse for wear. Flake kicked the herring out of the way and hauled Jasmine up.

'How are you feeling?' Flake asked her.

'I've been better,' Jasmine replied, sea water dribbling out of her mouth as she spoke.

Jacko wiped some muck off his face and the shoulders of his suit, then walked out from behind the bar to look around. Purgatory was fucked. All the tables and chairs were either busted or outside with most of the ocean water. 'Right then,' he said, squeezing some water out of the sleeves of his suit jacket. 'Who's cleaning up all this mess?'

At that moment, the batwing doors swung open and Elvis walked back in from the desert, along with Goober who had a big fish in his mouth.

'Can't you get Zilas up here to fix everything?' said Elvis as he tried to fix his hair. 'I think we could all use a sit down.'

'The phone is fucked,' said Jacko, pointing at the worktop behind the bar where the phone used to sit. 'I can't call anyone right now. But you've got a point. Let's have a break.'

Elvis walked over to Jasmine and lifted her off her feet. He carried her over to the upturned sofa, kicked it back into its upright position and laid her down on it. Then, realising how tired he was, he sat down beside her and placed her feet on his lap.

Flake picked up an unopened bottle of water that was rolling around on the floor, wiped some crap off it and then walked it over to Jasmine and Elvis. She handed it to Elvis.

'You know, you still haven't told us how you two got shot,' she reminded them.

'Elvis, you tell them,' said Jasmine. 'I'm too tired.'

Elvis removed the lid on the bottle of water and poured some of it into Jasmine's mouth. Then he took a swig from it himself and handed it back to Flake.

'Rex has got crabs,' Jasmine muttered.

'What's that?' said Rex, his hearing surprisingly good considering he was on the other side of the room.

'She's right,' said Elvis. 'In your hair. You've got loads of baby crabs.'

'Forget about that,' said Flake, slapping Elvis on the arm. 'I wanna know what happened to you and Jasmine.'

While Rex attempted to shake a bunch of crabs out of his hair, Elvis began to tell the tale of what he and Jasmine had been up to for the last twenty-four hours.

'It all started when me and Jas took a job from Calhoon,' he said. 'It sounded like it would be fun, but it went bad really fast.'

## Twenty-Eight

<u>Part Four – The El Guapo</u>

It was early afternoon when Elvis and Jasmine arrived at Calhoon's ranch. They drove there with the roof of Elvis's purple Cadillac down, soaking up the sun and the fresh country air. Jasmine had her seat reclined back as far as it would go. She was wearing blue denim cut-offs and a pink crop-top so she could soak up some sun rays. Elvis had gone for black pants and a mostly unbuttoned white shirt.

'Ready for some work?' Elvis asked as he parked the Cadillac outside Calhoon's house.

'When this is over, we should do a real vacation,' Jasmine replied. 'This road trip has been fun, just the two of us together. But we should do something even better. A real adventure.'

'Sounds like a great plan,' Elvis agreed. 'Where d'ya wanna go?'

Jasmine leaned across and planted a kiss on him. 'I'd like somewhere warm.'

'How about Jamaica?'

'Ooh, yeah, Europe. That's a great idea,' said Jasmine, her eyes lighting up.

Before Elvis could respond, Alexis Calhoon walked out of her house onto the wooden porch at the front. She greeted them with a warm smile. She was wearing a pair of red pants and a black shirt with a red neckerchief. The general had a seventies vibe to her when she wasn't in a work uniform, like she could have been Pam Grier's stunt double in *Foxy Brown* or *Coffy*.

'Great timing,' she said. 'I've just made some coffee.'

Elvis and Jasmine rolled out of the car and rocked up to greet her. Elvis shook her hand. 'You're looking good, Alexis.'

'You too.'

Jasmine planted a big and rather unexpected kiss on Calhoon's lips. 'Lovely to see you again,' she said.

'Likewise,' Calhoon replied, graciously, while she blinked her eyes a few times. Like everyone else, she'd gotten used to Jasmine over the years. 'Come on inside.'

While the general poured coffee into three large yellow mugs, Elvis and Jasmine sat down at her kitchen table and made themselves comfortable.

'How was your trip?' Calhoon asked.

'Spiffing!' said Jasmine.

'Spiffing?' Calhoon repeated.

Elvis cleared things up. 'It's a word she heard in a movie the other day. Now everything is spiffing.'

'Good to know,' said Calhoon. She placed their coffees down on the table, then returned to the sideboard and picked up a thick hardback book with a plain brown cover. She sat down in a chair opposite her two guests. 'Do you know what I've got here?' she asked.

'Is it a book?' Jasmine guessed.

'It is,' said Calhoon. 'But it's a book with medals in it.'

Elvis inwardly groaned, fearing the General was about to bore them shitless with stories of how she'd won silver medals in the shot put, or some other dull shit.

'Medals for us?' Jasmine asked, presumptuously.

'That's correct,' said Calhoon. She flipped open the book. It had no pages in it, just a thick blue felt material with six gold rings embedded in it. 'These are from the president, recognition of your work rescuing his daughter Arizona from the Bastard brothers. He can't give them to you in person, so the Attorney General, Navan Douglas asked me to present them to you.'

Jasmine stared into the box. 'They don't look like medals. They look like rings.'

'They are rings. It's a new thing the president has been doing for a while now. People keep medals in a drawer, whereas they wear rings all the time. So you now have medal rings. There's one for each member of the Dead Hunters. I have to fly out to Chicago tonight so I can be there in the morning to present Flake and Sanchez with theirs.'

'But we're first, right?' said Jasmine.

'You certainly are.'

Calhoon picked out one of the rings and checked the inscription on it. 'This one is yours Jasmine. It's inscribed with your name and a stars and stripes flag.'

Jasmine held out her hand for Calhoon to place the ring on one of her fingers. The General obliged, sliding the ring onto her middle finger.

'Wow,' said Jasmine, gawping at it. 'This is the nicest ring I've ever had.'

Calhoon pulled one out for Elvis and dropped it into the palm of his outstretched hand. He eyed it up and quickly came to the conclusion that it was decent. A gold ring with an American flag painted on one side, and his name inscribed on the other. Mustard.

'Thanks, Alexis,' he said politely, as he put the ring on his index finger. 'That's the good news over with, right? Now you're gonna give us a shitty job, yeah?'

'This job isn't from me,' said Calhoon, closing the book of rings. 'It's come directly from Navan Douglas, the Attorney General, so you're under no obligation to take it obviously, but I negotiated you a good fee.'

'Ooh, how much,' Jasmine asked.

'Ten thousand each, up front, in cash. And if you get the job done, another hundred thousand each.'

'Ooh, big bucks,' said Jasmine, still staring at her ring.

'Yes. It's a potentially tricky job though,' said Calhoon in a serious tone. 'Your mission is to hunt down and eliminate a man named Zero. He's a conspiracy theorist, one of those guys who spouts off uninformed bullshit on the internet.'

Elvis frowned. 'That's all? Why do you need us for that?'

'Well, apparently Zero is different to all the other conspiracy theorists.'

'He's got a girlfriend?' said Jasmine.

'Not that I know of. This guy is the source of many of the online conspiracy theories, but he's recently stopped using the internet altogether. The government got really close to catching him. It's spooked him, so now he's gone dark. He has no electronic footprint, and is hardly ever seen in public anymore. Navan Douglas informed me that the secret service sent a number of assassins to eliminate Zero. But, and this is the dangerous part of the job, all of them have fallen under his spell.'

'Spell?' said Elvis, remembering an unpleasant incident with a dirty witch.

'Yes, well, not a spell like in Harry Potter. This man is a serious threat to national security because he can hypnotise and control minds. All of the men sent to eliminate him have become disciples of his. If you meet him and make eye contact, that's it, he'll have you believing everything he says before he even says it. So, if you track this guy down, you have to kill him before he speaks. Do not hesitate. Gun him down straight away, or he will take control of your mind.'

'Awesome,' said Jasmine, picking up her mug and sniffing the coffee. 'This sounds like fun.'

'I have one question,' said Elvis. 'If the government wants this guy eliminated, then it must be because one of his conspiracy theories is true. So, which one of his theories has got the government spooked?'

Calhoon allowed herself a brief smile as she contemplated whether to answer the question or not. Eventually she relented. 'There is one theory online that is believed to have come from him, and I'm pretty sure it's true.'

'Ooh, exciting,' said Jasmine. 'What is it?'

'A few months back, Douglas came to me with a top secret item hidden in a secure box. He and I took it to a secret government bunker where it will remain forever, locked away, never to be opened. I believe it may have contained the coat of Benjamin.'

'Benjamin who?' Jasmine asked. Then her eyes lit up. 'Is it Benji the dog?'

'No, not the dog,' Calhoon replied. She took a sip of her coffee, which was still fucking hot, but she didn't wince when it hit her tongue. The woman was absolute nails. After swallowing the red hot brew, she asked them a question. 'Do you remember Joseph and his Coat of Many Colours?'

'I've always wanted to go see it,' said Jasmine. 'I love musicals.'

'I wasn't really talking about the stage show. I meant the story in the Bible. Jacob gave his son, Joseph, a coat of many colours, but Joseph's brothers became jealous and betrayed him, leaving him for dead. Jacob was distraught, so he prayed to God. And God gave him another coat, a coat with no colours. An invisible coat. Jacob gifted this coat to his new favourite son, Benjamin, who was younger than all the others. Jacob's thinking was that if Benjamin was ever in trouble, he could make himself invisible just by lifting the hood of the coat over his head.'

'I had an invisible coat once,' said Jasmine. 'I got it in Domino's party store a while back. It's not really invisible though, just see through.'

Calhoon took a big swig of coffee, possibly to hide the look on her face. After placing the mug back down on the table she ignored Jasmine's comment and carried on with her story. 'In a recent private meeting I had with the president, he confided in me about a failed assassination attempt. He claimed that a man in an invisible coat snuck into his hotel room. The attack was thwarted by bodyguards who retrieved the invisible coat. The president showed me a grainy photo of the man taken from a CCTV camera. It's Zero, the man Navan Douglas wants you to track down and assassinate. His real name is unknown. Zero is just a street name. It seems like he's been off the grid since the day he was born. This man is very dangerous, so if you take the job, you'd better be careful. If you lay eyes on him, shoot him immediately. There's one other thing. We're worried that he's somehow learned how to make more invisible coats. See, one invisible coat is bad news. Multiple invisible coats, that would be disastrous. So, are you in?'

'Oooh, exciting,' said Jasmine. 'Count me in.'

'Me too,' said Elvis.

Calhoon reached inside her breast pocket and pulled out a six-inch by four-inch photograph. 'This is the only picture we have of Zero. It was taken from a camera outside the president's hotel after the failed assassination attempt. Seconds after this picture was taken Zero jumped into an escape vehicle. And after that, he vanished underground again, but there are rumours all over the internet about him and the invisible coat. The president's people keep taking the articles down, but they're worried one of them could catch on and go viral. I know I keep saying it, but this man Zero needs to be gone. ASAP.'

'I like the sound of this,' said Elvis. 'Where do we start looking for this asshole?'

Calhoon raised her eyebrows and forced a fake smile. 'That's why we need you guys. You see, other than the photo, we don't have any leads. But you guys can find anyone, anywhere in the world, right?'

## Twenty-Nine

'This is so cool isn't it?' said Jasmine, her hair blowing behind her as they cruised along the highway with the Cadillac's roof down. 'A mission just for the two of us.'

'It'll make a nice change not to have to listen to everyone else bickering all the time,' said Elvis.

'I don't bicker.'

'I never said you did.'

'You implied it though.'

'No I didn't.'

'You did too.'

'Well, you don't,' said Elvis. 'In fact, I've never known you to bicker, ever.'

'I was only teasing,' said Jasmine, grinning.

'No you weren't.'

'Yes, I was, honest.'

'You were not.'

'I was too!'

It was Elvis's turn to grin. 'I'm just teasing.'

Jasmine rolled her eyes and tutted. 'Dickhead.'

'Skank.'

'Hey, I'm proud to be a skank, thank you.'

'And I'm proud to be a dickhead.'

'Good, because you are one.'

Elvis glanced over at her. 'Are you finished?'

'I believe I am. Are you gonna tell me how we're going to track down this Zero dude by just his photo?'

'Yes, I am.'

'Cool.' Jasmine leaned across and kissed Elvis on the cheek. 'How are we going to do it then?'

'Reach into my top pocket and pull the photo out.'

'Okay.'

'And Jasmine….'

'Yes.'

'Don't let the photo blow out of your hand.'

'As if!'

Jasmine slid her hand into the breast pocket on Elvis shirt and pulled out the photo. 'Okay, what now?' she asked, staring at the picture of Zero.

'Take a photo of it.'

Jasmine took out her phone and snapped a photo of the photo. 'Done. Now what?'

'Put the photo back in my pocket.'

Jasmine slid the photo back into its home. 'And?'

'Send your photo to Jacko, and ask him to do a facial recognition. He'll be able to check if Zero's face has showed up on any satellite or CCTV cameras recently.'

'Wow, Jacko's clever, isn't he?'

'Not really. The genius behind the operation is Eric Einstein, the ginger weirdo who used to work for Scratch. Remember him?'

'Yeah. He's got the hots for me.'

'I know. He can hook the Purgatory computers into any CCTV network in the world. If Einstein can find a few recent images of Zero, he'll be able to triangulate a position for us.'

'Triangulate?'

'What I'm saying is, he'll narrow down the area where we search for Zero.'

Jasmine gazed lovingly at Elvis. 'You are so clever.'

'Just send the text. Sooner it's done the better.'

Jasmine tapped away on her phone and sent the photo and message to Jacko. He promptly replied with a promise to get right on it.

'Awesome,' said Jasmine. 'He's doing it. What shall we do while we wait?'

'I'm thinking we stop off in the first motel we come across,' said Elvis.

'Are you hungry again?'

'Nope. But I figure once we start on this job, we ain't gonna have much spare time.'

'So you wanna fuck?'

'I absolutely do.'

'Good, because I've been wearing clothes for almost five hours now.'

Elvis honked the Cadillac's horn at an old lady riding a moped in front of them, then he yelled some abuse at her for going too slow.

'Jeez,' said Jasmine. 'Do you need a dick rub?'

'No, it can wait. Just see if you can find us a motel on your phone.'

'You got it, baby.'

The song "Going To California" by Led Zeppelin came on the radio, so Elvis turned up the volume and yelled some more abuse at the moped lady as he overtook her. Jasmine ignored him and searched for a local motel on her phone. There weren't many to choose from but she found one that sounded right up their street.

'Got one,' she announced. 'Six miles down the road.'

'What's it called?'

'Cheetah's Motel.'

'Really?'

'Yeah, it's got a good rating too.'

'That'll do.'

Ten minutes later Elvis turned off the highway into the parking lot for the Cheetah's Motel and pulled up in a "NO PARKING" zone. The motel looked decent, fairly modern. White exterior, black doors, clean windows, and plenty of vehicles in the parking lot, suggesting the place was popular. A sign above the entrance advertised it as having sixty rooms.

'My wallet is in the glovebox,' said Elvis. 'Why don't you take it and go book us a room?'

Jasmine looked surprised. 'You not coming in with me?'

'Nah, you might get a better price on your own.'

Jasmine opened the glove box and pulled out a shiny purple wallet. 'Do you want me to show them my tits?' she asked as she reached for the door.

'No, just be yourself. People like you.'

'They do.' Jasmine planted another kiss on Elvis, then vaulted out of the car without opening the door. 'Back in a minute,' she said, blowing him another kiss. 'Don't go anywhere.'

As soon as Jasmine was inside the motel, Elvis reached over to the glovebox and pulled out his big gold Desert Eagle 5.0 pistol. He tucked it down the back of his pants, opened the car door, rolled out, and then strolled across the parking lot to a blue Ford Bronco with two middle-aged white men in suits sitting in the front. The driver had thick blond hair, a matching moustache, and piercing blue eyes. His buddy was overweight, with grey hair that was thinning on top. Elvis headed for the blue-eyed blond and tapped on his window. The window duly rolled down.

'Can I help you?' the blond guy asked.

'Yeah. Fuck off. If you're still parked here when my girlfriend comes back out of the motel, I'm gonna shoot you both in the face. Understood?'

The blond man nodded. His friend closed his eyes and muttered the word, "shit" under his breath, but Elvis heard it anyway. They definitely got the message though, because Blondie started the engine on the Bronco, released the parking brake, and then drove out of the motel parking lot back onto the highway. When they were out of sight, Elvis headed back across the parking lot and into the motel reception area. He found Jasmine negotiating a price with an old lady behind the reception desk.

'Yo, Jas. I've changed my mind. This place is a shit-hole.' He faked a smile at the old lady. 'No offence, sweetheart.'

'I thought you wanted to fuck?' said Jasmine.

'I do. But not here. We gotta find someplace else.'

'Can I have my hundred dollars back please?' Jasmine said to the old lady.

Elvis pulled out his gun and pretended to polish it. The old lady saw it and duly handed Jasmine back her hundred dollars.

'Thanks,' said Jasmine. 'It was nice talking to you. I hope your husband gets his balls fixed.'

As they walked back out to the parking lot, Jasmine elbowed Elvis in the ribs. 'What the fuck was that about?'

'Two guys have been following us in a Ford Bronco.'

Jasmine looked around the parking lot. 'Where are they now?'

'I told 'em to fuck off. But my guess is they won't go far. Let's drive for an hour or so before we stop again. If we see them, we're gonna have to kill them.'

Jasmine shrugged. 'I get followed by guys all the time. What's the big deal?'

'These guys followed us from Calhoon's. My guess is, they're government.'

## Thirty

After leaving the Cheetah's Motel, Elvis and Jasmine drove for an hour before they found another motel they liked the look of. The El Guapo was a two storey motel with its own restaurant. Jasmine booked them a room on the upper floor, and before long they were settled in for the night with a few bottles of wine and a low budget movie called *The Naked Cage* (which thankfully wasn't a Nicolas Cage porno). When the movie ended they got down and dirty, then fell asleep in each other's arms.

After maybe two hours of sleep, Elvis was awoken by a buzzing sound. He looked across at Jasmine. She was lying next to him, out for the count. She could sleep through a plane crash. Elvis wished he was the same, but his years in the assassin trade had made him paranoid, edgy, a bit mental, and a few other things on top. He reached over to the bedside table and picked up his phone. He had a text from Jacko.

*"Call me when you're up."*

That just about did it. There was no way Elvis was getting back to sleep knowing that Jacko had some information for him. It was 3:20 a.m. He rolled out of bed. He had learned over time that there was no need to be quiet. Jasmine wouldn't wake until she'd either had seven hours of sleep, or could smell coffee.

Three bottles of wine. It wasn't a huge amount to drink, not by their standards, but it was enough for Elvis to feel a bit crap. He walked into the bathroom, took a piss, washed his hands, boiled the kettle, located his boxers from behind the television, then sat down in the lounge area with a cup of bland-as-fuck instant coffee, so bland the scent of it probably wouldn't wake Jasmine. After a few sips to sharpen him up, he made the call to Jacko. The master of Purgatory answered straight away.

'Hey Elvis.'

'Jacko, wassup?'

'Did I wake you?'

'Take a guess.'

'I'll say no. Anyway, here's the deal. The guy you're looking for, Zero. He's popped up on a few security cameras in a place called, wait for it....'

'Wait for it?' Elvis rubbed his head. 'There's a place called *Wait For It?*'

'No. A place called Santa Mondega. Your friend Zero is hanging out there.'

Elvis groaned. 'There's no getting away from that place is there?'

'If this guy really is wanted by the government, then Santa Mondega is the best place to hide out, after Purgatory.'

'Yeah, right.'

'Anything else I can do for you?'

'Which places in Santa Mondega have caught him on their cameras?'

'Mostly he's been seen at the launderette, the Nightjar, City Hall and the Wok and Roll restaurant.'

'Okay, it's a starting point. Thanks Jacko.'

'No problem. Let me know if you need anything else.'

Elvis ended the call. He walked over to the motel room's front window and peered through the blinds. The outside looked different to how he remembered it. He pulled up the last photo he'd taken on his phone. It was a photo of the parking lot, taken just before midnight. He stared at the photo, then through the window again. There was one new vehicle in the parking lot, a silver van, parked on the far side, near the entrance.

Elvis snuck back into the bedroom and rummaged through his suitcase. The item he was looking for was tucked in a flap inside the case. It was a black-handled switchblade, not a tool he used very often, but it was ideal for the current task. He wrapped himself in one of the complimentary blue bathrobes supplied by the motel, slid his feet into Jasmine's pink, open-toed fluffy slippers, then headed outside with the intention of slashing the van's tyres. The cold from the night air hit him as soon as he opened the door, clinging to him like the peanut butter he'd recently rubbed into Jasmine's nipples. He wrapped the bathrobe tighter, then climbed down a set of rattly metal stairs. Thanks to Jasmine's slippers he kept the noise to a minimum. When he reached the bottom, he ambled across the parking lot to the silver van, checking all around for anyone else who might be up and about at such a hideous hour. Everything seemed quiet.

At first glance, the van looked empty. Elvis peered through the driver's window. There was nothing much to see, no clues as to the identity of the van's owner, no food wrappers, nothing. He took one more look around the parking lot to see if anyone was watching. No one in sight. All good. Blade out. Into the front tyre. Hiss. Front tyre fucked. Suck on that, Mister Van-Driver. Round to the back. Blade into the rear tyre. Hiss. Two tyres fucked.

Two. That ought to be enough.

Fuck it. Why not make it three?

He walked around to the other side of the van. Blade into the third tyre. Hiss. Fuck it, may as well do the fourth one.

A light came on in the motel, five doors along from the apartment Elvis and Jasmine were staying in.

Elvis ducked behind the van and kept a keen eye on the window of the wide-awake apartment. After a while, a hand pierced the blinds on the apartment window. The face of a man peered through. He seemed to be looking Elvis's way. Could he see the flat tyres from that distance? It was possible.

Then the door to the apartment opened. The silhouette of a man stepped out onto the metal staircase. He was wearing a suit. He scurried along the landing to the apartment Jasmine was sleeping in. Elvis had left the door unlocked. The suited man pushed it open and stepped inside. Before Elvis could do anything, two more men came out of the man's apartment, also wearing suits. They made their way down the metal stairs to the parking lot, muttering to each other in hushed tones.

Damn, and shit, and fuck. Those weren't the names of the three suited men, they were the words racing through Elvis's head, over and over.

The first two men reached the bottom of the stairs and then marched across the parking lot towards the silver van, and Elvis.

## Thirty-One

Stakeouts were so fucking boring. Andrew Vadge had been watching TV in the motel room for three hours. Three hours of shit TV. Nothing was likely to happen now. The targets he and his colleagues were following were bound to be asleep. Vadge and his buddies had been on the tail of Elvis and Jasmine since two of their co-workers had blown the mission earlier in the day by following too close behind Elvis's Cadillac.

It didn't help that they were staying in a low budget motel. The furniture in their room left a lot to be desired. Vadge was sitting in an uncomfortable chair, the kind that usually ended up in an old people's home. He was slouched back in it, close to falling asleep because the rerun of *Moonlighting* he was watching was nowhere near as good as he remembered. His head was sliding to the side and his eyes were half closed. The suit he was wearing wasn't designed for comfortable naps. It was two degrees too hot to be wearing a suit anyway, but Simon Fodder the senior agent of the three, had insisted on it. The idiot. Vadge had argued that they should wear basketball shirts, or anything casual, but noooooooo, Fodder believed agents should wear suits at all times, even when undercover.

Fodder and the other agent, Carl Rosewood, were sitting around a coffee table in the middle of the room, playing cards. It was an uncomfortable game, not just because they were wearing suits, but because the table was so much lower than the chairs they were sitting in, and they were playing in the dark, with only the TV to shed any light on the cards. Vadge had quit playing after one hand, realising early on that he'd end up with backache and no money. There was no point in playing cards against Rosewood anyway because he was one lucky sonofabitch. Rosewood was a tall, slim thirty-eight-year-old with messy orange hair, a look that had earned him the nickname, Beaker. He was winning at cards, like he always did. He was one of those guys, born a winner. Cards, betting on horses, fruit machines, bingo, he won at everything. *The jammy bastard.* Fodder, on the other hand, was a fifty-two-year-old with weight issues, two chins, thinning brown hair and a permanent grouchy look on his face, and he never won at anything. He never quit though, not until he'd lost all his money. His persistence, while unhelpful in card games, was what made him a good agent. Vadge had learned a lot from both of his colleagues during his two years on the team. He was the youngest of them, a baby at thirty. Youngest agent in the whole unit. He was destined for the top one day. Then stakeouts and foul coffee-breath would be a thing of the past.

Vadge was moments away from nodding off when a beep from his phone reminded him where he was. He sat up straight, shook himself awake, then headed over to the window. He peered through the blinds at the parking lot. A few street-lamps lit everything up just enough for him to spot Elvis walking between two cars. Elvis was wearing a bathrobe and some pink slippers. Vadge blinked a few times. Pink slippers, really? Yes, really.

Vadge turned away from the window. 'Elvis is on the move!' he announced to his two colleagues.

Simon Fodder stood up, his knees creaking. 'What's he doing?' he asked, plodding up to the window to join Vadge.

'He's walking up to the van.'

'What?' Fodder slid his hand between the slats on the blinds and checked for himself. Sure enough, Elvis was giving their van the once-over.

Carl Rosewood threw his cards down onto the coffee table, then got up and joined them at the window, just in time to see Elvis stick a knife into one of the van's tyres.

'Asshole!' said Rosewood. 'He's slashing my tyres.'

'Told you not to bring the van,' said Vadge. 'It's an eyesore. I bet he had us rumbled the minute we arrived.'

'He'll see us now if we're not careful,' said Fodder.

With that in mind, the three men stepped away from the window. Rosewood flicked on the light.

'Don't switch the light on you moron!' said Fodder.

Vadge peered through the blinds again. Elvis clocked him and ducked behind the van. Vadge backed away from the blinds.

'Shit! I think he saw me.'

'Right, that's it,' said Rosewood 'I've had enough of these fucking Dead Hunter people. The guy's got a knife on him. That's all the excuse we need to kill him. We can tell Navan Douglas we did it in self-defence.'

'You dumbass,' Fodder groaned. 'We can't kill him until we've found Zero.'

'We could beat him up,' Rosewood suggested. 'See if he already knows where Zero is?'

'Ugh. No, we can't,' Fodder reminded him. 'Our job is to follow and observe, unless we see Zero.'

'What about Jasmine?' said Vadge.

'What about her?'

'She's alone in the room. We could take her hostage, couldn't we?'

'I like that idea,' said Rosewood.

Fodder groaned again. 'Here's what we're gonna do. Rosewood, you and me will go down to the parking lot and deal with Elvis. Vadge, see if you can get into their room and grab Jasmine. If Elvis sees you've got her, he'll tell us all we need to know. Then, *if, and only if,* we get what we want, we can kill them both, and be done with this fucking dumb mission.'

Vadge was mortified. 'We can't kill Jasmine,' he said. 'She's worth a fortune. She killed the pope, remember?'

'Okay. Rough her up a bit then. Don't underestimate her though.'

'I won't,' said Vadge. 'I've seen her video. I know what she's capable of.'

Rosewood grabbed his gun from the coffee table. 'Come on then,' he said, heading for the door. 'What are we waiting for?'

Fodder reached inside his suit jacket, unholstered his pistol, checked it was loaded, like he always did, then slipped it back in its holster. 'Okay, let's go,' he said.

Vadge was out the door first, scurrying across the landing to Jasmine's apartment. Rosewood and Fodder stayed a moment to argue about something, then they left the motel room and headed down a set of metal stairs to confront Elvis on the other side of the parking lot.

Vadge definitely had the better task, for once. He tried the door handle of Jasmine's apartment. Elvis had left it unlocked, *the sucker*. Vadge opened it up and crept inside, then he pushed the door back to an almost closed position to stop any draft from alerting Jasmine to his presence.

There was a table in the middle of the lounge with three empty wine bottles on it. A woman's sneakers were on the floor next to the table. Vadge crept across the room to the bedroom door, which was ajar. He nudged it open, and in the darkness he made out the sleeping figure of Jasmine. She was lying on her front on the near side of a king-size bed, her head facing outwards. Vadge reached inside his jacket and pulled out his pistol, then he moved over to the side of the bed. He looked down at Jasmine. Even asleep with hair across her face she was fucking gorgeous.

He pointed his gun at her head, just in case she was pretending to be asleep. He knew not to be complacent. He'd read all the files. With his free hand he reached down and switched on a bedside lamp on the table by her head. She still didn't stir. Vadge didn't want to slap her around the face to wake her up. He wanted to be more of a gentleman. The best thing to do would be to pull back the sheets, let her feel the cold night air on her skin. He reached down and dragged the sheets back, revealing Jasmine's naked body. He pulled it back far enough to get a look at her ass, not because he was a perv, but to make sure she didn't have a concealed weapon. That's what he told himself anyway.

Fucking hell. What an ass. What a body.

Still Jasmine didn't stir. There was nothing else left to do. He was going to have to slap her on the ass to wake her up. He lifted his free hand, but before he could swing it down onto the lovely fleshy buttocks, he was hit by a sharp pain in his testicles. He winced, almost cried out in agony. The pain didn't stop there though. It shot right through his body from his balls to his brain. Jasmine's ass vanished. Everything turned black. Vadge's legs gave up on him, and he slumped forward, his face landing on two soft cheeks.

Jasmine woke up and rubbed her eyes. 'Is it morning already?' she groaned.

No reply.

She rolled over onto her back. Elvis's side of the bed was empty, but someone was touching her. There was a hand on her stomach, and something heavy a little lower down. Her bedside light was on too. She lifted her head a few inches and looked around. There was a guy in a suit kneeling by the side of the bed. He was fast asleep with his head between her legs and his left hand on her tummy.

'Who the fuck are you?' Jasmine asked him.

She peeled his hand away and sat up. The guy didn't move. She grabbed a clump of his hair and lifted his head up. Man, his head was heavy. He looked drunk, really wasted.

'Elvis!' Jasmine called out. 'We've got another drunk guy in bed with us!'

No reply.

She pushed the man's head away from the bed. His whole body slumped onto the floor with a loud thud. She peered over the edge of the bed and saw him lying on his back in a kind of superman pose. There was a big patch of blood around the crotch of his pants, and it was spreading onto the floor.

Jasmine climbed out of bed and stepped over her new friend. 'Elvis?' she called out again.

Still nothing. She moved into the lounge. The front door was slightly open. She picked up an empty wine bottle from the coffee table and walked over to the open door. There were male voices talking somewhere in the parking lot. She recognised one of the voices. It belonged to Elvis. She walked out onto the landing outside the apartment. Elvis was down below on the far side of the parking lot, talking to two guys in suits. He was wearing a blue bathrobe and

Jasmine's pink slippers. The conversation looked heated, and the two men were pointing guns at him.

## Thirty-Two

Fodder and Rosewood marched across the parking lot to confront Elvis. He was clearly visible despite his feeble attempt to hide behind the van. Either he was a moron who genuinely thought they couldn't see him, or he was embarrassed about the pink slippers he was wearing.

'Leave the talking to me,' said Fodder.

'That's my fucking van,' Rosewood reminded him.

'And that's why I'm doing the talking. You're too emotional. Just let him see you're armed. That way he won't try anything.'

When they arrived at the van, Elvis stepped out from his shit hiding place behind it. He was holding the tyre-slashing knife by his side.

'Evenin' fellas,' he said. 'This your van?'

'What the fuck are you doing?' Rosewood asked, ignoring Fodder's demand that he stay quiet.

'Someone's slashed your tyres,' said Elvis, holding up his knife. 'Look. I found the knife they did it with.'

Fodder moved his hefty frame in front of Rosewood then reached inside his jacket, pulled out his pistol and pointed it at Elvis. Rosewood unholstered his gun, but then crouched down by the front of the van to get a better look at one of the ruined tyres.

'What are you doing out here at braindead a.m.?' Fodder asked Elvis.

'Like I said, someone slashed your tyres.'

'That doesn't explain why you're out here,' said Fodder. 'Unless you did it.'

Elvis shrugged. 'What reason would I have to get up in the middle of the night and slash your tyres? I don't even know you. I mean, it's not as if you're following me or anything is it?'

'Oh, we got ourselves a real fuckin' comedian here,' said Rosewood, standing up. His pale white face was positively glowing in the darkness.

'If you're not following me,' said Elvis, 'then I'm guessing you're just two smartly-dressed gentlemen who happen to be sharing a room in a motel, right?'

'You're the one wearing the pink slippers,' Rosewood reminded him.

'Listen,' said Fodder. 'Let's just cut to the chase. You're looking for a man named Zero. We'd just like to know if you've got any leads yet?'

'You *were* following me then?'

'Yeah. We were following you.'

'Don't forget he slashed my fucking tyres!' Rosewood complained. 'You're gonna pay for some new fucking tyres, asshole.'

'On the head,' said Elvis. 'Real hard.'

Both men frowned. 'What?' they said in unison.

CLANK!

THUD!

The thud was Rosewood's head hitting the side of the van. Fodder saw it out of the corner of his eye. Rosewood dropped his gun and slumped onto the ground next to the van.

Fodder forgot all about Elvis for a moment and twisted around, pointing his gun into the wind. He was greeted by the sight of Jasmine, who had made her way down to the parking lot, naked and holding a wine bottle in her hand.

'What the—'

Elvis swooped in behind Fodder. He pulled the tubby agent's gun-wielding arm down to his side, then with his other hand he pressed his switchblade against Fodder's chins. The senior agent dropped the gun onto the ground.

'She's cute, huh,' Elvis whispered into Fodder's ear. 'Now tell me, who are you working for?'

The blade was close, too close. Fodder didn't dare swallow in case he inflicted a cut upon himself. 'We were ordered to follow you by Navan Douglas,' he spluttered. 'He's the Attorney General.'

'Keep going,' said Elvis.

'I'm sorry,' said Fodder. 'It's hard to think with a naked woman in front of me.'

'Try,' said Elvis. 'Because if you don't, tomorrow morning someone will find you with that wine bottle up your ass, and your buddy giving you a reach-around.'

For a brief moment, Fodder visualised what Elvis was saying. He fought the instinct to shudder, and settled for chewing his lip instead. 'You've got quite an imagination,' he said.

'We like to try things,' said Jasmine. 'Now answer the fucking question because it's cold out here and my nipples are getting hard.'

Fodder sucked in as deep a breath as he could in the circumstances and tried not to stare at the nipples. 'Okay, it's like this. Douglas has got a real hard-on for you Dead Hunter people. He thinks you killed his friend, Michael Raffone.'

'We did,' said Elvis. 'Does that mean Navan Douglas wants you to kill us?'

'He just wanted us to follow you. You're going after this conspiracy theorist named Zero, right?'

'Yeah.'

'Our job was just to make sure that you killed him. If you didn't, we were to do it for you.'

Elvis tutted. 'And if we *were* successful with the assassination of Zero, I suppose you were going to try and kill us to clean the whole thing up?'

'It was an option. But it wasn't definite. I was against it.'

'Fuck him,' said Jasmine. 'These guys were sent to kill us when the job was done.'

'Did you hear that,' Elvis whispered in Fodder's ear. 'She thinks we should kill you.'

'I swear to God man,' said Fodder, 'we're on the same team. We could come with you, we could help.'

'What about the other two guys that were following us yesterday? Are they working with you too?' Elvis asked.

'Foster and McCabe. Yeah, they're part of our team.'

'Any others?'

'No, it's just us.' He glanced up at the motel's second floor. 'What happened to Vadge?'

'Is he the guy in our apartment?' Jasmine asked.

'Yeah. Is he okay?'

'No, he's not.'

'What did you do to him?'

'Never mind him,' said Elvis, pressing the knife harder against Fodder's lower chin and drawing a tiny amount of blood. 'Where are Foster and McCabe now?'

'They're at the next motel, five miles down the road.'

'You got a phone on you?'

'Yeah.'

'Get it out. I want you to send them a text.'

'Okay.' Fodder reached into his jacket pocket and pulled out his phone. He held it up in front of his face and pulled up a messaging service. 'What do you want me to say?' he asked.

'Nothing. Hand it to Jasmine. She'll type the message.'

Jasmine held out her free hand and Fodder pressed his phone into it. The overweight agent took a moment to admire her naked body. Unfortunately, that beautiful moment ended when Elvis slid the blade of his knife across Fodder's neck, ripping his throat apart. The overweight agent's mouth dropped open and his tongue slid out. Blood gurgled in his lungs. Elvis let go of him and stepped back. Fodder dropped to his knees, then slumped sideways. He was still alive when his face touched the cold ground, but with blood spilling out of his throat and filling up his lungs, he only lasted a few more seconds before the gods came calling.

Elvis leant down and stabbed Fodder's partner Rosewood in the throat to finish him off too. Rosewood made a choking sound, but died without a fuss. Elvis wiped his knife clean on Fodder's jacket.

'What am I texting to these other guys?' Jasmine asked.

'Nothing. I was just distracting this asshole. What happened to their friend who went into our apartment?'

Jasmine shrugged. 'That's what I'd like to know.'

'What do you mean? You knocked him out, right?'

'Well, no. I think what happened is, he snuck into the bedroom, and while I was sleeping he pulled the sheets back, took one look at my ass, and then his nuts exploded.'

'He jizzed in his pants?'

'No. His nuts exploded. There's blood all over his pants. And he's dead. It woke me up because his head was in my ass.'

Elvis scratched his head. 'Jas, what the fuck are you talkin' about?'

'I don't really know. You need to take a look at it.'

'Okay, but first, help me get these two assholes into the back of the van, then you can show me the guy with the exploding nuts.'

## Thirty-Three

'I don't believe it,' said Elvis. 'This guy's nuts have exploded.'

'I told you,' said Jasmine.

The two of them were in their motel bedroom, standing over the corpse of the man Jasmine had found with his head in her ass ten minutes earlier. They had pulled down the dead man's pants and shorts to get a look at what had happened. There was no other way of describing it, the guys testicles were a grisly mess, blown to pieces.

'Okay, explain it to me again,' said Elvis. 'And don't miss anything out.'

Jasmine sat down on the bed. 'Okay, so I was lying here, asleep.'

'Yeah, and then?'

'Then I felt something on my ass. I woke up, and I had a dead guy's face in my butt.'

'He was already dead when you woke up?'

'Yeah. I rolled over and his head just rolled with me. Then I pushed him off, he fell onto the floor, in exactly the position he's in now, and that's when I saw all the blood around his crotch.'

Elvis crouched down by the corpse. It was a grisly mess and he didn't want to get too involved with it. He inspected the crotch on the pants, which were pulled down to the dead man's knees. In the middle of all the blood, just below the zipper, there was a small hole, the size of a penny. It made no sense, so Elvis moved on from inspecting the pants and had a rummage through the man's jacket pockets. He found a phone and a slim wallet. The wallet contained an ID badge. "Andrew Vadge," Elvis said aloud. 'EBTC.'

'EBTC?' said Jasmine. 'What does that mean? Exploding balls, tiny cock?'

'Nice try,' Elvis said, reading the small print on the card. 'It's East Baltimore Tennis Club.'

'Damn, so close. Has he got any money?'

'Not much,' said Elvis, pocketing some banknotes from Vadge's pockets. 'I wonder if Calhoon knows about any of this?'

'Let's check their room,' said Jasmine. 'See what information they've got on us.'

'Hold on a sec,' said Elvis. 'Let's just think a minute. I never saw these guys tailing us. So how did they find us?'

Jasmine reached out and grabbed his hand. She ran her index finger and thumb around the gold ring on his finger. 'Maybe this is a tracking device?' she suggested.

Elvis stood up and looked up into Jasmine's eyes. His woman was sexy and smart. A lethal combination. Not everyone appreciated Jasmine's keen analytical brain. Most people just focussed on the fact she didn't know left from right and couldn't tell the difference between the pope and a zombie. 'You sexy beast,' said Elvis. 'If we weren't in a hurry to leave, and there wasn't a dead guy with no nuts on the floor, I'd bend you over that bed right now.'

'I know, sweetie.'

Elvis took off his new gold ring. 'Calhoon gave us these,' he said, staring at it. 'But she said she got them from Navan Douglas, who these assholes were working for. Looks like we're gonna have to kill him.'

'I love it when you get passionate like this,' said Jasmine. 'But what are we going to do with Mister Busted-nuts? We can't just leave him on the floor can we? Shall we put him in the van with his friends?'

'I don't fancy carrying a corpse across a parking lot,' said Elvis. 'Let's take him back along the landing to his own room.'

'Okay. Top or tails?'

'I'll take the top.'

Elvis slipped his gold ring into the pocket on his bathrobe then wrapped his hands under Andrew Vadge's armpits, while Jasmine picked up his feet. They carried him out onto the landing then hurriedly took him over to his own apartment. Once they were inside, Jasmine let go of his feet, and Elvis dragged him through a messy lounge into a bedroom. There was a single bed in the room, so Elvis chucked him on it and pulled the sheets over him to hide his bloody balls. Then he re-joined Jasmine in the lounge for a snoop around.

There wasn't much to see. There was a coffee table with an unfinished card game on it. A few empty coffee cups and food wrappers were lying around, and the television was on at a low volume.

'You know, I've been thinking,' said Elvis as he rummaged through a desk drawer for anything of interest. 'If Navan Douglas has all these agents tailing us, is it just because we killed his buddy Mike Raffone, or is it something else?'

'Like what?'

'Well, I'm thinking if we do find this Zero fella, maybe we should hear what he's got to say.'

'Even though he could hypnotise us?' said Jasmine, checking down the sides of a sofa.

'Maybe that hypnotism thing is bullshit?' said Elvis, thinking aloud. 'What if he knows something, something big? Something about the government, something they're desperate to keep under wraps? All these agents following us to make sure we kill him, it's just weird if you ask me.'

'I thought it was because he knows about the invisible coat, and he tried to kill the president,' Jasmine reminded him.

'Yeah, maybe it is.'

Jasmine left the lounge and headed into one of the bedrooms to look around. When she returned she had taken off her special gold ring from the president. 'What should we do with these rings then?' she asked.

'Leave 'em here,' said Elvis. 'Some other agents will be along to find them soon enough.'

Jasmine placed her ring down on the coffee table. 'I liked having a ring,' she said.

Elvis pulled his from his pocket and put it down next to hers. 'I like that we had *matching* rings,' he said.

The two of them shared a kiss that almost got out of hand. Jasmine ended the embrace by pulling away from her man just before the urge to slide her hand into his boxers took over. 'What now?' she asked. 'Shall we go to another motel? We can't stay here. I'm worried your nuts might explode.'

'If you don't put on some clothes, they just might.'

The two of them headed back to their own apartment to start packing up their stuff in readiness for finding another motel. Elvis cleaned the lounge up, while Jasmine cleared the bedroom. She was emptying a drawer by her side of the bed when she saw something on the floor next to the big patch of Andrew Vadge's blood.

'Hey, Elvis come in here,' she whispered.

Elvis poked his head around the door. 'Wassup?' he asked.

'Look,' Jasmine pointed at the pool of blood. 'There's a hole in the floor.'

Elvis approached cautiously. 'What is it? A peep hole?'

'No, I think it's a bullet hole.'

Elvis slapped his forehead. 'Shit. Of course.'

'What should we do?'

'Get away from it for starters,' said Elvis, beckoning her over to him. 'And let's get the fuck out of here. This place gives me the creeps.'

# Thirty-Four

## Back in Purgatory

'The presidential rings have got tracking devices in them?' Flake was incredulous. 'That explains how the cops tracked me and JD to the Gunslingers club!'

Elvis shrugged. 'That guy Navan Douglas has got it big for all of us.'

While Elvis and Jasmine had been telling the story of their hotel skirmishes, Zilas the hunchback and the cleaning staff from Hell (not a rock band, but an actual cleaning service) had mopped away most of the filthy ocean water and sprayed enough disinfectant around to get rid of the fishy smell.

The Hell cleaners had also been kind enough to bring up a couple of clean sofas and a rectangular wooden table, which they set down between the sofas. Elvis and Jasmine were snuggled up on one sofa. Rex, Flake and JD were on the other. Goober had to settle for lying on the floor by Flake's feet. The table was loaded up with drinks courtesy of Jacko. And with the door to the disabled toilets open, the heat from Hell was warming everyone up after the tsunami incident.

Elvis reached across the table to Flake and took hold of her ring finger. 'Yeah, you should probably get rid of that,' he said, eyeing up the engraved ring.

'Great,' Flake groaned. She pulled the ring off her finger. 'How am I supposed to get rid of it?'

'It doesn't matter,' Jacko called out from behind the bar. 'Nobody can track you to Purgatory anyway. They'll probably assume you've destroyed it.'

'Well, I don't want it,' said Flake. 'Can you chuck it into the flames of Hell or something?'

'If you like,' said Jacko.

Flake leaned back and tossed the ring to Jacko. Snippets of recent memories flooded into her head. Sanchez taking his ring from Calhoon, Sanchez ordering cheeseburgers in the president's hotel suite. She flinched and booted the images from her thoughts. To take her mind off Sanchez she turned her attention to Elvis.

'I wanna know who shot the government agent in the nuts,' she said. 'Did you not stop off at the motel room below you to find out who did it?'

'No, we didn't,' said Elvis. 'We were in a hurry to get out of there. Plus, whoever was down there had a gun. Could have been more government agents.'

Rex intervened. 'If it was government agents, they wouldn't be shooting one of their own in the balls, would they?'

'Who knows?' said Elvis, picking up a bottle of beer and taking a swig. 'Anyway, we left that motel behind and drove to Santa Mondega. It took fucking ages.'

'We had to take turns driving,' Jasmine added.

'And did you find Zero?' Flake asked.

'Holy fuck!' said Rex, butting in on the conversation. He climbed off the sofa and walked over to the television, carrying a half full bottle of Shitting Monkey with him. 'It says a nuclear missile hit San Antonio this morning!'

'Nukes have landed all over the place,' Jacko reminded him. 'This is the only safe place to be.'

'Yeah, but I was just in San Antonio when I got the call about Jasmine being shot,' Rex said, panic spreading across his face. 'I've gotta get back there.'

'You can't go now,' said Jacko. 'It's not safe.'

'I don't care. Send me back.' Rex's agitation was growing by the second.

'Why do you want to go to San Antonio?' Flake asked. 'Is that woman there, the boss's wife, what's her name, Selene? Did her husband find out about you sleeping with her? And what happened to Paige? Did you find her?'

Jasmine tentatively leaned forward and picked up a glass of lime and soda from the table. She was looking pretty good considering she'd been shot a bunch of times (and also thrown off a sofa by a tsunami). 'Go on,' she said. 'I wanna hear what happened to Paige.'

'I need to go back!' Rex said, pacing around the room, tugging at his hair.

'Look at the news,' Jacko reminded him. 'You *can't* go anywhere. It's not safe. The whole of San Antonio has been blasted to kingdom come. If anyone survived the initial blast, they're still gonna be fucked.'

Rex stared at the portal door on the men's toilets, then he hurled his bottle of Shitting Monkey at it. The bottle hit the door and smashed into a hundred tiny pieces, froth and beer spraying everywhere.

'Jesus Christ!' said Jacko, angrily. 'We've only just had this place cleaned! What's gotten into you?'

Rex did not reply.

'Come on, Rex,' said Elvis. 'Spill the beans. What's going on? What happened after Paige got kidnapped?'

**Thirty-Five**

<u>Part Five – Crazy Golf</u>

Rex and JD were both leaning against the side of the Mercedes, steadying themselves. JD was rubbing the back of his head, while Rex was wrapping his bandana around the bullet wound in his leg, and tying it into a knot to keep it tight. A minute had passed since Paige was kidnapped.

'We should call the police,' Rex said, wincing. 'They can put up road blocks and use helicopters to track the van.'

'We're not calling the cops,' said JD, who was still trying to get his vision back to normal.

'Paige's life is on the line,' Rex reminded him. 'And in case you'd forgotten, we're not exactly in the best shape of our lives here.'

JD walked over to the baseball bat on the sidewalk and picked it up. It was a thick, metal bastard. 'Did you actually see this thing swing at me?' he asked Rex.

'Nope. Never saw a thing until after Paige was lifted off her feet. The bat appeared out of thin air just before it hit the ground.'

'That means our invisible friend can make his weapons invisible too.'

Rex pointed at his bandaged leg. 'How else do you think I got shot? There was no gun anywhere. If I'd seen it I would have caught the bullet. Lucky they weren't shooting at my head.'

'Lucky for you, yeah.'

'You okay to drive?'

JD was still groggy from having his skull busted by the baseball bat. A regular person would have been hospitalised with potential brain damage. JD merely felt nauseous and very annoyed. 'Just gimme a minute,' he said.

While Rex hobbled around on the sidewalk to see if he could walk normally, JD steadied himself by pressing his hand against the Mercedes. Then he lowered his head and puked down the car's rear wing.

'You sure you're okay to drive?' Rex asked.

'Yeah. Get in the car. We've got to get moving.'

Rex took a look around. There were some people on the other side of the road staring at them. It was definitely time to leave the scene. 'That van is long gone,' he reminded JD.

'Yeah, but Antonio Rodriguez owes us an explanation. This is why he hired us. Invisible kidnappers. He knew about it, and he shoulda told us about it. I wanna know why he didn't.'

'So do I,' Rex agreed. 'Why would he withhold the one piece of information that could have helped us protect his daughter?'

'I don't know, but I think it's about that time.'

'What time?'

'That time where we go kill all the henchmen.'

Rex puffed out his cheeks and exhaled. 'I knew it.'

JD gathered up Paige's belongings from the sidewalk and stuck them in the trunk of the car. Then he staggered around to the driver's side and climbed in. Rex squeezed into the front passenger seat, trying to keep his leg from jostling too much. He reached back and grabbed his breakfast sandwich from the back seat. He took another bite from it. 'Do you want your sandwich?' he asked JD.

'No. Appetite's gone.'

JD started up the engine. The radio kicked into life and the song, "Comfortably Numb" by Pink Floyd came on.

As JD swung the car out into the road, the sound of police sirens rang out nearby.

'Get moving,' said Rex. 'We don't need to be killing a bunch of cops too.'

JD drove the car sensibly so as not to draw the attention of the cops. But before they made it to the first junction, two police cars raced up behind them.

'Fuck,' said Rex, checking his wing mirror. 'Are they coming for us?'

JD steered the car over to the side of the road, expecting the cops to park up behind him, but they didn't. Both police cars sped past, lights flashing, sirens blaring.

'That's lucky,' said Rex. 'Maybe they're going after Paige?'

JD pulled back into traffic and continued the drive back to the Rodriguez estate. A mile and a half later, the reason for the speeding cops became clear. A whole bunch of squad cars with blue and red flashing lights were blocking the road outside *Big Buns and Footlongs*. Police officers were swarming all around the forecourt of the sandwich shop. A traffic cop was redirecting cars down a side road.

JD drove right up to the police blockade and stopped the car.

'What the fuck is all this about?' said Rex, staring through the windscreen at the chaos in front of them. Cops were sealing off the area around the sandwich shop. Members of the public were crying in the street outside. In the twenty minutes since Rex had picked up the breakfast sandwiches, something terrible had gone down at Big Buns.

A traffic cop with a grey beard and a plaster over his nose approached the car. JD wound his window down and poked his head out. The cop recognised him and hesitated.

'It's okay,' said JD. 'Come here.'

The cop felt the plaster on his busted nose, thought for a moment, then decided to do as he was told. He walked up to JD's window, but stopped half a yard away in case he was lunged at.

'What's happened here?' JD asked him.

The cop, who according to his badge was Officer Nick Buckman, responded with some helpful information. 'The family that run the sandwich shop have been murdered. It's too early to call, but it looks like a professional hit.'

'A professional hit? On a sandwich shop?'

'I know, doesn't make any sense, right?'

'What do you know so far?'

Buckman looked around to see if any of the other cops were within hearing distance. Then he leaned a little closer and lowered his voice. 'Two members of the family weren't killed. The mother wasn't home, but, and this is the really strange part, the youngest boy, eye-witnesses say he floated out of the shop, screaming. Sounds stupid, right?'

'Nope. Did he float into a black van?'

Buckman furrowed his brow. 'Yeah. How did you know that?'

'Never mind. You said the youngest boy was taken. Is that Kai?'

Buckman nodded. 'Yeah, Kai, the autistic boy.'

Rex leaned across JD so he could speak to Buckman. 'Did you say autistic?'

'That's right,' said Buckman. 'They took Kai, the retarded one.'

JD reached out and grabbed Buckman's shirt. He yanked the cop forward, smashing his face into the frame of the car window, busting his nose open again. With the cop dazed and seeing stars, JD relinquished his grip on his shirt. Buckman crumpled into a heap on the road.

'Invisible people kidnapping autistic kids,' said Rex. 'That's a new one.'

JD wound his window up and reversed the car back. 'It's not new to Antonio Rodriguez,' he said. He turned the car around and sped off down a side road back to the Rodriguez estate.

## Thirty-Six

Antonio Rodriguez loved having his own golf course. It was great for working on his game, which was important with the annual invitational tournament coming up in a few weeks. He had his heart set on winning it. The fifty thousand in prize money didn't matter. It was all about the bragging rights. He'd finished as runner-up the year before and it had been eating away at him ever since.

After hitting a par on the first hole, Antonio was preparing to tee off on the second. He had all the best golf equipment money could buy, and the best clothing. His outfits were the envy of every golfer in the land. He was wearing a pink and blue checked sweater, bright yellow pants that were tucked into a pair of tartan socks, and a grey flat cap.

Standing a safe distance away from the tee was Antonio's head henchman, Lucas the cowboy, who was caddying for him. 'Watch for that wind, boss,' Lucas warned. 'It's blowing across from left to right.'

Antonio licked his index finger and held it up to get a sense of the wind direction. Lucas was correct. With that in mind, he took a few practice swings, convinced that some fade would be required. Confident that he knew what he was doing, he stepped up to the tee and lined up the shot. There was a big green fairway in front of him with a couple of deep bunkers in the middle of it. The only other hazard was the dense woodland on either side of the fairway. Or so he thought. He was just about to swing his club when Lucas broke his concentration by speaking again.

'What the fuck is *he* doing here?' the henchman said.

Antonio lowered his club, his irritation clear. 'Who?' he asked.

'Him.'

Antonio checked the fairway and the woods. There was no one in sight, but then again, Lucas wasn't looking at the fairway, he was focussed on something behind them. Antonio turned around to see what it was. The Bourbon Kid was heading their way.

'Hello, my friend!' Antonio called out, cheerfully. 'Fan of golf are you?'

'No.' JD walked straight up to him, ignoring Lucas. 'I want a word with you.'

Lucas lunged forward and grabbed JD's shoulder, spinning him around so they were face to face. 'He's busy playing golf, in case you hadn't noticed,' he said.

JD reached into the bag of clubs Lucas was carrying. He pulled out a thick-headed club and jabbed it under the caddy's Stetson hat, knocking it off his head. A second jab of the club hit Lucas under the chin, knocking him back a few steps. With sufficient distance between them, JD swung the club again, smashing it across the side of Lucas's face. The club head connected with his cheekbone. The caddy took a few sideways steps like a drunk on a rocking boat. JD swung the club again, this time into Lucas's gut. It doubled him over and he fell to his knees, holding his stomach. A kick to the face sent him sprawling onto his back.

'HEY!' yelled Antonio. 'What are you doing? That's an expensive club!'

JD flipped the club over in his hand so that he was holding the chunky wooden head, then he smashed the handle of the club into the fallen caddy's mouth. It broke a few of Lucas's front teeth as it headed into his throat. JD applied a little more pressure to see how far down the club would go. Lucas, whose eyes were bulging by this point, reached up with both hands and grabbed hold of the club in an attempt to pull it out of his mouth. His efforts were in vain. After a bout of gurgling and choking, he started spitting up blood. His cheeks initially turned red, but were quickly filled with branches of bulging blue veins. His legs wriggled around on the grass in desperation. It achieved nothing, and eventually as the club probed deeper into his oesophagus, he stopped breathing. His arms flopped to his sides, leaving him in a crucifix pose next to the bag of clubs. The whole brutal attack was over in thirty seconds.

JD let go of the club and turned back to Antonio, who was gawping at his dead henchman, and the golf club that was growing out of his mouth.

'You've ruined my favourite club, you asshole!' Antonio spluttered.

'Why did you hire me?' JD asked him.

'Do you know how much that club cost?' Antonio was about to protest some more, but then he caught sight of the serious look on JD's face. 'Sorry, what did you say?'

'Why did you hire me?'

'To drive Paige to school. I told you that already.'

'No. You said one of your henchmen had sent a death threat. But that was a lie. So tell me, why did you *really* hire me? And don't lie this time. You've got three seconds to spill, or I'm grabbing another club.'

Antonio recognised the seriousness of the situation and responded sharply. 'You're right, there was no death threat, but I was worried someone was going to kidnap Paige.'

'Not good enough.' JD grabbed a five-iron from the bag and wrapped both of his hands around the handle.

'I've got enemies.'

'Nope!' JD swung the club and hit Antonio in the arm, just above the elbow. Antonio dropped his own club, grabbed his arm with his free hand, and howled in pain.

'OWWW! What the fuck!'

'Paige has been kidnapped.'

'What?'

THWACK!

'OWWW! Stop doing that!' Antonio sat down on the grass. He had been smacked on both arms with his own five-iron. He attempted to rub each injured arm with the opposite hand. It wasn't a success. 'What do you want from me?' he pleaded. 'And where is Paige?'

'Paige is gone. Someone is taking autistic kids. And I think you know who. Tell me who took her, or I'll break your face in half.'

'All right, *all right*. I heard that there were some vampires coming to town and they were gonna target autistic kids. I thought you could protect her. Has she really been kidnapped?'

'Yes. Why would vampires target autistic kids?'

'I dunno, maybe they think autistic people are more trouble than they're worth. You know, like Hitler with the jews.'

JD swung the club hard, smashing it into Antonio's shoulder. The mob boss howled in pain again. The impact of the blow knocked him over onto his side, wincing and weeping. He held up a hand to defend himself.

'Next time the handle goes down your throat,' JD warned him.

'Please, listen. I was worried about my daughter. I heard that these vampires have a list of names of all the autistic kids in town.'

'I'm getting tired of repeating myself. Why do they want autistic kids?'

'I don't know, I swear!' Antonio cried. 'Please don't hit me again. I'm not that brave that I would lie to you. You've got to go and get Paige back. I'll pay you another hundred thousand, I promise.'

'Do you know where she is?'

'I know where the vampires are. They're at the travelling circus. Everyone in the circus is a vampire, at least that's what I was told. That's why I never let Paige go to the circus. These vampires are travelling around the country snatching autistic kids. That's as much as I know.'

JD smashed the club against one of Antonio's knee-caps. The gangland boss rolled over onto his back and grabbed at his knee with both hands, grimacing and sobbing all at once.

'What the fuck was that for?' Antonio whined. 'I answered the question.'

'How do you know this? Who tipped you off? And why keep it secret from me and Rex? Are you stupid or something?'

'The mayor told me. But it was in confidence. I had to swear I wouldn't tell anyone else. He's a good guy, the mayor. He was doing me a favour. I figured I could keep Paige safe and they'd just take all the other autistic kids in town instead. But now you're telling me they've got Paige. You have to go get her. She's my only child, please!'

'Why would the mayor only tell you?'

'I donated a lot of money to his campaign. Plus, I have photos of him doing coke with a couple of hookers. Please, go after Paige. Get my baby back. Take some of my henchmen. I'll come with you too.'

'There's one other thing,' said JD, lowering the golf club.

'What?'

'Rex fucked your wife.'

Antonio breathed a sigh of relief. 'Oh, yeah, that's okay. I know about that. It's fine. We have an open relationship. You can fuck her too if you want. I don't care.'

JD smashed the club onto Antonio's skull. The crime boss grabbed his head with both hands and rolled onto his side.

'Owww! Shit! Fuck! That hurts. What was that for?'

'I can't let you live.'

Antonio stopped sobbing and rubbing injured parts of his body. He sat up and stared wide-eyed in horror at JD. 'What?'

JD swivelled the club around in his hand so the handle was pointed at Antonio's mouth. The mob boss glanced over at his dead caddy, then held up his hands in an attempt to defend himself.

'Please, no. I'll pay you anything,' he begged.

JD kicked Antonio in the neck, knocking him onto his back again, then he stood over him and pressed his boot down on his chest, pinning him to the ground. Antonio tried to grab hold of the club to stop the end of it going into his mouth, which he wisely kept closed.

Fifty yards away, on the approach to the tee, a voice yelled out, 'NOOOOO!'

The cry came from Rex, who was hobbling across the golf course as fast as he could to try to stop JD from murdering their employer.

His plea for mercy was a wasted effort. JD rammed the handle of the golf club into Antonio's mouth, busted some teeth, and pushed his tongue back into his throat. It was more brutal than the assault on Lucas. Blood spurted out of Antonio's mouth, splattering all over the length of the club, accompanied by some delicious gurgling sounds. The gangster's eyes turned red and almost popped out of his head. He grabbed hold of the club with both hands but failed to do anything meaningful with it. By the time Rex arrived at JD's side, Antonio was dead, and he had a big piss patch on the front of his yellow golf pants.

'Great,' said Rex sarcastically. 'Now we're gonna have about a hundred henchmen trying to kill us.'

'It's not that bad,' said JD. 'There's never more than forty on duty at any one time.'

'Forty? Fuck. I was kidding when I said a hundred. We should get moving.'

'Don't you wanna know what I found out?'

'Tell me on the way out. If we get out alive.'

PING!

The caddy's golf bag made the pinging sound. Or more specifically, a bullet that ricocheted off it made the pinging sound.

'Oh fuck,' said Rex, looking back at the main house. 'Here they come.'

Ten heavily armed henchmen were heading their way. Most of them were overweight so they weren't coming in at any great speed, but even so, ten fatties with rifles was still a problem.

'One of them's got an M16!' said Rex, backing away towards the fairway.

The incoming henchmen were certainly angry and ready for action. Every few steps one of them would stop and fire off a shot. None of them were exactly hotshots, but there were ten of them and they had plenty of ammo. These chunky fuckers meant business, and they were seemingly unaware of the golden rule that all henchmen are supposed to die in a gunfight.

To add fire to the flames, someone started shooting at Rex and JD from the fairway ahead of them. Rex spun around. Two henchmen on horseback were flanking them, and they had shotgun rifles.

'We're fucking surrounded!' said Rex, pulling out a pistol and firing a shot back at the men on horseback.

PING!

Another bullet hit the caddy's bag.

'I wouldn't worry too much,' said JD. 'I think they're shooting at the seven-iron.'

'Goddammit! We're sitting ducks!' Rex hissed back at him. He fired a few shots back at the foot-soldiers approaching from the house. All ten of them dropped to the ground, but then started shooting back.

'Don't just stand there!' Rex yelled at JD. 'Help me out here.'

'Head for the woods,' JD replied, pulling up his sleeve and checking the number of darts that were loaded into a miniature crossbow device he had on his arm. 'By the way, there's a sniper on the roof.'

Rex looked up at the roof of the main building. Sure enough there was someone up there, lining up the sniper rifle, aiming it in their direction.

'Ooh, fuck me!'

Rex and JD both ducked down and started running for the woodland, firing off shots in both directions. Bullets whizzed past them. JD made it over to the woods in good time, but Rex was struggling because he'd already been shot in the leg earlier in the day, so running was kinda difficult.

One of the men on horseback had his rifle aimed at Rex. He was taking his time, following Rex as he ran, lining him up in his crosshairs. Rex fired off a few warning shots at him, but running and gunning wasn't as easy as it looked in video games. He missed and missed again. The horseman bided his time, waiting for the precise moment to shoot.

SPLAT!

It didn't make much sense to begin with, but the man Rex was worried about suddenly had a bit of a face-lift. Or more specifically, a head-lift. His head lifted off his shoulders, turned to ketchup and blew away. Then his rifle slipped from his hands, and he fell off his horse.

SPLAT!

Two seconds later, the other armed rider died the same way, leaving his horse covered in brains and blood. The two horses had more sense than the dumb fucks who had been riding them. They turned and bolted. Horses, cleverer than henchmen. FACT.

Rex successfully hobbled into the woodland without taking any damage. He ducked behind a big tree and reloaded his gun. JD was three rows of trees into the woods, taking cover behind a large oak, while he stared up at the house.

'Was that you?' Rex yelled at him, convinced JD must have used his Headblaster gun on the two dudes on horseback.

'No. You must have really made an impression on Mrs Rodriguez,' JD replied, pointing at the house.

'What?' Rex poked his head around the tree and stared up at the sniper on the roof. He squinted with his one good eye to get a better look. 'Fuck me, is that Selene?' he said, gobsmacked.

'It is,' said JD. 'I'm guessing she's on our side. Either that, or she's a terrible shot.'

## Thirty-Seven

Selene was still glowing from her night of passion with Rex. An early morning swim in her private pool was followed by a healthy fruit and yoghurt breakfast in the kitchen. She managed to avoid bumping into Antonio who probably had his breakfast in bed with one of the local slags.

It was almost lunch time and she was in the middle of reading the morning paper when she heard a ruckus in the hallway outside. It sounded like a school corridor during recess. When she went to investigate, she was greeted by mayhem. Henchmen, armed with rifles and handguns, were running along the corridor yelling all kinds of indecipherable nonsense at each other. Selene pressed her back up against the wall to avoid being crushed in the stampede. These assholes seemed to have forgotten she was the lady of the house.

She grabbed the arm of one of the henchmen, a bearded-lumberjack-type named Larry, and pulled him away from the group. 'Larry, what's going on?' she asked him.

'You don't know?' he asked.

'No, that's why I'm asking.'

'It's those two new bodyguards, one of them has killed Antonio on the golf course. We're going to get 'em.'

'My husband is dead?'

Larry hesitated, his mouth open and his eyes shifting from side to side as if suddenly realising he'd broken some life-changing news to the wife of the boss. 'Gotta go,' he said. 'Sorry for your loss.'

And that was that. Larry sprinted after the others (to what would probably be certain death), rather than face the awkwardness of comforting Selene.

Well fuck him. And his henchmen friends.

Selene ran over to a set of stairs and bounded up them as fast as she could. Her asshole husband was finally dead. She'd waited years for this moment. She just wished she'd been there to see it. But how had it happened? Who did it? Rex or JD?

She followed the stairs all the way up to a door that led out onto the flat section of the roof. From there she scampered over to the big sniper rifle which was covered by a sheet of tarpaulin. She threw the sheet off and laid down on the concrete floor, pressing her eye up against the sighter on the rifle. It offered the best view of the golf course. She moved the rifle around until she spotted Antonio. He was on his back on the grass by the second tee. And he had a golf club sticking out of his mouth. His useless caddy, Lucas was dead too, a few feet away.

Rex and JD were standing over the bodies, engaging in what looked like an argument. The argument was abruptly interrupted by gunfire. The henchmen were mobilising on the first fairway. Not only that, a couple more goons on horseback were coming up from the third tee.

Rex and JD eventually stopped bickering and made a break for it. They ran to the woods at the side of the course. Rex was hobbling like he'd hurt his leg. He needed help. And Selene was just the person for the job. She grabbed a pair of nearby ear-defenders, slipped them on, loaded the rifle and lined up one of the horse-riding henchmen in its crosshairs. It was a man she recognised. Angelo was a patronising piece of shit who thought he knew more about horse riding than she did. He was lining up to shoot at Rex. Unlucky, Angelo, you smug fuck. Selene fired off the first shot.

It took Angelo's head clean off.

The kickback from the rifle hit her right at the same moment she realised she'd just killed a man. Selene had never killed anyone before. Was this what it felt like to take another life?

Yes. *It felt fucking awesome.* She lined up the other rider in the crosshairs. Smug Neil. Selene disliked him even more than she did Angelo. He was one of those assholes who frequently told her, "cheer up love, it might never happen".

*Well, Neil, it's about to happen.*

Two for two. Neil's head left his shoulders and landed on the fairway, adding a delightful touch of red to all the green.

This was fun. Selene began to wonder why she'd never tried killing henchmen before. After all, they existed solely to be killed for fun.

Who next?

She lifted her head and peered over at the golf course. JD and Rex were in the woods. Henchmen were heading their way in large numbers. She lined up another in the rifle's crosshairs.

Ozzy. What reason did she have to execute Ozzy? Easy. *"Any chance you could make us a coffee, sweetheart?"*

Selene had never actually made him a coffee, but it didn't stop him asking her at least once a week. Time to die Ozzy. *Make your own coffee in Hell.*

She shot Ozzy in the back. He went straight down like he'd been blindsided by Lawrence Taylor of the New York Giants. His blood spattered all over another goon who was dithering behind him, unsure which way to turn. Before Selene could target the other goon, he went down too. Someone in the woods had shot him. Either Rex or JD.

Selene looked for her next target, her bloodlust growing with each kill. This was suddenly a race against time, or more specifically a race against Rex and JD. There weren't enough henchmen to go around.

Paul the perv. Easy choice. Shot in the crotch.

Carl. Sexist and condescending. Shot in the face.

Mike. *"Busy today Selene?"*. He'd said that to her too many times. Prick. She shot him in the chest. He did a wobbly walk for a few seconds, then fell into a bunker. The bunker had three faceless assholes taking cover in it. Selene blasted them each in the head, one after the other.

Larry was next. The idiot who had just informed her of her husband's death. He could die just for being a dumbass. It was time to get creative. Selene took his left leg off just below the knee. When he hit the ground she blew his guts out. *Sorry for your loss, Larry.*

By this time, even the dumbest of henchmen had headed for the woods despite knowing that death was waiting for them in there. Selene scoured the trees for one she could take down.

There he was. Candy Andy. The fat henchman in the blue overalls was hiding behind a big tree in the woods. And as usual he was chomping on a candy bar. The dumb fuck's life was on the line but he still couldn't control his sugar cravings. He was actually the nicest of all the henchmen. Selene tried to think of a reason to kill him. It took a while, but it came to her eventually.

He was the fucker who'd stolen the big piece of chocolate from Paige's advent calendar the previous Christmas. *Time to die, candy man.*

Selene lined up his snack bar in her crosshairs.

One squeeze of the trigger and the tasty snack exploded over Andy's overalls. And Andy exploded all over the tree behind him.

Game over.

Selene removed her ear defenders and took a few deep breaths. Shooting henchmen.

Brilliant fun.

## Thirty-Eight

'I think that's all of them,' said JD.

Dead henchmen were splayed out all around the woodland. The fairway on the golf course was just as bad. Several henchmen had taken cover in the bunkers, but each time one of them had poked his head up to look around, Selene had blown them away with a shot from her sniper rifle. Rex counted eleven victims of Selene's sniping. It was quite a turn-on.

'We should probably make a move,' he said to JD. 'Hanging around here isn't an option.'

JD walked onto the fairway and kicked one of the corpses that still had a head, just in case it was faking death. It wasn't. 'Our next stop is the circus,' he said.

'The circus?'

'Yeah. Rodriguez says we were hired to protect Paige from the circus. They're taking autistic kids.'

'Why? What do they do to autistic kids at the circus?'

'He didn't know, but he said it's a vampire circus, so let's face it, it ain't gonna be good.' JD checked his watch. 'It's nearly two hours since she was taken. We've got no option but to go straight there and kill everyone.'

Rex disagreed. 'We don't have to go in all guns blazing. Our first job has to be to find Paige, otherwise we might fuck it up. I say we go stealth, not guns blazing.'

'Guns blazing usually works well for me. I fuckin' hate the circus.'

'Let's discuss plans on the way there,' Rex suggested.

As they began the walk back to the main house, Rex looked up at the roof. The sniper was gone.

'Can we just wait for Selene?' he said. 'She might know a bit about the circus.'

'She's not coming with us.'

'She could be useful.'

JD shook his head. 'They saw women in half at the circus.'

'Quit being funny. Here she comes.'

Selene had climbed aboard a horse and was riding across the golf course towards them. Her horse hurdled over the bodies of her dead husband and his caddy, and rode down to join Rex and JD on the fairway.

'Nice work!' said Rex as she neared them.

The horse stopped, and Selene dismounted. Even after shooting eleven staff members, and riding a horse over her husband, she still looked good. She was wearing tight blue jeans and a black shirt with the sleeves rolled back to her elbows. There wasn't a blot on her makeup either. 'Are you two okay?' she asked, her demeanour very casual considering what had just happened.

'We're fine,' said Rex. 'How about you?'

Selene shrugged. 'I'm okay. I was just wondering why we were killing everyone though?'

'You mean you didn't know?' Rex asked, surprised.

'No, but I figured it must be bad.'

'I like her,' said JD. 'She's more fun than you.'

Rex answered Selene's question. 'JD found out why we were hired,' he said, gazing into her eyes. 'The circus you told me about the other day, it seems like they're here to kidnap autistic kids. They took Paige this morning.'

'They took Paige?' Selene repeated, her casual demeanour vanishing. 'How? Weren't you with her?'

'An invisible man hit JD with an invisible baseball bat,' said Rex. He pointed at his injured leg. 'Then the invisible asshole shot me with an invisible gun.'

'What on earth are you talking about?' Selene asked, eyeballing them both like she thought they were making fun of her.

'Your husband was tipped off about it,' JD added. 'He admitted everything to me before I rammed a golf club down his throat. These invisible dudes are taking autistic kids, but Antonio didn't know what they want the kids for. Whatever it is, it's a good enough reason for us to go kill the circus. They took a kid called Kai too. He worked in the sandwich shop.'

'Big Buns and Footlongs!' said Selene, her eyes filled with horror. 'Kai is a really nice boy. His mother is a friend of mine. The whole family are good people.'

'The whole family is dead,' said JD.

'What?'

'I think the mother is alive,' Rex added. 'But the rest of the family are definitely dead.'

'Are you sure?' Selene asked.

'It happened around the same time Paige was taken,' said Rex. 'It must have been a coordinated operation.'

Selene's expression switched from horrified to mighty pissed. 'We're going to get the children back, aren't we?' she said.

'*We* are,' said JD. 'But you should stay here. You can tell the cops me and Rex did all the killing on the golf course.'

'But I can help,' said Selene.

'The circus is run by vampires,' said JD. 'That's our field of expertise.'

'He's got a point,' said Rex.

Selene put her hands on her hips, and tilted her head to the side while she eyeballed Rex. 'Don't you want me to come?' she asked him.

JD sighed. 'We're wasting time. Look, what we're talking about here is invisible vampires. Invisible vampires that use guns. That makes this very fucking tricky.'

'Yeah,' Rex agreed. 'This is dangerous. And I'm not sure we'll have time for you to set up your sniper rifle.'

Selene turned away and climbed back on her horse. 'I'm coming with you,' she said.

'No deal,' said JD. 'We don't know you well enough. You did great with the sniper rifle, but one mistake at the circus and you could fuck up the whole thing.'

Selene smiled. 'You do know I have an armoury here, right? Let me come with you, and I'll let you help yourselves to as much firepower as you can carry.'

'We've got plenty of ammo,' said Rex.

'Have you got a rocket launcher?' Selene asked. 'Or a flame thrower? XM25 grenade launcher? HK416 assault rifle? Chainsaw? Samurai sword?'

'You've got all those things?' JD asked, surprised.

'Those and lots more.'

JD looked at Rex. 'Looks like she's coming with us.'

'She could get hurt,' Rex reminded him. 'Invisible vampires with guns, remember?'

JD ignored him. 'Let's get tooled up.'

## Thirty-Nine

<u>Back in Purgatory</u>

'Invisible vampires with guns?' said Flake. 'How many of them were there?'

'It was hard to count them,' said Rex. 'Because they were fucking invisible! How else do you think I ended up with a bullet in my leg?'

Jasmine put her drink down on the table. 'Did you find out why they were taking autistic children?' she asked.

'No,' said Rex.

'Well, I know why,' Jasmine replied. 'And so does Elvis.'

'You do?' said JD, joining in the conversation.

'Yeah, we know,' said Elvis. 'We found that guy Zero we were looking for. He explained everything.'

Rex was perplexed. 'How the fuck could you know about the autistic kids?'

'That's what our mission was,' Elvis replied. 'We found Zero and he told us all kinds of stuff. Basically the government want him dead because he stumbled onto something big, something the government has been covering up for years.'

*'Years?'* said Jasmine. 'I think you mean *centuries!'*

'What was it?' Flake asked. 'Come on, spill it. Does it have anything to do with the assassinations of all the world leaders?'


\*\*\*\*\*\*\*\*\*\*\*\*\*\*\*\*\*\*\*\*\*\*\*\*\*\*\*\*\*\*


Meanwhile, after a tediously long helicopter flight, Acting President, Navan Douglas and his new best friend, bodyguard Cedric O'Malley, finally landed on the White House lawn. They were greeted by a team of military guards and Julie Giannini, the new White House Chief of Staff. Giannini was a Harvard graduate, smart as a button. Douglas was grateful she was around. She looked tiny next to all the big, burly soldiers in their khaki uniforms. She was five-feet-nothing with a hairstyle currently unknown because the propellors on the helicopter were blowing her blonde locks all over the place. And her blue suit jacket was puffed out behind her like a miniature parachute. She greeted Douglas with a nod of the head while she held onto her hair, then joined him on the walk up to the west wing.

'Julie, what's the latest?' he asked her, thankful that the helicopter was drowning out his voice so that none of the soldiers could hear. It felt like half the army was escorting him to the building, when all he really wanted was Cedric, who was walking two steps behind him.

'I have some good news, sir,' said Giannini. 'The nukes that were headed for Washington and Chicago were all shot down.'

'They were? That's wonderful.'

'Yes, sir. Our defences have also shot down missiles headed for California, New York and Iowa. But Texas, San Antonio and Virginia have all been hit. I think you should make a statement for television. Let the Russians know we're not standing for it.'

'We're not?'

'Sir?'

'Yes, of course. Of course we're not standing for it. Bloody Russians. Fuck 'em. What's our strategy?'

'That's your call, sir. So far, all we've done is follow defence procedures, but any retaliation will require your approval. I've arranged a meeting for you in five minutes in the war room. All the heads of national security will either be there in person or by video call, sir.'

'That's good work, Julie. Well done.'

'Do you have a strategy, sir?'

'Of course, I do,' he said, lowering his voice as they neared the building. The helicopter was no longer drowning out their conversation, and he didn't need any of the minions hearing his bluster. 'Out of interest, what do you think we should do?'

'If it was me, sir. I'd have the Russian president taken out.'

Douglas felt a flutter in his chest. 'Can we do that?'

'It is possible, sir. I suggest giving Alexis Calhoon a call. She can arrange it. She has assassins everywhere.'

'Oh, yes. Good old Alexis. Will she be in the meeting?'

'She will be joining via video link. She's still at the Poseidon hotel.'

'Ah, of course she is. That's good to know. I'll speak with her in private then, after the main meeting.'

'Yes, sir. Good idea. And, er, there's one other thing. Ever since the president was murdered we've been tracking the assassin Flake Munroe via the device you had fitted into her gold ring.'

'Excellent, have you pinpointed her location?'

'It's strange, sir. After she and the Bourbon Kid escaped the hotel, we tracked them to an underground bikers club, but when our agents showed up at the club, they were gone. And the tracker stopped working.'

'That's a shame.'

Julie Giannini stopped at the edge of the lawn and tugged at Douglas's sleeve, stopping him too. 'Thing is, sir, we assumed she'd destroyed it, but then a short while later the tracker popped in the Pacific ocean, in a place called Medicine Island. It's weird because there's no way she could have gotten there that quickly. But after a few minutes there, the tracker went dead again, and it hasn't come back up.'

'What's on Medicine Island these days?'

'Not much. Our satellites show the island was hit by a tsunami caused by some of the Russian nukes.'

Before Douglas could respond, Cedric O'Malley tapped him on the shoulder. 'Sir, we need to keep moving.'

'Of course.'

Douglas and Giannini stepped onto a path and headed for the west wing lobby, speaking in hushed tones as they went.

'That's odd,' said Douglas. 'What about the others, Elvis and Jasmine? How did our trackers do with them? Did they find Zero?'

'I'm still waiting to hear on that, sir,' said Giannini, leaning in closer to avoid being heard. 'Although I'm told they ditched their gold rings at a motel. We have three dead agents at the scene too.'

'Do we have any idea where they went?'

'Yes, sir. They went to Santa Mondega.'

'Elvis and Jasmine went to Santa Mondega?'

'Yes sir.'

'Hmm. And then what?'

'It's hard to know, sir. That area is currently uninhabitable on account of the Russian nukes.'

'Okay. Thank you, Julie. You've been very helpful. Keep an eye on the Elvis and Jasmine situation though.'

'My team are all over it, sir. By the way, should I start calling you Mister President?'

Douglas was contemplating how to answer that question when his phone rang. He hooked it from his pocket. He had an incoming call from Diago. The dastardly vampire was alive, and finally returning calls. Douglas waved Julie Giannini away and headed through a door into the west wing lobby. He ducked into a corner and took the call, speaking in a hushed tone.

'Diago, where the fuck have you been?'

**Forty**

## Part Six - Bobby's Trains

Finally, after an epic cross-country drive, Jasmine saw a busted, "WELCOME TO SANTA MONDEGA" road sign. She had been driving for the last three hours while Elvis took his turn sleeping in the back. She reached over the seats and prodded him in the leg to wake him up.

'Honey, we're here,' she said, cheerily.

Elvis sat up and rubbed his eyes. 'Sheesh, how long have I been out?' he asked.

'Since you fell asleep.'

'Right. Do you remember the way to City Hall?'

'I surely do.'

Elvis fixed his hair and straightened out his crumpled blue suit, then he climbed through the gap between the front seats and squeezed into the passenger side. He pulled the sun visor down and stared at the road ahead. It was blindingly bright, so he put his gold-rimmed sunglasses on and peered over at Jasmine. She was wearing a purple catsuit that looked like a Batgirl outfit, only instead of a Bat Logo it had the words, "PORN STAR" emblazoned in black letters over a yellow oval shape on the chest. The outfit was topped off with a yellow utility belt that had a gun holstered on one side and a pair of handcuffs on the other.

When they arrived at City Hall Jasmine parked the Cadillac in a bus lane out front. The streets weren't very busy, probably because the population had taken a bit of a hit in recent times due to the invasion of zombies, skeletons and other undead bastards.

Elvis pointed at a security camera that was positioned over the front doors of City Hall. 'That could be one of the cameras that picked up footage of Zero.'

'What now then?' Jasmine asked. 'Sit here and wait for him to walk by again?'

'That could be a bit boring,' said Elvis. 'You know, it's a shame Sanchez isn't still the mayor. He could have been useful for once.'

'You should call him anyway. No one knows this city better than him. And he must know the sort of places where someone would hide out.'

Elvis checked his watch. 'What time are him and Flake meeting the president?'

'I think it was ten-thirty. They should be finished by now.'

'Good.' Elvis pulled up Sanchez's number on his phone and made the call. Two rings and the tubby former mayor answered the call.

'Hey Elvis, wassup?'

'Sanchez, hi. How was your meeting with the president?'

'I'm still in the lobby. The lazy asshole is keeping us waiting.'

'Aah, too bad. Hey, listen, me and Jas are in Santa Mondega. We're looking for some kook who's hiding out down here.'

'Kook?'

'Yeah, you know, a conspiracy theorist. Any ideas where someone on the run from the government would hide out in Santa Mondega?'

'My guess is they'd go underground.'

'Yeah, but where?'

'The best place to hide out underground would be the old Chinese ruins. Remember them?'

'No.' Elvis was puzzled. 'When the fuck has there ever been Chinese ruins in Santa Mondega?'

'They were originally the Aztec ruins,' said Sanchez.

'The Aztec ruins? Why didn't you just say so, for fuckssake?'

'Because they've been built over. They're now under Chinatown.'

'Chinatown?'

'Yeah, a bunch of Chinese people moved into the city about eighteen months ago. They built their own part of town on top of the Aztec ruins. Now people call them the Chinese ruins because the Chinese ruined the ruins.'

Elvis groaned. 'That's stupid.'

'I don't make the rules,' said Sanchez. 'I'm just passing on information. Anyway, I've gotta go, Flake is doing the laser-eyes thing at me.'

'Okay, just one last thing, Sanchez. Do you know how to get down to the ruins? Is there still an entrance anywhere?'

Sanchez took a few seconds to deliberate before replying, 'It'll be under one of the shops in Big Wang Street.'

'Big Wang Street?'

'Yeah, it's a narrow street with a few terrible shops on it. I think there's a voodoo place and the Wok and Roll café. There's a snake charmer there too, although I have to be honest with you, she's not really much of a charmer. Quite rude if you ask me. You know there was this one time—'

'Say hi to the president for me,' said Elvis, ending the call before Sanchez could launch into a rant.

'Where are we going then?' Jasmine asked.

'First stop is the Wok and Roll café in Chinatown. Jacko said Zero had been caught on camera at the Wok, and also at a launderette. If we can find them I think we'll be close.'

'You wanna give me directions?' Jasmine asked.

'We're heading for what used to be the ruins, so go straight on, then take the second right.'

Jasmine started up the car, pulled out into the street and followed Elvis's directions to Chinatown. When they arrived in the district, which wasn't actually labelled as Chinatown anywhere, they drove around a few backstreets until Elvis spotted a place called the Fook Hin Launderette. Jasmine parked up across the street so they could check it out. It was shitty. The whole street was shitty. Really shitty.

'That's got to be the launderette we're looking for,' said Elvis. 'Can you see the Wok and Roll anywhere?'

'I see it,' said Jasmine, pointing at nothing in particular. 'Look, there's a sign in the alley next to the Fook Hin Launderette. It says Wok and Roll café.'

Elvis spotted the sign. It was shitty. A shitty sign in a shitty alleyway in a shitty neighbourhood.

'Let's take a walk, act like sightseers,' said Elvis. He climbed out of the car, walked around to the sidewalk and opened Jasmine's door for her.

'Where exactly are we gonna go?' she asked, looking around as she stepped onto the sidewalk.

'I'm not sure,' said Elvis. 'It all looks different to how I remember it.'

'Okay,' said Jasmine. 'Which of these shops looks like it would have a secret underground entrance?'

Elvis puffed out his cheeks. 'At a guess, I'd say the launderette. Those sort of places are always used as a front for something else.'

Jasmine smiled and slapped Elvis on the arm. 'You're so predictable,' she said. 'Let's check out *Bobby's Miniature Trains.*'

'Bobby's what?'

*'Miniature Trains.'*

'Where's that?' said Elvis, looking around.

'Over there, next to the launderette.'

'That place is a dump. I didn't even notice it.'

'Exactly. It's perfect for an underground gang of conspiracy theorists.'

Elvis was confused. 'It is?'

'Yes. Stop thinking like you, and think like a nerd. Conspiracy theorists are nerds.'

'That doesn't automatically make it the train shop.'

'It does when the train shop is the only one with no customers. Look around you. All these other places are busy, and they have Chinese names. See, there's the Shi Te drugstore, Yung Ho's Acupuncture, Easy Lei's massage parlour. All of these stores are busy and have Chinese names. But Bobby's Trains? Firstly, it's a crap non-Chinese name, and second, only nerds like trains.'

'Rod Stewart likes miniature trains.'

'Rod Stewart can lick my ass.'

Elvis sighed. 'Okay, we'll try the train shop.'

Jasmine slid her arms around Elvis, squeezed his butt and kissed him on the lips. 'Let me do the talking in here,' she said. 'Nerds are my speciality.'

'Okay, after you.'

Jasmine led the way up to the train shop and pushed open the front door. A bell chimed to announce their arrival. The place was fairly big inside, bigger than it looked from the outside. There were miniature village displays on both sides of the store, with trains chugging their way around them. At first glance it didn't look like anything was actually for sale. There were a few small items by the counter, which was manned by a young man in ripped blue jeans and a black sweater. He could have passed for a non-nerd, but he was wearing a rather naff, blue train driver's cap on top of a long mane of greasy brown hair. A dead giveaway that he was a nerd.

'Hello, how can I help you today?' he asked.

'We're looking for the secret entrance to the underground,' Jasmine said, approaching him with a smile.

The young man frowned. 'I'm sorry, what?'

'The secret underground entrance. You know what I'm talking about.'

'I'm afraid I don't.'

Elvis took up the interrogation. 'Listen buddy, we're looking for a guy called Zero. Lives underground. We've got some juicy information for him.'

The man stared at Elvis, then at Jasmine. 'Oh my God!' he said, gawping. 'Are you Elvis and Jasmine from the Dead Hunters?'

'That's right,' said Jasmine. 'So, why don't you tell us what we need to know?'

'About the secret underground thing?'

'Yep. Where is it?'

The young man shrugged. 'I'm sorry. I still don't know what you're talking about.'

Elvis tapped Jasmine on the ass. It was his way of telling her to do her thing. So Jasmine did her thing. She leaned over the counter so the shop assistant could get a good look at her cleavage. ''What's your name?' she asked him.

'Neville.'

'Neville. I love your hat. Maybe we could do a swap? I give you my underwear, and in exchange, you give me your hat, and tell me where the underground entrance is?'

Neville swallowed hard and looked Jasmine up and down. 'Umm, I'm sorry,' he said eventually. 'I really can't. I'm sworn to secrecy.'

'Sworn to secrecy? About what?'

'Nothing. Honest.'

Jasmine moved away and let Elvis take over. He stepped up and grabbed a fistful of Neville's sweater. He dragged the nervous nerd halfway over the counter.

'You're messing my woman around,' Elvis said, his breath on Neville's face. 'And it's beginning to annoy me.'

'I'm sorry. I....I... I didn't mean to be rude,' Neville stammered.

'Have you seen Jasmine's porno?'

'What?'

'You know what I mean. The film clip where she bashed a guy's cock and balls to pieces with a club.'

Neville looked over at Jasmine. She was admiring his miniature village. She bent over to take a closer look at one of the tiny trains that wasn't moving. Neville's cheeks burned red as he stared at her ass. 'Yeah, someone showed it to me once,' he admitted.

'Well, think about this, Train Boy. You could be in her next video. The whole world will be watching Jasmine destroying your asshole with a toy train. Now, one last time, where's the entrance?'

Neville hesitated for just long enough to annoy Elvis. The hitman grabbed the shop assistant's nose and squeezed it with his thumb and forefinger, twisting it one way and then the other.

'Okay, okay,' Neville pleaded in a squeaky voice. 'It's out back. I'll show you.'

Elvis smiled. 'That wasn't so hard was it?' he said, releasing Neville.

Neville straightened up and glanced over at Jasmine while he rubbed his sore nose. 'Could you put that train down please?' he asked her. 'It's a collectible, worth a lot of money.' He noticed Elvis glaring at him, so he stopped rubbing his nose and forced a fake smile. 'Before I take you to see Zero, you'll have to turn off your phones,' he added. 'The government could be tracking you.'

While Elvis was switching off his phone, Jasmine carried the toy train over to the counter and put it down in front of Neville. 'If I'd stuck this train up your ass it would have been worth a lot more,' she said.

Neville gulped.

'Anyway,' Jasmine went on. 'Seeing as we're all friends now, why don't you close up the shop, and then show me your secret entrance?'

## Forty-One

After Neville locked up the store and put the CLOSED sign in the front window, he took Jasmine and Elvis through to a back room that had been converted into a miniature replica of Santa Mondega, but with train tracks all around it. It was kinda quirky because there were no trains in Santa Mondega.

'Wow,' said Jasmine. 'Is this a council project?'

'No,' said Neville. 'It's just how we think Santa Mondega would look if it had a train service. See that over there?' He pointed at a narrow street on the east side. 'That's where we are now.'

'But we're over here,' said Jasmine.

Neville wasn't sure how to respond, so he changed the subject. 'What do you want to speak to Zero for anyway?' he asked.

'We just want to hear some of his conspiracy theories,' said Jasmine.

'Most of them are all over the internet,' said Neville.

'Yeah, but the internet is full of cunts,' Elvis reminded him. 'Better to hear the story direct from the source.'

Neville stepped into the replica city, treading carefully to avoid the train tracks. 'Follow my steps,' he said. 'Don't break anything or you'll set off the alarm.'

'Will we be electrocuted it we step on the tracks?' Jasmine asked as she looked for a safe place to plant her foot.

'No,' said Neville as he walked past the miniature City Hall. 'It's perfectly safe.'

Elvis and Jasmine trod a careful path through the city, keeping close behind Neville. The nerdy store clerk stopped next to the miniature Nightjar bar, bent down and poked a finger through one of its upstairs windows.

'What are you doing?' Jasmine asked him.

'Opening the secret door.' Neville pointed at a bookshelf on the far wall. It was filled with shit books about trains. While Jasmine and Elvis were looking at it, it slid to one side, revealing a set of stairs behind it that led down into darkness. 'Those stairs will take us down to what we call, Ground Zero,' Neville said. 'Because it's where Zero lives.'

Elvis muttered the word, "cunt" under his breath.

'Is it true Zero can hypnotise people?' Jasmine asked in an attempt to lighten the mood.

Neville rolled his eyes. 'Zero doesn't hypnotise people,' he said. 'He enlightens them. He will show you the truth about the world you're living in.'

Elvis scoffed. 'Why don't you just call him Morpheus and be done with it?'

'Because his name is Zero,' said Neville, showing a distinct lack of humour. 'Now, follow me.'

He tiptoed across the rest of the miniature city to the secret stairs. Jasmine followed carefully in his footsteps, whereas Elvis walked through a miniature post office, razing it to the ground, like he was Godzilla.

Neville stopped at the entrance to the stairs, and turned to Elvis and Jasmine. 'Whoever comes in last has to pull the bookshelf back across the entrance,' he said. 'We can't leave it open. It's a security risk.'

'I'll do it,' said Elvis.

Neville and Jasmine stepped onto the stairs. Elvis joined them and dragged the bookshelf back across the entrance as promised. At the bottom of the stairs they found a dark, narrow corridor, which was lit up by a set of dim blue lights that were fitted into panels in the walls. It gave the place a cool (or uncool depending on how you looked at it) sci-fi look, like something from an underground rebel base in a Terminator movie.

'Why do the government think Zero is a hypnotist?' Jasmine asked Neville as they proceeded along the corridor.

Neville stopped and turned to face them. 'If the government told you that, then you must be here to assassinate him,' he said. 'They told you to kill him before he speaks, didn't they? And they said if you let him speak, he would brainwash you.'

'No,' Elvis lied. 'The government hates us, dipshit. We're top of the FBI's Most Wanted list.'

'You were,' said Neville. 'Now it's Zero. He has shown us all the way.'

'Is he a hypnotist though?' Jasmine asked. 'I've never been hypnotised before. I'd be keen to try it.'

Neville turned away and carried on walking along the corridor. 'He's not a hypnotist,' he said. 'He's a truth teller. In recent months the government has sent several assassins to kill him. The most recent ones were told he was a hypnotist and to kill him before he could speak. The government doesn't want you to know the truth.'

'What truth?' asked Elvis. 'That Zero had an invisible coat and used it to try to assassinate the president?'

Neville groaned. 'You're right about the invisible coat,' he admitted. 'But if Zero wanted to kill the president, he could have. But he's not a killer. I'll let him explain it to you. He's better with words than I am. Just don't do anything stupid like shoot him before he can show you why the government is so afraid of him.'

At the end of the corridor was an open door into a room with black walls. Strange flashing blue and yellow lights flickered inside the room like there was a disco going on inside. The lights were accompanied by the sound of gunfire.

'What the fuck is that?' Elvis asked, while checking his jacket to make sure his gun was still there.

'That's headquarters,' said Neville.

'It's a games room!' said Jasmine. 'Is that Call of Duty?'

Neville stopped again. 'You play video games?' he said, impressed.

'No, but I slept with a lot of guys who did. I like gamers, they're hot.'

And with that remark, Neville was completely smitten, putty in Jasmine's hands. 'Really?' he said, his eyes lighting up.

Elvis shoved Neville in the back. 'Keep walking, numbnuts.'

Neville walked through the open door into the games room, and stepped aside so that Jasmine and Elvis could enter.

Jasmine squeezed in ahead of Elvis and took a look around. 'Wow, this place is cool,' she said, admiring what she saw. There were sofas dotted around the sides of the room, as well as a few desks furnished with computers, like in an internet café. In the opposite corner of the room was a strip curtain that led into another room or corridor. And to the left of the entrance was a statue of Alicia Vikander dressed as Lara Croft from *Tomb Raider*. In the centre of the room, sitting on a scabby sofa was a young man with greasy brown hair. He was playing a shoot-em-up game. A large screen on the wall in front of him showed he was gunning down vampires and zombies.

'Cool game,' said Jasmine. 'Can we play?'

'You are playing,' said the gamer without looking around. His onscreen character was a sexy, dark-skinned babe in a red catsuit. She was in an underground lair shooting at undead creatures. After blowing the heads off of just about everything, she took down the final zombie by performing a somersault and then ripping its head off. At that point the young man playing the game paused the action and looked around. 'Nice to meet you,' he said. He looked Jasmine up and down. 'Wow, you're even sexier in person.'

'We're looking for Zero,' Elvis butted in.

'That's me,' said the young man. He put down his video game controller and jumped up from the sofa. He was wearing blue sweatpants and a baggie black hoodie. 'I'm so excited to meet you. Really glad you found me. I've got so much to tell you.'

Elvis reached into his jacket and unholstered his gun. He pointed it at the young man. 'There's no fucking way you're Zero,' he said. 'How about showing us where he is?'

'Exactly,' the man replied. 'No one believes I'm Zero. That's how I've evaded so many assassination attempts. I don't look threatening. Did they tell you I'm a hypnotist? Because I'm not. But I am Zero. It's an honour to meet you. Do you like the video game? I made it myself. The hot girl on screen is Jasmine.'

He spoke fast. Too fucking fast for Elvis to keep up. Annoying little, nerdy bastard. Jasmine on the other hand, was most intrigued by the video game. She was staring at the frozen screen. The babe in the red catsuit had a much bigger ass than her, and tits that were so big they made no sense at all.

'That doesn't look like me,' she said, frowning.

'Oh, hey wait, check this out,' said Zero. He ran back to the sofa, sat down and grabbed the controller again, then he pressed a combination of buttons that caused the on-screen version of Jasmine to discard her clothes and perform somersaults all around the screen. 'Cool, huh?' he said, smiling.

'That's more like it,' said Jasmine.

'I've got characters for all of the Dead Hunters. I call the game *Santa Mondega*,' Zero said, looking round at his guests. 'I found out all about you guys from the locals when we moved here. So I made a game about you. Cool, huh?'

Elvis lowered his gun. 'What do I look like on here?' he asked.

'Show him Nev.'

Neville moved past Elvis and Jasmine and grabbed a second controller from a coffee table next to the sofa. He sat down next to Zero and then joined the game as the character of Elvis. The onscreen Elvis was wearing a white jumpsuit that made him look fat. He had some decent karate moves on him though, and he carried a gold Desert Eagle, like the one Elvis had in his hand. The onscreen version of the King approached the Jasmine character, and the two of them engaged in a fight that ended with Jasmine choking Elvis by wrapping her thighs around his neck.

'Ha! My character is tougher than yours,' said Jasmine, elbowing Elvis in the ribs.

'We should try that later on,' said Elvis, momentarily mesmerised by the onscreen action.

'What's Rex like on here,' Jasmine asked. 'Does he jerk off with his metal hand?'

Zero frowned. 'Why would he do that? Is that his thing? I can incorporate it into the game if it is.'

'Then do it,' said Jasmine.

'Enough, already,' said Elvis. 'We've been sent here to assassinate you, Mister Zero. But, despite being advised not to let you talk, I'm gonna give you five minutes to convince me we shouldn't blow you away.'

Zero didn't seem in the least bit fazed. 'Wait 'til you hear what I've gotta tell you,' he said. 'It'll blow your fucking mind. Can I get you some beers?'

'Are you old enough to drink?' Elvis asked.

Zero quit the video game, got up from the sofa again and walked up to Jasmine. 'You truly are the most beautiful woman I've ever seen,' he gushed, while staring at her chest.

'Easy there, Gameboy,' said Elvis.

Zero offered his hand to Elvis. 'You've always been my favourite member of the Dead Hunters,' he said.

'Bullshit,' said Elvis. He tucked his gun away and shook Zero's hand, confident that he wasn't being hypnotised.

'Is it just you two?' Zero asked.

'Yeah,' said Elvis. 'And if anything happens to us, the other members of the gang will find you, and you'll be fucked.'

'Oh yeah?' Zero said, smirking. 'Will Sanchez come and beat us up?' He and Neville spent a few seconds laughing at their private joke before Jasmine joined in, which made them laugh even more.

'That's enough,' said Elvis. 'At least Sanchez doesn't have a fucking Lara Croft statue in his lounge.'

'That's not just a statue,' said Zero. 'Poke Lara in the eyes and a secret door behind her opens up.'

'What's behind the secret door?' Jasmine asked.

Zero looked at the floor as if he was embarrassed. 'It's just the toilet. But it's cool, right?'

'No. It's stupid,' said Elvis. 'Come on. Start talking. What do you know that makes you so dangerous the government wants us to kill you?'

Zero switched from goofy to serious in an instant. 'I know what the president does in his spare time,' he said, his eyes shifting around the room as if he was paranoid that someone might be listening in.

'Go on.'

'Can I get you guys a drink or anything?'

'You already asked that. Get on with it.'

'Okay, okay. Come, take a seat.'

Zero gestured for them to sit on one of the sofas by the wall. While they were getting comfortable, he grabbed an office chair with wheels on it and dragged it over to the sofa so he could face them while he spoke. 'Let me start at the beginning,' he said, getting comfortable. 'I'll keep this brief. About a year ago, me and my guys cracked an ancient code in the gospel of Susan. It led us to a secret underground tomb in Havana. We got through some serious Indiana Jones-style booby traps, and that's when we found the Coat of No Colours that Jacob gave to his son Benjamin.'

'Thank you for keeping that brief,' said Elvis.

'No problem,' said Zero, chewing on one of his fingernails. 'We took turns using the invisible coat to spy on people, like our favourite celebrities, you know, to see what shit they got up to. Turns out celebs are generally fuckin' boring.'

'Bullshit,' said Elvis. 'I bet a million bucks you were spying on chicks in the shower.'

'Would you just hear me out?' said Zero raising his arms defensively. 'After I'd been doing it for a few months, I got braver. I started following the president. One day, when he was staying in the penthouse suite of a hotel, I managed to sneak in. Got past his security team because they couldn't see me, and I squeezed through the door into his room. I'll tell you man, it was scary as fuck. My heart was going like crazy. Now, thing is, I just wanted to see if the president was into kinky shit or something. But I got way more than I bargained for. What I saw, it scarred me for life, man. I can't un-see it.' Zero shuddered momentarily as if he felt a spider on his shoulder. He soon continued when he saw the impatient look on Elvis's face. 'I'm telling you man, I couldn't believe my fucking eyes. So I got my phone out and started filming him. But I fucked up and dropped the phone. The president saw it before I could pick it up. Next thing you know, he calls all his security up, and those guys, *shit!* I mean, wow! They knew straight away that there was an invisible presence in the room. They came after me in a big way. I guess they're ready for anything. Anyway, I made like a fucking tree and got outta there, but one of the guys, he was all over me like a rash. I'm running down stairs and he's right behind me. But, by the grace of God, I got away, except my invisible coat got caught in the fucking fire door as I went through it. I had to leave it behind. Lucky for me, Neville was waiting outside in a getaway van. We got away, but it was a close fucking thing. I think I got caught on a security camera because they've been after me ever since. They already knew who I was, but *now*, now that I know what the president does in his spare time, *fuck* man, I'm a walking bullseye.'

Jasmine was intrigued, even if Elvis was unsure about it all. 'What did you see?' she asked. 'What was the president doing that was so bad?'

'You're never gonna believe this. It's huge.'

## Forty-Two

'The president is part of a massive international paedophile ring.'

Elvis and Jasmine stayed silent for a few seconds following Zero's revelation. After processing what he'd said they both responded at the same time, but with very different words.

'Bullshit!' said Elvis, shaking his head.

'Of course,' said Jasmine. 'It's so obvious. You can tell just by looking at his face.'

'I'm now seeing why we were told to shoot you before you spoke,' said Elvis. 'That's quite some accusation.'

'We should tell Arizona,' said Jasmine. 'She'll be shocked. Imagine that, finding out your dad is a child toucher.'

'You've met Arizona Petersen?' said Zero, gobsmacked. 'Most people don't even believe she exists.'

'She's a friend of ours,' said Jasmine. 'We rescued her a while back when she was kidnapped by these three guys who kept taking turns to jizz on her feet.'

'The Bastard brothers!' said Zero, his eyes widening as he stared into space. 'I was warning people about them for years. But the government did nothing because those perverts were working for them.'

'Wait a second,' said Elvis, waving his hand in front of Zero's face. 'If the president was a paedophile, there's no way he could keep it secret. Someone would have snitched on him by now.'

'How can you be this naive?' Zero asked, a look of scorn on his face. 'You can't become president *without* being a paedophile. Think about it. Haven't you ever wondered how paedophile gangs exist? You know, you hear about these groups of perverts who exchange photos and movies online, or meet up and pass kids around. Haven't you ever asked yourself how they get away with it? Or how do they meet each other in the first place? I mean, you can't just go up to someone in a bar and say, *"Hey, I've got some kidnapped kids at home. Fancy coming round and watching me fuck 'em?"*. You'd get your head kicked in.'

'Fuckin' right you would,' Elvis agreed. He took a second to process his thoughts. 'Wait a second. Just dial this back a minute. What exactly did you see the president do?'

'I saw him watching a live streamed movie of a gang of people doing vile shit to kids.'

'Like what?' Jasmine asked, not sure if she really wanted to know the answer.

'I'll get to that later,' said Zero. 'But the point I'm making, is that paedophiles go to places where they are protected. There are paedophiles everywhere. The dumb ones get caught real easy because they're usually loners walking the streets, offering sweets to kids. Those guys are amateurs. The next level up is the scout leaders, school teachers, the entertainment industry, and stuff like that. Those lot are still idiots, but they had just enough sense to hide in a place where they're trusted to look after kids. Then there's the ones who hide in organisations like the church. They're protected because the church cares about its reputation and doesn't want the world knowing they've got a few perverts in their ranks, even though it's a lot more than a few. And then there's the *really* clever ones, the millionaires, the billionaires, and the politicians. The ones who own private islands where they can do all this vile stuff undetected. The president is one of *them.*'

Elvis still wasn't convinced. 'But the president would be open to blackmail. There's just no way.'

'There *is* a way,' Zero replied. 'Have you ever heard the theory about the lizard people who run the world?'

'Oh God, not this,' Elvis groaned.

'Lizard people?' said Jasmine, wide-eyed.

'They aren't really lizard people,' said Zero. 'But they are from a different race of humans, a superior race that was believed to be extinct, from the lost city of Atlantis.'

'Atlantis?' said Elvis. "Didn't that place sink to the bottom of the sea?'

'The ocean actually,' said Neville, who was still sitting on the gaming sofa, but was now flicking through music channels on the television rather than playing games.

'The president has gills and webbed feet,' Zero continued. 'I've seen them. Everyone in his paedophile ring has them. The Atlanteans only breed with their own kind. They see regular humans as inferior. Almost every world leader or billionaire is a descendant of Atlantis. And get this, the whole left versus right argument in politics, it's all organised by these assholes. They do it to turn the rest of us against each other so they can carry on doing what they do. Everyone else is so busy blaming each other for the world's problems that they just don't see what the elite are really up to.'

'Webbed feet?' said Jasmine. 'Didn't Bobby Ewing in Dallas have webbed feet?'

'He did,' said Zero, 'when he was in the *Man From Atlantis.*'

'I must have missed that episode,' said Jasmine, grimacing. 'I don't remember Bobby having sex with a man from Atlantis?'

Zero looked confused. 'Patrick Duffy *was* the man from Atlantis,' he said.

'And he slept with Bobby Ewing?'

'No! Bobby Ewing and Patrick Duffy are the same person. *The Man From Atlantis* was a whole other TV show, and Patrick Duffy was the star.'

Elvis was ready to blow. 'Can we forget about the fucking *Man From Atlantis?*' he ranted.

'Fine,' said Zero. 'But listen, I can't bring this paedophile ring down on my own. I don't have the muscle. But you guys, and your friends Rex and the Bourbon Kid, you guys could do it. You could smash this operation and expose these perverts for what they really are.'

Elvis still wasn't totally buying it. 'Who else is in this paedophile ring with the president?' he asked. 'Any other politicians?'

'All of them!' said Zero. 'Well, almost all of them. That's why they want me dead.'

'Okay,' said Elvis. 'You've seen the president smashing one off to some kiddy porn, but you haven't seen anyone else, have you?'

'Not exactly, no, but, I know where the paedophile movies are made, and who makes them. If you can track them down, you could destroy the president's ring.'

'Destroy the president's ring?' Jasmine said. 'What does that mean exactly?'

'The president's paedophile ring. We're fairly certain it's made up of politicians, royal family members and people who run newspapers and the big news channels. The members of MAWF who were killed at Riverdale Mansion a while back, they were part of it. The Atlanteans are everywhere. They even act like they're the biggest philanthropists in the world. They finance movies and use them to push their agendas, to divide the public, pit us all against each other. Shit, even the biggest internet companies, some of which were started off by regular humans, have been either bought out by Atlanteans, or infiltrated. They run everything. They can get to anyone. It's a matter of time before they get to me. I move around but they keep finding me.' He paused for breath. 'How did you guys find me?'

'You're a nerd and you're hiding under a toy train shop, you fucking clown,' said Elvis.

'Hey, trains are cool,' said Zero. 'But, I get your point. Thing is, see, I'm autistic. I've been into trains and video games since I was old enough to know what they are.'

'You don't seem autistic,' said Elvis.

'Yes he does,' said Jasmine. 'He's not made eye contact with me yet, and he lives in a dark dungeon playing and designing video games.'

'The government knows I'm autistic too,' said Zero. 'It's one of the few pieces of information about me that was available online. And unfortunately, it's made things worse for other autistic people.'

'How so?' said Elvis.

'After I caught the president jerking off to kiddy snuff movies, I started doing some research into how and where it was happening. I worked it out. See, they've been doing it for years, but before I found out about it they were just kidnapping homeless children, orphans, kids no one cared about. But since they hacked my network, they've switched. Now they only kidnap autistic kids. It's a bit more high-profile, but they're the elites so they can still get away with it.'

'Hold on a second,' said Elvis. 'Slow down. You think they're kidnapping autistic kids to get back at you?'

Zero shook his head. 'No. But it's a well-known fact that the best conspiracy theorists on the internet are autistic. Neurotypical conspiracy theorists generally just make shit up. Autistics don't do that. We research, we analyse, and we gather evidence. The elites have realised this, and now they've shifted their policy. For their snuff movies they've started going after autistic kids instead of homeless kids, simply because they now see autistics as a real, genuine threat. Autistic brains aren't wired to the same frequency as everyone else, so we're less susceptible to the bullshit spouted out by these Atlantean frauds. So now, the elites, the Atlanteans, they've decided that one way to cut down the number of autistic people is to round them up and use them in their snuff movies. All over the world, countries are starting to actively identify autistic people. It's become a priority. They're monitoring all of us, locking adults up in mental hospitals, and killing the kids in these snuff movies. It's a matter of time before they do a mass culling of all autistic people.'

'That's quite a theory,' said Elvis. 'Can you actually prove it though? I mean, can you prove they're kidnapping autistic kids?'

'I know who does the kidnapping,' said Zero. 'It's a travelling circus. We've been tracking their movements and syncing them up with all the local reports of missing children. I have a whole database of information to back up what I'm saying.'

'Can you show us the database?' Elvis asked. 'And what's the name of the circus?'

'I can show you the circus,' said Zero, standing up. 'It's called Diago's Travelling Circus. I have footage of it on the video I filmed of the president.'

## Forty-Three

Jasmine and Elvis joined Zero standing behind the gaming sofa while Neville, who was sitting on the sofa, flicked the television over to a blank screen.

'Give me a second,' Neville said. 'I hope you guys have strong stomachs because you're about to watch the president of the United States jerking off to a snuff movie.'

It was quite a revelation. Elvis shuddered at the thought of it. 'Oh, God. How graphic is this going to be?'

'It's bad,' said Zero. 'But there's only about fifteen seconds of it because that's when I dropped my phone and gave away my position.'

'Hang on a sec,' said Elvis. 'If you've got this footage, why haven't you posted it online?'

'Oh, we did,' said Neville. 'It got taken down within seconds.'

'It's true,' said Zero. 'They own the online world. They were just waiting for us to upload it. They found it real quick, and once they knew what the footage looked like, they built an algorithm that made it impossible to post it again.'

'Yeah, plus they can pinpoint our location if we try it,' said Neville. 'After the first time we posted it and it got taken down, we relocated immediately. Security cameras showed a bunch of agents turning up at our old place within minutes of us leaving. The second time we tried to post it, it wouldn't go, and someone took control of our fucking network. After that, we had assassins looking for us, asking around town if anyone knew where we were. That's when we made the move to Santa Mondega. We figured this city is the safest place on earth for criminals.'

'None of the assassins actually found you then?'

'No. If they had we'd be dead,' said Zero. 'We certainly wouldn't have been able to hypnotise them, contrary to what you've heard.'

'All right. Just show us the fucking video,' said Elvis.

'Here goes nothing,' said Neville, looking over his shoulder at them. 'You ready?'

No one replied, so Neville turned back to face the television screen. He brought up a clip of some poorly framed camera footage. The picture was clear enough though, and the image it brought up was undoubtedly grim. The president of the United States was sitting in an armchair with his shorts around his ankles and his dick in his hand, gently stroking himself off while he watched TV. After a few seconds, the camera moved away from the cock-tugging and focussed on what was he was watching on his telly. It was horrific stuff. Elvis looked away.

'Why the fuck is he jerking off to that shit?' he asked.

'This is what the Atlanteans get a kick out of,' said Zero. 'It's why God sent Atlantis to the bottom of the ocean. These assholes have no soul. They care nothing for regular humans. They see us all as inferior beings to be ruled over. They brought Atlantis to its knees with their greed and narcissism. And now they're doing the same to the whole world. These selfish assholes have profited from all the things that are destroying our planet.'

Zero's rant was interrupted by a loud buzzing sound. He covered his ears with his hands and closed his eyes. The buzzing noise was accompanied by a flashing red light on the wall beside the television. Neville leapt up from the sofa and sprinted across the room to one of the computer desks. The computer had a packet of digestive biscuits next to it. He grabbed a biscuit and started munching on it while he tapped away on the computer keyboard.

'Is it more assassins?' Zero asked him.

Neville brought up a live camera feed on his computer screen. 'They've found us!' he cried, panic on his face.

Zero looked up at Elvis. 'You've led them right to us!'

'Led who?' Elvis asked.

'The fucking FBI, the secret service, the Atlanteans. Who do you think? They're here. They'll kill us all.'

Elvis stayed calm. 'How many of them are there?' he asked.

Zero screamed at Neville. 'Put it up on the TV!'

Neville followed orders, and a few seconds later the big TV screen started showing a live feed from the security cameras in the train shop above them. A group of men and women dressed in casual clothes were walking around on the miniature model of Santa Mondega.

'Shit!' said Zero. 'There's loads of them, and they've got a fucking great big sniffer dog.'

'Sniffer dog?' said Elvis. 'Are you dealing drugs here or something?'

'No. But they've brought a fucking great big dog. Look!'

Elvis checked the screen. There was a big Alsatian patrolling around the train shop, sniffing around for a trace of something.

'That dog's gonna lead them right to us,' said Elvis. 'I bet it can smell everything we touched upstairs.'

Zero screamed at Neville again. 'Pull the plug, we're getting outta here!'

On the TV, one of the female assassins poked her fingers through the windows of the miniature model of the Nightjar. She'd found the button that opened the secret entrance. This was serious.

'What's your escape plan?' Elvis asked Zero. 'It better not be shit.'

'We blow up the fucking shop!' Zero replied.

Following Zero's earlier order to, *"pull the plug",* Neville left his computer desk and sprinted over to the corner of the room. He grabbed a metal chain that was hanging from the ceiling and yanked hard on it three times.

BOOM!

The ceiling shook. The floor beneath their feet shook. The fucking walls shook. Chairs rolled away from desks, computer screens went blank, desks bounced up, bits of the ceiling crumbled and dropped to the floor.

'THIS WAY!' yelled Zero. 'Follow me!'

Elvis checked the TV screen to see what had happened to all the agents. A series of small explosions had destroyed the model city of Santa Mondega, and thrown some of the government spooks off balance. The bombs were pretty shit though. No one was even seriously injured, let alone dead. Elvis had a sneaky feeling Zero and Neville were actually pacifists. Fucking nerds and their rubbish bombs. Elvis had half a mind to give them both a good kicking. Unfortunately, there wasn't time.

Neville vanished through the strip curtain in the corner of the room. Zero sprinted after him. Elvis grabbed Jasmine's hand and they scampered after the two panicking nerds. Before they reached the strip curtain, gunfire broke out on the other side of it. The government spooks had found the escape route too. Elvis held Jasmine back and poked his head through the curtain. There was a dark corridor on the other side with more electric blue lights in the walls. Halfway down it, Zero was lying on his back with a hole in his head. Neville was a little further on in a similar condition. To make matters worse, a big fucking dog came bounding along the corridor towards them, and a bunch of red laser sighters appeared, looking for more nerds to kill. One of them settled on Elvis's chin.

'Fuck!'

The big Alsatian took a running jump at Elvis and knocked him back through the curtain just as the first shot was fired. Elvis and the dog landed in a heap on the floor. Elvis drew his gun from its holster and contemplated shooting the big mutt. Thankfully, there was no need, because Jasmine found a better way of dealing with the situation. She threw the dog a biscuit from the packet on Neville's desk. The dog leapt off of Elvis and pounced on the treat, giving Elvis time to roll away and fire a warning shot through the curtain.

'Any ideas, Jas?' he shouted, without looking at her.

'JACKO!' she yelled over the din of gunfire. 'GET US OUT OF HERE!'

Elvis glanced her way. She'd switched her phone back on and used it to make a call to Purgatory. With the phone pressed against her ear she shouted instructions at Jacko while she ran over to the wax statue of Lara Croft on the other side of the room. She prodded two fingers into Lara's eyes. A secret door slid open in the wall by the side of it, revealing a small bathroom with just a toilet, a washbasin and a towel rail in it. Jasmine ducked into the room and yelled at Elvis.

'Come on! Let's go.'

The Alsatian must have thought she was talking to him, because he bounded across the room and leapt into the bathroom with her. Elvis took a little more time. He had his gun trained on the strip curtain just in case anyone came through it.

'HURRY!' Jasmine yelled at him. Her dog friend barked as if he agreed.

Elvis continued edging towards the bathroom. Before he reached it, an assassin in full body armour, wielding an assault rifle, stepped through the strip curtain and looked around for someone to shoot at. Elvis was ready for him.

BANG!

Nailed the bastard. The bullet hit the assassin's helmet, knocking him back a step. He fell back into the curtain, hindering one of his colleagues who was coming through it behind him.

Elvis ducked into the bathroom with Jasmine and the dog, then he slid the secret door back into place before anyone saw them. 'Any luck with Jacko?' he asked Jasmine.

'He's put me on hold.'

'On hold?'

'He's busy apparently.'

Jasmine stroked the Alsatian's head and fed him another biscuit to keep him quiet.

'Some fucking sniffer dog he is,' said Elvis.

'Don't be mean,' said Jasmine. 'He's just chosen to swap sides because we've got biscuits, haven't you Goober?'

'Goober? What kind of— fuck! We didn't get a copy of the video!'

'Screw that!' said Jasmine. 'Why would you wanna watch that again?'

'I don't, but it was the only evidence we had.'

The sound of agents piling into Zero's gaming room silenced them both for a moment. There were a lot of boots pounding on the ground outside the bathroom.

'This is bad,' Elvis whispered. 'If they've got infrared gear they could see us through this secret door.'

Jasmine put her finger over her lips to silence Elvis because Jacko was back on the phone, asking for their location.

Elvis pointed his gun at the door while Jasmine quietly gave Jacko some instructions.

'A bathroom underground in Chinatown,' she whispered. 'Underneath Bobby's Trains.'

It was a vague description. But it was all she had.

If Jacko didn't grasp the seriousness from her voice, the sound of gunfire peppering the bathroom door would have alerted him to the situation. The agents had spotted them and were shooting at the door, making dents in it. Elvis glanced over his shoulder at Jasmine. She was facing the back wall, waiting for it to vanish and offer them a route into Purgatory, courtesy of Jacko.

'WHAT'S HE WAITING FOR?' Elvis yelled over the sound of bullets hitting the bathroom door.

Jasmine tucked her phone into the belt on her catsuit and unholstered her pistol from her hip. She stepped up alongside Elvis and pointed her gun at the door. The gunfire from the other side stopped suddenly.

'Uh oh,' said Elvis. 'They're looking for another way of getting through the door. What's Jacko doing? Can't he find this place?'

'He said give him a minute.'

'A minute? This'll be over in seconds.'

## Forty-Four

### Back in Purgatory

'And that's how you got shot?' Flake asked.

The whole gang were sitting around the new table in Purgatory, drinking and listening to Elvis and Jasmine recount their tale. Jasmine was almost back to her normal self, thanks to JD's blood transfusion and the healing powers of the Eye of the Moon.

'Yep, that's it,' said Elvis. 'They shot the door to pieces and boom, we were sitting ducks. Jas got hit a bunch of times, as you know. I took a couple in the gut. We fired back, took a couple of them down, but then Jas hit the deck and I couldn't even see what I was shooting at. Those fuckers were blasting away at us even though their fucking dog was in the bathroom with us.'

'Don't be rude about Goober,' said Flake. The big hound was sitting on the floor by her feet, licking his injured leg.

'I thought we were done for,' Elvis continued, 'but God bless him, Rex came through the portal and dragged us outta there. Five more seconds and we were done.'

'They planted a tracker on your car, didn't they?' said JD.

'Huh?' Elvis hadn't had time to consider how the assassins had found them. 'My car?' Suddenly it all made sense. 'Those motherfuckers. They must have done it in the motel parking lot. Fuck! Why didn't we think of that?'

Jasmine agreed. 'That pisses me off. We ditched the gold rings and they had a tracker on the car anyway. Dammit! I want my ring back.'

Jacko was behind the bar, staring up at the television, watching the news. 'It looks like there's a ceasefire,' he said, changing the subject. A scrolling bar along the bottom of the screen claimed the Russians had agreed to a temporary truce.

'I wouldn't believe that,' said Rex. 'Fucking Russians. Sneaky fuckers.'

'I can't believe the president was a paedophile,' said Flake. 'What was on the video Zero showed you?'

Elvis and Jasmine looked at each other. They both winced. Neither really wanted to talk about what they had seen. Elvis was the one who answered eventually.

'We saw the president beating himself off,' he replied. 'Then the camera moved and we saw what he was watching. A young boy, no more than ten years old was being ripped apart by lions, while a bunch of people watched and cheered.'

Flake recoiled in horror. 'That's what the president was masturbating to?' she said, covering her mouth.

'Lion porn,' said Jasmine. 'Not something I ever want to see again.'

'The boy was still alive,' said Elvis. 'It was grim. One second of that shit was too much. I'll never get it out of my head. That's what goes on at a circus after the main show ends.'

'Diago's Travelling Circus,' said Rex. 'That's where it all happens.'

Elvis leaned across the table and tapped Rex on the arm. 'Please tell me you killed all those circus assholes,' he said. 'And you saved the kids, right?'

Rex didn't answer.

Elvis looked at JD. 'You did save Paige and the boy from the sandwich shop, didn't you?'

## Forty-Five

### Part Seven - The Circus

'The last performance ends at eight p.m.,' said Rex, reading the information on his phone. 'What time is it now?'

'It's seven-twenty-five,' Selene replied, keeping her eyes on the road ahead. The recently widowed wife of Antonio Rodriguez was driving Rex's van because she was the only one who knew where the fucking circus was. Rex was sitting up front with her. JD was in the back, drinking bourbon and admiring the heavy artillery they had recently acquired from the Rodriguez estate.

'They won't kill Paige or Kai while the show is on,' said Rex. 'They'll do it afterwards, when the paying public have gone home.'

'That's obvious,' said Selene, rolling her eyes.

'Hey, I'm just thinking out loud.'

When they arrived at Dinosaur Valley Park it was seven-thirty-five and the night sky had drawn in. A giant circus tent, which was almost the size of an arena was lit up and filled with the sounds of people cheering at whatever act was currently performing. Behind it, rows of trailers that belonged to the circus folk were parked up in a field.

Selene manoeuvred the van into a space between a pair of buses in the public parking area. The parking lot was almost full, with roughly a hundred cars and another seven or eight buses. Plenty of idiots wanted to see the circus.

Rex stared over at the trailer park with all the circus vehicles in it. 'We've got about twenty-five minutes to search those circus trailers for Paige,' he said.

'What happens if we walk into a trailer and someone there raises the alarm?' Selene asked.

'We kill them *before* they can raise the alarm,' said Rex.

'And if we find Paige and Kai? What then?'

JD came up from the back and poked his head between their seats. 'If we can get Paige and Kai out before the show finishes, you two can get out of here. I'll stay and kill all the circus fuckers.'

'Or we could report them to the police?' said Selene. 'If we've got the children with us, they'll be able to tell the cops everything they've seen.'

Selene's suggestion was met with a deathly silence. After about ten seconds, she compromised.

'Or, we could forget about the police and just kill everyone?'

'That's a good idea,' said Rex. 'Okay, JD, you do the first trailer we come across. Me and Selene will take the second one. Then we keep going from trailer to trailer until we find the children.'

'I have one question,' said Selene. 'It might seem trivial, but if we find the children, where are we taking them? We can't take Paige home because you've rammed a golf club down her father's throat and killed all his henchmen. And Kai's family are all dead too.'

'I think Kai's mom is still alive,' said Rex 'But for now, let's just find them and worry about the rest later.'

'This will be over in ten,' said JD. 'And remember we need to be quiet. No guns.'

While JD ducked back into the armoury at the back of the truck, Selene looked to Rex for confirmation about the "no guns" thing.

He nodded. 'You sure you're okay with this?'

'I am,' said Selene. 'Just kiss me and tell me it'll be okay.'

Rex leaned over and pressed his lips against hers. She was a great kisser. Their lips locked together like they were made for that reason and nothing else. It was a long kiss that ended when someone knocked on Selene's door. She looked around and saw JD, hood up over his head, standing by her window. She wound it down.

'It's okay, we're coming,' she said.

JD spoke in a voice gravellier than before. He issued her with one final piece of advice. 'If you have to use a gun, then use it, but know that all hell will break loose, and we'll have to kill everyone here, including all the families that have come to watch the show.'

Selene baulked at the idea. 'Why would you kill all the families?'

'Because that's what we do.'

Selene looked over at Rex. 'Really?'

'Not exactly,' said Rex. 'It's just what *he* does. Don't give him an excuse. Just stick with me, and stick to the plan, okay?'

'Got it.' Selene reached into her jacket and pulled out a pistol that had a silencer on it. 'If I have to shoot someone, this should be okay though, right?' she asked.

Rex gawped at the gun. 'You've got a gun with a silencer?' he said, failing to mask his surprise. 'I wish I'd thought of that. Are there any more?'

'There were loads in the armoury,' said Selene. 'Didn't you see them?'

Rex winced. 'I guess not. Never mind. Let's move.'

Under the cover of darkness, the three of them headed over to the trailers. JD was carrying a chainsaw. It was a cumbersome weapon for sure, and bound to be noisier than Selene's gun. But it was a weapon that struck terror into those confronted by it. He had a handful of other quieter weapons tucked away inside his coat. Rex had a machete and a baseball bat strapped across his back. Selene had the small pistol with the silencer on it, and a knife sheathed on her belt.

JD headed straight to the first trailer. It was a long, grey, rusty piece of crap with two steps out front that led up to a rickety door. JD bypassed the steps, grabbed the door handle, twisted it and pulled it open. He stepped inside and closed the door behind him.

'No turning back now,' Rex whispered to Selene.

He ducked down and scampered along to the next trailer. Selene followed, her heart racing. Killing henchmen with a sniper rifle had been fun. She hated most of them anyway. But getting up close to kill a bunch of vampires? That was a totally different ball game.

The next trailer along was in better shape than the previous one. It had an orange front door with a small window in the top.

'You open the door,' Rex whispered to Selene. 'Then step aside. I'll go in.'

Selene crept up to the trailer door. Her hand hovered over the handle for a moment. She wanted to take more time, to think about what she was doing, but Rex was watching, and the Bourbon Kid might reappear from the first trailer at any moment, so she had to do it, and do it fast. She pulled at the handle. It clicked. She yanked the door open and ducked behind it. Rex snuck into the trailer.

'Who the fuck are you?' said a man's voice from inside.

THUD!

Selene peered around the door. There was a man lying on the floor, wearing only a pair of shorts. He was dazed, but not quite unconscious. Fuck it. Selene climbed into the trailer and closed the door.

There was an orange curtain across the middle of the trailer. A light was on behind it, revealing the outline of a person on the other side. Rex yanked the curtain to one side. The figure standing behind it was a naked woman in her early thirties, with straw-like blonde hair. As soon as she saw Rex, she opened her mouth ready to scream, but Rex moved in quick and head-butted her. She fell back onto a pull-out bed and lay there, blinking and groaning.

Selene loomed over the dazed man on the floor and pointed her gun at him. 'Don't make me shoot you,' she whispered to him. The man looked frightened, and thankfully he didn't make any effort to get up from the floor.

'Okay,' said Rex, addressing both of the trailer's residents. 'Where are the children you people kidnapped?'

'What children?' the man replied.

Selene planted her boot on the man's chest and pointed her pistol at his nose. 'The girl who was taken from outside her school this morning, and the boy from the sandwich shop. Tell us where they are and we'll let you live.'

'I don't know what you're talking about.'

'Can you hear that?' said Rex.

Selene hadn't noticed it before, and neither had the man at her feet. A buzzing sound was coming from a nearby trailer, accompanied by some muffled screams.

'What the hell is that?' the man asked.

'That's our friend, the Bourbon Kid. My guess is he's using his chainsaw to cut the face off of someone who didn't tell him where the missing children are. So, if you want to keep *your* face, start talking.'

The man's response was not what Rex was hoping for. His cheeks tightened and blue veins rose to the surface of his skin. His eyes turned yellow and a set of vampire fangs sprouted from his upper jaw. He looked ready for a fight. Selene pressed her boot down harder on his chest. Keep that fucker down.

'Fuck you, you bitch!' the vampire hissed at her.

'Last chance, dickhead,' said Rex. He unsheathed his baseball bat. 'Tell us where the children are, or I bash your girlfriend's brains all over your nice trailer.'

'You wouldn't dare!'

Rex swung the bat down onto the woman's head. It made a sweet connection (and a delightful CLONK sound) that turned her into a dead-weight instantly. Her arms fell down by her sides and blood started seeping from her ear.

'That's just for starters,' said Rex. 'Now tell me where the children are, or your girlfriend's brains are going for a walk.'

'She's not my girlfriend,' the man replied. 'I just met her in the parking lot half an hour ago.'

Selene glanced at Rex. He glanced back. There was no way of knowing if the vampire was bullshitting or not.

Rex took a second, then composed himself. 'Okay Selene, shoot that asshole in the face. We'll try the next trailer along.'

The vampire panicked. He grabbed Selene's leg with both hands and forced her boot off his chest. It threw her off balance and she fell back against the door. The bloodsucker leapt to his feet like he was bouncing back up from a trampoline. He opened his mouth wide, showing off his razor-sharp fangs, then he lunged towards Selene, looking for a bite of her throat.

Not a problem.

Selene straightened her arm and stuck her pistol into the vampire's incoming mouth. The silencer slammed into the back of his throat. She squeezed the trigger. The report from the gun was muted, but the damage was *to the max*. Blood spattered up the sleeve of Selene's leather jacket as the undead fucker's brittle head exploded and went for a ride around the trailer. Eyeballs, teeth, tongue, ears, hair, it all went towards redecorating the dead vampire's home.

Selene wiped some vampire goo from her face. 'How'd I do?' she asked Rex.

'I think you're natural. Ready for the next trailer?'

'Yep. What about her?' Selene asked, nodding at the unconscious female on the bed.

'She's unconscious.'

'Was she a vampire though?'

'Probably. Can't wait around here to find out though. We gotta get moving, or JD will have all the fun.'

## Forty-Six

Chopping people up with a chainsaw was tiring work. Five trailers. Three had been empty. Two now contained dead vampires. Vampires who were dead because they were either too dumb to tell the Bourbon Kid what they knew, or because they just didn't know anything. The first vampire he encountered lost both arms, which traumatised the poor bugger so much that he didn't even remember what the questions were. His head had to come off in order to keep him quiet. The other occupied trailer had two naked female vamps in it. They were in the middle of something intimate when JD burst in on them. What followed was a battle between a chainsaw and two dildos, with a brief cameo from a set of anal beads. The chainsaw was victorious, but at a cost. While ramming it up a vampire's asshole it snagged on something hard and its engine cut out. Without time to fire it up again, the second vampire had to be strangled to death with her own anal beads. It was a loud and messy fight. The noises coming from the circus drowned out most of it, but it was highly likely the fight had been heard by some of the nearby trailer folk. The smell wasn't great either.

JD left the chainsaw and the anal beads behind and headed to what would be his sixth trailer. Trailer number six contained just the one vampire, a fat, stoned-out-of-his-brain loser in green shorts and a red vest. He was sitting cross-legged on the floor when JD entered his domain. He had a peace pipe on the floor next to him, with smoke fizzling out of the end of it.

JD got down to business right away. He whipped a machete out from inside his coat, hacked the stoned vampire's right arm off at the elbow, then picked up the severed arm and started slapping him around the face with it.

'I wanna know where Paige is,' JD said, giving the guy a backhand slap with his own hand.

'I don't know who Paige is,' the stoned vampire replied, tears already flowing down his cheeks from the unpleasant arm-removal incident. 'But I can show you where the kidnapped children are.'

'Don't show me. Tell me.'

'It's hard to describe.'

'Are they in one of the trailers?'

'Yeah.'

'Which one?'

'It's a red and black one.'

'Where?' JD handed him back his severed arm. 'Point this in the right direction.'

The vampire's bottom lip trembled. 'This was my favourite arm!' he blubbed.

And that was the end of that interrogation. The one-armed, stoned-out-of-his-brain vampire couldn't point his own hand at anything. He just sobbed and wailed. JD hacked the cry-baby's head off with his machete.

*Red and black trailer.* That was enough information. JD wiped his knife and hands clean on the dead vampire's curtains then headed back out to the trailer park. Rex and Selene were just about to enter the next trailer along, which was not red and black.

'It's not that one!' JD whispered loudly to them.

'Huh?' said Rex, stopping.

JD moved silently over to them. 'Look for a red and black trailer,' he said, looking around. 'That's where Paige is.'

'Red and black?' said Rex, looking around.

'Over there,' said Selene, pointing at something out of JD's view. He walked up alongside her. There was a red and black trailer visible through a gap between two much smaller trailers.

'We'd better hurry,' said Rex. 'I'm pretty sure the late show just ended.'

'The three of them hot-footed it over to the red and black trailer. JD tried the door. It was locked.

He looked back at Rex. 'Can you unlock this quietly?' he whispered.

'I absolutely can,' said Rex, stepping up to the door. He pressed his magnetic metal hand against the lock and wiggled his fingers one way and then the other. After a gentle click to indicate it was unlocked, Rex turned the handle and pulled the door open for JD to storm in.

It was dark inside, but seemingly free from vampires. JD turned back to Rex. 'You two wait here,' he whispered. 'Keep watch.'

'Sure, why not?' said Rex. 'You go do all the exciting stuff. We'll just stand around out here doing—'

Selene slapped him on the arm. 'Quit moaning, would you?'

'Hey, I was just saying. He always does this.'

Selene grinned. 'I can't believe how much fun this is. It's exhilarating. Do you guys really do this sort of thing all the time?'

A light went on in one of the smaller trailers nearby. 'Keep it down,' Rex whispered. 'The natives are restless.'

Inside the red and black trailer, JD was beginning to think the stoned vampire had lied to him. There were no vampires, no acrobats, no dancing bears, no dildo sisters, nothing. The trailer had a living space, a small kitchen and bathroom etc. After a few seconds of looking around, he deduced that what he was looking for was at the far end of the living space. There was a large square object in the corner that was covered by a red sheet. JD moved towards it, checking for potential enemies, or booby traps. But nothing tripped him, jumped out at him, or threw anal beads at his head. He grabbed a clump of the red sheet and yanked it off. The sheet had been covering a four-feet-high cage. Sitting on the floor of the cage was Kai. He was wearing blue pants and a brown T-shirt. His arms were bound behind his back, and he was rocking back and forth. He didn't even look up at JD. His face was pale and drawn, his hair greasy and unkempt, and his mouth had a strip of tape over it to prevent him from making any noise. JD reached through the bars on the cage and ripped the tape off Kai's mouth. The boy didn't react, didn't even look up.

'Kai?' said JD. 'You okay?'

No reply.

'Have you seen Paige?'

Kai nodded, but continued rocking back and forth.

'Would you like to go home?'

Nodded again.

'Okay, I'm gonna get you out of here. Don't panic. I'm just gonna bust this lock.'

The cage door had a big padlock chained to it. JD pulled out his machete and smashed it down on the padlock. It made a loud "clank" that echoed around the trailer and made Kai wince. The padlock busted and JD pulled open the cage door. Kai continued rocking.

JD reached inside the cage and used his machete to cut the plastic that was binding Kai's hands together. Kai immediately wrapped his hands around his legs and continued rocking back and forth. JD offered the boy his hand. 'Come on. You're safe now. I'll take you home.'

More rocking. No intent to take the hand of friendship. After ten seconds of coaxing, JD lost patience. This was a job for Selene. Or maybe even Rex.

'Okay,' he said to Kai. 'Wait here a sec.'

He walked back to the open door and stepped out onto the grass. Rex was nearby, standing on a male midget's head while Selene was kicking the little fucker in the face. JD walked over to Selene and tapped her on the shoulder.

'Kai from the sandwich shop is in there,' he said. 'I can't get him to come out. Can you try?'

Selene stopped kicking the midget in the face. 'Why me?' she asked.

'I figure you're good with little people,' said JD, staring at the bloodied and almost unconscious face of the midget.

'All right,' said Selene. 'I think I'm done here anyway.'

She gave the midget one last kick, this time in the nuts, then left the scene and vanished inside the trailer to find Kai.

'Any sign of Paige?' Rex asked.

'She's not there.'

'You think we're too late?'

'HEY!' a high-pitched voice called out. 'What are you doing to Roger?'

JD spun around to see who had yelled at them. A female midget dressed as one of Snow White's dwarves was standing outside a tiny trailer. She was staring angrily at Rex and JD, with her hands on her hips.

Fighting with midgets. This was a new low in a history littered with lows. Rex reacted first. He reached back over his shoulder, unsheathed his baseball bat and hurled it at the female midget, all in one fluid move. The bat spun end over end, until it hit Dopey in the face. The impact knocked her off her feet. She landed with a thud on the grass, her arms and legs splayed out.

'Let's not tell anyone about this,' said Rex.

'About you assaulting midgets?'

Rex didn't bite. 'Where do you think Paige is?' he asked.

'I don't know,' said JD, looking around. 'But she ain't in there. Kai is in there, locked in a cage, but he won't say shit. Poor fucker is traumatised.'

Selene reappeared at the trailer door. Kai was with her, holding her hand. The two of them walked over to JD.

'Kai says Paige is in the Big Top,' said Selene. 'I'm going to take him to a police station. Hopefully they can reunite him with his mother. Rex, do you mind if I take your van? I've still got the key.'

'Take him to a drive-through first,' said Rex. 'Buy him a burger. That way, by the time you get to the cops, we'll be all done here. I'll call you when we need a ride.'

'Got it. I'll see you soon.'

Selene escorted Kai back to the van, bumping fists with Rex as she went past him. Rex watched her and the boy walk away then turned back to JD.

'What now then?' he said. 'Stealth? Or all guns blazing?'

'We left the big weapons in the van,' JD replied. 'So it's gonna have to be stealth. Let's find a back entrance into the Big Top and take these fuckers down quietly. But before we do anything, hide those fucking midgets.'

## Forty-Seven

Tears streamed down Paige's cheeks. She was still in her school uniform, but instead of sitting in a classroom, she was in a filthy cage in the backstage area of the Big Top. Her hands were bound behind her back and she had tape over her mouth.

There were two other cages in the backstage area. One, which was much closer than Paige would have liked, contained a pair of lions. The male lion stared at her like she was a Happy Meal. This was no Aslan, Simba, or Clarence the cross-eyed lion. This was a proper, big, scary, jungle VIP. The other cage was home to a big, grizzly bear, wearing a pink hat. He looked sad and embarrassed, the poor bastard.

The most recent live performance in the Big Top had ended and the audience had slipped away. It was time for the after-show party.

The three cages were wheeled through a short tunnel into the bright lights of the circus ring. The seats all around the ring were empty. There was a new audience now. A big cinema screen had been positioned in front of one of the seating stands. A block of squares filled the screen. Each square had a person in it, watching, waiting for the late night ritual that was to come. The faces belonged mostly to old men, although there were a few women dotted around too. In all, there were close to a hundred faces, and almost all of them were staring at Paige.

Unfortunately, the people on the screen were the least of her problems. Circus performers were lined up all around the perimeter of the ring. One of them, a young, attractive, dark-haired woman in a green dress was standing next to a giant upright wheel opposite the big screen. The wheel had segments all around it like those on a roulette wheel. An arrow marker beside the wheel would decide Paige's fate.

Diago the ringmaster was standing in the centre of the ring in a purple suit and top hat. He was holding a cane, which he used like a baton to conduct his audience. He waved it at the other circus folk as he called for quiet. When everyone's eyes were on him, he launched into his opening monologue.

'Ladies and gentlemen, tonight's offering is a young lady named Paige.' He pointed at her. 'Paige in a cage!' he bellowed, chuckling to himself like he'd made the best joke ever. It didn't get much of a response, so he cleared his throat and carried on. 'Kratos, bring her over.'

Kratos, a giant, greasy-haired oaf in a blue wrestling singlet, unlocked the padlock on the cage door and reached in to grab Paige. She pressed her back up against the bars at the back and kicked out at him. It didn't help matters at all. Kratos had done this a thousand times. He grabbed Paige by one of her ankles and dragged her out onto the sand and sawdust on the circus floor. He tore off the wire that was binding her hands together, then with a firm grip on her arm, he ripped the sticky tape off her mouth. Paige screamed but no one paid her any mind.

Diago addressed the TV audience again, then pointed his cane at the woman in the green dress. 'Athena, spin that wheel!' he cried with great enthusiasm.

There were eight categories on the wheel. BEAR, KNIFE THROWERS, FIRE EATERS, FIST FIGHT, GANG BANG, LIONS, SWORD SWALLOWING and SAWED IN HALF. Athena grabbed a handle on the side of the wheel and spun it hard. Round and round it went, the arrow-shaped pointer on the side making a ticking sound as each section went past it. The wheel gradually slowed. Paige's mouth was dry, she could barely swallow. All of the options were horrific. There wasn't one that she would have preferred above the others. It was hard to decide which was even the worst. It wasn't a hundred percent clear what would happen on some of them, but one thing was certain, they all sucked. The bear? Maybe the bear was the best option? He was wearing a hat and he seemed depressed more than he seemed dangerous. But even so, he was still a fucking, great big grizzly bastard.

The wheel eventually slowed up. The options became easier to read as they crawled around towards the arrow-shaped marker. The arrow ticked past BEAR and into KNIFE THROWERS. For a second it looked like it would stop there, but then it flicked over one more time into the section marked FIRE EATERS.

Diago's lips broke into a sly smile. 'Tonight will be a game of fire!' he hollered. 'Are you ready to watch Paige fight fire with nothing? Prepare to hear her screams as our fire eaters take her down.'

The reactions from the people on the big screen ranged from small cheers to big grins and light applause, and in one instance, a man licking his lips.

Paige's heart was beating at a million miles an hour. She made a fruitless attempt to wriggle free from Kratos's grip. She kicked him in the shins, spat at him, bit his arm. None of it bothered him, he just tightened his grip on her arm.

Two performers in skin-tight white outfits stepped forward from the outer circle. One was a male who looked like an eighties rocker with a big perm. His female companion was a short-haired blonde, who looked like a ballet dancer. Each of them was holding a long metal rod that they used in their fire-eating act. The male approached Diago and held out his rod. With a flick from a petrol lighter, Diago lit the end of the rod up in flames. The elegant female fire-eater held hers out, and

Diago lit that up too. The two fire-eaters walked away to opposite sides of the ring and waited while Diago addressed the people on the screen again.

'Ladies and gentlemen,' he announced. 'Let this evening's Ludus Mortis begin!'

Diago bowed to the audience, then strolled past Paige and Kratos to take up a safe position at the side of the ring. He gave Kratos a nod of the head, which was the signal for the giant oaf to let go of Paige's arm. Kratos then made a hasty retreat, taking up a position alongside a group of clowns who were blocking off the exit to the backstage area. Paige had earmarked the exit as her best chance of escape. With that route gone there was no easy way out of this.

The two fire-eaters standing across the ring from each other bowed down like they were members of Cobra Kai preparing for a fight. When they came back up, the game was on. The two of them closed in on Paige from both sides. She had to run. It's what the audience wanted. It's what the fire-eaters wanted, and it was what Paige had no choice but to do. That's where the entertainment was for the audience. If she stayed still and let the fire-eaters walk up to her and set her on fire it would be anticlimactic, for them and the audience anyway. But Paige didn't want to die, certainly not without trying to escape. Run and hope for the best, that was her only option. There wasn't a single escape route available to her. The performers forming the circle around the ring's perimeter would never let her past them. And even if by some miracle she squeezed through their barrier, they would catch her again easily. Apart from the midgets. Yes, the midgets. Paige could outrun a midget. That was her best option.

She started running, initially just away from the fire-eaters, but then towards a midget in a grey jump-suit, who was standing next to a slender, silver-haired woman in a shiny blue outfit. But as she closed in on them, the midget, the woman, and every other person guarding the perimeter underwent a physical transformation. Every single one transitioned from their human form into a bloodsucking vampire. Their pale skin thinned, showing off blue veins all over their arms, faces and any other parts of skin that were visible. Paige screamed. She planted a foot down and changed direction. She almost ran straight into a huge gust of fire. It blew past her face, causing her to stop and change direction again. But then a coconut whizzed past her shoulder. She ducked down and ran back towards the centre of the ring. The vampire audience had started hurling things at her. Coconuts, tennis balls, fruit, trash, it was all coming her way, further diminishing any chance of escape.

Horrid, cackled laughter filled the air. Paige was getting a taste of what it was like for a wild animal when it was hunted by a pack of bigger, stronger, predators.

She ran around in circles, changing direction every few steps when something or someone showed up in her way. Everything was closing in on her, and she was tiring fast. Eventually, Paige got taken down. Not by the fire, but by a fucking coconut of all things. It rolled into her path, and she trod on it, twisting her ankle and tumbling over onto the dusty floor. A huge cheer went up from the crowd. Paige's head landed on another small but solid object. It dazed her, and her vision clouded.

The two fire-eaters moved in from opposite sides. This was it. The moment Paige had been dreading ever since she was kidnapped. Her eyes filled up with water. How could anyone be this cruel? How could this many people get a kick out of watching a child set on fire?

The female fire-eater pressed her foot down on Paige's arm, pinning her to the floor. Paige tried to wriggle free, but to no avail. The fire-eater leaned back and held up her flaming rod, then she lowered the burning end into her mouth, swallowing the flames, and preparing to spit them back out again. Her male companion took up a position behind Paige's head. He looked down on her face, a wicked grin across his. He tilted his head back and swallowed the flames from his burning rod.

Paige closed her eyes and sobbed. She had never been burned before, not even a little. And to her surprise, when the flames hit her body, the feeling was nothing like she imagined it would be. It was hot for sure, but also sticky, and wet. Very, very wet.

The cheering crowd went silent. A new sound filled the circus ring. Screams. Roars. Gunfire. A pair of loud thuds as the two fire-eaters crumpled to the floor nearby.

Paige opened her eyes a tiny bit, wincing, still expecting burning flames to rage down upon her. But the fire-eaters were gone, and Paige wasn't covered in flames. She was covered in goo. Vampire goo. Brains, innards, blood, bits of bone. But no hot flames. She glanced to the side and saw the female fire-eater lying beside her. Minus her head.

One thought went round and round in Paige's mind.

*What the hell is happening?'*

Someone on the big screen actually said those words out loud. 'What the hell is happening?'

The next voice Paige heard was a familiar one. It yelled out, *"Paige, stay down!"*

She did as she was told. She stayed on her back, initially staring up at the roof of the enormous tent, but after a severed arm flew by overhead, she decided to look around. After all, she had only been told to stay down. No one said anything about not looking around. And when she looked around she saw who had come to her rescue. It was her chauffeur and her backseat buddy, armed and dangerous.

## Forty-Eight

Paige had always felt deep down that she was unique. Things happened to her that didn't happen to other people. Being kidnapped by an invisible man who turned out to be a vampire was one such thing. But there were others. The carnage taking place all around her in the circus was a perfect example. Her chauffeur and her back-seat escort had showed up to kick some ass. The chauffeur was a wanted mass-murderer with a drink problem. The back-seat buddy was a Hell's Angel with a metal hand and one eye. And now, these two absolute darlings were destroying a group of circus vampires.

Paige stayed flat on her back in the centre of all the carnage. She covered her ears with her hands because all the high-pitched screaming from the vampires was driving her insane. She wanted to get up and run, but JD had told her to stay down, so that's exactly what she was going to do, until told otherwise. She counted to a hundred in her head, and concentrated on her breathing. *This will all be over soon. Please let it be over soon. And please, for the love of God, stop hurling severed limbs around because the blood keeps landing on me.*

It was a curious oddity, not being able to hear much, other than muffled screams interspersed with loud bangs. The bangs made her shudder, but they weren't as frightening as seeing a severed head fly past overhead, its dead-eyes staring at her as it went. Someone's arm bounced off her at one point too. And Rex leapt over her in pursuit of one of the vampires. He was swinging something around above his head.

After counting to a hundred, Paige twisted her head to the side to get a better look at the corpse of the female fire-eater. The burning rod the vampire had been chasing Paige with had been rammed up her asshole, hot end first. Smoke was drifting out of the hole where her head had once been. She smelt bad too, like her insides were cooking. Barbecued vampire liver. Not a good smell.

The giant figure of Kratos slithered into Paige's vision next. He bellyflopped onto the floor nearby. His face had been caved in. It reminded Paige of the time she kicked a punctured football and it flattened in on itself. When it was someone's face, rather than a football, it was an ugly sight. But Paige didn't like Kratos, so the sight was perfect.

She looked back up at the roof of the tent, just in time to see one of the trapeze artists fly overhead. He had a knife sticking out of his chest, and even though Paige only got a brief look at him as he zipped by, she was fairly certain he had no eyes or nose.

She lifted her head a few inches off the floor and looked around. The first thing that caught her eyes was a purple suit. Diago, the man who had kidnapped her, was fleeing the carnage. He was running through the tunnel to the backstage area, most likely with the intention of fleeing the circus completely. Neither JD nor Rex saw him leave. Rex was too busy with a machete, slicing Athena's legs off at the knee. It served the bitch right for spinning the wheel of misfortune. JD was ripping the saddle off a unicycle. For a moment, Paige couldn't think why. But then she saw him grab a clown whose pants had fallen down. He lifted the clown up and sat him down on the unicycle. With no saddle on it, the clown's ass went down a long way.

The assault on the clown came to an end when someone threw a knife at JD's head. He plucked it out of the air with his free hand, then hurled it back in the direction it had come from. Someone took it in the face and fell down. Probably the knife-thrower. It was a rare sight, someone at the circus throwing a knife and actually hitting the person they threw it at.

All around the circus ring, corpses were burning up, smouldering, disintegrating. A giant pair of upturned shoes were all that remained of one of the clowns. A couple of nearby midgets were skewered on a sword, like meat chunks on a kebab stick. Paige recognised the sword. She had seen Yoga the sword-swallower rehearsing with it earlier, back when he was a whole person. At some point in the last two minutes, Yoga had been cut in half. The bottom half of him was on the floor of the bear cage. His top half was in the bear's mouth. It brought a smile to Paige's face to see the bear looking happier as he chomped on the sword-swallower's ribcage. There was another corpse nearby. It belonged to Dexter, one of the acrobats. Paige recognised him because he was Diago's brother. Or rather, he used to be. Right now he was on the ground, melting like a plastic bag on a barbecue.

When there were no other circus folk to chase after, Rex came over to see Paige. He had a comforting smile on his blood-specked face. His lips moved, but Paige didn't hear what he said because her hands were covering her ears. She lifted them away, inviting in all the strange, wonderful sounds of the circus.

'I said you can take your hands away from your ears now!' Rex said, rather loudly.

'Is it over?' she asked.

'Yeah, it's over.'

'I think Diago got away.'

'Who?'

'The ringmaster. The one in the purple suit.'

Rex looked around. 'Did he go down the tunnel?'

'Yes.'

'Don't worry about it then. JD's gone after him.'

Rex offered her his hand, the non-metal one. Paige's smaller hand vanished into it, and the Hell's Angel hauled her up to her feet.

'Let's go get a burger,' he said. 'Would you like that?'

'I'd like some strawberry custard.'

'Then I'll get you some strawberry custard. Anything else?'

Paige contemplated the offer while the smell of burning vampires and bear lunch wafted around in the air. Lion's dinner too. She hadn't noticed that at first. The lions were in their cage fighting over someone's leg. The lioness had the thigh in her mouth, her male counterpart was pulling on the foot. It reminded Paige of the scene in Lady and the Tramp when the two dogs are eating spaghetti, only there was more blood in this.

'I'd like to thank you,' Paige said to Rex. 'I'd be on fire if you hadn't showed up when you did.'

'How about a hug?' said Rex, moving in for an embrace.

'No. But you can hold my hand on the way out.'

'Okay. Deal.'

Rex and Paige walked hand in hand through the decaying corpses of the circus performers and back out into the fresh air. By the time they reached the far end of the parking lot, the circus tent was fully on fire. Any evidence of the vampires would soon be erased.

'Selene should be along in the van any minute now,' said Rex. 'I'll just give her a call. See where she is.'

'What about my dad?' Paige asked.

'Your dad?' said Rex while bringing up Selene's number on his phone 'Umm, I don't know where he is, actually. Ask Selene when she gets here.'

'Is he okay?'

'Hang on, phone's ringing.'

Thankfully, Selene answered the call before Rex had to think up a response to any of Paige's awkward questions. 'Hi, Selene, how's it going?'

'Did you get Paige?' .

'She's right here with me. Everything went smoothly. Can you get back here and pick us up? The circus is burning down so time's not on our side, if you know what I mean?'

'I'll be with you in about a minute. I had to drop Kai off outside the police station. I couldn't go in because we're all over the news.'

'We are?'

'Yeah. Apparently every cop in the city is at my house right now, going through security camera footage of everything that happened on the golf course. I don't think I can go home.'

'Then come with me to Santa Mondega.'

'Where exactly is that?'

'It's a twelve-hour drive from where we are. We might need to spend the night somewhere while we work out how to get over the border.'

'Sounds like fun,' said Selene. 'Count me in. See you in a minute.'

Rex ended the call and looked around for any sign of JD. While he was looking, Paige poked him in the thigh, not far from where he'd been shot earlier. He resisted the urge to yell at her, and sucked up the pain like it wasn't there.

'Rex,' said Paige.

'Yes, my love.'

'Can I ask you something?'

Rex took a deep breath. 'Go on then.'

'Would you be able to go back to the circus tent and get the bear and the lions out?'

Rex breathed a sigh of relief. 'Don't worry,' he said. 'They'll be fine. We unlocked their cages when we threw some circus folk in with them. They're probably out and roaming around the countryside by now.'

'Isn't that dangerous?'

'Yes it is. But it'll keep the cops off our tail for a while.'

'What about JD though?'

She had a point. 'I'll call him,' said Rex. He pulled up JD's number on his phone and made the call. At the point where it looked as though the call would go to voicemail, JD finally answered.

'What's up?' he said abruptly.

'Where are you?' Rex asked. 'We're about to leave.'

'I'm checking the trailers for more vampires.'

'Well, hurry up. The cops will be here any minute now.'

'You can go on without me.'

'What? How are you gonna get out of here?'

'I'll take one of the circus cars.'

'Okay. Watch out for the lions and the bear though.'

'Shut the fuck up.'

It wasn't the reply Rex was expecting. 'What?' he said, confused.

'Not you, Rex. I gotta go.'

The line went dead. Rex stared at his phone. It confirmed the call was over. JD was an awkward character sometimes.

'Is he coming?' Paige asked.

'No. I think he's busy.'

## Forty-Nine

Paige snuggled up to Rex in the twin passenger seat of the van while Selene drove it to Santa Mondega. Within minutes of the journey commencing, Selene delicately explained to Paige that her father had died, choking to death on a club sandwich. The girl took it surprisingly well. No tears, just a period of silence followed by a request that Rex and Selene promise not to take her to an orphanage. Then she rested her head on Rex's shoulder and closed her eyes. Rex turned the radio off, and the journey continued in silence to allow Paige to catch up on her sleep. It gave Rex plenty of time to reflect.

Over the course of the last two days, he had transitioned from a lonesome biker, into a passenger on a road trip with a woman he had fallen head-over-heels for, and her step-daughter, who had turned out to be pretty amazing too. Throughout the late night drive, Selene repeatedly looked over at Paige and smiled. Every time she did, she then looked up at Rex, and smiled some more. The newfound sense of calm was something Rex had never realised he needed. The silence was beautiful. Four hours of it flew by before Paige eventually woke up.

'What time is it?' she asked, rubbing her eyes.

'It's half past two,' said Rex. 'You've been fast asleep.'

'I'm still tired,' said Paige.

'How about some music?' said Rex. 'That'll keep you awake.' Paige didn't protest so Rex switched on the radio and found the song, "When the Morning Comes," by Hall and Oates.

A few miles down the road, Selene spotted a motel. After a short debate, it was agreed that it looked ideal for their needs. Selene swung the van off the road and into the motel parking lot.

'See if we can park around the back,' said Rex. 'The more discreet we are the better.'

Selene drove around to the back of the motel and reversed the van into a space next to a large dumpster. Rex jumped out, breezed into the reception and booked them an apartment with two bedrooms. Twenty minutes later, he and Selene were asleep in a king-sized bed in the main room, and Paige was tucked up in bed in the smaller room.

There was just one problem for Paige. She wasn't tired anymore. Her mind was turning over and over again like the wheel of misfortune. Everything that had happened to her in the last twenty-four hours kept playing on a loop. She'd been kidnapped, spent time in a dark cage with Kai from the sandwich shop, almost been burned alive by fire-breathing vampires, then after being rescued, she'd been informed that her father was dead. She loved her dad. She regretted that the last time she'd seen him, she'd been cross with him.

And she knew enough to know that he didn't choke on a sandwich. She wasn't stupid. She knew her dad wasn't a good guy. But he was her dad. And now—no matter how kind people were and how safe she felt with them—they weren't hers and she wasn't theirs.

She couldn't go back home now, which meant her future belonged in Santa Mondega with Rex and Selene. That also meant a new school, new friends, new mean girls to steal her lunch. Not forgetting the fact that all of her possessions were at home. She didn't want to start over. She didn't even want to be where she was. And while she didn't *want* to remember the last twenty-four hours, what those fucking vampires did would torture her for eternity. How in God's name was she ever going to get those images out of her head? They were ingrained there forever. And forever was way too long to be remembering those things. And in the early morning quiet, the wheel of misfortune turned, and turned, and turned.

It was too much.

And then, a new thought came. And a calm settled over her. She got up and crept into the lounge. On the floor by the sofa, there was a sports bag containing a bunch of weapons. Rex had brought it in with him, fearing it would be irresponsible to leave so much firepower in the van outside. Paige knelt down beside the bag and unzipped it, careful not to wake the others. The item she was looking for was right on top of everything else. The pistol with the silencer. She gazed at it for a while, then reached out for it. Her fingers tentatively wrapped around the handle. It was a good weight. Not too heavy, but not lightweight either. She took it and zipped the bag back up. No sound came from Rex and Selene's room. They had to be asleep. Paige tip-toed back to her room and sat down on the end of the bed. She stared at the gun. This would make the wheel of misfortune stop turning. This would take away the pain. It wasn't like anyone would miss her. If you can't get bad memories out of your head, you can blow them out.

Paige stroked the silencer. She wanted to do this right. The angle, the position, the intention—all of it had to be perfect.

She tried out every possibility, finally settling on sticking the gun under her chin. But even then, it needed to be at the correct angle, aimed towards her brain. She was sure she'd read horror stories of people who had shot themselves in the face but missed the brain, leaving them deformed and in more pain than before.

With the tip of the silencer tickling her chin, she rested her finger lightly on the trigger. One squeeze and all the pain and suffering would be gone. Life would be over. Her future didn't matter, because at best, it was an imagined one. What she knew right now was that everything hurt too much and this was the only way to get rid of it.

The images flashed through her mind again. The vampires cackling, showing off their fangs. Another turn of the wheel. The dark cage. Kratos the giant. The bear eating one of the vampires. Even the good stuff was bad. And then she pictured her father. His smiling face. Gone forever. He would be waiting for her in the afterlife, for sure.

To hell with it. Just do it.

She caressed the trigger with her finger. All that was required was a little pressure. She closed her eyes and took a deep breath.

BANG!

Paige jerked at the sound, realizing it hadn't come from her, and that she was still very much alive. A motel room door had slammed up above her, followed by the clanking of boots pounding on metal stairs outside. People were coming.

SHIT!

Paige panicked and yanked her head away from the gun. But at the same time, her finger pressed down on the trigger. A round fizzed out of the gun barrel, passed through the silencer, then zipped past her face on its upward trajectory. At least the silencer did its job, muffling the sound of the shot. Paige breathed a sigh of relief. But then a sprinkling of thick powder landed on her head. New problem. She held her breath. Then she leaned back and looked up at the ceiling.

Bullet hole.

Shit.

THUD!

Uh, oh. Someone hit the floor in the room above. Had her stray bullet just shot someone? No. Bullets don't shoot people. People shoot bullets. Holy fuckballs. *She had just shot someone.* Someone in the room above.

A drop of blood fell from the hole in the ceiling and landed on her nose. Shit, shit, SHIT!

She jumped up from the bed. Could this day get any worse? Had she just killed someone? Should she expect a knock at the door? How the fuck do you explain that you didn't mean to shoot a hole in the ceiling with a gun you weren't supposed to have?

Light footsteps clonked around on the floor above, followed by more footsteps on the metal staircase outside. Lighter steps. Someone was creeping down the stairs.

What the fuck? Paige was paralysed by panic. If she'd shot someone in the room above and someone else was coming down the stairs to complain about it, then Rex and Selene would find out what she had done. She was in for the mother of all telling-off's.

She scampered back into the lounge, unzipped the sports bag and slid the pistol back inside where she had found it. Then she tiptoed back to her room, quick sharp. She waited. She listened. There was no knock at the door. Had she gotten away with it?

She reached out to the blinds on her bedroom window and separated two of the slats so she could peek at what was going on outside. Just like everything else in the last twenty-four hours, what was happening could only be described as bizarre. There was a naked woman strolling across the parking lot with a wine bottle in her hand. She was approaching a silver van with three men standing beside it. Two of the men were in suits. The third guy, an Elvis lookalike in a bathrobe and pink slippers, was chatting away to them.

CLANK!

The naked chick bashed one of the suited men on the back of the head. He went down like a sack of spuds. His buddy turned around, only to find himself with a knife pressed against his throat courtesy of the Elvis lookalike. Paige closed the blinds and scrambled back onto her bed. This was a strange motel. Thankfully, no one had complained about her shooting a hole in the ceiling. Not yet anyway. She dived under the sheets of the bed and pretended to be asleep. After a while she heard more footsteps on the metal stairs outside. She heard a man and a woman discussing something right above her. The words were muffled. And all the while, every few seconds a drop of blood fell from the hole in the ceiling. A patch of it was forming on the toe end of the bed.

For the next few minutes, Paige listened to the muffled voices, and to more footsteps going back and forth on the landing, and she hoped and prayed no one would come knocking. No one did. Even when some people came back down the metal stairs, they didn't knock on the door. Eventually, someone started up a car in the parking lot and drove off. After that, there was nothing but silence.

Paige let out the breath she'd been holding for an age. It was as if this final, violent, and definitely bizarre experience had been a metaphysical defibrillator. She'd hit the bottom of what life could throw at her. Whatever happened next could only be better.

# Fifty

It was late in the morning when Rex woke up. Selene was gone, and his phone was ringing. He reached over to the bedside table and grabbed it. It was a call from Flake. He rubbed his head. What the fuck could Flake possibly want? He stretched his arms out and yawned before accepting the call and pressing the phone to his ear. A hissing sound on the other end made it sound like Flake was in a moving car.

'What's up Flake?'

'Rex, thank God. Me and JD are in trouble. Where are you?'

Rex let the words sink in for a moment. 'JD?' he said, rubbing his head. 'What the fuck's he doing with you?'

'Sanchez is dead.'

Rex woke up like he'd just downed five espressos. 'Put me on speaker. I wanna speak to JD.'

'Done,' said Flake.

'Where the fuck are you?' Rex asked. 'What's going on?'

JD's voice came through. 'Rex, listen, we're being chased by the whole fucking world. They think Flake killed the president.'

'Whaaaaat?'

'No time to explain. You got a biker hideout round here anywhere?'

'Where are you?'

'Downtown, Chicago, not far from the Poseidon hotel.'

'Poseidon,' said Rex, repeating the name. He knew the place all right. And he knew a biker hideout near it too. 'Yeah, I know a place near there. It's called the Gunslingers. You could be there in ten. Just don't let the cops track you there. You lead the cops to these guys and……… well, they won't like it.'

'Where is it?'

'It's underneath a pizza place called "Another One Bites the Crust". Pull into the underground parking lot there. There's a secret entrance. I'll tell the boss man there to expect you. They'll take you in. Okay?'

'You're the best, Rex,' said Flake.

''Good luck. And I'm sorry about Sanchez. If you get any problems just call me again.' He was about to end the call when he remembered what they'd said about the president. 'Is the president really dead?' he asked.

'Yeah,' JD replied. 'It's all over the news.'

'Shit. Speak to you later. Good luck.'

Rex made a quick call to Axl, the boss man at the Gunslingers, asking him to take Flake and JD in, then he rolled out of bed and slung last night's clothes on while he listened to the radio. According to the news, a whole bunch of important people had been assassinated overnight, but the president was the big one for sure. Rex couldn't fathom why anyone would think Flake had killed the president though. It was insane. When he was finished dressing, he sprayed on some deodorant and left the bedroom. Selene wasn't in the lounge either. Where the fuck had she gone?

The answer was on the coffee table in the middle of the room. A piece of paper with a handwritten message on it, from Selene.

*"Paige and I have gone for breakfast. You were fast asleep.*
*See you soon Big Guy, love Selene."*

Rex was very interested in a breakfast with the two new women in his life. He would have gone straight to the motel restaurant to join them, but his phone rang again. This time the caller was Jacko.

'Fuckssake,' Rex groaned to himself. 'What now?'

He answered the call, but before he could even say hello, Jacko started talking at a hundred miles an hour.

'Rex! It's Jacko. *Emergency!* Jasmine and Elvis are in trouble. People are shooting at them. They're locked in a bathroom somewhere underground in Santa Mondega, but I can't find the place. Can you come back to Purgatory and help?'

*What a morning this was turning into!*

'Yeah. Shit!' Rex's mind sharpened up. 'I'm in room forty-two of the El Guapo Motel in San Antonio. Open the portal and I'll come through. Are they hurt?'

'I don't know. HURRY!'

The bathroom in the motel was very basic. It had a toilet, a shower and a wash basin. Rex walked in and started counting in his head. Time was precious. Every second mattered. He'd counted to four when the toilet vanished along with the wall behind it. Rex ran through the new opening into Purgatory. Jacko was behind the bar tapping away on a keyboard.

'WHERE ARE THEY?' Rex yelled at him.

'Underneath Bobby's train shop in Chinatown,' said Jacko. 'But Einstein can't find it on the map!'

Rex hadn't even noticed Einstein. The crazy scientist was sitting at a round table near the bar, staring at a laptop screen. Rex stayed by the portal and called over to him.

'Yo, Einstein, look for Barbie's Nails. That's the old name. The train shop moved in a few months ago.'

Einstein tapped away some more on his keyboard. To his credit, he typed fast. 'GOT IT!' he yelled.

The sound of gunfire burst into Purgatory from the portal. There was no time to question what the fuck was going on. Rex turned just in time to see a great big Alsatian limp past him. The motel bathroom in the El Guapo was gone, replaced by a poky little room. Jasmine was laid out on the floor right in front of him, her catsuit peppered with bullet holes and blood. Elvis was standing between her and a fucked-up door that was being shot to literal pieces. Big chunks of the door had been blown out, and Elvis was making it worse by shooting back at whoever was on the other side.

Rex jumped straight into action. He crouched down and slid his hands under Jasmine's armpits. He dragged her into Purgatory and away from the line of fire. The big dog started barking, possibly at Elvis to get a move on, possibly at Jasmine to wake her up, and possibly at Rex. Rex ignored the dog and checked Jasmine for signs of life. There were trails of thick blood on the floor from the portal, all from her injuries. She wasn't speaking. She was barely breathing. The only thing likely to save her was the Eye of the Moon. Lucky for Rex, he had an idea where it was. It was with Flake, and she was heading for the Gunslingers. He poked his head around the portal entrance and yelled as loud as he could above all the gunfire.

'ELVIS! COME ON!'

## Fifty-One

Selene left Rex sleeping soundly in bed. After showering and dressing she walked into the lounge where she found Paige watching cartoons on the television, with the volume muted. The poor girl looked like she hadn't slept much, and she was still wearing her school uniform from the day before, which was covered in dried vampire blood. Not only did Paige need new clothes, she needed a good meal too, so Selene did the decent thing and insisted on taking her out for a late breakfast.

The obvious place to go was the motel restaurant, but it didn't look very good and it was full of people smoking, so Selene took Paige to a place across the street, a diner called *Coffee and a Crepe.* The place was moderately busy, with customers eating late breakfasts and lunches at window booths, or at the lunch counter.

Selene and Paige entered and headed over to a window booth with spongey red seats on either side of it. They sat down opposite each other.

'Order whatever you like,' said Selene, picking up a table menu.

Paige picked up a menu, but didn't say anything. She looked anxious and very tired, and her right leg was bobbing up and down under the table. It was hard to know what to say to the poor girl. Selene had plenty of problems of her own but they paled in comparison to what Paige had been through. The young girl looked like she might burst into tears if she tried to talk about anything that had happened.

'I'm not really hungry,' Paige said eventually, putting the menu down.

'Order something anyway. It doesn't matter if you don't eat it. I'll bag it up and take it back to the motel for Rex. He's bound to be hungry.'

A short, middle-aged, blonde waitress came over to their table. Her blue and white checked dress had every possible sauce stain on it. She gave the two of them a genuine smile, and held up her note pad and pen. 'What can I get you two ladies?' she asked.

'I'll have a large coffee, white, two sugars, please,' said Selene. 'And a tuna salad. Paige, what would you like?'

'Just a coffee please,' Paige said, without even looking at the waitress.

'How'd you like that, miss?' the waitress asked her.

'Black, three sugars, please.'

'How about we share a plate of fries?' Selene suggested.

Paige nodded. 'Okay.'

'Fries as well, please,' Selene said to the waitress, with a polite smile.

'Coming right up.'

A few minutes later the waitress returned with the two coffees. She placed them down on the table, along with two sets of cutlery wrapped in serviettes. 'Food will be along in a few minutes,' she promised. Then she headed off to take someone else's order.

'Do you think I'll ever be able to forget what happened?' Paige asked without looking up.

It was a tough question. Selene didn't think Paige would ever forget what happened, but at the same time, she wanted to give her some encouragement. 'I hope so,' she replied. 'Things will definitely get easier over time, I'm sure of that.'

'Will we ever be able to go home?'

'I don't know. It's possible, but it depends on a lot of different factors.'

'If we can't go home, will we live with Rex, or JD?'

'We might live with Rex. Would you like that?'

Paige bit her bottom lip. 'Yes, it would be okay. Do you think you'll marry Rex?'

Selene laughed. 'Let's not get ahead of ourselves. I do like him though.'

'I know. I can see it.'

Paige stared out of the window, so Selene glanced up at a television behind the counter. A news reader was looking very downbeat. There was too much noise from other customers to hear what was being said, but a scrolling yellow bar revealed the day's big news. The president had been assassinated in his hotel room.

'Oh my God,' Selene whispered. 'Paige have you seen the news? The president has been murdered. And so have several senators.'

Paige looked around at the television, but said nothing.

'Wow,' said Selene, reading more of the headlines. 'The British prime minister is dead too. What the hell is going on?'

While they waited for their food to arrive, Selene checked her phone for more information about the assassinations. It seemed like most of the major world leaders had been killed, with the exception of the Russian president. The only possible positive Selene could take from any of it, was that the cops and the FBI weren't likely to give a shit about the murder of her husband Antonio, or his henchmen, or the circus people.

The waitress eventually returned with their food. She placed a rather bland looking tuna salad in front of Selene and a bowl of soggy fries in front of Paige.

'Will that be all?' she asked.

'Yes, that's great thanks,' said Selene.

The waitress left them to enjoy their tasteless food in peace. Selene was pleased to see Paige reach for a squeezy bottle of ketchup to pour over the fries. A few seconds into covering the fries with sauce, Paige stopped.

'Do you mind me putting ketchup on these?' she asked.

'Nope. You do whatever you like.'

Before either of them could actually start eating their food, a dazzling flash of white light from outside almost blinded them. It was over in a second, but it left a weird visual echo, where Selene felt like she kept re-seeing it. She blinked a few times to get her vision back, but even though the white flash had been fleeting, the aftermath of it seemed to have left a white glow on everything in the diner.

'What the hell was that?' she muttered. Almost everyone else in the diner said the same thing. And they were all looking around for an explanation.

Paige stared out of the window again and whispered something that sounded like, *"What's that?"*

Everyone in the diner started panicking. Voices were raised, chairs scraped back on the floor. People were staring through the window at what Paige had already seen. Selene turned her head to get a look at what had gotten everyone so intrigued.

A huge wall of fire, fifty metres high, was heading their way. It stretched as wide as the eye could see. As it raced towards the diner, it engulfed everything in its way. Buildings, cars, people, street-lamps, nothing evaded it. And within two seconds of Selene seeing it, it swept through the diner, destroying everything and everyone in it. It turned furniture to ash. It melted the skin off the staff and the customers, turned their bones into dust, and wiped the diner off the face of the earth. All in less than a second.

## Fifty-Two

A week in Purgatory was a long time. Long enough for Jasmine, Elvis and Rex to fully heal from their gunshot wounds, with a little help from the Eye of the Moon. The mental scars were far from healed though. The loss of Sanchez was difficult for everyone, particularly Flake.

News outlets still had no idea who was responsible for the mass culling of world leaders, although it was unanimously believed that Flake had murdered the US president, with the Bourbon Kid as her accomplice. There was a great deal of speculation about the involvement of the Russians, on account of their president being the only major world leader still alive. The fact he had fired nukes at several countries who had lost their leaders only made him look more guilty. One news outlet was even claiming Flake was a Russian spy, or the Russian leader's secret lover, on account of her track record for dating pudgy-faced men.

Every country was suspicious of their enemies. And all the new leaders were paranoid they might be killed next. That feeling of unease and distrust spread onto the streets of many major cities. All over the world, in cities not destroyed by Russian nukes, there was a fight for survival. Overnight, food became scarce. People were living without gas and electricity, clean water, fuel for their cars, and chocolate. Gangs of thugs were looting stores. The strong were killing the weak. The whole world, with the exception of Russia, and a handful of smaller countries, had become a lawless hellhole. Smalltalk, flirting and handshakes were becoming a thing of the past, replaced by rape, murder and early signs of cannibalism.

Since the passing of the tsunami, the ocean had returned to its own domain. It gave the gang time to fix up the research centre on Medicine Island. There was plenty of ocean filth to clean away, and more than a few dead fish. A few people from Hell were summoned to assist with the project. Plumbers, electricians, cleaners, gardeners, anyone who could help tidy up the island was given a brief holiday from Hell to work on the research centre. Most of them were in Hell because they had been overcharging customers. That couldn't happen on this job because they weren't getting paid. One of the most useful helpers was Eric Einstein, the fuzzy-haired scientist who had built the travel portal in Purgatory. He oversaw the installation of everything from basic electricity to internet and satellite receivers.

In the quieter moments when no one else was paying attention, Rex would wander into the desert outside Purgatory. Even though he knew it was futile, he kept making calls to Selene. Her phone was dead. Deep down, Rex knew it wasn't just the phone. Selene was gone and not coming back, just like Paige, and like Sanchez. People all over the world had lost loved ones. It was a hard time for everyone.

At two o'clock one afternoon, Rex was sitting on a stool in Purgatory drinking coffee when his phone rang for the first time in over a week. His heart missed a beat. He naively hoped it would be Selene. It wasn't. It was Alexis Calhoon. He took the call anyway, grateful to speak to someone different.

'Alexis, hi.'

'Hello Rex. I'm sorry for the radio silence. As you know, a lot of shit has been going down. How are you guys? Is everyone safe?'

Rex took a sip of his coffee before replying. 'Well, I'm guessing you know about Sanchez?'

'Yes. The whole thing was a mess. I'm so sorry. How's Flake?'

'She's shaken up. We all are. But she's pulling through. She didn't kill the president, y'know.'

'I never thought she did. Apparently she did shoot the First Lady though.'

'Yeah, that was an accident. Did you know Jasmine and Elvis got shot too?'

'By Flake?'

'No, by a bunch of agents that tracked them using those rings you gave them.'

'Say again?'

'Those rings you dished out from the president. They had tracking devices in them. A bunch of government spooks followed Elvis and Jas to the hideout of that Zero fella you sent them to find. The spooks wiped out Zero and his people, and tried their best to get rid of Elvis and Jas too. Jasmine took a few in the gut but she's back on her feet now.'

'I'm so sorry, Rex. I had no idea.'

'I know you didn't. Who gave you the rings? Was it Navan Douglas?'

'It was.'

'And he's now the president. Everything worked out well for him, didn't it?'

'It did,' Calhoon said evenly. 'I'm not convinced he planned it that way though. He's totally out of his depth.'

'He's lucky we haven't killed him yet.'

'I realise that, but Rex, there's another job come up. It's *from* Navan Douglas, but I'm really hoping you'll take it. It's important, and it's a job only you guys can do. Would you be interested?'

'Go on.'

'The Russians have grown in strength off the back of all that's happened. The rest of the world is at their mercy. They could wipe out the West in an afternoon if they really went for it. Our intelligence is indicating that there is a very real possibility they will launch another nuclear strike any day now.'

Rex knew what was coming. 'You want us to kill the Russian president?'

'Yes. It's not ideal, but it looks like it's our only play, our only option. We need to eliminate him, and leave a message so that whoever takes over from him knows that if they attack us, we can get to them too. How would you feel about a job like that?'

'That sounds like *something*,' said Rex. 'Something very risky.'

'Could it be done?'

Rex looked around him. He was still alone. Purgatory was a quiet place. The world was a quiet place. Having recently lost a chance at a life with Selene, he really had nothing to lose. 'Fuck it,' he said. 'We've killed the Devil and the Four Horsemen of the Apocalypse. This should be a piece of cake.'

Calhoon breathed a sigh of relief on the other end of the phone. 'Great. I'll let the new president know. When do you think you can do it?'

'I'll have to check with the others, then I'll get back to you. But, Alexis, there's one thing I'd like to discuss with you before you go.'

'Shoot.'

'That guy Zero that you sent Elvis and Jasmine to assassinate. He told them some interesting stuff, right before your people assassinated him.'

'They heard him talk?'

'Yeah, turns out the guy's no hypnotist at all. What he said was that most of the world leaders are descendants of Atlantis. That sound reasonable to you?'

'Atlantis? Did he have any evidence to back that up?'

'No, but he claimed the Atlanteans run the world. And our man Jacko in Purgatory has confirmed that the rulers of Atlantis were power-hungry narcissists, and they're not extinct.'

'I guess if Jacko says it, it's got some credence. He's in the know, isn't he?'

'He has a hotline to God, so yeah. Now, there's something else I gotta tell you. Six months ago when Zero broke into the president's hotel room wearing the invisible coat, he said he saw the president jerking off to a kiddy snuff movie at a circus.'

'A what? Kiddy snuff movie?' Calhoon sounded bewildered. 'Can it be proved? Do you believe it?'

'I do believe it, because I was recently on the set of one of those snuff movies. It was at a circus, and they were killing kids in the name of entertainment. It was being streamed out to an audience of perverts.'

Calhoon let out a deep sigh. 'And you think the president was one of them?'

'I don't know, but it's possible. I saw some faces watching it on a big screen, but I didn't recognise any of them. And they all disappeared just after me and JD showed up.'

'Circus vampires? Jesus, Rex. This just gets worse.'

Rex took another sip of his coffee. 'Jacko says the Atlanteans did a deal with the vampires hundreds of years ago. They used the vampires as assassins to hunt down and kill anyone that threatened the Atlantean rule. In return, the vampires were given their own city, a city that was never to be included on any maps.'

'Santa Mondega?'

'Exactly. It looks like the elites, the most powerful people in the world were all Atlanteans, up until recently anyway.'

Calhoon went quiet for a moment. As usual, she was quick to figure things out. 'Is it possible the vampires have killed the elites?'

'You tell me, General. I haven't had time to think about it. It's been a rough week. But out of interest, have you checked Navan Douglas for gills and webbed feet?'

'Gills and webbed feet?'

'Yeah, that's how you can tell if they're from Atlantis. Maybe if you can check the autopsies of any of the high-profile victims, you could confirm it? Any of those senators, or even the president? You can get a look at the bodies, can't you?'

Calhoon paused again, taking a moment to let the revelations sink in. 'Give me some time,' she said eventually. 'I'll look into it. While I'm doing that perhaps you can talk to the others about assassinating the Russian president?'

Rex heard movement over his shoulder. He looked around and saw Elvis walk in through the portal from Medicine Island.

'Hang on, Alexis. Let me put you on speaker.' Rex put his phone on speaker so Elvis could join in the conversation.

'Yo, Elvis, I got Alexis on the phone. She wants us to assassinate the Russian president. What do you think?'

Elvis walked up to the bar, reached over it and grabbed a bottle of Shitting Monkey beer. He cracked the lid off with his teeth, took a swig, then answered the question. 'I don't see why not. But it'll have to be tomorrow. It's burgers and beers on the beach tonight. Flake's cooking.'

'That sounds like fun,' Calhoon replied. 'Tell you what, I'll call you again in the morning and let you know what's what, okay?'

'Sounds good, General,' said Rex. 'We'll be ready.'

## Fifty-Three

### Part Eight – The Russian

The research centre on Medicine Island was finally beginning to look like a home, not just for Flake but for Elvis, Jasmine, Rex, JD and Goober the dog. The gang had a place to call their own. And it was better than the Tapioca.

The first night in the new home had to be a party, because that's the rules. Jacko joined the gang on the beach for burgers, sausages, chicken, fries and salad, all cooked and prepared by Flake. There was also plenty of alcohol too, courtesy of the never-ending supply in Purgatory.

For several hours everyone let loose and had a good time. A beach barbecue with music and good friends was just what was needed after all the crazy shit that had gone down. Eventually, when the night sky drew in, and all the food was long gone, Jacko headed back to Purgatory with a few crates of empty bottles.

Flake hadn't had as much to drink as everyone else, but she was definitely feeling a little tipsy, so shortly after Jacko left, she headed back to the medical centre to clean up the new kitchen. The beach party and the alcohol had helped her to forget about the loss of Sanchez for a few hours. When the sting of loss did come back, she was glad that it was Goober who was beside her. Flake liked to think he followed her around because she was his favourite person, rather than just his best chance for more food. With the devoted dog by her side Flake was beginning to feel normal again.

Cleaning the kitchen with help from Goober and his penchant for licking food stains off the floor was therapeutic in its own way too. It wasn't hard to make it look brand new again, because it *was* brand new. It took her and Goober less than half an hour to have the place almost spotless. When there were only a handful of plates left to wash up, someone finally joined her, although not to offer any help. Jasmine, slightly worse for wear and wearing just a black bra and panties, poked her head around the kitchen door.

'Hey, Flake, what'cha doing?'

'Just cleaning up.'

Jasmine stepped inside the sparkling clean kitchen. She was wobbly on her feet, and feeling around like a blind person. 'Need a hand?'

'No, it's okay. I'm almost done.'

'Good,' said Jasmine, 'because we're all going skinny dipping. You coming?'

'You're *all* going?' said Flake, eyebrows raised.

'Yep, don't be a square!'

'A square?' Flake groaned. 'What are you, twelve?'

'At least,' Jasmine replied with a drunken smile. Then she turned around a few times looking for the door. Eventually, after she managed to grab hold of the door frame she staggered back out into the corridor and headed back to the beach while slurring the words to Neil Diamond's, "Red Red Wine".

Flake took a moment to think about what might be occurring on the beach. Knowing Jasmine and Elvis, skinny dipping probably did mean getting completely naked. That wasn't something Flake generally did in public. Or even among her close friends. She'd seen Jasmine naked a bunch of times. Who hadn't? And she'd seen Elvis's dick more times than she could remember, simply because it was often in Jasmine's hand, or he was pissing up against something. She'd never seen Rex or JD naked. And none of the guys had ever seen her without her clothes, bar one incident months ago when JD and Elvis saw her in her underwear.

She thought about it for a minute. A beach skinny dip could be fun.

No. No way. Definitely not. Bad idea. The sea would be cold. Plus, she'd been drinking and would probably regret it in the morning.

She filled the sink with warm water and began washing a plate that was covered in grease and barbecue sauce. Skinny dipping. She just didn't have the nerve for it. It would be liberating though. She had never done it before, after all.

'Yo, Flake!'

Rex walked into the kitchen. He was wearing a pair of black jeans, but his shirt was long gone. The man had muscles on his muscles. Flake glanced at his ripped torso momentarily then looked back at her dirty plate.

'I'm just washing up,' she said.

'Come on, we're going for a midnight swim.'

'Yeah, Jasmine just told me.'

'Then what are you waiting for?'

'I told you. I'm washing up.'

'Don't be a prude. Everyone's doing it.'

'Jasmine said you were all skinny dipping.'

'That's right.'

'As in, completely naked?'

'Yep.' Rex's slurred voice took on a slightly more serious tone. 'Flake, you've got a great body. Nothing to be embarrassed about. We're all friends here. And the state the world is in right now, I think we could all do with letting our hair down a bit!'

'I'll think about it.'

'Don't think too long. If the last week has taught me anything, it's that life is very short. If you're not careful you could miss all the fun stuff.'

Flake looked up at him and smiled. 'Yeah, I know.'

Rex smiled back in a way only drunk people can. 'Okay, I'll leave you to it.' With that, he left the kitchen to rejoin the others on the beach.

Flake turned back to her washing up, but before she'd wiped the first grease stain off the plate in her hand, something landed on the floor behind her. She leaned back from the sink and saw Rex's jeans on the floor. Then a pair of black boxers landed in the hallway outside the kitchen door.

Flake put the dirty plate down and walked over to the door. She poked her head around it. Sure enough Rex was naked and running along the corridor to the exit. He had a pretty great ass too. When he burst through the main door that led outside, the sound of people singing and laughing down on the beach filtered into the medical centre. Goober brushed past Flake's leg as he walked out of the kitchen. The dog didn't follow Rex. He strolled across the corridor into Flake's bedroom instead. He curled up in a basket at the end of the bed and closed his eyes. He'd certainly had enough.

Flake walked back to the sink and picked up another dirty plate. "Life *is* short," she thought. "Why am I washing up while everyone else is being silly and having fun?"

She finished washing the plate and set it down on the draining board.

*Oh hell, why not?*

She flung off her apron, peeled her T-shirt over her head, slipped out of her sneakers, dropped her cut offs and then raced after Rex in just her underwear. When she was halfway down the path to the beach she saw Rex running across the sand towards the ocean waves. It was dark but she could hear the others in the water cheering him on.

When Flake's feet touched the sand she went for it. Her bra came off easily. Pulling down her underwear meant slowing down a little in order to avoid tripping over, but what the hell, this was liberating. Free from all of her clothes, she ran into the ocean.

It was warmer than she expected.

'Woo-hoo! Flake, get you!' Jasmine cried.

Jasmine and Elvis were far enough into the ocean that the water was up to Elvis's waist. Rex waded out to the same area. The whole thing was much less embarrassing than Flake expected. Until that is, she saw Eric Einstein in the shallow water, wading towards her. He was only in up to his knees.

'Hi, Flake,' he said, waving at her.

'Oh hi,' she replied, before glaring at Jasmine and asking, 'What's he doing here?'

'This was his idea,' said Jasmine. 'He came down just after you left. And he made a bet that me and him could beat Rex and Elvis in a drinking game. Losers had to strip. Me and Eric lost, so then we all decided to go skinny dipping.'

'It's fun, right,' said Einstein, grinning at Flake. He was standing with his hands on his hips. He had a puny, pasty white body that practically glowed in the moonlight.

'Where's JD?' Flake asked, looking around.

'No idea,' said Jasmine. 'Elvis, do you know where JD went?'

Elvis shrugged. 'Haven't seen him.'

Rex dived down under the water and started swimming away. Flake decided to follow suit, especially with Einstein staring at her with his eyes bulging and his nostrils flared. As it turned out, swimming naked in the sea was just what she needed. As each minute passed she felt less self-conscious, and the fresh water and cool air seemed to sober her up a little. The only downer was Eric Einstein's presence and his constant ducking down under the water when he was close by. After a while everyone congregated together to sing some songs. The singing was bad. After a terrible rendition of, "Show Me the Way to Go Home", Rex came up with a better idea.

'Maybe we should play Marco Polo or something,' he suggested. 'Have we got anything we can use as a ball?'

'Best put that on our shopping list for Jacko,' said Elvis.

'Maybe we could play a game of tag?' Eric Einstein suggested. 'You have to slap someone on the ass and then they're IT.' He moved towards Flake, an excited look on his face. He slid his hand under the water towards her ass, but at the last moment, Rex reached over and grabbed his arm, pulling him away.

'Maybe tag's not such a great idea,' Rex said. 'And besides, I'm not sure Flake wants your hand on her ass.'

'Hey, I'll grab a coconut,' said Flake, spotting a coconut tree that was still upright on the edge of the woodland. 'We can play catch with one of those.'

She swam away from Eric, and when she neared the shore she ran out onto the beach and headed for the coconut tree. As she jogged across the sand, a voice in the darkness said her name.

'Flake, that you?'

She stopped and looked around. It didn't take long to spot the outline of a man approaching her from the woodland. It was JD. He was wearing jeans and a T-shirt.

'Oh. JD.' She inadvertently held her breath for a while before casually adding, 'Hi.'

'Caught you at a bad time?'

There were only two ways to deal with this situation. Cover up and die of embarrassment, or play it cool. Play it cool was definitely the only way to come out of the situation with any credibility.

'We're all skinny dipping,' she replied, wiping some wet hair away from her face and avoiding using that arm to cover herself. "I was just looking for a coconut that we could throw around.'

'Right.'

'You not joining us?'

'I was actually just looking for you.'

'Me? What for?'

'I've just been up by the waterfall. It looks great at night. Thought we could hang out up there.'

'The waterfall? Really?' Flake said. What she was really thinking was, "hang out with *me? Really?*" JD, the Bourbon Kid, the guy who never wanted to hang out with anyone, was asking *her* if she wanted to hang out.

'It's only a minute away,' he said, pointing into the woodland. 'I go there sometimes to get away from all the madness.'

Having a conversation with someone when you're naked and they're not, and they've never seen you naked before? Jeez, *awkward*. Flake wanted it over quick. But she also liked the idea of hanging out with JD, despite her lack of clothes. He'd been a rock for her since she'd lost Sanchez.

'Yeah, cool,' she said, as nonchalantly as possible. 'Okay. Let's do it.'

JD glanced down at Flake's naked body. 'Am I overdressed?' he asked.

'If we're going to a waterfall, then yes, you are.'

JD took her by the hand. 'Come on,' he said, leading her into the woodland. 'You're gonna like this.'

## Fifty-Four

'Wow, that was some night,' said Jasmine staring in the mirror at her reflection. She was in one of the freshly decorated bedrooms in their new home on Medicine Island. Elvis was still lying in bed, his hair a shaggy mess. He opened one eye and looked over at her. She was wearing gold hotpants and a tight-fitting pink sleeveless vest, and she was in the process of tying her hair back into a ponytail.

'Shit, I don't remember anything after the skinny dipping,' Elvis replied. He reached over to his bedside table and picked up a glass of water he'd put there the night before. He took a swig and felt the texture of his tongue change from "stale feet" to "damp carpet". 'How come you're up so early?'

'It's not early. It's nine o'clock.'

'That's early. We didn't go to bed until five.'

'Yes, well I've got to help Flake with the breakfast.'

'Huh?' Elvis rubbed his head. 'Since when did you ever help Flake with breakfast?'

'Since she hooked up with JD.'

'What?'

'Oh, come on. Keep up. Didn't you notice Flake went off to get a coconut and never came back.'

'A coconut?'

'To play catch with. She came skinny dipping with us, then she went back to the beach and vanished. JD never showed up either. I'm telling you, they totally did it last night. And I want the lowdown from Flake, so I'm helping her with breakfast. How does my ass look?'

Elvis checked Jasmine's ass. Then he shook his head. Why was he even looking? Her ass always looked great. 'Yeah, you look fine. Your ass is great. Hold on a sec, slow down. Flake and JD? Seriously?'

Jasmine turned around. 'We talked about it last night while you were asleep. Don't you remember anything?'

'I remember seeing Flake naked.'

'We talked about you not mentioning that.'

'Did we?'

'Yes, while you were asleep. Do you remember the game of truth or dare?'

'Oh God, no.'

'Yes. Remember when it was Rex's turn, and he chose a dare?'

Elvis closed his eyes and covered them with his hands. 'I just had a flashback.'

'Can you believe he did it?'

'No. Stop talking.'

'I've never seen a guy jerk off with a metal hand before.'

'For the love of God, stop talking.'

'I filmed it too. Totally got the evidence.'

Elvis took his hands away from his eyes. 'What were you saying about Flake and JD?'

Jasmine sat down on the edge of the bed and started putting on her sneakers. 'They hooked up. I poked my head around her door half an hour ago. She never slept in her room last night.'

'That doesn't mean they hooked up.'

'Then I looked in *his* room.'

Elvis perked up. 'You did?'

'They were fucking.'

'Shut. Up. No fuckin' way. You're bullshitting.'

'Nuh, uh,' said Jasmine, shaking her head. 'Why else would I be making breakfast? I've gotta hear all about it from Flake.'

'Can you let her do all the cooking?'

Jasmine finished tying her laces and leaned back to get a closer look at Elvis's face. 'Wow, you are grumpy this morning, aren't you?'

'No, I'm just tired.'

'I've got a few minutes. I can give you a morning blowie if you like?'

Elvis laid back on his pillow and closed his eyes. 'Can I pretend to be asleep?'

'Sure you can. Lay back and think about Rex jerking off with his metal hand.'

'Forget it. Go make the breakfast.'

'I'll call you when it's ready.'

Jasmine leaned over and gave Elvis a smacker on the lips, then dashed off to the kitchen to work out how to use the toaster.

When she arrived in the kitchen she was surprised to find it empty. Flake was late. This was unprecedented. Flake was always up early to make breakfast. The simple solution was to wake her up by playing some loud music. Jasmine connected her phone to a speaker on the kitchen sideboard and turned on the song, "People Get Up" by James Brown. Within ten seconds at least three voices had yelled out variations of the phrase, "Turn the fucking music off!"

Jasmine persevered, and eventually Flake showed up. She was wearing a dark blue, fluffy bathrobe. Her hair was a screwy mess, and she had dead zombie eyes.

'Morning Flake,' said Jasmine. 'I thought I'd make breakfast this morning. Want some?'

Flake ignored her and walked over to the speaker on the sideboard. She turned the volume right down until James Brown was a mere whisper.

'Big night last night, huh?' said Jasmine.

Flake grunted something that made no sense and headed back the way she came.

'I watched Rex jerk off with his metal hand,' Jasmine called after her. 'What did you do?'

Flake stopped just short of the doorway. She turned around and looked at Jasmine. 'What?' she muttered, squinting.

'I saw Rex jerk off with his metal hand. Can you top that?' Jasmine asked. 'You kind of disappeared when you went to get a coconut. I just wondered what you got up to?'

Flake sighed. 'I hooked up with JD. We did it four times. Anything else you want to know?'

'Hell, yeah. What was it like? Was it good?'

Flake nodded. 'Yep. You're gonna have to make breakfast for everyone because I'm going back to bed.' With that, Flake turned around and sleepwalked back to where she came from.

'Have a nice sleep,' Jasmine called after her.

Flake didn't reply. Jasmine contemplated the idea of making breakfast, but swiftly decided that there was now no need. She had the information she required. It was time to go back to bed. She tiptoed past JD's room and ducked back into the room she shared with Elvis. She stripped off again and slid into bed with him. He was fast asleep, so she snuggled up against his back and gave him an intimate squeeze to wake him up.

'They did it,' she whispered in his ear. 'Flake and JD. They did it. Four times.'

'Good for them. Can I sleep now?'

'Yeah, by the way, I didn't make you any toast, sorry.'

'Good.'

## Fifty-Five

At eleven a.m. Rex awoke to the sound of music coming from the kitchen. Julie Andrews to be precise, singing "The Sound of Music". It was the second time he'd been woken up. A few hours earlier it had been James Brown. Thankfully that hadn't lasted long. Julie Andrews on the other hand was showing no sign of shutting up. He sat upright in his bed. Ouch. Headache. Flashback to the night before.

'Shit.'

He closed his eye. A multitude of images from the previous night flashed through his mind. It had been quite an occasion. But he was now awake in his new bedroom, with no recollection of how he got there. He rolled out of bed, opened a chest of drawers and picked out a pair of boxers and a black vest, then grabbed some blue jeans from his closet. His clothes from the night before were somewhere else, possibly on the floor outside the kitchen where (if his memory served him correctly) he'd stripped off before going skinny-dipping. While he tied up the laces on his boots, the smell of coffee and bacon wafted into his room, accompanied by a new song, "Maid of Orleans" by Orchestral Manoeuvres in the Dark. The bacon was a sign that Flake was up.

Rex staggered out of his room, bumping into the door frame as he went. It was hard to walk in a straight line. While occasionally steadying himself by pressing his hand against the wall, he eventually arrived at the kitchen, where the music and the bacon smell were coming from. Flake was not there though. Elvis, Jasmine and JD were making the breakfast. Elvis was at the grill doing the bacon and eggs. Jasmine was laying the table, and JD was standing with his back up against a sideboard next to the toaster.

'Morning, folks,' said Rex. 'Any coffee going?'

'I'll get you one in a sec,' said Jasmine. 'Take a seat. How's your dick this morning?' The question was followed by sniggers from Elvis and JD.

'It's fine, thanks,' said Rex. 'How's your mouth?'

Jasmine was in the process of laying a knife down on the table. She stopped and stared at Rex, a puzzled look on her face. 'It's fine. Why?' she asked.

'You don't remember?'

'Remember what?'

Elvis stopped flipping rashers of bacon and looked around. JD perked up too.

'Where's Flake, anyway?' Rex asked.

'She's still in bed,' Elvis replied.

'Really? She left early last night though. She was barely in the sea five minutes.'

Jasmine brought Rex up to speed as she poured him a mug of coffee from a recently brewed jug. 'Flake's shagged out.'

'Excuse me?'

'She's been doing it all night. I'm surprised you didn't hear her.'

'She's been what?' He'd barely finished asking the question when the answer came to him. He stared at JD. 'No fuckin' way!'

'Four times,' said Jasmine, handing Rex his coffee. 'Flake's in a starfish pose in bed, fast asleep.'

'Ugh,' Rex groaned. 'That's too much information.'

Jasmine laughed. 'Remember truth or dare last night? You jerked off in front of me with your metal hand.'

Rex frowned. 'You don't remember what *you* did, do you?'

Jasmine walked over to help Elvis at the grill. 'The whole night's a blank after watching you pleasuring yourself,' she said, turning a sausage over with a set of metal tongs.

'Is it really?' said Rex, sniffing his coffee.

'Morning everybody!' a voice called out from behind Rex. The bright ginger perm belonging to Eric Einstein appeared in the doorway. The crazy scientist strolled into the kitchen with a beaming smile on his face. 'What's for breakfast?'

'Whatever you like,' said Rex, slapping the scientist on the shoulder. 'Did you have fun last night?'

'Best night ever,' Einstein replied. 'We should play Truth or Dare more often.'

The catch-up on the previous night's events was interrupted by Rex's cell phone ringing. He checked the display, saw it was Calhoon and answered it immediately.

'Alexis, how's it going?'

'Hi Rex. Are you guys ready to go?'

'Always, what's the plan?'

'We've got good information about the location of our primary target.'

'The short, fat guy with the crap haircut?'

'Yes, the Russian president. Now, listen, you didn't get this job from me or anyone in government, understand? Anything goes wrong and you're on your own.'

'Nice.'

'I know that's shit, but for the sake of the free world, we can't have the Russians thinking we had anything to do with this.'

'It's okay, Alexis, I understand.'

'Can you use your portal to get into his palace in Moscow?

'Yes, we can.'

'All we need you to do is get into the palace in the middle of the night. We figure it will be easier to get to him while he's asleep. Just cut his throat, stab him in the heart, whatever it takes. Quick in and out job. And leave a note saying, "End the war or we'll be back". Don't sign it though. I want whoever takes over from him as president to be paranoid, to not know who did it.' After a short pause for breath, Calhoon made a promise. 'I'll see to it that you're paid well for this, at some point anyway.'

'As long as it's not any more special rings from the president.'

'Definitely no rings, I swear.'

'Let me just check with the others.' Rex put the phone down by his side and covered it with his metal hand. 'Guys, Calhoon wants us to kill the Russian president tonight. Whadda ya say?'

Elvis spoke first. 'I'm in.'

Jasmine gave Rex a thumbs-up sign.

There was no response from JD. Rex looked at him. 'You in?'

JD shook his head. 'I've got plans.'

'Like what?' Rex asked, stunned.

'I like it here. I'm gonna hang out on the beach.'

Jasmine gasped. 'Oh my God. With Flake! JD and Flake, sittin' in a tree, F-U-C-K-I-N—'

JD interrupted her. 'You and Einstein can join us if you like.'

Jasmine frowned. 'Einstein? Why would I...' She stopped in mid-sentence as if suddenly remembering something from the night before. Einstein beamed a smile at her.

'Wanna borrow some mouthwash?' Rex asked Jasmine. Without waiting for a response from her, he returned to his call with Calhoon. 'General, I think me and Elvis and Jasmine can take care of this one. That okay?'

'What about the Bourbon Kid?' Calhoon asked.

'I think he's busy.'

'Really?'

'Yeah.'

Calhoon shrugged off any disappointment she might have felt. 'That's fine,' she said. 'Call me if you need anything. Thanks a lot.'

'No problem.'

'Oh, and Rex. One last thing. Can you tell Jasmine not to send me rude videos at four o'clock in the morning?'

'Jasmine sends you rude videos?'

'You didn't know?'

'No. Should I?'

'Uh, well, you were in it. Not something I particularly needed to see if I'm honest. Anyway, speak soon. And good luck tonight.'

## Fifty-Six

With the night drawing in and the moon shining over the calm ocean waters, JD and Flake found a secluded cliff on the upper part of the island. They sat down on the grass, drank beer and watched the ocean waves lap on the beach below. Medicine Island was a beautiful, relaxing place to be at night, especially with no one else around.

'I wouldn't have minded if you'd gone with the others,' Flake said, after several minutes of silence. 'It sounds like the Russian president deserves what's coming to him.'

'I'm sure he does,' JD agreed. 'But to be honest, I've done enough killing. I need a break from it all.'

Flake took a sip of her beer. 'Life's been crazy for too long, hasn't it?'

'Life's always crazy. You just have to enjoy the quiet moments when they come along.'

After another prolonged silence, Flake asked a question that had been on her mind for a while. 'I know you'll never get over Beth,' she said, cautiously, 'but after you lost her, was there a point where it started to get easier?'

'I'm over it.'

'Really?' Flake was surprised by the suddenness of his answer. He'd said it without giving it any thought.

'I made my peace with it after we killed Scratch. If you can't move on after that, you'll never move on.'

Flake smiled. 'We certainly gave Scratch a good death, didn't we?'

'You still thinking about Sanchez a lot?'

Flake stared at the grass by her feet. 'I feel guilty about it.'

'That'll pass. It's just part of the grieving process.'

'I know, but, he's not been gone long and I've already….. well…… you know.'

'Yeah.'

'Last night, was that just two friends getting drunk and hooking up, or what? I mean, what do you think? What are we doing here?'

JD flipped the question back on her. 'What do *you* think?' he asked.

Damn, he was hard to get an answer from. Flake felt she understood him better than the others did, but even so, she had no idea how he felt about what they were doing.

'You know,' she said, 'we've fought the undead, the Devil, Cain and the Four Horsemen and all that stuff, but what we did last night, that was the most alive I've ever felt. From the minute I stripped off to go skinny-dipping to the moment we woke up together this morning, that was the most amazing, crazy, unexpected night I've ever had.'

JD looked across at her, his mouth curling up at the corners. 'It was just a regular week night for me,' he said.

Flake elbowed him in the arm. 'Don't be a dick!'

He looked up at the moon and took a long pull on his beer, but he said nothing more, so Flake approached the subject from a different angle.

'If Jasmine wasn't with Elvis, would you have hooked up with her?'

JD put his beer down on the grass. 'What's with the Jasmine insecurity?'

Flake shrugged. 'Would you though?'

'No. I like Jasmine, but I've seen her pull a phone out of herself. And she's naked all the time. Whereas you, you're sexy when you're cooking, when you're kickin' some guy's ass, when you're sticking up for yourself, when you're calling people out on their shit. And yeah, when I saw you naked last night, that definitely did it for me.'

It was just the answer Flake was hoping for. 'I always thought you were cool,' she said. 'But I couldn't understand why, because you know, you're an asshole sometimes. But ever since I've known you, when you look at me, I fucking melt inside.'

She paused and thought about Sanchez and everything they'd been through together. 'I never had that with Sanchez,' she began carefully. 'And I don't think I really understood that until last night. Don't get me wrong. I loved him. Truly. But … I wonder if I loved him because he loved me and because he needed me, and because he definitely had the hots for me. And he made me laugh.' She smiled at a long-forgotten joke. 'And he was there—when I really needed him.' She looked up at the stars. 'But he and I never had what you and Beth had.'

JD stared out at the ocean again as he considered his response. 'Me and Beth met at a crucial point in our lives,' he said, after a long pause. 'Neither of us had anyone else. We went through a lot of rough times when we were apart, and also when we were together. The relationship was never easy. But you and me, we're sitting on a desert island together, drinking beers and looking up at the stars like we don't have a care in the world. We've earned this. The things we've been through together over the years, you and me, we've done a lot. Sanchez needed you, and Beth needed me, and we were there for them through thick and thin. I don't need you, but I like being with you *more* than I like being with anyone else.'

'I like being with you too.'

They leaned in and kissed under the light of the moon. It all felt right. When they parted, Flake asked him another question.

'Did you know I lost my mom when I was sixteen?'

'No, I didn't know that.'

'I never even knew my dad. After my mom died, it took me a while to work out what to do with my life. Then after I turned seventeen, I went travelling in the hope of finding my true self, and working out who I wanted to be. Somehow I ended up as a waitress in Santa Mondega, and I met Sanchez and all you guys. You were the first real family I had after my mom died.'

'It's a crazy ass family, that's for sure.'

Flake took another swig of beer only to find the bottle was empty. Instead of reaching for another she took a moment to stare at the label on the bottle. It was a picture of a defecating monkey. 'You know, when Sanchez was being an ass, I often thought about leaving him,' she said, as if the monkey on the label had reminded her of some of Sanchez's worst attributes.

'Really? I never thought you would.'

'Every couple have their rough times though, right?'

'I guess.'

'Do y'know why I never left?' She picked at the label on the bottle. 'It's because if I did, I would have had to leave the Tapioca, and then I would have lost all my friends. And I might never have seen *you* again. I always thought about that when I'd had an argument with Sanchez.'

JD nodded like he understood. 'Do you remember the first time we met?' he asked.

Flake laughed. 'Yeah, you pointed a gun at me, and sprayed black paint over my face.'

'I was going to kill you. But then I saw you had that book, the one with no name that killed vampires, and you'd painted it black. Your plan was to use it to save Sanchez from Jessica the vampire queen.'

'That's right.'

'I knew right then you were cool. You and me, we saved Santa Mondega that night. Maybe even stopped the vampires from taking over the world.'

'Yeah, but then you disappeared, and Sanchez offered me a job at the Tapioca. Plus, you were in love with Beth.'

'It's a long time ago.'

JD reached over and slid his hand around the back of her neck. He pulled her in close and kissed her again. Flake melted into his arms, just like she had the night before. Island life was good.

## Fifty-Seven

Finding the Russian president was never going to be easy. The skills of Eric Einstein were imperative if it was to work. The crazy scientist had previously demonstrated excellent capabilities when it came to hacking into security systems in places all over the world. While Elvis, Rex and Jasmine were sitting at the bar in Purgatory, drinking beer and chatting to Jacko, Einstein was at his usual table, tapping away on his laptop computer, searching for maps and images of the Russian president's palace.

In readiness for the assassination attempt, the gang were all dressed to kill. Elvis had on a slim black suit. Rex was in jeans and a brown leather waistcoat, and Jasmine had gone for a black catsuit, which looked like a gimp suit but without the mask.

It was approximately 2 a.m. Russian time when Einstein made a breakthrough. 'Okay people, I've got a way in,' he announced, sitting back in his chair with a self-satisfied look on his face. 'Are you ready?'

'As we'll ever be,' said Rex, standing up. 'This is it then. Is this asshole on his own?'

'I can't be one hundred percent sure if he's alone,' said Einstein. 'But based on the images available to me, it's a safe bet he is. At most he'll have one or two people with him. From what I've read, this guy is a paranoid nutcase. He doesn't like anyone near him at the best of times, especially people with guns. He knows a lot of people in his country hate him, so he's terrified of being assassinated. That should make it easier for you to get to him without encountering any armed guards.'

'Wow,' said Jasmine. 'You're quite impressive sometimes, Eric.'

'I know,' said Einstein, winking at her. 'The location I've chosen for your arrival in the palace is a bathroom not far from the president's bedroom.'

'How near is not far?' asked Rex. 'Is it an en suite?'

'No,' Einstein replied. 'I don't think he has an en suite. I've got you a bathroom at the end of a corridor that I *think* leads to his bedroom.'

'You *think?*' said Elvis.

'Take a look for yourself,' said Einstein, pointing at his screen. 'I've done my best. You're just gonna have to hunt him down when you get there. It shouldn't be hard. According to the national spy network, he smells of baked beans most of the time.'

Elvis walked over to Einstein's table and peered over his shoulder at the screen, which was showing crystal-clear colour footage of a corridor, but not much else. 'That's it?' he groaned.

'I'll be right here watching everything while you're there,' said Einstein. 'Let me worry about the cameras. You just do your thing. And don't forget to turn your earpiece on.'

Elvis tapped his ear. 'It's on.'

'This'll be fun,' said Jasmine. 'I've never been in a real palace before. I mean, I lived in the Beaver Palace for years but I don't think it counts as a real palace.'

'The Kremlin palace is probably very similar,' said Elvis. 'Just with less jizz on the carpets.' He walked back to the bar, picked up his beer and downed what was left of it. 'Are we ready to go, or what?' he asked the others.

'Let's do it,' said Rex. He picked up a semi-automatic pistol from the bar and tucked it into a holster by his ribcage. He also had a hunting knife on his belt. Jasmine had a pistol holstered on each hip. Elvis was packing two Glocks inside his jacket and a knife on his belt. He also had a length of rope wrapped around his shoulder.

'Good luck, guys,' said Jacko as he cleared their empties from the bar. 'Just remember, if anything looks off, come right back. Don't take any chances.'

'Yeah, yeah, we know,' said Rex. 'Elvis, check your earpiece one last time.'

'Einstein,' Elvis called out. 'Whisper sweet nothings in my ear.'

Einstein slipped a headset on, which looked disastrous on his curly ginger hair. He spoke into the mouthpiece. 'Ground control to Major Elvis.'

'Yep. It works,' Elvis confirmed.

Rex barked one more order at Einstein. 'You watch those cameras, and if you see us walking into any trouble you tell Elvis, right.'

'Yes sir,' Einstein replied, with a mock salute.

'I'm not fucking kidding,' said Rex. 'Once we go through that portal you can't get up and go for a piss or anything. Your eyes are glued to those screens. Understand?'

Einstein saluted again, which didn't impress Rex.

'He knows what he's doing,' said Jasmine defending the crazy scientist. 'So quit giving him a hard time. Let's go.'

The three of them walked over to the portal. They looked badass.

'Good luck!' Jacko called out.

Jasmine swivelled around and blew Jacko a kiss. 'Don't worry,' she said. 'We'll be in and out of there.'

Elvis stood in front of the portal door, pistol drawn, ready to shoot at anyone who might be taking a piss on the other side. Jacko opened the portal from behind the bar. The door slid to the side and they were greeted by the sight of a huge bathroom where all the fittings were made of gold. The floor and walls were made of black marble.

'No one in there!' Elvis announced with a sigh of relief.

Jacko called out from behind the bar. 'I'll close it up behind you. But I'll make sure it's open again before you come back.'

Elvis stepped into the bathroom first, his gun pointed at a door on the opposite wall. Jasmine and Rex followed him in, then Jacko closed the portal back up.

'Wow,' said Jasmine, looking around at the bathroom. 'Sanchez would have loved this place.'

'Good job he ain't here,' said Elvis. 'He'd have stunk the place out already.'

'Sssshhhh,' said Rex. 'We gotta be quiet, remember.' He walked straight up to the exit door and turned the handle. Elvis and Jasmine pointed their guns at the door, waiting for Rex to open it and step aside. This was some serious shit.

Rex pulled the door open a few inches and peered around it. 'Fuck,' he whispered.

'What is it?' Elvis asked.

'Long corridors.'

'Should we split up?' Jasmine asked.

'Are you fucking nuts?' Rex whispered. 'We're sticking together!'

'After you then,' said Elvis.

Rex pulled the door open and the three of them stepped out into a corner where two corridors met. Everything looked ludicrously expensive. Even the floors were a gold colour. The red walls were adorned with gold-framed paintings every few metres. All of the paintings were of ugly old men with creepy eyes.

'Which way do we go?' Jasmine asked.

They had two options. Go straight ahead to a set of golden doors, or go right to a set of red doors with gold trims.

'This way, I reckon,' said Rex pointing to the red doors on the right.

'What does Einstein think?' Jasmine whispered to Elvis.

'He ain't said shit,' Elvis replied. 'Can you see a camera anywhere?'

'No,' said Jasmine. 'Does it matter though? Isn't Einstein disabling the cameras?'

'I'm not sure. He just said not to worry about them.'

'Let's just get a fucking move on,' said Rex. 'If the cameras are still on, then this could be a very short mission.'

'Einstein knows what he's doing,' said Jasmine. 'Stop fussing, and start moving!'

Rex did as Jasmine suggested. He moved briskly towards the set of red doors, which were about fifty metres away. Jasmine followed closely behind, admiring the paintings as she went and looking for anything she could take as a souvenir. Elvis covered the rear, pointing his gun back down the corridor in case anyone showed up behind them. They arrived at the big red doors without encountering any obstacles.

Rex, gun in hand, reached for the door handle. And at the same time, Elvis finally heard Einstein's voice in his ear. The scientist said just one word.

*'Shit!'*

## Fifty-Eight

'Shit?' said Elvis, repeating what Einstein had just muttered in his ear. 'What does that mean? Please tell me you've just spilt coffee on yourself.'

Rex held off opening the door. 'What's going on?' he asked.

'Shush!' said Elvis.

'Don't shush me.'

Elvis ignored Rex and concentrated on what was coming through on his earpiece.

*'There's a guard heading your way!'* said Einstein.

'Fuck,' Elvis whispered. 'Einstein says we've got company.'

Rex stepped away from the red doors. Jasmine was already pointing her pistols down the corridor. Elvis and Rex lined up on either side of her, guns at the ready. The sound of footsteps floated around the corner towards them. Someone was heading to the bathroom they had just come out of.

'What do you wanna do?' Elvis asked.

Jasmine kicked him in the shin. 'Shush.' She stared disapprovingly at her two comrades. 'Did neither of you two bring a silencer?' she whispered.

Neither Elvis nor Rex had noticed before but Jasmine had a silencer on the end of each of her pistols.

'Dammit,' Rex whispered. 'Can you handle this, Jas?'

'Obviously.'

The owner of the approaching footsteps revealed himself as he rounded the corner up ahead. He was six feet tall and looked like a soldier. He was wearing a smart, dark blue uniform, a silly oversized hat that had a flat top, and epic boots that were almost knee high. Neither Rex nor Elvis got a good look at his face because Jasmine, ever the lethal shooter, put one right through his nose before he even saw them. The smack of his head on the floor sounded like someone dropping a billiard ball.

'Nice shooting,' said Elvis, squeezing Jasmine's ass to demonstrate added approval.

'Do we just leave the body there?' Jasmine asked. 'Or should we hide him in the bathroom?'

'Fuck it. Let's just find the president and get this done,' said Rex. He grabbed the handle on the door again and twisted it. It wasn't locked, so he shoved it open and marched into the room on the other side, waving his gun around, looking for anyone worth shooting at. Elvis and Jasmine snuck in after him, pistols at the ready.

The room was big, and its centrepiece was a long (actually *fucking* long) marble table with a seat at either end. The walls were white and undecorated, with the exception of a giant painting of the president himself. The image had beady eyes that stared directly at the three intruders.

Jasmine closed the door behind them. 'What now?' she asked.

Right at that moment, a short, tubby man in a pair of black, silky pyjamas and red slippers walked into the room through an arched opening on the left. His hair was badly thinning on top but he'd let it grow a bit on the sides so he could sweep it over to hide his baldness. His face looked kind of squashed too, like he was wearing stockings on his head to disguise his features in readiness to rob a bank. He stared at the three intruders for half a second before his eyes revealed that he'd seen their guns and knew he was in deep shit. If he'd really been wearing stockings on his head they would have split. He yelled something in Russian that sounded like, "moye litso ogromno". Then he turned tail and minced his way back through the archway into a lounge area. The lounge had a couple of red armchairs in it and a coffee table. There was a bottle of vodka on the table and a tall glass that was half full of the stuff.

Jasmine was about to shoot the little tyrant, but Rex ran after him and inadvertently obstructed her view. Elvis lowered his gun and ran after Rex.

'Is it him?' Jasmine asked, chasing after Elvis.

'YES!' Rex yelled. 'It's him.'

The tubby Russian didn't get far before Rex grabbed him and dragged him back through the archway over to the long table. One quick shove and the president's forehead smashed into the edge of it.

Elvis leapt up onto the table and walked along it until he was in front of the balding dictator, then he kicked him in the face. The terrified little weasel whimpered and begged for mercy, or possibly more vodka. It was hard to know for sure what he was saying. Rex grabbed the Russian by his hair and stood him upright.

'Anyone know what he's saying?' Elvis asked.

'I used to know a little Russian,' said Jasmine.

'Really?' Rex asked, surprised.

'Yeah, his name was Ivan, he was a client at the Beaver Palace. 'The only word I learnt from him was "minyet".

'Minyet?' said Rex. What does that mean?'

'Blowjob, I think.'

'For fuckssake!' Rex slammed the Russian president's head down hard onto the marble table. It knocked the little bastard out cold. His body went limp and became remarkably heavy for such a little person. Rex let go of him and he slid to the floor like a drunk break-dancer.

'Is he dead?' Jasmine asked.

'Unconscious,' Rex replied.

Elvis unhooked the length of rope from around his shoulder. 'Let's hang him from something.'

The three of them looked around for something to hang their captive from. Nothing caught anyone's eye.

'What do you normally hang people from?' Jasmine asked.

'I don't know,' said Elvis. 'Never done it before.'

'Then why bring the bloody rope?' said Rex, exasperated.

'Oh, fuck it,' said Elvis. 'Let's just shoot him in the head and get the fuck out of here.'

'Has Einstein said anything? Have we been compromised?' Rex asked.

Elvis shook his head. 'Not a word. Not since he warned us about the guard in the hallway.'

'Okay. We've got time then,' said Rex. 'Let's take him to his bedroom.'

'What for?' said Elvis.

'Because that's where people always kill themselves. No one does it in the dining room.'

'Are you sure?'

'No, but can you do just do as I say for once?'

'Hang on a sec,' said Elvis. 'Why are we making it look like suicide anyway?'

Jasmine left them bickering and hot-footed over to a big black door at the back of the lounge. She pulled it open and pressed a light switch on the wall inside. 'Found it!' she called out. 'There's a big four-poster bed in here.'

'Help me carry him,' Rex said to Elvis.

'Can't you lift him on your own?' Elvis asked.

'I can, but he's short, fat and heavy, so grab his legs and we'll carry him together.'

Rex and Elvis lifted up the chunky tyrant and carried him into to the bedroom. Jasmine was on the bed staring up at a mirror on the ceiling.

'I've got an idea,' she said, sitting upright and rolling back off the bed so they could chuck the unconscious fat guy onto it. 'Why don't we get the guard from outside and bring him in? Make it look like he killed his boss, then killed himself?'

Rex and Elvis slung the unconscious despot onto the bed. 'That's a pretty good idea,' said Rex. 'Frame the guard. I like it.'

'Okay,' said Elvis. 'I'm into that. Let's go get him. Jas, can you keep an eye on this asshole in case he wakes up?'

'Sure thing, sweetie.'

'Great. We'll be right back.'

Rex and Elvis exited the room and ran back down the corridor to where the dead guard was splayed out on the floor in a pool of blood. Rex picked up the guard's big hat and tucked it under his arm, then they grabbed a leg each and dragged his body back along the corridor to the president's apartment. The guard's wounded head left an unfortunate trail of blood that led all the way up to the president's private quarters.

'That blood kind of fucks things up, doesn't it?' said Rex.

'Who cares?' said Elvis. 'It'll just confuse whoever finds the bodies. That's no bad thing, right?'

'I suppose.'

They dragged the body through the dining room and the boozing room and into the bedroom. Jasmine had already removed the president's pyjamas and positioned him in a rather compromising pose on the bed, with one hand behind his head and the other down by his crotch. Without his slippers on, he had a pair of hideous webbed feet. Typically, that wasn't the freakiest thing. Jasmine had also found an inflatable male sex doll, which she had placed on the bed with him. It had a pathetic inflated penis, and openings in its mouth and ass for penetration.

'Yikes!' said Elvis wincing. 'That's not a pretty sight.'

'Where did you find the sex doll?' Rex asked.

'It was under the bed with all his other sex gear.'

Elvis leaned down and sniffed the sex doll. He recoiled in disgust. 'Woah, the ass on that thing smells like baked beans.'

'For fuckssake,' said Rex. 'Why are you sniffing the ass? Forget it, don't answer that. Can we just get on with this?'

'What exactly is it we're doing now?' Elvis asked, rubbing his nose.

'Well,' said Jasmine, 'I figured we could strip the guard off too and lay him next to the president, make it look like they were spooning. Then we can shoot the president in the back of the head and it'll look like his mate shot him while he was bumming him.'

Rex and Elvis were both taken aback.

'You thought that up while we were outside?' said Rex.

'Uh huh. I've done this sort of thing before, you know, for role-playing when I was a hooker. I didn't do it with dead people though.'

'How does the sex doll fit in with this?' Elvis asked.

'I thought we could have the president bumming the sex doll, which adds motive, like the guard was jealous of the attention the sex doll was getting.'

'Or maybe it'll look like the sex doll was the killer?' said Rex, ridiculing the idea.

Jasmine scowled at him. 'Don't be silly. This is serious stuff.'

Elvis pursed his lips for a while, then spoke. 'You know, I'm really proud of you, Jas. This is excellent work.' He looked closer at the naked president. 'Those webbed feet are a bit rank aren't they? Has he got gills too?'

'He has,' said Jasmine. 'Wanna take a look?'

'No thanks.'

'But you like my plan?

'Yep,' said Elvis. 'It's a winner.'

'Okay, what the hell,' said Rex, tossing the guard's hat onto the floor. 'Let's get this guy's clothes off.'

Over the course of the next five minutes, the three of them undressed the guard and manoeuvred him into various different positions with the president and the sex doll. They took photos of each scenario to show to people at dinner parties, then when they found a position they all liked, Jasmine pressed her silencer against the back of the president's head and blew his brains out. Blood splashed all over the pillow and the sex doll. Jasmine wiped the gun on the bedsheets to get rid of her fingerprints, and planted it in the guard's hand.

'Great job,' said Elvis, admiring the work of art they had created with the two dead Russians and the blow-up doll. 'Now let's get the fuck out of here.'

'Wait a sec,' said Rex. 'Calhoon wanted us to leave a note saying we'll be back if they try any more of that nuclear shit.'

'Can you write in Russian then?' Elvis asked.

Rex closed his eyes. 'No.'

'Then what the fuck are you talking about? Let's get outta here.'

As they were leaving the bedroom, a crackling noise broke out in Elvis's ear, followed by Einstein's voice.

'Guys, I don't know where you are,' Einstein said, 'but they're onto us. I've been booted out of the security system, which means the Russians are back in it. If they follow protocol, they should look back at all the footage they missed while they were locked out of the system. If they don't already know you're there, they will pretty soon. Jacko says head for the portal, and be quick!'

## Fifty-Nine

Rex, Elvis and Jasmine left the Russian president's private quarters and headed back out to the corridor. Within seconds they were confronted by the sound of marching boots coming from the adjacent corridor. It sounded like a whole platoon was headed their way. Nothing needed to be said. All three of them heard it.

Jasmine was the quickest to react, sprinting way ahead of Elvis and Rex. She was lighter on her feet so she could run faster without making much noise. When she arrived outside the bathroom she looked around and saw a troop of soldiers marching towards her. They were all in military uniform, black shirts and pants with a red lining, stupid big hats, high boots. And every single one of them had a pistol holstered on his hip.

There was one soldier marching ahead of the rest, like he was the leader. He had a silver moustache and a square jaw. He stopped marching and stared at Jasmine, his mouth agape. The others all followed his lead and stopped immediately. Captain Square-jaw pointed at Jasmine and yelled something in a deep, booming Russian accent. It sounded like, "Posmotrite na sis'ki etoy zhenshchiny. Oni udivitel'ny". Jasmine had no idea what it meant, but it sounded aggressive. She opened the bathroom door and ducked inside, leaning her ass against the door to keep it open for Rex and Elvis.

Elvis and Rex arrived outside the bathroom with guns drawn. Elvis fired off three quick shots at the gobsmacked soldiers, then shoved Jasmine fully into the bathroom and leapt in with her before any of the Russians could fire back. Rex backed in after him, holding up his metal hand to catch any bullets that might come their way. Three of the soldiers in the front row hit the deck after being shot by Elvis. That snapped their comrades back into reality. They stopped staring at Jasmine's ass and unholstered their pistols. Rex kicked the bathroom door shut just before the Russians opened fire and peppered the door with bullets.

The portal was already open at the back of the bathroom. Jasmine sprinted through it into Purgatory with Elvis and Rex close behind. The portal entrance closed up as soon as they were through.

'Phew, that was close,' said Elvis.

'Yeah, let's not do that again,' said Rex, strolling up to the bar and accepting a bottle of beer from Jacko.

'Everything go to plan?' Jacko asked.

'We killed him,' said Elvis, hopping onto a stool next to Rex.

Jasmine moved in beside Elvis and slid her arm around his waist. 'The Russian president had gills and webbed feet,' she informed Jacko. 'And we left him in a great position. Elvis, show him the pics.'

Elvis pulled up the photos on his phone and slid it across the bar to Jacko. The bluesman flicked through the photos of the Russian president being serviced by one of his bodyguards and a blow-up sex doll.

'Nice,' said Jacko, shuddering. 'Is he being rimmed in this one? And, what the hell is that? How did you get his whole fist up there? Which one of you got the president hard?'

'He got hard on his own,' said Jasmine, 'even though he was unconscious. He obviously enjoys a good fisting.'

Jacko eventually came across a photo taken after the president had been shot in the head, at which point he handed the phone back to Elvis. 'Was it really necessary to try so many different things? You could have been caught.'

'Yeah, but we can blackmail him with those photos,' said Jasmine.

'You could if you hadn't killed him,' Jacko pointed out. He reached down into a fridge below the bar and pulled out a bottle of Shitting Monkey for Elvis. 'What are you drinking, Jas?'

'I think I'll try a Black Russian.'

Jacko grabbed a glass and started making the drink.

'What do you think'll happen now?' Elvis asked. 'Have we just ended the war, or will it get worse?'

Rex pulled out his phone. 'Calhoon might be able to answer that question,' he said, taking another pull on his beer while he called her up. She answered straight away, but didn't bother with a greeting.

'Rex, is it done?' she asked.

'It's done.'

'Thank God. You're a legend. How did you do it?'

'Jasmine did it actually. She shot him in the back of the head.'

'How did it all go down? Tell me everything.'

'Well, we found him in his private quarters. He was a real pussy. After we knocked him out, we stripped him naked and put him in a compromising position with one of his guards and an inflatable sex doll. We made it look like the guard destroyed his asshole, then shot him in the back of the head to get revenge for the president cheating on him with the sex doll.'

Calhoon sighed. 'Of course you did. I don't suppose you took any pictures did you?'

'Actually yeah, Elvis did. Oh, and that's the other thing. He had gills and webbed feet, so he must be another one of the Atlanteans.'

'Can you send me the photos that prove that?' Calhoon asked. 'I need to show them to president Douglas.'

'Are you sure you wanna do that?' Rex asked.

'How do you mean?'

'Seems to me like *all* of the world leaders have got gills and webbed feet. What's to say Navan Douglas isn't one of them? I wouldn't want you to disappear.'

'I'll take my chances,' said Calhoon. 'Just text me through the pictures. I'll take it from here.'

## Sixty

One week later

'It worked. I can't believe it,' said Elvis.

Jasmine, Elvis and Rex were sitting at a table in Purgatory watching the television. The breaking news was on every channel. World War 3 was over. The rather excellent execution of the disgraced Russian leader had worked out even better than they could have hoped. A new ruler had taken over in his place and negotiated peace with the other world leaders.

'You know we won't get any credit for this,' said Rex.

'I guess everything will gradually go back to normal now?' said Elvis.

Jacko called over to them from behind the bar. 'More drinks anyone?'

Jasmine shook her head. 'Not for me. I'm gonna go tell Flake the good news about the war. And I quite fancy having a bit of a sunbathe on the beach.' She kicked her chair back and stood up. 'You coming with me?' she asked Elvis.

'I'll be along later,' he replied. 'I just want to watch a bit more of the news. Be nice if we got some kind of mention for what we did.'

'Well, when you're ready, I'll be sunbathing on the beach. I need to work on my all over tan,' she said with a wink.

Jasmine was wearing a pair of denim cut-offs and a blue bikini top. Elvis eyed her up, then checked his watch. 'Okay, ten minutes and I'll be there.'

Jasmine kissed him on the cheek then headed through the portal into the research centre. She couldn't find JD and Flake anywhere in the building, so she headed outside to look for them. It was a warm day and there was a pleasant breeze blowing in from the ocean. Jasmine got a waft of barbecued chicken and followed it down to the beach where she found Flake and JD with Goober. Flake was wearing knee-length jeans and a white frilly top. JD was in shorts and a T-shirt (a look he would never have considered a few weeks earlier). He was turning over some chicken breasts on the barbecue while Flake was laying out a picnic blanket on the sand. Goober had one corner of the blanket in his mouth, which was causing a problem because he seemed to think the blanket was his.

'Hey, guys!' Jasmine called out as she set foot on the sand. 'How's it going?'

Goober stopped fighting Flake for the blanket and bounded over to greet Jasmine.

'Hey, Jas. Wanna stay for some food?' Flake asked.

'I don't want to intrude,' Jasmine replied, while Goober licked her face. 'I just came to tell you the war is over. There's a new Russian president and he's agreed to end the fighting.'

'That's great news,' said Flake. 'Did the news people say anything about you?'

'Not a word,' said Jasmine as she walked over to the grill to see how JD's chicken was cooking. 'They didn't even mention the sex doll or the reach-around.'

Flake laughed. 'Maybe you can post some of your photos of it online?'

'I dunno,' said Jasmine. 'I don't want to embarrass the blow-up doll. But at least now that the war is over we can all go back to the real world.'

JD responded to her suggestion. 'We've already decided to stay here.'

'What, forever?' Jasmine asked.

Flake grinned. 'We love it here,' she said. 'Do you want to some chicken? We've got enough food for everyone.'

Jasmine pondered the offer. She didn't want to be a third wheel but the food did look good. 'Okay, if you don't mind? Elvis is coming down here in a minute too.'

'No problem,' said Flake. She walked over to JD, slipped her arm around his waist and planted a kiss on his cheek. 'I'll go and get the fries from the oven,' she said. 'They should be about ready.'

'Don't be long.'

Flake left the beach and headed up the path to the medical centre, leaving Jasmine with JD and the barbecue.

'You need a hand with anything?' Jasmine asked.

'Nah, it's okay,' JD replied, as he tossed a few raw beefburgers onto the grill.

Jasmine stroked Goober and contemplated asking JD something that had been on her mind for a while. 'Can I ask you a question then?' she ventured.

'About me and Flake?'

Jasmine rolled her eyes. 'No, I always knew you two would end up together. It's been brewing for a while now. The pair of you are so transparent. I think I know more about your relationship than either of you.'

JD sighed. 'What do you want then?'

'Have you told Flake yet?'

'Told her what?'

'That you killed the president and all the other world leaders?'

JD stopped what he was doing and looked across at her. 'Who told you that?'

'No one. It just crossed my mind when we were killing the Russian president. The easiest way to kill all those powerful people is to use the portal. Calhoon's theory about multiple invisible coats, it doesn't work for me.'

'Why not?'

Jasmine scoffed. 'Because, a bunch of people with invisible coats dotted all around the world coordinating multiple assassinations? I can't see it. Whereas just before all the assassinations, you and Rex were saving children from a vampire circus. I know you well enough to know that you'd kill everyone that was involved, including all the perverts who watched it. I mean, come on, it's obvious you did it.'

JD stopped turning the meat and looked at Jasmine. There was a troubled look in his eyes. 'Yeah, I killed them all,' he said. 'And they fucking deserved it. It wasn't supposed to be a secret. But then Sanchez got killed, and Flake got blamed for it all. I didn't want to add to her pain by telling her it was me, not right away anyway. Then, of course, she and I hooked up, and so telling her became a problem with no solution.'

Jasmine smiled. 'I won't say anything to anyone,' she said. 'But, you know, if I can work it out, then it's just a matter of time before everyone else does. And Flake isn't stupid. She'll figure it out.'

'I know. I'll tell her when the time is right.'

'Come on then, tell me how you did it?'

'How I killed the elites?'

'Yeah. Come on, spill the beans.'

'Flake will be back in a minute,' JD reminded her.

'Then tell me quickly,' said Jasmine. She picked up a set of tongs and used them to flip over a chicken breast on the grill. 'And don't let this cook for too long,' she warned him. 'You don't want fuck it up.'

# Sixty-One

<u>Part Nine - Killing the Elite</u>

*The night before the president's murder*

Diago had always known the day would come. The day some idiot cop or FBI agent, (or worse still, a vigilante mob armed with guns) came looking for the vampire circus. That day was here. But the enemy was way worse than the cops or the FBI. It was a vigilante mob, a mob of only two men, Rodeo Rex and the Bourbon Kid.

The kidnap of Paige Rodriguez had been a success. Except it hadn't. When Diago had smashed Paige's chauffeur across the head with a baseball bat earlier in the day, he hadn't bothered to get a good look at the driver's face. Worse still, he'd left him alive. It was a chauffeur after all. And kidnappings need to be done quickly, even when wearing an invisible coat. But the second man who exited the vehicle from the back seat, Diago had recognised him straight away. It was Rodeo Rex. He managed to shoot Rex in the leg before making his escape. He'd felt confident that it would be enough to debilitate him. But it hadn't been enough, because the chauffeur turned out to be the Bourbon Kid. And now Rodeo Rex and the Bourbon Kid were at the circus to rescue the Rodriguez girl. The destructive duo turned up just as she was about to be burned alive by fire-eaters. And true to form, they were killing everyone. When Diago saw his brother Dexter blown to bits, he made up his mind to get the fuck out of there.

His only hope was to get to his invisible coat, which was in his trailer. A hasty retreat was needed for that. He hurdled the dead and dying on his way out of the Big Top. By the grace of God he made it outside in one piece and headed straight for his trailer. Its door was already open. He charged in, ready to fight anyone he found inside. There was no one. The place hadn't even been ransacked. He moved quickly to the closet and pulled it open. His invisible coat was still there, on a hanger where he'd left it. He breathed a sigh of relief. Thank the Lord!

He grabbed the coat and wrapped it around his shoulders while he looked in the mirror. Every time he put it on he feared it might not work its magic anymore. He need not have worried. As soon as he pulled the hood up over his head, his reflection in the mirror melted away. Now what to do?

The screams of his circus friends didn't just pierce his ears, they pierced his heart, his vampire soul. His family was being slaughtered.

The loss of each one was like being stabbed by a hot poker dipped in acid.

But the enemy was the one Diago feared the most. The Bourbon Kid, slaughterer of thousands upon thousands of vampires. And Rodeo Rex was with him. God's own bounty hunter.

Fighting wasn't an option. Not without a plan. And Diago had no plan. And he had no idea if his invisible coat was bulletproof because at this point, no one had shot at him when he was wearing it. Now wasn't the time to test it out either. There were more important problems to be fretting about, like how to get out of the trailer park alive.

Diago left his trailer, only to see the Bourbon Kid walking out of the Big Top, gun in hand, looking around, *looking for him.*

Fuck.

There was only one thing to do. Stay still, stay invisible and stay quiet, which was actually three things, but who the fuck is counting at this point? Diago held his breath and stayed deadly still, afraid of making even the slightest sound. The Bourbon Kid stopped a short distance away from him. Beneath his black cowl, his eyes darted one way then the other, as if he could sense the presence of Diago. Eventually after what felt like an hour, but was probably only twenty seconds, the Kid moved on, heading toward another trailer. Diago let out a deep breath.

*Escape. Get the fuck out.*

Hanging around when the Bourbon Kid was on the hunt was not an option, even in an invisible coat. The Kid and his friends were rumoured to have killed the Devil, the medusa, Frankenstein, the pope, the cast of the Planet of the Apes TV show, and countless other supernatural entities.

Diago crept back into the Big Top to see if anyone else had survived. The sight before him was a tableaux of death and ruinous mayhem. Everyone was dead. Athena, Dexter, Kratos, Takemi, the clowns, all of them were gone. Some were smouldering on the ground, others were missing important parts of their anatomy, like their arm, or their head. Some poor soul was being eaten by the bear, and the lions were fighting over someone else's leg. In the middle of the arena, one of the perpetrators, Rodeo Rex, was comforting the Rodriguez girl, whom the fire-eaters had been chasing around only minutes earlier.

All of the people who had been watching on the big screen had vanished too. Who could blame them? They were important people. Now they would all be in a panic.

Diago was all alone, a vampire without friends or family, or even a home. It was time to leave, to get the fuck out of town, find some new allies, and then plot his revenge. He took one last look at the destruction all around him, then he snuck out and vanished into the night.

■■■■■■■■■■■■■■■■■■■■■■■■■■■■■■■■■■■■■■■■■■■■■■■■■■■

Diago wasn't the only vampire to escape the Big Top during the massacre. Pollox, one of the acrobats, had swung his way out and then scrambled to his trailer to collect his personals, with a view to getting the fuck out of town. If he'd had just a little more sense he would have forgotten all about his belongings and just concentrated on escaping.

His trailer had been broken into, but thankfully nothing seemed to have been taken. Pollox headed straight to his sleeping area and packed everything of value into a sports bag. It took a minute to fill it to the brim, then he zipped it up and bolted back out of his trailer, right into a fist. It busted his nose, and knocked him back into the trailer where he fell onto his back. The man who had hit him was the Bourbon Kid. He stepped into the trailer and loomed over Pollox..

'I'm not one of them,' Pollox lied. 'I'm not a vampire.' His bullshit was stinking the whole trailer out.

'I'm not here to kill you,' the Bourbon Kid replied.

'You're not? I mean, good. Thanks.'

'Get up. Take a seat.'

Pollox backed away and scrambled to his feet. He nervously pulled a cushioned sofa out of the wall and sat down on it. The Bourbon Kid closed the trailer door and turned back to face him. His promise not to kill the acrobat was curiously followed up by him reaching inside his jacket and pulling out a sharp knife.

'We're going to discuss a few things,' the Kid said. 'You can start by giving me the names of everyone who was watching on the big screen.'

Pollox swallowed hard. 'Oh, God. They're the most powerful people on earth. If I give them up, I'm done for.'

The Kid took a half-step towards him, his knife pointed menacingly at Pollox's heart. 'All of your friends are dead. Consider that for a moment, and think about how lucky you are that you have this opportunity to live.'

'Right. Yes. Of course.' Pollox's mind was racing, going through every possible scenario. There was only one way out of this. Start spilling the beans. 'I'll tell you everything you need to know,' he said, generously.

'I want names. Every single one.' The Kid reached into his jacket with his free hand and pulled out his phone. He held it up so that Pollox could see the display. He'd taken a photo of all the people on the big cinema screen in the circus arena. There were a lot of famous faces on there. Powerful people.

'I guess you know some of them already?' Pollox suggested.

'I do. But I wanna know the names of everyone in this photo, and everyone else whose ever been involved in this shit. You got a list? A database? What?'

'There is a database. My laptop over there. I can get you the names and positions of everyone who logs into the events.'

'And why are you killing autistic kids?'

'Umm, oh, that's a new thing,' said Pollox. 'I'm not sure of the reason why. I wasn't told.'

The Bourbon Kid paused the interrogation to take a phone call, which Pollox presumed was from Rodeo Rex. It sounded like Rex was waiting in the parking lot. But the Kid wasn't going to join him. Halfway through the conversation, Pollox raised his hand and spoke without waiting for permission.

'While you're on the phone, shall I go get my laptop?' he asked.

'Shut the fuck up!' the Kid snapped at him, before muttering to his phone, 'not you, Rex. I gotta go.' He ended the call then switched back into interrogation mode. 'The president of the United States was on that screen,' he said. 'How is that possible?'

Pollox grimaced. 'Have you ever heard of the Atlanteans?'

'Not really, but you're gonna tell me about them.'

For the next half an hour, Pollox told the Bourbon Kid everything he wanted to know. He gave him all the names, titles and addresses of the Atlantean elites who regularly tuned in to watch the vampires torture and kill young children.

When the interrogation was over, Pollox breathed a sigh of relief and slid towards the end of the sofa, ready to grab his bag and get the fuck out of there. Unfortunately for Pollox, the Bourbon Kid stepped across him, blocking him from getting up. He was brandishing his knife. The intent was clear.

'You said you'd let me live if I told you everything!' Pollox protested. 'You promised!'

'I lied.'

Those were the last words Pollox heard. He felt the knife plunge into his stomach and twist before being pulled out again and plunged into his midline, drawing up, filleting him. His screams filled the night.

When the kill was complete, JD made a phone call to Jacko. The bluesman answered the call in his usual cheery manner.

'Hey man, wassup?' he said.

'I'm in a circus trailer park,' JD replied. 'Get me into Purgatory. We're gonna use the portal for something. Something big.'

## Sixty-Two

Jacko knew from the tone of the Bourbon Kid's voice that his day was about to go from boring to crazy-stressful. By the time the phone conversation was over, he missed being bored. He switched the location on the portal to a public toilet outside the circus and waited for the Bourbon Kid to show up. He didn't have long to wait. The Kid walked in, his long black coat covered in blood.

'You know, this isn't Star Trek,' said Jacko, as he pressed the button to close the portal back up. 'It's not my job to beam you up from wherever you are, any time you want.'

The Bourbon Kid ignored Jacko, made his way behind the bar, grabbed a bottle of bourbon from the worktop, flipped the lid off and took a swig straight from the bottle. There was a lot of blood on his hands.

'Help yourself,' Jacko said, nodding at the bottle of bourbon. 'Don't mind me. I just run this place.'

The Kid put the bottle down on the bar, lowered his hood, then walked around to the customer side and pulled up a stool. He reached inside his jacket and tossed a rolled-up notebook over to Jacko, who didn't really want it, but caught it anyway.

'What's this then?' Jacko asked. 'Shopping list?'

The Kid picked up his bottle of bourbon and drank some more. Then he lit up a cigarette just by sucking on it. Bad sign.

Jacko flipped open the notebook. The first page had a list of names on it. Next to each name was a small writeup, things like job titles and addresses. He turned the page. Same thing. He recognised some of the names. 'Please tell me this isn't a hit list,' he said, looking back up at the Kid.

'I want you to find the locations of all the people in that book. Then I'm going to kill them. All of them.'

'You *are* shitting me? Please tell me you're shitting me.'

'This is no fucking joke. Get Eric Einstein up here.'

'Einstein? What for?'

'Don't play dumb. He can hack into any security network in the world. He's done it before. He can find these fuckers, then I can go through the portal and take them down one by one.'

Jacko put the notebook down on the bar in front of the Kid. 'You're going to have to tell me what these people have done. I can't partake in a bunch of high-profile assassinations like this, not without running it by God first.'

'You won't need to run it by God.'

'You don't know God like I do. He can be tetchy about things like this.'

JD pulled out his phone and held it up so that Jacko could see a photo he had taken. It was a photo of a circus ring, with a giant cinema-sized screen at the back.

'What's this?' Jacko asked.

'See the big TV screen?'

Jacko looked closer. 'Is that a zoom call? Or Celebrity Squares?'

The Kid was not amused. 'All the people on that screen were watching a live execution of a twelve-year-old girl. It's something they do regularly. They get off on it.'

Jacko winced. 'No way. That can't be right….. can it?'

'A travelling circus has been going around the country picking up kids and murdering them for the viewing pleasure of these rich cunts.'

'The president of the United States was on that list,' said Jacko.

'He's in the photo too. So is the leader of the opposition, a bunch of senators, the Russian president, a bunch of European leaders, kings, queens, princes, you name it. Well, today, I'm bringing 'em down. And you're gonna help me do it. You and Einstein.'

'JD, what you're talking about here is insane. You need to take some time, clear your head. Breathe in some air.'

'I've been breathing in air my whole fucking life. Get this done, or I'll add you to the list.'

'I'm already dead,' Jacko said, rolling his eyes.

'I don't care.'

'Do Rex and the others know about this?'

'No. Get Einstein.'

'All right, all right.' Jacko turned around and picked up the old-fashioned red phone on the worktop behind the bar. He made a call down to Hell. Zilas, the deformed hunchback who worked on reception down there answered the call.

'Yes, boss,' Zilas said.

'I want Eric Einstein up here, now.'

Jacko slammed the phone back down. 'Happy?' he asked the Kid.

'It's a start.'

'You know, nothing good will come of this,' Jacko pointed out. 'These people are evil, sure. But if you kill them all, you're going to destabilise the whole world.'

'I'm going to make the world a better place.'

'Hey, I don't want to argue with you, but think on this for a while. If you kill these people, they'll be replaced by others just the same as them.'

'Child killers from Atlantis?'

Jacko furrowed his brow. 'Atlantis? The underwater city?'

'You know about it?'

'I know a little. Scratch had historical records about the place. The Atlanteans were known for their narcissism and hunger for power. God grew tired of their cruel behaviour to people worse off than them. That's why he sent Atlantis to the bottom of the ocean.'

'Didn't kill them all though, did it? According to a vampire I just killed, some of the Atlanteans survived because they'd evolved, grown gills and webbed feet. They were one step ahead of God.'

'Don't tell him that. It's a touchy subject apparently.'

The Kid took a sip of his drink. He had blood around his lips, some of which went down with the bourbon. 'Those Atlantean fucks are still doing what they always did, ruling over the masses, treating everyone like they're worthless shit.'

Jacko poured himself a glass of rum from a bottle while he tried to think. He took a sip of the rum, then sensing the Bourbon Kid's impatience, he started talking. 'From what I know of them, they hide in plain sight. They only breed with each other. Any Atlantean that conceives a child with a regular human is exiled from society. Although, sometimes the most powerful get away with it. Take the US president for example, he's got his daughter Arizona, who he keeps secret.'

JD took a drag on his cigarette. 'When they get exiled from society for breaking the rules, where do they go?'

'Back to the ocean, I think. It's a while since I read about this. Oh, and you should know, there are Atlantean vampires too.'

'Vampires with gills and webbed feet?'

'Yeah. In daylight hours they can avoid the sun by staying underwater. They're known to prey on people who go diving to explore shipwrecks.'

'Well, these circus vampires are kidnapping kids in the daytime. One of them has an invisible coat.'

PING!

The elevator doors at the back of the room parted and the crazy scientist Eric Einstein stepped out, carrying a laptop computer under his arm. He was wearing a long white coat, grey shirt, black pants and grubby brown shoes. His curly ginger hair was out of control. They needed better barbers in Hell, or he needed to visit one a little more frequently.

'Hey fellas,' he said, a broad grin across his face. 'What can I do for you?'

'Wipe that fuckin' smile off your face,' said the Bourbon Kid. 'And get onto your laptop. I've got a list of powerful people for you to track down. We're going to kill them one by one. Understand?'

Einstein's eyes lit up. 'Oh, I'm in,' he said. 'Who's first?'

'The president of the USA,' the Kid replied.

'Oooh, I like it.'

'Wait a second,' said Jacko. 'Aren't Flake and Sanchez due to meet the president tomorrow morning?'

JD thought for a moment. 'What time are they meeting him?'

'I don't know, I think it's at about nine a.m. Or it could be ten. He's giving them both the medal of honour. Flake's really looking forward to it.'

The Kid handed his notepad to Einstein. 'Fine,' he said. 'All the names are in here. We'll start with the Russian president instead.'

Einstein sat down at one of the tables. He put his laptop down, then flipped open the notepad. After a few seconds he raised his hand like a child in school.

'What?' said the Kid as he took another cigarette from his pack.

'The Russian will be the hardest one to find. The Kremlin security network is always on the fritz. Besides, wouldn't it be best to start off with some of the less high-profile figures?' He scoured the first page of the notepad. 'Like senator Baynard. Kill him first and the press won't hear about it for hours. In fact, some of these people have families that will need to be informed before it hits the news. Some won't even announce the deaths for at least twenty-four hours. But if you kill a president first, all the others will be rushing out to meetings about it. That'll make 'em hard to get. Whereas right now, most of these people are probably tucked up in bed. You do this right and you could kill them all by lunchtime.'

'He's got a point,' said Jacko.

'Just get on with it,' said the Kid. He put his cigarette in his mouth, and it lit up on its own. 'I want the location of the first target within five minutes.'

'Jeez,' said Einstein. 'While I log onto the computer, could someone get me a vodka and tonic?'

The Bourbon Kid blew some smoke at Jacko. 'What are you waiting for?'

## Sixty-Three

Senator Baynard was sitting in a high-backed armchair in his lounge at home, drinking cognac and flicking through all the news channels on his television. It had been a long, stressful day spent voting on new laws to help poor people stay poor. Being a senator was tedious work sometimes, especially when he had to pretend to care about job losses among his voters. The late-night glass of cognac was one of two things he'd been looking forward to after such a hard day. The other was watching the Ludus Mortis. There had been a problem though. The Wheel of Misfortune event had been interrupted when two psychos turned up and started killing the circus vampires. As soon as Baynard realised it wasn't part of the show he logged off. Ever since then, he'd been waiting for someone to call him and tell him not to worry, because right now he was worried. Fucking worried. One of the men who showed up at the circus to kill the vampires had taken a photo of the big screen that Baynard's face was on.

His phone didn't ring until 10.45 p.m. It was the secretary of defence, Rebecca Howe. Baynard was so desperate to take the call and mute his television at the same time, that he fumbled with the phone, almost dropping it. When he composed himself he put the phone to his ear, skipped the pleasantries and got straight to the point.

'Rebecca, what the hell happened?'

'I don't know any more than you,' she replied. 'I logged off as soon as the shooting started. But yes, one of the men took a photo of the screen with all of us on it, so it's bad news.'

'Who were those men? Were they cops? Feds?'

'Navan Douglas is going to call Alexis Calhoon,' Rebecca replied. 'He thinks it could have been her people, in which case, she's gotta go.'

'Calhoon's people? Who are Calhoon's people?'

'I don't know for sure, but rumour has it they killed Mike Raffone last year.'

'Mike hung himself, didn't he?'

'That's what the papers went with, but actually no, he went missing at Calhoon's ranch. Only reason the president let it go is because he's afraid of Calhoon's people. Apparently they did a top secret job for him once, although no one knows exactly what it was.'

'Fuck. I tell you, since the president won his second term, he's gotten sloppy. We need him replaced.'

'Richard, calm down. If anyone hears you say that, you'll go the same way as Raffone. Just sit tight. Stop calling everyone, have a drink, and let it all blow over, okay.'

'Blow over? BLOW OVER?' The other end of the line went quiet. 'Hello? HELLO? REBECCA? BITCH!'

The secretary of defence had long since hung up.

Baynard slammed his phone down onto the small table beside his armchair. He took another sip of his cognac and unmuted the television. No amount of booze would get rid of this awful feeling of dread. This was the mother of all fuckups. He wriggled in his chair, trying to get comfortable as he continued watching the news, dreading the possibility of any mention of what had happened at the circus.

'Was that the secretary of defence?' an unfamiliar voice asked from behind him.

Baynard leapt out of his armchair and looked around. He was greeted by the sight of a man in a long black coat standing in his lounge. The man's hood was up, casting a shadow over his face. 'Who the fuck are you?' Baynard asked, his heart racing.

'I'm the man you were just talking about. The man who took your picture while you were on the big screen.'

'Oh Jeezus. How the fuck did you get in here?'

'I can get in anywhere.'

Baynard took two steps back. 'I can have my security guards up here in five seconds flat,' he bluffed.

'I'll kill them too.'

'Who are you?' Baynard asked, his bluster and bravado fading fast.

'I'm the man you've had nightmares about. You've always known the day would come when someone found out about all your shit. Well, Senator Fuck Head, today's the day.'

'I, I'm not part of it. I just logged on by mistake. I was appalled by what I saw.'

The Bourbon Kid reached into his coat and pulled out a machete. 'You politicians just can't tell the truth can you? You just don't know how. It's hardwired into you to fucking lie, isn't it? Well, not anymore. Your bullshitting days are over.'

Baynard turned and ran towards a big oak door in the corner of the room. He didn't make it. He didn't even come close to making it. The Kid grabbed his shoulder and dragged him down to the ground. He rolled Baynard over onto his back, then slammed the machete into his crotch. The blade ripped through the senator's torso, opening him up from his nuts to his neck. It was a painful way to go. Baynard wailed in pain for a moment before passing out. His security team would have heard it, but the Kid would be long gone before they showed up.

One down.

The Bourbon Kid left Baynard paralysed on the floor of his lounge, struggling for breath, the blood and the life oozing out of him. He exited via the senator's exquisite bathroom, wiping his blade clean on one of the towels on his way through.

Jacko and Einstein were waiting for him in Purgatory. Jacko was behind the bar, strumming away on a blues guitar, which was something he did when he needed to relax. Einstein was at a round table nearby, staring over his laptop. He was wide-eyed with excitement at what was to come next. Jacko was much less enthusiastic.

'That's one,' said the Kid.

Jacko stopped strumming his guitar. 'One could be all that's needed?' he suggested. 'It might send a message to the others. They might stop what they've been doing.'

The Kid looked at Einstein. 'Where next?'

'Switzerland,' Einstein replied. 'The weird one from the royal family is out there in a ski lodge. Latest camera footage suggests he's gone to his room, but he's probably not alone.'

'I don't care if he's got ten Roman gladiators in there with him. The guy's going down. Switch the portal.'

Einstein offered half a smile. 'It's already done.'

'Good. I'll be back in thirty seconds. Get the next one ready.'

## Sixty-Four

'This is a fucking disaster.'

'Stay calm, Mister President. I've got our best people working on it.'

'Don't fucking tell me to be calm. I told you Baynard was just the beginning. Every five minutes now someone new is assassinated. And every single one of them was watching the Ludus Mortis last night. I'm telling you, those men who killed the circus vampires, they're behind all of this. We need to find out who they are and what they want.'

Navan Douglas had never seen his boss so animated, so stressed out. Shit, he'd not been this fidgety during the election campaign or any of the overseas conflicts that had taken place during his presidency.

'Sir, as long as you stay here, you'll be perfectly safe. We need to present an image that we're not panicking. Just get this next meeting out of the way, and I'll go sort out a press conference for you. The American people need to see you speak in public about this.'

The president tugged at his tie, which had seen a lot more tugging than usual and was hanging loosely around his neck like a noose. 'Fine,' he said eventually. 'Who am I seeing at ten-thirty?'

'It's actually eleven-fifteen now, Mister President, but you're seeing two of the people who helped rescue Arizona a few months back, remember?'

'Arizona?'

'Your illegitimate daughter.'

'Oh, right, yes, her. And who are these people that rescued her?'

Douglas patted him on the shoulder. 'Sanchez Garcia and Flake Munroe.'

The president's brain was frazzled. Fortunately, Douglas was kind enough to give him a little coaching about what to expect in his next meeting, as well as informing him that he had some food between his teeth.

With the prepping done, the Attorney General excused himself and headed for the exit. As soon as Douglas was out the door, the president headed for the bedroom to freshen up. He had a feeling there were patches of sweat in the armpits of his shirt, to go with the food stuck in his teeth. Fucking people wanting medals. For fuckssake. Fucking medals and gold rings. Pieces of shiny metal that made humans feel important. Christ, the public were so fucking stupid. Gullible sheep. Dumb fucks. And the name *Flake*, it had better not be short for snowflake. Rewarding her and her friend Sanchez for rescuing his illegitimate daughter, Arizona, *pfft*. The world would be a better place if the brainless bitch was dead anyway. He should never have slept with a non-Atlantean in the first place, let alone do it without protection. The fucking abortion laws hadn't helped either. He should have had Arizona sent to the vampire circus. Oh well. Too late now.

He checked his reflection in his bedroom mirror. His face was pale, rusty even. The shittest thing about being president, and there were plenty of shit things about it, but the really shitty thing, was all the assassination attempts. Every cunt was out to kill him. And at this point, he was one of the only surviving members of the previous night's Ludus Mortis. He'd been enjoying watching some poor girl chased around the circus by a couple of fire-eating vampires, and then POW! The whole world had gone to shit. Someone was going to lose their job over this. He just hadn't decided who it would be yet.

His inner rantings eventually subsided. He liked to grant himself a minute of ranting approximately three times a day. That was all he ever had time for. His priority right now was freshening up for his next visitors. He gritted his teeth and opened his mouth. There it was. Shit between his teeth. A toothpick was required He walked over to the bathroom and pushed the door open.

'Going somewhere?' said a gravelly voice. It belonged to a tall, shadow-like figure that was standing right in front of him in the bathroom.

'Huh?' The president was staring into the chest of the shadow. He leaned his head back and looked up into the face of a man wearing a dark hood over his head.

'I saw you on TV this morning,' the gravelly voice said.

'What?' The president took a step back. 'Oh, shit.'

The shadow grabbed the loose-hanging tie around the president's neck and yanked it hard, pulling the shorter man towards him.

THUD!

A headbutt.

It was a great many years since anyone had head-butted the president. Man, head-butts fucking hurt. The president was out on his feet. He would have dropped to the floor, but his attacker was still holding his tie.

'This is for all the kids who died at the circus,' said the shadow.

The president's instincts kicked in. Bullshit began to flow freely from his mouth in spite of his dizziness. 'Hey, it wasn't what it looked like,' he blustered. 'We hacked into their server. I was going to send the

FBI down there to kill those circus freaks myself. You did us a favour. I should pay you. How much?'

The Bourbon Kid let go of the president's tie, and the old man staggered back into the bedroom. The corner of a window sill dug right into his spine, causing him even more pain.

'I can see why you've got so many bottles of mouthwash in here,' said the Kid. 'The constant stream of shit coming out of your mouth must ruin your breath.'

'I'll give you anything you want.'

'I want to see the colour of your heart.'

'What?'

The president tried to think on his feet. Normally someone in his ear told him what to do when he was dithering, but he didn't have the earpiece in. The only way out of this was to run, to call for help. He made it as far as the double-bed in the middle of the room. Then a hand grabbed his arm and twisted him round. Everything was already a blur, and the twisting only made it worse. Dizziness, nausea, dry mouth. And then came the attack. It happened so fast, the president barely saw it. But he felt it. The tip of a blade ripped through his balls and sliced upwards to his chest.

'Oh, God.'

The president's blood and guts squirted out of his belly and through his shirt. Specks of blood splashed up into his face. His legs lost every ounce of strength they had. His knees buckled under him and he flopped back onto the bed, his vision wobbling in and out of focus as he stared up at the ceiling. Then his head lopped to the side and he watched the black shadow of his killer retreat back into the bathroom and then disappear.

## Sixty-Five

'Have you located the Russian president yet?' Jacko yelled across to Einstein.

The fuzzy-haired scientist was tapping away on his laptop, with his fourth vodka and tonic of what had been a long shift in Purgatory. 'Almost,' he replied. 'The network is harder to hack into out there.'

'Well fucking hurry up. The Bourbon Kid will be back any second and he'll be really pissed if you haven't found it.'

Up on the television, the news hadn't yet reported on the death of the president of the United States. The Bourbon Kid had killed him almost twenty minutes ago, and he was currently doing the same to the leader of North Korea.

As if to add to Jacko's stress levels, his cell-phone started ringing. 'Oh, for fuckssake, this job's a nightmare,' he groaned as he fumbled around in his pocket for the phone. He pulled it out and checked the display to see if it was worth answering. The call was from Flake. Jacko couldn't really imagine a scenario where Flake would have an emergency on her hands, but he answered it anyway, simply because it was Flake and she was one of the only people who never pissed him off.

'Hello Flake. What's up?'

'Jacko. Help me! Sanchez is dead. I'm trapped in a hotel and I need to get out. People are trying to kill me. Can you get me out?'

*Sanchez dead?* The words went round and round in Jacko's head. What the fuck? It didn't make sense. But Flake wasn't one for bullshitting. This had to be real. Then something flashed through Jacko's thoughts. Was this something to do with the Bourbon Kid killing the president? Please no. Jacko closed his eyes and mouthed the word, "shit" for no one's benefit but his own. Unfortunately, there wasn't time to dwell on what might have happened, because Flake was in trouble. Big trouble. Deep fucking shit. Time to stay calm.

'Sure thing,' Jacko replied as coolly as possible. 'What hotel?'

'Umm, oh shit,' Flake blabbered. 'It's the… uh, Poseidon Hotel, in Chicago.'

'The Poseidon?' Jacko repeated. 'Is that where the president is staying?'

'Yes. But he's dead too. And I accidentally used the Eye of the Moon to kill the First Lady and a couple of bodyguards. Jacko, get me the fuck out of here. PLEASE!'

A chill went right through Jacko, from head to toe. 'What floor are you on?'

'I don't know. I'm in the stairwell heading down to the lobby. I'm about five flights from the top, I think. But I don't know what to do. Should I get off on the next floor or what?'

There was a ringing sound in the background on Flake's end of the line.

'Is that a fire alarm I can hear?' Jacko asked.

'Yes. They're onto me. Fuckin' hurry. This is an emergency.'

It was a tough call because the portal was currently in use. But, as luck would have it, before Jacko had a full-on panic attack, the Bourbon Kid returned from killing the North Korean president, Chunki Phat Fuk, or whatever his name was.

'Hold on,' Jacko said to Flake. 'Just wait one second.' He muted his phone so Flake couldn't hear, then he yelled at the Bourbon Kid. 'JD, FUCK! We've got a problem!'

It was Einstein of all people who replied first. 'I've found the Russian president!' he announced.

'Forget that!' Jacko hissed at him, before turning back to JD. 'Flake is in trouble. She's at the fucking Poseidon. She says Sanchez is dead and she's accidentally killed the First Lady. Oh, and people are trying to kill her, obviously.'

JD looked shocked. 'I thought their meeting with the president was hours ago?'

'Does it matter? Just put two and two together for fuckssake. This is our fault, well-- actually it's *your* fault.'

'What floor is she on? I'll go get her.'

'Right, yeah. Good thinking.'

Einstein called out again. 'There's fifty-four floors in that place!'

'*I know that!*' Jacko snapped. 'I haven't forgotten. Wait, hang on, that's actually useful. Flake said she was five floors from the top and heading down.'

'In that case I'll set the portal to come out in one of the rooms on the fortieth floor,' said Einstein.

'Okay, good.'

JD yelled at Einstein. 'Hurry up, you dumb fuck! This is urgent.' He turned and faced the portal, ready to go through it when the location changed. He reached into his coat and pulled out a pair of handguns, then pointed them at the door, ready for action.

Jacko unmuted his phone and put it to his ear. Flake was rambling away on the other end.

'Okay, Flake, you've got fifty-four floors in that place. Get off on floor number forty.'

'Forty? Why forty?'

'Just get to forty. You must be close to it by now. Get there and wait for help.'

'That's it? Wait for help?'

'Flake, get moving! I'll stay on the line.'

Einstein called out to Jacko. 'Confirm forty please!'

'Confirmed!'

Einstein pressed a button on his computer keyboard. 'It's ready,' he said.

The Bourbon Kid pressed the button beside the portal door. It slid open. Before he walked through it, he looked back at the other two. 'No one can know what we've been doing here today,' he said.

'Well, no shit!' said Jacko. 'I told you this would all end in tears. Now Sanchez is dead, and Flake will be too if you don't get a move on.'

'My lips are sealed,' Einstein added.

'GO!' Jacko yelled.

JD, who was not normally one to take orders, stepped through the portal into the Poseidon hotel. Jacko put his phone to his ear again. Flake was babbling away on the other end. He missed part of it, but heard her say, "What do I do? I've gotta move."

'Where are you?' he asked her.

'I'm on forty, but I've got to get off.'

'Stay where you are.'

'They're pointing guns at me. I've gotta go.'

Jacko stared at the portal and whispered the words, *"Hurry up JD, for fuckssake!"* About ten seconds later the sound of gunfire filtered in through the open portal. In some ways it was a relief to know JD was doing the business, but it did also mean *more dead people*.

Jacko looked across at Einstein. 'This is the mother of all fuck ups.'

'You're telling me,' the scientist replied. 'Should we keep the portal open? Or close it and wait for him to call?'

'Hang on a sec,' said Jacko. 'I'll take a look.' He climbed over the bar and ran up to the portal. On the other side of it was a hotel bathroom with a toilet, a washbasin and a shower in it. 'It doesn't look like there's anyone in here,' he called back to Einstein. He stepped into the bathroom and walked through it to an open door just past the shower unit. More gunfire rang out nearby. And screams. Lots of screams. Jacko poked his head around the bathroom door. The hotel room was empty, apart from the furniture, which consisted of a television, a small table and some comfy chairs. The main door into the room was open, and lots of hotel guests and staff were running past it in a panic. But then to add to Jacko's woes, two people stumbled through the open door into the hotel room. The first was an elderly lady in her seventies with wrinkly white skin. She was wearing a black and orange patterned dress, and she looked terrified. Her companion, a man of similar age followed her in. He was pale and wrinkly too, and he was wearing light blue pants and a grey sweater.

Aa soon as they were inside, the man slammed the door shut and backed away from it. Jacko ducked back into the bathroom and closed the door, before either of them saw him.

'Fucking hell,' he whispered to himself.

He backed away towards the portal, hoping not to draw the attention of the old couple. But to add to the increasingly long list of the day's fuck ups, the old lady opened the bathroom door and looked straight at Jacko. She saw the opening in the wall behind him too. And to top things off, she screamed.

'Brian! There's a black man in our bathroom!'

Jacko leapt back through the portal into Purgatory, but not before the old man saw him too. This was a shitshow. The portal closed up, courtesy of Einstein using some initiative.

But things were about to get worse.

Einstein had taken up Jacko's usual position behind the bar. He had the receiver from the big red phone against his ear.

'Who the fuck are you talking to?' Jacko asked him.

'It's God,' said Einstein.

'God?'

'Yeah, and he wants to talk to you.' Einstein placed his hand over the mouthpiece on the receiver. 'He sounds really pissed. He said something about you misusing the portal. He wants it closed off.'

*When it rains, it shits down.*

'Tell him I'm on the other line,' Jacko said.

Einstein looked horrified. 'What? You want me to lie to God?'

Jacko pressed his own phone against his ear. Flake was no longer there. The line had gone dead. But then it started ringing again.

*Undisclosed number.*

Jacko answered it. 'Flake?'

'No fuckface. This is God. Since when do you not take my calls?'

'Aah, God. Great to hear from you. How's things?'

'What the fuck have you been doing with the portal?'

'Ummm.'

'The most powerful people in the world are dead, apart from a few of the really psychotic ones,' God continued.

'Ummm.'

'No wait, hang on, the fat kid from North Korea is dead too.' God sounded more agitated every second. 'And on top of all that,' he said, his voice lowering to indicate how agitated he was, 'an elderly couple in the Poseidon hotel have just seen you, *and* Purgatory. What the fuck kind of operation are you running down there?'

'I'm sorry, God. It's the Bourbon Kid. He went on a killing rampage, wiped out a load of Atlanteans. I thought you'd be pleased.'

'You thought wrong. No more using the portal without my permission. Got it?'

'What about Flake and the Bourbon Kid? They're stuck in the Poseidon and everyone is trying to kill them.'

God had no sympathy. 'The Bourbon Kid caused this mess,' he said. 'Let him find his own way back.'

'What about Flake?'

God wasn't much of one for goodbyes, so a simple click signalled the end of the call.

'Was he angry?' Einstein asked.

Before Jacko could tell Einstein to go fuck himself, his cell rang again. It was Flake. Again. So he answered it. Again.

'Hi, Flake.'

'Jacko, me and JD are in the hotel room, but the portal is closed. Can you reopen it?'

'I'd love to, but God has just banned me from using it. You've got to find your own way out of there.'

'You're fucking kidding me?'

'I wish I was. Sorry.'

Flake had a similar phone etiquette to God. Simple click. Call ended. Rude.

'What's happening then?' said Einstein.

'No more portal without God's permission.'

'Shall I make you a drink?'

Jacko let out a deep sigh. 'Rum and coke. You know, I'm starting to understand why Scratch was always angry, *and* drinking. This job drives you crazy.'

Einstein poured out a rum and coke in a tall glass, and set it down on the bar top. Jacko hopped up onto a barstool, turned his phone onto vibrate and put it down next to the rum and coke. He wiped some sweat off his brow, then picked up the rum and coke. Just as the glass touched his bottom lip, the inevitable happened. His phone started breakdancing on the bar top. Incoming call. *Motherfucker.*

'Ugh. What now?' Jacko put the drink down and picked up the phone. The display showed the caller was Jasmine. Jacko answered it. 'Hi, Jas. How's it going?'

'JACKO, GET US OUT OF HERE!'

Jacko winced and moved the phone away from his ear a little. 'Out of where?' he asked.

'Santa Mondega. It's an emergency. Me and Elvis are being shot at. We need you to open up the portal. Get us out of here. We're sitting ducks!'

'Where exactly in Santa Mondega?'

Jasmine lowered her voice. 'A bathroom underground in Chinatown. Underneath Bobby's Trains.'

Jacko rubbed his head in frustration. How the fuck was he going to explain to her that the portal was out of action? Best idea. Don't tell her. 'Bobby's Trains?' he said, in his calmest voice. 'Okay, give me a minute. I'll see what I can do.' Jacko covered the phone. 'Einstein! Start looking up a place called Bobby's Trains in Chinatown. We need to open up the portal for Jasmine and Elvis. There's an underground bathroom there somewhere.'

'What about God? Didn't he *just say* you couldn't use the portal?'

'Would you just look up Bobby's Trains!'

'Yes, sir.'

Jacko returned to his call with Jasmine. 'Hey, Jas. Just give me a minute. We're having some technical problems here at the moment. I'll sort it as soon as I can.'

Einstein raced out from behind the bar and dived onto a chair at the small round table where he'd left his laptop. He opened it up and started tapping away on the keyboard. 'Bobby's Trains?' he said, a confused look on his face.

'Yeah. Bobby's Trains. In Chinatown.'

'There is no Bobby's Trains in Chinatown.'

Jacko put his phone back to his ear. All he could hear on the other end was gunfire. 'Jasmine? JAS! CAN YOU HEAR ME?'

No answer. Fuck.

'EINSTEIN! HAVE YOU FOUND IT YET?'

Einstein's goofy top teeth were chewing on his bottom lip. 'I'm telling you, there's no Bobby's Trains in Santa Mondega!' His voice was cracking, like he was going to cry.

Jacko had to make a snap decision. *Who knew Santa Mondega best?*

*Sanchez. No good, he's dead.*

*Flake? No, unavailable.*

*Rex? Rex might know.*

Jacko terminated the call with Jasmine and made a hasty call to Rex. Thankfully, the big man answered his phone. There was no time for small talk though, so Jacko got right down to business.

'Rex! It's Jacko. *Emergency!* Jasmine and Elvis are in trouble. People are shooting at them. They're locked in a bathroom somewhere underground in Santa Mondega, but I can't find the place. Can you come back to Purgatory and help?'

'Yeah. Shit!' Rex started talking fast, which was exactly what was required. 'I'm in room forty-two of the El Guapo Motel in San Antonio. Open the portal and I'll come through. Are they hurt?'

'I don't know. HURRY!' Jacko covered the phone and yelled at Einstein again. 'Room forty-two at the El Guapo Motel in San Antonio. NOW!'

While Einstein tapped away on his keyboard, Jacko leapt over the bar, grabbed the big red phone on the worktop and pressed the white button in the centre of it. The call went straight through to God who answered with a tired, "Yes?"

'Jasmine's in trouble. Need to use the portal!'

'Jasmine? Okay.'

Jacko hung up the phone. It was lucky Jasmine was God's favourite member of the Dead Hunters. In fact she was possibly his favourite person, period. The mere mention of her name was the best way to get God's approval for just about anything.

When Jacko turned around, Rex was already walking through the portal into Purgatory.

'WHERE ARE THEY?' he yelled at Jacko.

'Underneath Bobby's train shop in Chinatown,' Jacko replied. 'But Einstein can't find it on the map!'

'Yo, Einstein,' said Rex, pointing at the scientist. 'Look for Barbie's Nails. That's the old name. The train shop moved in a few months ago.'

Einstein tapped a few more keys at lightning speed. 'GOT IT!' he yelled back after a couple of seconds.

The portal door slid shut behind Rex, then immediately reopened. Gunfire filled the air. Rex turned around just in time to see a great big Alsatian limp past him. Jasmine was laid out on the floor inside a poky little room, her catsuit peppered with bullet holes and blood. Elvis was standing between her and a fucked-up door that was being shot to literal pieces. Big chunks of the door had been blown out, and Elvis was making it worse by shooting back at whoever was on the other side.

Rex jumped straight into action. He grabbed Jasmine and dragged her into Purgatory and away from the line of fire. To add to all the chaos, the big dog started barking at nothing. Jacko leaned over the bar to get a look at Jasmine. She was in a bad way.

Rex left Jasmine and yelled at Elvis to get a move on. It worked because Elvis stopped shooting at the knackered door and dived into Purgatory. Rex hit the button beside the portal and the door slid shut, silencing all the gunfire.

'Whose fucking dog is that?' said Einstein.

'Who cares?' said Rex, leaning over Jasmine and checking her pulse. Jasmine's purple catsuit was full of bullet holes. It was her best catsuit too, the one that said *Porn Star* on the chest.

'Oh, Jesus,' said Jacko. He didn't dare say much else for fear of incriminating himself. He felt partly responsible for the whole shitstorm.

Elvis looked over at him with pleading eyes. 'You gotta get Flake!' he said. 'She's got the Eye of the Moon.'

Jacko rubbed his forehead. 'Flake's got problems of her own. I'm not even sure where she is right now.'

'I know where she is,' said Rex. 'Set the portal for the Gunslingers bar in Downtown, Chicago.'

As ever, Einstein was on the ball. It took him next to no time to locate a men's washroom in the Gunslingers. Rex reopened the portal door and dashed through it to look for Flake.

Jacko was as close as he'd ever been to having a panic attack. Every second that passed after Rex went through the portal felt like an age. Time was not on Jasmine's side. She was going to die at any moment, Jacko was sure of it.

DING-DONG!

What the fuck?

Jacko looked over at Einstein. The crazy scientist had heard the doorbell ring too. And he looked as confused by it as Jacko was.

'Was that a doorbell?' Einstein said, echoing Jacko's thoughts.

'It was,' Jacko agreed, frowning. 'But we don't have a doorbell..... do we?'

Einstein shrugged, then he yelled at the top of his voice. 'COME IN.'

'What are you doing?' Jacko asked, exasperated. 'Are you mental? We don't know who's out there!'

'We do now,' Einstein said, pointing at the batwing doors at the front entrance.

A cheery-looking female postal worker strolled in through the doors. She was a petite young thing in a pair of brown shorts and a red jacket with a satchel over her shoulder. She spotted the big Alsatian curled up on the floor by the bar, gave him a wide berth and made her way up to the bar.

'Delivery for Jacko,' she said, holding up a large padded brown envelope.

This day really couldn't get any weirder. Not only had Purgatory never had a doorbell before (not that Jacko knew of anyway) but there had never been a postal service in the Devil's Graveyard either.

Jacko forced a smile. 'I'm Jacko,' he said.

The postal worker handed him the padded envelope and a small piece of paper. 'Sign here please,' she said.

Jacko looked at her name badge. He name was Cindy. 'Excuse me, Cindy. How did you get here?' he asked.

'I drove,' she said. 'Sign please.'

'Right, yes, of course.'

Jacko signed the piece of paper and handed it back to her.

'Thank you,' said Cindy. 'Have a nice day.'

'Err, yeah. You too,' Jacko called after her as she strolled back out through the batwing doors.

Einstein got up from his table and walked over to the bar. 'What is it?' he asked, eagerly eyeing up the envelope.

Jacko ripped open the brown envelope and pulled out an empty syringe and a small piece of paper with a handwritten note on it. The note said – *To Jacko, from God.*

'Why has he sent me a syringe?' Jacko muttered.

'Maybe he wants you to inject yourself with the plague?' Einstein suggested. 'You know, because you've really annoyed him today.'

Jacko ignored Einstein's snide remark and looked over at the portal to see if Rex was on his way back. There was no sign of him. He looked down at Jasmine. She was draped across Elvis and she didn't appear to be breathing. Elvis looked like he was asleep, or maybe even unconscious.

To make matters worse, the sound of gunfire burst through the open portal again. It woke Elvis back up. He looked around like he'd forgotten where he was. Jacko closed his eyes. *Please let Flake, JD and Rex be okay.* He put the stupid syringe down under the bar. God's cryptic message was wasted on him. When he looked back up he saw Rex, Flake and JD charging in through the portal.

'What took you so long?' Jacko asked, failing to hide how nervous he was.

No one answered him. Instead, Flake dived down onto the floor and pressed the Eye of the Moon against Jasmine's injuries. She and

Elvis tried to work out the best way to use the blue stone while the others watched on anxiously. Seeing as no one was speaking to Jacko he closed up the portal, just in case any more dogs came bounding in through it.

Eventually Rex asked Jacko, 'Do we have any bandages?'

'All out,' Jacko replied. 'You could try a T-shirt?'

That idea went down like a lead balloon. Although, after a while Elvis did take off his shirt and wrap it around Jasmine's torso like it was a bandage. Nothing seemed to be working though. Eventually, JD left the others and walked up to the bar. He clicked his fingers at Jacko, then pretended to inject himself in the arm with an imaginary syringe.

*Aha! So that's what the syringe is for. Wow, God really does like Jasmine.*

Jacko reached down under the bar and picked up the syringe. He handed it to JD who was using a knife to slice open his hand, drawing out some of his holy blood.

'I hope this works,' Jacko whispered to him. 'Because if it doesn't, God will never forgive us.'

## Sixty-Six

<u>Four months later</u>

Alexis Calhoon had played a major part in ending the war. Only a handful of people knew that her assassins were responsible for the execution of the Russian president. One of the people who knew was President Navan Douglas. It had taken him four months to finally invite Calhoon to the White House to thank her for her efforts.

She and her husband Roger had put on their best clothes for the meeting. The General wore her white dress uniform, and her husband rocked up in his best formal wear. They waited in the reception area for twenty minutes before one of the president's staff, a young black man in a grey suit came to fetch them.

'Hello, General,' he said. 'I am Jeff Brooks. The president is ready to see you now.'

Calhoon and her husband both stood up and simultaneously smoothed out any creases in their clothing.

'Sir,' said Brooks, addressing Roger Calhoon. 'If you don't mind, you'll have to wait here for a while. The president needs to discuss some official business with the General first. When that's done, I'll come get you.'

'No problem,' said Roger, graciously. He patted Alexis on the arm and wished her good luck, then sat back down to wait a little longer.

Brooks and Calhoon walked along a corridor to the president's office, exchanging quick-fire banter like they were in an episode of *The West Wing*. When they arrived outside the oval office, Brooks made some chit-chat with the secretary, then he knocked on the president's door, opened it and stepped aside to let Calhoon in.

President Douglas was perched on the edge of his desk, looking casual. Blue suit pants, shirt undone, no tie. The guy seemed to be taking to the job quite well.

'Alexis,' he said, greeting her with a smile and walking across the room to shake her hand. 'I trust your journey here went well.'

'Yes indeed, Mister President. My husband and I would like to thank you for the private jet and the car. They made the journey so much more comfortable.'

'Good, I'm glad. Please take a seat.'

Douglas walked around to the leather seat behind his desk and slouched back in it. Calhoon sat in one of the chairs on the other side of the desk, but stayed in an upright, less comfortable position.

'Great, *great* work your people did with the Russian,' Douglas said, leaning forward. 'Your country owes you a debt of gratitude.'

'That's very kind of you, sir. Just doing my job of course, serving my president.'

'I don't know where the world would be without your assassins,' Douglas said. He leaned back in his chair again and smiled at her, but he said nothing more.

'I think the world is thankful for your leadership in such tough times,' Calhoon said, generously.

Douglas continued smiling at her. This was bad. Calhoon's decades of service in espionage, counter-intelligence and phantom ops meant that she knew when something was amiss quicker than most people. She glanced to her left, then to her right. She'd already checked the room upon entering. They were alone. Except, maybe they weren't. Calhoon had that feeling, like there was a creepy-crawly on the back of her neck.

'Is everything okay, Mister President?' she asked.

'Absolutely.'

And there it was. The insect bite on the base of her neck. Except this was no insect. She reached up to swat it away, but her hand never made it that far. Her fingers touched the collar of her shirt, but then her hand slipped back down to her side. Her head felt heavy. She'd been injected with something. A pair of invisible hands steadied her head and let it fall back against her chair. Her mouth dropped open like an old person falling asleep in front of the TV after a big lunch.

'You've had that coming for some time,' Douglas said, his smirk broadening. 'That's for my old friend, Mike Raffone. Remember him? I know you had your people kill him last year.'

Calhoon was completely paralysed. She could see and hear everything, but she couldn't move a muscle, not even her eyes, which were staring at the curtains behind the president's head.

President Douglas stood up from his seat and walked around the desk. He perched on the edge of it again and leaned forward to get into Calhoon's eyeline. He reached out and lifted her bottom jaw, closing her mouth up. As soon as he withdrew his hand, her mouth fell open again.

'It fascinates me,' he said. 'Seeing people paralysed like this. You can do stuff to them that you would never normally be able to do to anyone.' He ran his finger across her cheek. 'Don't worry though,' he continued. 'The paralysis will be over soon. In about two minutes you'll have a massive heart attack. Thank you for your service to your country.'

Before Calhoon got to experience the massive heart attack, she witnessed the unveiling of her killer. The invisible man lowered the hood on his coat, revealing himself to her. He was standing beside the president's chair. He was a pale-skinned, forty-something man wearing a purple shirt and pants beneath a fuzzy, black and white coat. In his hand was the murderous syringe that had injected Calhoon with a deadly poison.

'Oh, this is the man who killed you,' said Douglas. 'His name is Diago, and your people killed everyone he cared about, including his brother.'

Douglas closed up Calhoon's mouth again just for fun, then he walked back around the desk, ushering Diago away from his chair.

'That's my part of the bargain done,' said Diago, moving away but then pulling up a chair next to Calhoon. 'Now tell me where to find these Dead Hunter people.'

'It's complicated,' said Douglas, sitting back down in his own chair. 'We didn't have a tracking device on either of the two men who murdered your circus friends.'

'Rodeo Rex and the Bourbon Kid,' said Diago. 'One of them killed my brother, Dexter. That I cannot forgive.'

'Don't worry. We had a tracker on their friend, Flake Munroe. She was wearing it when she and the Bourbon Kid fled the Poseidon Hotel after the murder of my predecessor. We tracked them to an underground biker bar in Chicago called the Gunslingers. Unfortunately, when our people got there, they'd vanished.'

'Vanished? How?'

'It's hard to say. At around the time our people raided the club, Flake's tracking device went on the fritz.'

'On the fritz?'

'Yes. One minute she was at the Gunslingers, then she and the Bourbon Kid both vanished off the face of the planet. At first, the assumption was that they had discovered the device and disabled it, but then about an hour later the tracker showed up on an island in the Pacific ocean.' Douglas winced, then added, 'but ten minutes later it vanished again. It must have been a glitch because there's no way they could have gone from Chicago to the Pacific ocean in such a short time.'

Diago wasn't convinced. 'What was the name of the island?'

'Medicine Island. It's uninhabited these days, but it used to be a testing site for vaccines.'

'I know it,' said Diago. 'Orto McTavish was exiled there some years ago. Maybe he would have seen them?'

'I'm certain they weren't there,' said Douglas. 'And even if they were, the island was hit by a tsunami that was triggered by the Russian nukes. If you really want to find them, my gut is telling me the bikers at the Gunslingers club know more than they're letting on.'

Diago leaned across the desk, opened his mouth and bared his fangs. 'You made me wait all this time, only to tell me they're probably dead?'

'It's all I have, sorry.'

The vampire reached back over his shoulder and pulled his hood up over his head, making himself invisible again.

'What are you doing?' Douglas asked. 'Diago? What are you doing?'

Diago did not reply verbally. Instead he moved around the desk and introduced the new president of the USA to his vampire fangs. He chewed off Navan Douglas's nose, ripped his tongue out of his mouth, and then skinned him alive. The message was clear, never double-cross a vampire, especially one with an invisible coat.

## Sixty-Seven

Since losing a chunk of its clientele in a recent massacre, the Gunslingers club had become a rather quiet place. Tina the barmaid had always preferred it busy. But since the massacre she was perfectly happy for it to be quiet. Quiet and dull, that suited her just fine.

It was midday on a particularly quiet Thursday lunch-time and there were only two customers in the club. Carmine, the new club president and his buddy, Bony Jim. They were playing pool when a non-member walked in through the main doors and sauntered up to the bar. He was a tall, pale gentleman wearing a strange fuzzy black and white coat over a purple shirt and matching pants, a real joker's outfit. He had long dark hair, yellow eyes and a rather effeminate way about him. Tina eyed him with suspicion. He didn't look like the sort of customer the doorman Kurt would allow into the club.

'Good day to you,' the man said, as he hopped onto a stool at the bar.

'How did you get in here?' Tina asked him.

'I glided in.'

'Rik let you in?'

'Yes.'

'Rik don't work here. Kurt's on the door, and he don't let strangers in. Who are you, mister? And how did you get in?'

'My name is Diago,' the man replied. 'And my job is to hunt down the people that attacked your club.'

'You mean the Bourbon Kid?'

'That's right. I understand he was here a few months ago with a lady named Flake?'

Tina squinted her eyes at him. 'How do you know so much?'

'I'm educated,' Diago replied with a waft of arrogance. 'But I am correct, am I not?'

'Yeah, they were here. And Rodeo Rex showed up too. The three of them shot the place to pieces. The cops and the FBI have been looking for them ever since. What makes you think *you* can find them?'

'Because I'm awesome,' said Diago. 'I will see to it that they pay for what they have done.'

'You gonna buy a drink?' Tina asked, her curiosity piqued.

'No I am not. What I want is to know where the Bourbon Kid and his friends went after they left this place?'

'They just vanished,' said Tina.

'Vanished?'

'I was here, behind the bar. The cops don't believe me, but I saw it. They went into the men's toilets and they never came back out.'

'So they escaped through a window?'

'Nah. Ain't no windows in those toilets.'

Diago stroked his chin as he deliberated what Tina was saying. 'Explain it to me again,' he said eventually. 'From the beginning. They arrive, they come to you for a drink, and—'

'They didn't come to the bar,' said Tina. 'I had to go over and take their order. And to begin with it was just the Bourbon Kid and his girlfriend. He had a glass of bourbon, she had a gin and tonic. Then a bunch of cop cars showed up outside. That's when some of the guys confronted them. We don't like cops round here.'

'Who does?' Diago agreed.

'Right, so then some of the guys confront the Bourbon Kid. That's when Rodeo Rex shows up out of nowhere. That's to say, he came in through them toilets.' Tina pointed to the men's room at the back of the drinking area.

'Rex was already here then? But he was in the men's room?'

'No,' said Tina, pushing her bottom lip out with her tongue. It was something she did to people when she thought they were dumb. 'That's what I keep tellin' people. He wasn't here, hadn't been here in years, but then he comes in through the men's room.'

Diago scratched his temple. 'Wait a second. He came in through the men's room? Is there a way into the club through the men's room?'

'Are you listenin' to me? There ain't no windows in the men's room. There ain't no doors in the men's room. It's one way in and out. He never went in there, but he sure came outta there.'

Diago pursed his lips while he took the information on board. 'Okay,' he said after a few seconds. 'Then what?'

'Then the pretty little lady started firing blue electricity from her hands, and the Bourbon Kid started shootin' at everyone. They killed a lot of people.'

'And you saw this?'

'I ducked down behind the bar. I only heard most of it. But when the shootin' was done I looked up, and I saw them go into the men's room. All three of 'em. And that's the last we saw of 'em. Cops burst in a couple of minutes later, and I told 'em what I just told you. But they went into the men's room and there was no one there.'

'Okay,' said Diago. 'What do you think happened when the Bourbon Kid and his friends went into the men's room?'

'I *know* what happened,' said Tina. 'They got beamed up.'

'Beamed up?'

'I'd heard about it. Rumours and such, y'know. For years now, people been sayin' Rodeo Rex, he can switch continents in a matter of seconds. One minute he's here, next minute he's there.'

'There?'

'Australia, Europe, Asia, anywhere you like.'

Diago lowered his eyebrows. 'How does he do that?'

'I don't know. But I know it's going on. I'm not the only one what saw him go in that men's room. I'm tellin' you now, it's the work of the Devil. They can travel to any place they want, anywhere in the world.'

'Like a desert island?'

Tina repeated herself, extra loud for Diago's benefit. 'ANYWHERE IN THE WORLD.' Her raised voice attracted the attention of the two bikers who were playing pool. They stopped and looked over.

'Thank you,' said Diago. 'You've been very helpful.'

Carmine, a six-footer who had a partially shaved head with a two-inch high tuft of hair growing out of the top of it, walked over from the pool table. He was wielding a pool cue like he was ready to use it. His buddy, Bony Jim, a skinny, toothless fella with one eye lower than the other, followed him over, cue in hand.

'Hey, asshole,' said Carmine, addressing Diago. 'Who told you, you could come in our club?'

Diago slid off his stool and glared at Carmine. Then he lifted the hood of his coat over his head and vanished into thin air. Tina looked at Carmine to see if he'd witnessed it. He looked back at her. The pair of them were dumbstruck. Had the weird, pale man really just disappeared?

'Where did he go?' Carmine asked.

Before Tina could respond, Carmine started doing a weird dance, like a tango but without a partner. Then blood squirted out of his neck. To begin with it looked like he'd been stabbed with a pair of scissors, but then the hole suddenly erupted. The skin on the front of his neck peeled away. Blood spurted everywhere. Carmine's throat had been ripped out. Bony Jim reacted by swinging his club at where he thought the invisible killer might be. But midway through his third swing, the cue flew out of his hand, disappeared for a second, then reappeared as it clattered onto the floor.

'What happened?' Tina asked. 'Did you get him?'

Bony Jim didn't get a chance to respond. His hands dropped down to his sides, and he started wiggling his legs like he was doing an Irish jig. Then he twisted his head past his shoulder. A loud crack signalled the end of the routine. Bony Jim dropped to the floor, his neck broken.

Tina had no intention of being Diago's next victim. She turned on her heels and ran back to the club's storeroom where she grabbed a short-barrelled rifle that was kept in a cupboard for emergencies. When she returned to the bar area, she waved it around like she was ready to use it.

'Show yourself you fuckin' coward!' she screamed, her hand trembling on the handle of the gun.

There was no reply. She walked out from behind the bar, both hands on the gun, threatening to fire. She prayed to God that the invisible man was gone.

He wasn't. The gun was snatched from her grasp. As soon as it left her hands it disappeared. Tina backed away.

'I wasn't gonna shoot,' she said. 'It's not even loaded.'

Diago didn't care for her lies. He smashed the butt of the gun into her mouth, knocking several of her teeth out. A second blow to the side of her head knocked her unconscious. Diago didn't believe in loose ends so he hit her a few more times with the gun until her brains were all over the floor.

## Sixty-Eight

'That's our next job,' Rex announced. 'We find the people who killed Calhoon.'

The gang were sitting around the kitchen table in the medical centre having a late lunch after working up an appetite playing volleyball on the beach. Flake had cooked up some fillet steaks and French fries for everyone, and laid out a mixture of "help yourself" sides on the table. There was much to discuss because in the last twenty-four hours they had heard about the deaths of Alexis Calhoon, Navan Douglas and a few more members of the Gunslingers club.

Elvis responded to Rex's announcement through a mouthful of meat and fries. 'How the fuck are we going to find out who did it?'

Rex had given the matter plenty of thought. 'I'm convinced that whoever killed Calhoon and Navan Douglas is responsible for what happened at the Gunslingers,' he said. 'It's too much of a coincidence. Someone is probably trying to track down JD and Flake.'

Flake swallowed a chunk of steak without sufficiently chewing it. It made a loud gulping sound. 'Who would want to do that?'

'I don't know,' said Rex. 'But it's the only thing that makes sense.'

JD stopped eating and looked across the table at Rex. 'No one knows we're here. If someone was looking for us, the trail would go cold at the Gunslingers.'

Rex picked up a bread roll from a basket in the centre of the table. But before he could do anything with it, his phone beeped, indicating an incoming text. He put the bread roll down on his plate and checked his phone.

'Who's texting you?' Jasmine asked him.

Rex looked deep in thought as he read the message. 'Ask for help and God sends you a text message,' he said.

'God texted you?' said Jasmine.

'No, it's Denise, an old friend of mine.'

Elvis was about to shove a handful of fries into his mouth, but he hesitated. 'Denise?' he said. 'Carmine's old lady?'

Rex nodded. 'I've got a funeral to go to.'

Elvis was still holding his fries. 'Carmine's dead?'

'Yep, he was in the Gunslingers yesterday.'

'Text her back. Ask her who killed him,' said Elvis, finally shoving his fries into his mouth.

'Jeez, I never would have thought of that,' said Rex, rolling his eyes. He then proceeded to text Denise back, expressing his condolences and asking if she knew who was responsible for the latest Gunslingers slaughter.

Everyone else carried on eating, saying nothing as they waited for Rex to get a reply from Denise. It arrived just as Rex was about to eat a juicy piece of steak. He put his fork down and checked his phone.

'She doesn't know,' he said after reading the message. 'She says the security cameras didn't pick up anyone going in or out of the club.'

'That's a bummer,' said Elvis.

'And she wants me to give a speech at Carmine's funeral. Shit.'

Elvis took a swig from a bottle of cola and swilled it around in his mouth before replying. 'I dunno if that's a good idea, man. Aren't those guys gunning for you now?'

'They might have been,' said Rex. 'But by the sounds of it, all the Gunslingers are dead. The funeral will be made up of bikers from other clubs. Carmine was a popular guy.'

'I wouldn't go,' said Elvis. 'It could be a trap.'

Rex was torn. 'Denise is a good friend of mine. And so was Carmine. I feel like I should.'

'When is it?' Elvis asked.

'It's on Thursday. In Oakland.'

'California? That's a long ride.'

'It's okay. I'll use the crossroads.'

Flake swallowed a French fry and looked up. 'Use the crossroads? What does that mean?' she asked.

'It's a new thing,' said Rex. 'Jacko got Einstein to create another portal. This one is at the crossroads. Unlike the bathroom portal, you can go through this one in a vehicle, and it'll take you to any parking lot in the world. I like it better than showing up in people's bathrooms.'

'It sounds dangerous,' said Flake. 'You could crash straight into something on the other side.'

Jasmine grabbed one of the fries from Elvis's plate and nibbled the end of it. 'Me and Elvis will go to the funeral with you,' she said. 'Just in case there's any trouble.'

'It's Hell's Angels only,' said Rex. 'Everyone has to show up on two wheels. Then when the ceremony is done, we take over a highway and go for a long ride together.'

'I've ridden with your people before,' said Elvis. 'I'm an honorary biker. I can go, can't I?'

'That would be okay,' said Rex. 'It could be like old times.'

'Can I really *not* go?' said Jasmine. 'Not even as a plus one?'

'Elvis will have to be *my* plus one,' said Rex. 'I can just about get away with taking him with me.'

Elvis rubbed Jasmine's shoulder 'You should stay here. We'll only be gone a day anyway, right Rex?'

'Actually,' said Rex. 'I was thinking, after the funeral we could hit the road again and head to Calhoon's ranch, speak to her husband, Roger. See if he has any idea who killed her. Whadda you think?'

Elvis slid his arm down to Jasmine's waist and gave her a squeeze. 'How do you feel about that, sweetie?'

'It sounds shit,' said Jasmine. 'But I think you two deserve some guy time. Go on your big bike ride, and when you find out who we're going to kill, then you can come get me. I'll stay here and work on my all-over tan.'

Goober barked, as if approving of the idea. What he actually wanted was for the gang to quit chattering and throw him some fucking meat. Flake did the honours, tossing him a chunk of steak from her plate. It was wolfed down in half a second.

When lunch was over, and Goober had licked all the plates clean, Rex, Elvis and Jasmine headed to Purgatory for some afternoon drinks while JD and Flake stayed behind to clean up.

JD cleared the table and retrieved the plates from Goober while Flake filled the sink with hot water.

'You know, I had a thought,' Flake said.

'What's that?'

'Rex said that when his friend was killed at the Gunslingers, the cameras didn't pick up anyone entering or leaving the premises.'

'Yeah.'

'Do you think maybe it was one of these invisible assassins? You know, like the one who hit you with the baseball bat, or the ones who killed all the world leaders?'

JD had a stack of plates in his hand. He put them down on the table. 'About that,' he said, clearing his throat. 'There's something I need to tell you.'

'Yeah, I know. You need to get it off your chest.'

'You know?'

'Yeah, I know. I think everyone else knows too. It's kind of obvious.'

JD picked up the plates again and carried them over to the sink. He set them down next to it and looked Flake in the eye. 'If I'd known Sanchez would get killed, I wouldn't have done any of it.'

Flake looked away and turned off the hot tap. She ran her hand through the water in the wash basin to check the temperature. 'I'm still sad that Sanchez is dead,' she said. 'And I wish he was still alive. And I wish the whole world hadn't fallen apart and millions of people hadn't died because of what you did. But the fact remains, what happened has led to this, to us living on this island together. And this is the happiest I've ever been. Sometimes I feel guilty about all of it, but in spite of everything, it feels like it was all meant to be.'

JD placed his hand on her back. 'Sometimes, good things come out of very bad situations. I wish I hadn't killed all those people. But if I hadn't, I wouldn't be here right now. And I wouldn't know I was in love with you.'

'You know, you're an idiot,' said Flake, turning to face him. She slid her arms around his waist even though her hands were wet. 'But I love you too,' she said, gazing up at him. 'So let's finish cleaning up, then go to the beach.'

## Sixty-Nine

Jasmine was standing outside Purgatory in a "barely-there" brown bikini. She looked up at the sky. Dark red clouds were forming, as if a downpour of acid rain was incoming. She was there to wave goodbye to Elvis and Rex, who were heading off to a funeral. Rex was sitting on a custom-made Harley Davidson chopper at the roadside, revving the engine. He was wearing black leather pants and a leather jacket that had a picture of an eagle on the back. The eagle was smoking a cigar and wearing a stars-and-stripes bandana, just like the one Rex had wrapped around his head. There was a second, riderless chopper next to Rex. It belonged to Elvis, who was taking his time leaving Purgatory.

'Come on, hurry up!' Rex yelled.

Elvis strolled out of Purgatory through the batwing doors at the front. He was in a plain black leather suit. He ignored Rex and went straight up to Jasmine. The two engaged in a passionate embrace that ended when Rex cleared his throat as loudly as he could.

Jasmine ran her hand down Elvis neck as they parted. 'Aren't you gonna wear a helmet?' she asked him.

'And ruin my hair?'

'Of course. Stupid question. That's my guy. Hair first, safety never.'

'I'll be back in a couple of days,' said Elvis, pressing his crotch against her and grabbing her ass as if he'd forgotten about the recent embrace. 'I'll bring you back a present. Anything in particular you want?'

'Just bring yourself back. That'll do me just fine.'

'You got it.' Elvis leaned in for another kiss, which got out of hand again like always. It ended when Rex shouted, "Get to the chopper!" at him.

Jasmine and Elvis removed their hands from inside one another's clothing, then Elvis headed over to his chopper. He climbed on and took a little while to get comfortable. Boners and leather pants don't mix well with choppers.

When Elvis finally started the engine, a drop of rain fell onto his cheek. He looked up at the sky as the second and third raindrops landed on his shoulders, swiftly followed by a torrential downpour.

'This is your fault!' Rex snapped at him. 'You took too long.'

'Fucking hell,' Elvis groaned. 'This rain's gonna ruin my hair and my suit, man.'

Rex shook his head in disgust. 'You wouldn't last five minutes in a biker gang. You'd be strung up for saying something like that.'

'I'm not in a biker gang,' Elvis reminded him. 'Because I don't much care for riding a bike in shitty weather.'

'I'm not gonna tell you again. It's a chopper.'

'Chopper shmopper,' said Elvis as the wind and rain whipped up and started to fuck with his hair. 'If it's raining in Chicago, I'm ditching the bike and hiring a car.'

'CHOPPER!'

Jasmine yelled at them through the wind and rain. 'WOULD YOU TWO JUST GO FOR FUCKSSAKE!'

Rex needed no second invitation. He revved his engine again then sped off down the highway. Elvis took one last look at Jasmine, blew her a kiss, then hit the road, riding straight into the dirt and debris that Rex had left in his wake.

A couple of minutes later, Rex arrived at the crossroads. He stopped and looked around. Elvis was half a mile back, riding with caution in the heavy rain. Rex sighed. Riding with non-bikers was tiresome stuff. Elvis eventually cruised up alongside him, looking like someone had thrown a bucket of wet sand in his face.

'What happens now then?' Elvis asked as he wiped some dirt off his face.

Rex pointed at the four-armed signpost at the roadside. One of the arms had CHICAGO on it in red letters. 'Road to Chicago,' he said.

'Sounds like a crappy Bob Hope movie.'

Rex ignored the sarcastic remark. 'Once we take the turn we'll be transported straight to Chicago,' he reminded Elvis. 'It won't be raining there.'

'Yeah, right. Like it never rains in Chicago.'

Rex jammed on the throttle and sped onto the road to Chicago. A few sparks of lightning crackled around him, then his chopper disappeared like he was in a cheap B-movie rip-off of *Back To the Future*.

Elvis sighed. 'Why the fuck is he going fast?' he muttered to himself. He rolled the throttle on his ride and cruised at a sensible speed towards the spot where Rex disappeared. He didn't see or feel the electrical fuzz that he'd seen when Rex went through the new invisible portal. The empty road ahead just disappeared, replaced by a dark building with cars parked on all sides. And no torrential rain, thankfully. The crossroads had transported him to a parking garage. Rex was up ahead waiting for him, his engine ticking over.

'Where now then?' Elvis asked him.

'Just follow me.'

## Seventy

Jasmine spent an hour in Purgatory with Jacko, drinking tonic water and watching the news, which was showing a press conference by the newest president of the USA. In the wake of Navan Douglas's murder, a new acting president had taken over. Her name was Ophelia Cox. One of the first things she did was call for the capture of the Dead Hunters, who she believed were responsible for murdering her predecessors. She was particularly keen to see Flake and JD apprehended and tried before a judge.

'She sounds like a lot of fun,' said Jasmine.

'You should let Flake know about this,' said Jacko. 'This bitch sounds serious.'

Jasmine waved a dismissive hand. 'They've been trying to catch us for years. Sheesh, I bet they've been after JD for decades.'

'True,' Jacko agreed. 'But you should still let them know.'

Jasmine slid off her bar stool. 'Fair enough. I was going for a swim anyway. Can you switch the portal for me, please?'

'Already done.'

Jasmine left Jacko and headed through the portal into the research centre. She was greeted by the sound of Olivia Newton John singing "Physical". She followed the tune until it led her to the utility room, where she found Flake doing some ironing. There was also a washing machine rumbling away behind Flake as it tossed dirty laundry around in its drum.

'Hey Flake, need a hand?' Jasmine asked, knowing full well that Flake would not want any help from her with the domestic chores.

'No, it's okay,' Flake replied. 'I'm nearly done. Have Elvis and Rex gone yet?'

'Yeah. They left about an hour ago. I've just been watching the news. There's a new president in America. She just gave a speech where she said her top priority is finding you and JD.'

Flake groaned. 'Thanks, got any other cheerful news?'

'No, that's all,' said Jasmine. 'I'm off for a swim now. You wanna come?'

'Maybe later,' Flake replied as she folded up a pair of shorts. 'I'll be down on the beach in a bit to hang out the washing. I think Goober is down there at the moment though. He might go for a swim with you.'

'Okay. What about JD? Where is he?'

'He's probably on the beach too,' Flake said, before hastily adding, 'He won't want to go swimming with you though.'

'Why not?'

'He likes to walk around the island in the morning, so don't bother him.'

'Fair enough. I'll see you later then.'

'Yeah, have fun.'

Jasmine grabbed a towel and strolled down to the beach. Goober was there on his own, playing with a giant red, white and yellow beach ball.

'Hey Goober, where's JD?' Jasmine asked him.

Goober responded by nudging his beach ball in her direction. It was his way of saying, "quid pro quo". *Play ball with me, and I'll give you answers.*

Jasmine kicked the ball around with Goober for a few minutes, only for him to renege on his promise to tell her where JD was. Rude dog.

When the kickabout ended because Goober decided to keep the ball to himself, Jasmine slipped out of her bikini and ran into the ocean for a swim. It was the perfect day for it. Warm sun, cool breeze, cooler water, and no one around to tell her to put some clothes on.

After fifteen minutes in the sea where she practised the back stroke, breast stroke, front crawl, butterfly and doggie paddle, Jasmine swam back towards the shore to do some sunbathing on the beach. Goober was on the sand barking furiously at his beach ball.

'Okay, boy, I'm coming!'

Jasmine reached the shallow water and started walking back to the beach. The breaking waves splashed into the back of her thighs, and the warm sun made the droplets of water on her skin glisten. She wiped her hair back and let the water trickle down her shoulders. Island life sure was good, although it would be a lot better if the dog stopped barking.

Goober had become agitated, his beach ball no longer of interest to him. He leapt around on the sand, snarling at nothing.

'What's the matter, Goober?' Jasmine asked him. 'Is it a fly?'

As the ocean water washed back past her feet, she saw something in the wet sand in front of her.

*Footprints.*

They weren't hers from when she had walked into the water. These footprints were facing towards the beach. Someone else had recently walked out of the water.

Someone with webbed feet.

## Seventy-One

It had been a long time since Diago had travelled across the ocean. His journey to Medicine Island started when he stowed away aboard a cargo vessel. His invisible coat made it easy to get aboard. It was also easy to kill sleeping crew members in order to drink some fresh blood to keep his spirits up. Eventually, when the ship reached a point where it was only twenty miles away from Medicine Island, Diago leapt overboard and swam the rest of the way. The sharks and other ocean predators could sense his presence but they couldn't see him.

When he reached the island he knew straight away that it was inhabited. His first clue was the beautiful naked woman swimming in the water not far from the shore. Being invisible meant Diago could get close to her without her knowing. He had a good look at her. A real good look. And it didn't take him long to recognise her. She was one of his favourite porn stars, Lady Sack-punch aka Jasmine. After ogling her for a while, he reminded himself that he had a job to do. Lady Sack-punch could be ravaged later.

He swam to the shore and waded out onto the sandy beach where he saw a big Alsatian playing with a beach ball. There was a washing line on the beach too, and some deck chairs. Diago was certain there were more people living there, it couldn't be just a porn star and her dog.

Typically, the Alsatian got a whiff of vampire scent almost immediately. The big dog quit playing with its ball and started barking in Diago's general direction. Diago hated dogs. Couldn't stand them. Dogs didn't like vampires, and the feeling was mutual.

The barking drew the attention of the swimming porn star. She wandered out of the ocean like a naked goddess. Diago forgot about the dog for a moment and focussed his attention on her. She was a major distraction. The temptation to ravish her before hunting down the Bourbon Kid was almost unbearable. While he was ogling her incredible body, he saw her look down at the sand. She saw his footprints.

Shit!

That was it. There was no way he could let her raise the alarm. He had to do something. He pulled a dagger from its leather sheath on his hip and moved towards her.

She looked over at the barking dog. 'What's the matter, Goober?' she said. 'Is it a fly?'

Diago edged closer, careful not to make a sound, grateful for the crashing waves and the barking mutt drowning out the sound of his feet

297

on the sand. But when he was almost within touching distance of Jasmine, she looked down. She saw the disturbance his feet were making in the sand, and she started running.

Awesome. Diago loved it when a conquest tried to flee. It added to the thrill of the kill. He sprinted after her. She was easy to catch. Far too easy. Diago grabbed one of her arms and pulled her towards him. She swung at him with her other arm, catching him across the face. This bitch liked it rough.

His intention was to pin her to the ground, press his knife against her throat and then have his wicked way with her. Unfortunately, the fucking dog had other ideas. It blindsided Diago, leaping onto him and sinking its sharp teeth into his arm. It caused chaos. Diago, Jasmine and Goober crashed to the ground in a messy heap. Diago's knife plunged into Jasmine's arm, just below her shoulder. She screamed out in pain. Diago yelled too because the fucking dog sunk its teeth into the side of his face.

The three of them rolled around in the sand. Jasmine was trying to break free and run, Goober was trying to rip Diago's face off, and Diago was trying to fight the dog off.

'FLAKE, HELP!' Jasmine yelled.

In the blur of everything, Diago successfully thrust his knife into the dog's side. Goober screamed. Diago yanked his knife back out of the mutt, ready to stab it again if necessary, but Goober rolled away, whimpering. Diago composed himself and climbed to his knees. A foot kicked him in the face. Now Jasmine was on the attack. Despite the blood seeping out of her arm, she was no longer trying to flee. She was blindly kicking out in Diago's direction. The bitch. He hauled himself up, brandishing his knife, ready to stab her again. His intentions towards Jasmine were no longer sexual. Now he just wanted her dead.

■■■■■■■■■■■■■■■■■■■■■■■■■■■■■■■■■■■■■■■■■■■■■■■■■■■■

Flake finished ironing and put the clothes away in the appropriate closets and drawers. When that chore was complete, the next one announced itself. A beep from the washing machine signalled that its cycle had ended. Island work was never done. She unloaded the washing machine and put all the wet clothes in a wicker basket, then she grabbed a tub of clothes pegs and headed down to the beach to hang the washing on the line.

When she reached the beach she saw Jasmine and Goober rolling around on the sand. Jasmine was naked, as usual. But it looked like Goober was attacking her, and not in a fun way. This was aggressive. Jasmine looked up and saw Flake.

'FLAKE, HELP!' she yelled at her.

The whole thing confused Flake at first. But then Goober screamed out in pain and flung himself away from Jasmine. His high-pitched screams made Flake shudder. Then Jasmine started kicking out at nothing. Flake saw blood streaming down her arm too. What the fuck was going on?

Jasmine provided the answer.

'FLAKE! INVISIBLE MAN!'

Flake dropped the basket of washing. The first thing that crossed her mind was to do the same thing as Jasmine. Call for help.

She screamed at the top of her voice. 'JD! HELP! INVISIBLE MAN!'

That was just instinct. The second thing that crossed her mind, a millisecond later was, *"What can I do?"* It's not every day you see your friend and your dog being attacked by an invisible person.

With her hands free from carrying the washing basket, the answer soon came to her. She raised her hands and pointed her palms at the area Jasmine was throwing punches and kicks at. It was time to test out the old reflexes.

ZAP!

She fired off a pair of blue laser bolts from her hands. The bolts hit the sand near Jasmine. It scared the shit out of Goober if nothing else. The injured dog jumped back in a panic. Jasmine to her credit, carried on kicking out in all directions. Flake tried to work out where the invisible man was. It was impossible. She fired more blue laser bolts at the sand. It didn't seem to achieve anything.

And then the weather stepped in to complicate matters. As if encouraged by her lightning bolts, a clap of thunder from high above signalled the start of a downpour of heavy rain.

Flake took a few cautious steps onto the sand, firing off more electrical blasts at areas where she thought the invisible man might be. But there was no way of knowing if she was hitting anything.

## Seventy-Two

JD was taking a walk around the island. It was a warm day and he was wearing a pair of black cargo pants and some sneakers, but nothing else. The peacefulness of walking around the island on his own was therapeutic. City life with cars, buses, angry people and all the noise that came with those things was nothing compared to the bliss of island life.

He was on a patch of grass by the waterfall when he heard Goober barking at something on the beach. That was followed by Jasmine calling out to Flake for help. He sat up and cocked his ear. Jasmine yelled out Flake's name again, followed by the words, *"Invisible man"*.

JD leapt to his feet and started running through the woodland towards the beach. He was in the thickest, darkest part of the woods when a loud clap of thunder from above signalled an imminent downpour. Heavy rain was a regular occurrence on Medicine Island. It came from nowhere and usually lasted just a few minutes. The first drops landed on JD's face as he was halfway down to the beach. By the time the ocean was in sight he was in the middle of a major downpour.

He burst out of the woodland onto the beach, looking for the danger. Jasmine was doing naked kung-fu kicks on the sand. Goober was hobbling around nearby, barking and growling. Flake was on the edge of the beach, like she'd just come from the research centre. Her T-shirt was already soaked through and glued to her skin. As he laid eyes on her, she fired a blast of lightning from each of her hands. The blue laser bolts hit the sand near Jasmine. JD took it as a useful sighter as to where the invisible problem was.

He charged across the sand towards Jasmine, without any idea what he was going to do when he got there. He had no weapons, or indeed anything that could scare an invisible assassin. But he had to do something. And fast.

Jasmine had blood gushing down her arm from a deep cut on her shoulder. She was spinning around, throwing punches and kicks in all directions. But she was visibly tiring. Her hair was soaking wet and stuck to her face and shoulders, and the wind and rain was pummelling her.

'LOOK FOR FOOTPRINTS!' Jasmine yelled at JD. 'YOU CAN SEE WHEN THEY APPEAR!'

JD stopped and stared at the sand. Through the heavy rain it was hard to see anything, let alone a footprint. He quickly came to the conclusion that Jasmine's tactic of punching and kicking at nothing in particular was actually the best thing to do. He followed suit, and began throwing punches and kicks at the rain. He hit nothing. This was exasperating.

'WHERE DID HE COME FROM?' JD yelled at Jasmine.

'THE OCEAN!' she yelled back. 'HE'S GOT WEBBED FEET!'

JD took up a position behind Jasmine, covering her back, while she covered his. Looking for footprints wasn't working though, so JD watched Goober's eyes. The sniffer dog had a better idea where the predator was than any of them. JD pulled Jasmine with him as he moved towards an area that Goober was growling at.

Flake yelled at them. 'MAKE A RUN FOR IT. I'LL COVER YOU!'

To reiterate her point she blasted off some more laser bolts at the sand near their feet. JD pulled Jasmine across the sand towards Flake, with the intention of heading back to the research centre, and then Purgatory.

*'Shit!'*

The cry of *shit* came from Flake. She was still thrusting her palms out, but the laser bolts weren't firing anymore. JD let go of Jasmine and threw a few more punches at nothing. Initially it looked like Flake had lost the ability to shoot electricity, like the time she was at the Gunslingers club. But it soon became clear that this was something different. The necklace that held the Eye of the Moon had slipped off her neck and fallen onto the sand. Flake looked down at it, but instead of picking it up, she reached back and rubbed the back of her neck like she'd been bitten by something.

JD yelled out. 'FLAKE! RUN!'

Flake pulled her hand away from the back of her neck and checked her fingertips. There was blood on them. JD knew it before she did.

'RUN!'

He charged across the beach towards her, cursing the stupid sand, wind and rain that made it hard to run at full speed.

A patch of blood appeared on the front of Flake's T-shirt. It started off the size of a pea, but transitioned swiftly into a golf ball and then a tennis ball. Flake stopped looking at her fingertips. Her arm dropped back down to her side. She stared at JD, panic in her eyes. Then she dropped to her knees in the sand. Blood dribbled from her mouth.

JD caught up to her and threw a hail of punches and kicks at the area all around her, hoping to hit something, or at the very least keep the invisible threat away. He hit nothing. He was wasting time.

Flake was hurt bad. What she needed more than a bodyguard was the Eye of the Moon and its magical healing powers.

The blue stone was partially submerged in the hardening wet sand. JD stopped swinging at nothing and instead reached down to grab it.

Too late.

It vanished. It was there, then it was gone.

Jasmine's claim about the footprints in the sand was correct though. JD saw them. He started throwing punches at the air above the footprints. But still he hit nothing. He was always a step behind. It was infuriating. He needed to retrieve the Eye of the Moon. Not in a minutes time, not in twenty seconds time. Right fucking now, because Flake was laid out on her side in the sand, not moving, not crying for help, just blinking.

Jasmine mustered up enough energy to stagger over to help JD fight. She stopped near him and threw some half-hearted punches with her good arm. Her other arm was pumping out blood, and she could barely lift it. She hit nothing either.

And then there it was. Right in front of Jasmine. The clue JD was looking for. The outline of his enemy was there after all. It had been there all along. The rain was landing on the invisible person's head and shoulders, but then disappearing, revealing the outline of a man in the rain. JD lowered his shoulder and took a run at it. He connected with the invisible figure, not cleanly, but enough to knock it over. The tip of a blade dug into JD's ribs. He ignored it like it was a scratch from a needle. There was no time for pain because the Eye of the Moon was visible again. It had slipped from the invisible man's grip and landed in the sand.

'JASMINE! THE EYE!' JD yelled. He followed up the yell with an anguished cry as the knife in his ribcage took a sharp turn towards his armpit.

JD rained down punches at what he hoped was the other man's face. One sweet connection induced a muffled yelp from his enemy, and a crunch that had to be some teeth breaking. JD had the enemy pinned down. He ran his hand around the man's face, feeling it with his palm, identifying parts until his fingers finally grasped hold of some cloth. The invisible hood. While his enemy stabbed repeatedly at his ribs, JD pulled the hood back, revealing the face of Diago, the ringmaster from the vampire circus.

JD punched him in the face again with greater accuracy, busting his nose. Through his hazy vision and the torrential rain, he saw Jasmine pick up the Eye and run over to Flake. And all the while, Diago was stabbing JD in the side.

JD grabbed the vampire's knife-wielding hand and pushed it away. He peeled Diago's fingers off the knife handle, causing the vampire to drop it. As soon as it hit the sand, JD grasped hold of it and raised it above his head. With one mighty swing, he slammed it down into Diago's eye. The tip of the blade sliced through the eyeball and slammed into the vampire's brain. Diago wriggled and kicked out, but it was to no avail.

With the kill almost complete, JD pulled the knife out and thrust it into the dying vampire's heart. Diago screamed and writhed around some more, then his skin began to burn. JD rolled away from him. The vampire's body exploded into flames. He thrashed around for a few more seconds, until he eventually disintegrated into smoke and ash. His remains blended in with the sand and rain, filtering away like he'd never existed, making him invisible once more.

JD sat back on the sand and took in a few deep breaths as the adrenaline from the kill began to subside. He looked down at the blood that was pumping out of his side. Seeing it reminded him of the pain. Being stabbed hurts, beating stabbed multiple times hurts a lot. His vision began to swirl around, a sign that he was losing blood. He saw Goober lying in the sand a few feet away.

'JD!'

The cry came from Jasmine. JD twisted his neck and looked over at her. She was crouched down next to Flake pressing the Eye of the Moon against the pool of blood around her chest and stomach.

JD crawled on his knees across the sand towards them. Jasmine was panting heavily and staring at him, her mouth open, her chest heaving. Flake was now on her back, her head lopped to one side, not moving.

When JD reached them he took over the job of pressing the Eye of the Moon against Flake's stab wound, in the hopes of stemming the flow of blood.

'How bad is it?' he asked.

Jasmine put her hand on JD's shoulder. Even though she was exhausted, she managed to muster up two words to answer his question.

'She's gone.'

## Seventy-Three

'This is my fault.'

Although JD hadn't noticed it, the rain had already stopped and been replaced by a blue sky and a hot sun. He was sitting on the sand beside Flake cradling her head in his hands. Jasmine was close by, using the Eye of the Moon to tend to Goober's injuries. The Eye had many powers, but bringing Flake back from the dead wasn't one of them.

After a few minutes of love and care from Jasmine, Goober was back on his feet. He limped over to Flake and licked her face. It wouldn't bring her back to life, but the dog tried anyway.

Jasmine pressed the Eye of the Moon against the injury on her own shoulder. 'I can't believe this,' she said. 'It all happened so fast. I wish I hadn't called for help. I should have just run away. Then Flake would be okay.'

JD looked up at Jasmine. 'This isn't your fault. I did this.'

He laid Flake's head down in the sand and stood up. He limped over to the invisible coat, holding his injured side as he went. The coat was crumpled up on the sand where Diago had been destroyed. JD picked it up and shook away the dust and ash that were once part of the vampire.

'What are you going to do with that?' Jasmine asked.

'Destroy it.'

'Are you sure? It could be a useful thing to keep.'

'All it could ever be used for is spying on people, or killing them. I don't need it for either of those things. Do you want it?'

Jasmine shook her head. 'No. But I would have thought you'd want to use it to kill everyone that vampire ever cared about.'

JD stared at the strange translucent coat he was holding. 'I already killed all the people he cared about,' he said.

Jasmine pulled the Eye of the Moon away from her shoulder, and winced as she was reminded of the pain of her stab wound. 'Who was he?'

'He was the ringmaster at the vampire circus.'

'Oh.'

'It was all for nothing. I killed the vampires, I killed Antonio Rodriguez and his goons, and I killed the people behind it all, the elites. And what did it achieve? It caused the death of Sanchez. It started a war that killed Paige and Selene and a million other people. And now Flake is dead, all because of what I did.'

Jasmine walked over to him and pressed the Eye of the Moon against his ribcage. 'You need to rest,' she said. 'Blaming yourself won't change anything.'

Goober barked at them. It wasn't a warning bark this time. It was a plea for help. The dog was still standing over Flake, trying to wake her up.

'Sorry, boy,' said JD. 'She's not coming back.'

Jasmine pressed the Eye of the Moon into JD's hand so he could use it on himself, then she walked back to Goober and knelt down beside him to give him a hug.

JD winced as he pressed the Eye against one of his open wounds. 'That vampire came here for revenge,' he said. 'He came for Flake.'

Jasmine wiped a tear from her eye, then she stroked Flake's face. 'It's over now then,' she said. 'There's no other circus people to kill is there?'

'I don't think so.'

JD slung the invisible coat over his shoulder and walked back to Jasmine. He handed her the Eye of the Moon. 'You need this more than me,' he said. 'I've got holy blood.'

'I've got some too, remember?' Jasmine said, forcing a smile. 'You injected some into me.'

JD knelt down beside Jasmine and took another look at Flake. She was so pale. He leaned in and pressed his lips against hers. They were cold and dry, nothing like before.

Jasmine reached across and wiped some hair away from JD's forehead. 'She loved you,' she said. 'I never saw her so happy as she was these last few months.'

'Yeah, I loved her too.' After a prolonged silence, JD stood up. 'I'm gonna go get rid of this coat,' he said, 'Can you stay here for a while?'

'Of course. Don't be gone forever though.'

JD left the beach and hobbled up to the research centre that had become his home, his and Flake's. He headed straight for a storage room that contained all the weapons he thought he would never use again. The room had a sideboard with a bunch of cupboards above it, one of which contained an old-fashioned radio. He switched it on and turned up the volume. The theme tune to the TV show *The Waltons* was playing. He flicked to another station and found "The Mark has Been Made" by Nine Inch Nails. A much better choice in the circumstances.

He opened a storage closet and found all the things he was looking for. A pair of boots, a black vest, a shoulder strap with holsters on either side, and a gun belt. He grabbed as many loaded weapons as the holsters could take, and a couple of sheathed knives. When he had as much as he could handle he looked at the most important item in the closet. His long black coat. It had a multitude of pockets and compartments in it for carrying weapons. But he wouldn't need it. Not this time.

Instead, he slid his arms into the invisible coat and wrapped it around his shoulders. It was a shitty looking coat. Not the kind anyone would want to be seen out in. But when he lifted the hood over his head, he vanished completely, along with all of his weapons.

He pulled the hood back down, making himself visible again, then he checked his reflection in a mirror on the inside of the closet door. 'Remember me?' he whispered. The reflection whispered the words back at him.

Convinced that he had enough armoury for what lay ahead, JD left the storage room and headed for the portal into Purgatory. It was already open, inviting him in.

Jacko was behind the bar as usual. The bluesman had already set out a bottle of bourbon and a whiskey glass on the bar top.

'I heard the news,' he said.

'Then you'll know why I'm here.'

## Seventy-Four

Rex rode through a set of large steel gates into the Saint Columbanus memorial cemetery. It looked like Carmine's funeral was about to begin. There were lots of choppers and motorcycles parked up outside the funeral parlour. Rex parked his chopper away from the others, closer to the front gates. Elvis rolled up alongside him.

'That's a lot of Harleys,' Elvis remarked.

'Carmine was a popular guy.'

'Is this really a cemetery for bikers only?'

Rex climbed off his chopper. 'Clue is in the name. Saint Columbanus is the patron saint of bikers. Look around,' he said, pointing at the graveyard. 'Everyone of those graves is for a biker. I'll be buried here one day.'

'Let's hope it's not today,' said Elvis, climbing off his bike and fixing his hair.

'Don't bring bad vibes to a funeral,' said Rex.

'All I'm saying is, if anything looks amiss when we walk into this place, we should get the fuck out. At least you can say you showed up. And if we leave early you can blame it on me.'

Rex slapped Elvis across the arm. 'Are you forgetting something? I'm the King of the Hell's Angels.'

'Yeah, and I'm the King of Rock 'n' Roll.'

'Look, nobody wants to ruin a funeral by starting a fight, okay? It'll be fine.'

'If you say so. You go in first. I'll cover the rear. Anyone looks at you funny, I'm spitting at 'em.'

'You're not funny.'

Rex marched up to the funeral parlour with Elvis just behind him. From the outside, the parlour looked like an aircraft hangar, nothing fancy, just grey and functional. The inside was much more in keeping with a traditional funeral parlour.

'I think it's already started,' said Elvis as they walked into an unmanned reception area. 'We're late.'

'Would you calm down!' Rex snapped. 'You're making me nervous.'

'Let's just stand at the back.'

'I can't. I've gotta say a few words, remember?'

'Fine. I'll stand at the back and laugh at your jokes. Hey, what's that music?'

Rex stopped and listened. The song, "Memorial" by Michael Nyman was playing nearby.

'Do they play the music before the ceremony or during it?' Elvis asked.

'Shut up.'

Rex followed a sign to the main hall with Elvis tagging along behind. They walked through a set of tall wooden doors into the funeral hall. The ceremony was already underway. There were roughly fifteen rows of seats on either side of the main aisle. Every seat was taken by a Hell's Angel, or a biker chick. At the far end of the hall, past all the pews was Carmine's coffin. It was draped in a black flag with a pair of white angel's wings sewn into it. Just past the coffin, a preacher was standing behind a lectern. He nodded at Rex and Elvis as they walked in. Everyone in the aisles looked around to see who the late arrivals were. There were a lot of solemn faces. Rex raised his hand and bowed his head as a mark of respect. Elvis took his sunglasses off and tucked them into his top pocket.

'Is that Denise?' Elvis whispered in Rex's ear.

The lady he was referring to was in the front row waving at Rex. She was in her forties, kinda butch with a thick brown mullet and cheeks a hamster would be proud of. She was wearing double denim, and a red neckerchief.

'That's her,' said Rex. 'Wait here.'

Rex walked down the aisle, keeping his focus on Denise. Everyone stared at him as he went past, which was normal for Rex at a biker event. The other folks were in awe of him, always had been, always would be.

Denise had saved a chair for Rex next to her on the front row. He took it and sat down between her and an old guy with a white beard and cloudy eyes.

'Thank you so much for coming,' Denise whispered. 'Carmine would be so happy. He really missed you these last few years.'

'I missed him too,' Rex whispered back. 'How are you keeping? Is there anything I can do for you?'

'Just being here is enough,' said Denise, squeezing Rex's human hand. 'You'll do a little speech, yes?'

'Of course.'

When the music came to an end, the preacher cleared his throat to get everyone's attention. Then he launched into a rather dull homily about death and religion and going to a better place, and all that kind of stuff. After a few minutes, when everyone was close to falling asleep, he invited Rex up onto the stage to make his speech.

Rex stood up and made his way over to the lectern. The preacher gave him a polite nod of the head then moved aside. Rex took a deep breath and grasped the lectern with both hands before looking up at the audience. The first thing he saw was Elvis at the back, texting someone on his phone. He looked around at the rest of the audience. The only person looking at him was Denise. Everyone else was either looking at their feet, their prayer book, or at the person next to them. Something wasn't right, Rex could sense it. The vibe was bad, like something was going to happen. He checked the faces of the men. One of them, a young fella that Rex didn't recognise glanced up at him, but quickly looked back down at his hands. Rex was beginning to wish he'd listened to Elvis and stayed away. He glanced back at Denise. She was giving him a "why aren't you saying anything?" look. She had a point. It was getting awkward. So Rex launched into his speech, while keeping his eyes on the audience.

'Good day to you all,' he said. 'For those of you that don't know me, my name is Rodeo Rex. I knew Carmine back when we were both young men. He was bigger than me back then, and he was known for his ability to....NOOOOO!'

A man dressed in black came in through a side door at the back of the hall. He had a pistol in his hand. He marched towards Elvis, and lifted the gun, aiming it at Elvis's head.

Rex's shout of "NOOOOO!" was meant to act as a warning to Elvis of what was coming. The cry was drowned out by a gunshot. Rex went silent. This was bad. Not as bad as he initially feared because Elvis was a step ahead of the game. He may have looked like he was texting someone but he actually had a gun behind his back. When the armed intruder entered with the intention of killing him, Elvis whipped out his gun and fired first. Straight into the other man's chest.

It was the cue for the funeral to go bonkers. Every single biker in the funeral parlour pulled out a piece. Half of them had their eyes on Rex, the others spun around to get Elvis in their sights.

Rex ducked down behind the lectern and whipped out his own semi-automatic pistol. He winced in readiness for the incoming hail of bullets. But it didn't come. He peered around the lectern. The reason for the lack of incoming fire became clear. Elvis had grabbed hold of a fourteen-year-old boy from the back row and was using him as a human shield. The boy had thick black hair, like a young Ralph Macchio, and he was wearing black jeans and a brown leather jacket. Elvis had his gun pressed against the boy's head.

'Put your fucking guns down or I blow this kid to kingdom come!' Elvis bluntly informed the congregation.

A whole bunch of people started yelling back at Elvis. The young boy was obviously popular. But with so many people shouting at the same time, nothing really made any sense. It was just incoherent yelling, like a bad thrash metal concert. Rex stood up and fired his gun in the air.

BANG!

That shut everyone up.

'Okay, listen everyone,' said Rex. 'If y'all put your guns down, Elvis will leave the building, and let the boy go. Okay?'

'You two drop your fucking guns!' a heavy-set biker with long grey hair yelled back at Rex.

BANG!

Elvis shot that guy in the back of the head. It had the desired effect, assuming the desired effect was to stun everyone else momentarily then get them all to point their guns at Elvis and start yelling again.

With no one aiming any weapons at Rex anymore, he saw an opportunity. He caught Elvis's eye and pointed at a side door not far from the lectern. It was the only logical escape route for Rex. Elvis had the back doors as his way out. The only person between Rex and his escape route was the preacher, and even he was pointing a gun at Elvis.

Elvis gave a subtle nod of his head, then started dragging the boy with him towards the exit, keeping his gun against the young lad's head, and making sure no one could get a clean shot at him.

Rex snuck up on the preacher, grabbed him and relieved him of his gun. He pressed his hand over the preacher's mouth to silence him, then barged through the side door with the holy fucker in tow. The door led into a short corridor and another door marked EXIT. Rex smashed the preacher's head against a wall, knocking the divine bastard out cold, then he bolted through the exit and headed for his chopper.

Meanwhile, Elvis was dragging his young hostage through the reception area hoping to make a clean getaway. A bunch of gun-toting mourners were tentatively following, waiting for a chance to shoot.

'Listen up!' Elvis yelled at them. 'Everyone turn around and count to a hundred. By the time you get there, I'll have let this boy go. But if anyone comes after me before the hundred count is up, I'll shoot this little fucker in the head. Got it?'

There was a pregnant pause while the angry biker mob mulled over Elvis's demands. He had to hope they went for it because it was the only bluff he had. Sooner or later he was going to have to let go of his hostage, and make a break for it. If anyone was close by when that happened, Elvis was getting shot, no two ways about it.

Elvis pressed his gun harder against the boy's head, acting like he was losing patience. After an uncomfortable delay, one of the bikers turned around and started counting out loud. God bless him. Elvis could have hugged the dumb bastard. By the time the count was up to five, every single one of the bikers had turned around and started counting aloud. It was likely to take them a while too, because from the sound of things, half of them didn't know what number came after seven.

Elvis didn't wait around. He dragged the boy outside and looked around for Rex. The roar of a chopper engine nearby alerted him to the sight of his friend. Rex was on his chopper, twenty metres away, facing the exit. He looked back at Elvis.

'GET ON!' he yelled. 'WHAT ARE YOU WAITING FOR?'

Elvis bashed his young hostage over the head with the butt of his gun. The poor little biker boy went down like a sack of shit. Elvis took off, running as fast as he could over to Rex. He tucked his gun away, leapt onto the back of Rex's chopper, wrapped his arms around his buddy's waist, then hung on for dear life as the chopper sped away.

Unfortunately the angry mob of bikers never counted to a hundred (some of them didn't even count to eight) because at the sound of Rex's chopper speeding away they all raced out of the funeral parlour. Some started shooting at the escaping pair, others headed for their steel horses and hit the road in pursuit.

**Seventy-Five**

## Part Ten - Undoing a Good Deed

Back when God gave Jacko the job of overseeing what went on in Purgatory, the bluesman had felt honoured. All of Jacko's friends were pleased for him too, except for Sanchez who had warned him that God was a "stitch-up-merchant". Sanchez's gripe was something to do with a dodgy fire-truck God had lent him once. Naturally, Jacko dismissed Sanchez's rantings out of hand. Sanchez was always moaning about stuff. But things had changed. Sanchez had been right. The job in Purgatory was looking like a stitch-up too. Jacko was beginning to regret taking it.

The Bourbon Kid was sitting at the bar smoking a cigarette and working his way through a bottle of bourbon. It took him five minutes to drink the whole damn thing, then he slid it back across the bar to Jacko and stubbed the cigarette out on the bar. 'Where is he?' he asked, impatience building in his voice.

'He'll be here in a minute,' Jacko said.

The "he" in question was Eric Einstein, the only man who knew how to build a travel portal. More specifically, the only man who had ever built one that could send people back in time. He'd done it before, sending JD and Beth back in time at Coldworm abbey, albeit without their approval, because the Devil had made him do it.

The big red telephone on the worktop behind Jacko started ringing. He reached back for it, picked it up, then set it down on the bar in front of JD. 'That's for you,' he said.

JD took a deep breath, then answered the phone. 'Yeah.'

'You wish to ask me something?' said the voice of God.

'I want Einstein to send me back in time.'

'Of course you do.' God sounded very calm. 'This was always going to happen. When you used the portal to kill the elites, you messed with the natural order of things, and now fate has come back to bite you.'

'I don't need the lecture,' said JD, sensing that God was going to ramble on a bit.

'But you must know by now, if you go back in time, your destiny still does not lie with Flake.'

'If I go back to yesterday, I can get her off the island before that invisible prick shows up.'

God's answer was not what JD was hoping for. 'You're not listening. Your time with Flake is at an end. When you killed the circus people, you allowed Diago to escape. He saw what you did to his brothers and sisters, and he swore revenge. You see, revenge only leads to more revenge. And when you used the portal to kill the world leaders, you changed Flake's future. Sanchez died because of what you did. Your actions also led to the extermination of millions of innocent people.'

'How was I supposed to know that?'

'Have you learnt nothing? You have *my* blood in your veins. That makes you and your loved ones a target for those who want destruction. Your children understood it. Their mother Beth understood it too. They tried to lead quiet, uncomplicated lives, but they all died because of you. Your actions always lead to the death of those you love. And yet, knowing this, you started a relationship with Flake.'

'I fell in love with her.'

'Indeed you did. But now you must reset the clock. The world must go back to the way it was.'

'The world was run by assholes.'

'As it always is. You killed them, and made things worse. Nothing you did benefited anyone other than you. You saved Paige from the circus vampires, but then because you killed the world leaders, she died anyway.'

'I killed a bunch of murdering paedophiles.'

'Atlanteans. You killed Atlanteans. They were voyeurs, narcissists. They craved power, power that gave them access to all of life's pleasures. They had so much of what men crave that they became desensitised, bored by the things that once excited them, and they sought out more extreme ways to get an adrenaline fix. A few thousand years ago, I made the same mistake as you. I tried to kill the Atlanteans to punish them for their wickedness. But by then they had evolved, and as I already knew, when you kill those in power, nothing changes. Power vacuums draw in evil. Atlantis sits at the bottom of the ocean, but evil spreads. It grows from nothing. It is a parasite. It can never be fully eradicated.'

'What can I do now then? How can I fix things?'

God took a short pause, possibly irritated by being interrupted in the middle of an educational history lecture. When he resumed, he spoke in a kinder tone. 'If Einstein can make it happen, I will allow you to travel back in time, into your own body on the night the circus arrives in San Antonio, two days before you started working for Antonio Rodriguez. The vampires always do a rehearsal of the show on the night they arrive in a new place. You will go to the rehearsal, kill Diago and retrieve the invisible coat. If you can do that, and return the coat to me, along with the one you are wearing, then I will allow you to go back to your old life, but if you fail to retrieve the invisible coat, you will be brought back to this time. Flake will be dead, the world will be in ruins, and it will be because of your actions and your failure to make amends. The invisible coat has no business in the world anymore. Those damn vampires were even trying to replicate it, which could have been disastrous. You have one chance to get it back, one shot to fix the mistakes you made. Do you understand?'

'I understand.'

'You should also know that whether you succeed or fail, there will be no more time travel. *Not ever*. If you succeed, Eric Einstein will be granted passage into Heaven for his contribution in ending the war you started. And if you fail, he will languish in Hell for the rest of eternity. There will be no more visits to Purgatory for him.'

'I don't give a fuck about Einstein.'

'I'm just making sure you understand the consequences of the choice you are making.'

'I do. Can I go now?'

'Yes, you can.'

JD replaced the receiver on the phone and slid it back across the bar to Jacko.

'It's on then?' said Jacko.

'It's on.'

Jacko smiled. 'Thank God for that.'

A cheery voice called out from the back of the bar. 'Morning folks!'

JD looked over his shoulder. Einstein was walking in from the disabled toilets. 'You need me to do the time travel thing again, yes?'

'That's right,' said Jacko.

'Okay, give me half an hour.'

Jacko handed JD another bottle of bourbon. JD flipped the lid off and raised the bottle to his mouth. Before he took a sip of it, he asked Jacko a question. 'Is this the first time I'm doing this?'

'Drinking bourbon?'

'Don't be a smartass. Have we had this time travel conversation before?'

'Not that I recall, no.'

'You sure about that?'

'God said you get one shot,' Jacko reminded him. 'So don't fuck it up.'

'I won't. I've killed Diago once already, and I'll kill him again. It'll be easy.'

Einstein called over to them. 'What about Jasmine? She's still on Medicine Island. Why don't you take her with you? She could help.'

'No.'

Jacko leaned across the bar. 'If you leave her on the island, she will cease to exist in this reality.'

Before JD could voice his opinion on the matter, Jacko's cell phone rang. He sighed, then checked the display. 'It's Elvis. I gotta take this,' he said. He put the phone down on the bar top and answered it, putting it on loudspeaker.

'Hey, Elvis, wassup?'

'JACKO! GET US OUTTA HERE!'

Jacko glared at JD, as if to say, *"Look what you've done now!"*

The other end of the line was a mess of chaotic noise. Screeching tyres, revving engines, Rex yelling in the background, and then most alarming of all, gunfire.

'What's going on?' Jacko asked.

'We're being chased by a fucking biker gang!' Elvis replied. 'Can you get us outta here?'

'Can you get to a bathroom?'

'NO! Can you get us a portal back to the crossroads! SHIT!'

Elvis's cry of shit was followed by something that sounded like a crash. More gunfire followed.

'Elvis?' said Jacko. 'You still there? Elvis?'

The line went dead.

Jacko stopped staring at the phone and looked up at JD. 'That's your fault too,' he said.

JD took a sip of his bourbon. 'That settles it then,' he said. 'Jasmine stays here.'

'How does that settle it?' Jacko asked, confused.

'Because it does.'

'I've lost all sense of logic at this point,' said Jacko, mulling things over. 'If Rex and Elvis are dead, then I guess when this is all over, if it hasn't worked, then it's just you and Jasmine from now on. But, if by some miracle you succeed, everyone will be alive, but you and me will be the only people who remember anything about the last four months.'

'What about me?' Einstein called out. 'I want to remember everything too. These last few months have been brilliant. I don't ever want to forget the time Jasmine gave me a—'

'For goodness sake!' Jacko hissed. 'Of course you'll remember everything. I meant to include you in what I was saying.'

'Oh, thank fuck for that,' said Einstein.

JD eyed Jacko with suspicion. 'I'm the only one going back in time. Surely, I'm the only one who will remember anything about what's happened?'

'No,' said Jacko. 'If this works, Einstein will know why he's in Heaven. And I'll know why he's not here. That's how it works. I will remember everything.'

'Then all of this will be our secret.'

'Yes, it will,' Jacko agreed.

JD picked up his pack of cigarettes and placed one between his lips. He sucked on it, lighting it up. 'Is the portal ready yet?' he asked Einstein.

'Just be patient,' Einstein replied. 'I have God's instructions. He wants you back in your own body on the night the circus arrived in San Antonio. Do you know where you were at that time?'

'No.'

'Well, wherever you end up when I send you back in time, you'll have to head straight to the circus. The sooner you get there—'

'I know the plan, fuckface.'

'He knows the plan,' said Jacko, in an effort to be agreeable. 'Just remember, JD, there's no second chances. If you fuck this up, nothing will go back to how it was. It'll just be you and Jasmine living on a desert island together, so be careful.'

**Seventy-Six**

## Back In Time

When the circus vampires weren't killing children to entertain the world leaders, they spent their time putting on performances for the public, or rehearsing for those performances. No one actually enjoyed rehearsing something they had done a thousand times before. Rehearsing sucked. The only good thing about it was that everyone did it in their gym clothes. There was no point in getting dressed up for a show that no one was going to see.

It was almost 7:30 p.m. and everyone was ready for the rehearsal to begin. Everyone except Diago. The ringmaster was absent. The others were waiting in the backstage area for the opening ceremony to begin. The ceremony involved marching into the Big Top, then parading around the ring to give the audience a taste of what was to come later. The ringmaster always went first, followed by the midgets and the knife-thrower.

After fifteen minutes of waiting for Diago, his brother Dexter, one of the acrobats who was known to hate tardiness, snatched a phone from Athena the contortionist and dialled up Diago. For a while it looked like the ringmaster wouldn't answer his phone, but Dexter had no intention of ringing off, so eventually the call was answered.

'What?' Diago snapped.

'Everything is set up and ready to go, brother,' Dexter said, through gritted teeth. 'We're just waiting for you.'

'Crack on without me,' Diago replied. 'I'm running late. I'll be there in a few minutes.'

Dexter ended the call without replying and handed the phone back to Athena. Then he put his finger and thumb in his mouth and whistled to get the attention of everyone else. When they all finished muttering among themselves, he launched into an announcement. 'Everyone! Diago says we should get started without him. He'll be along later.'

Athena stamped her foot. 'Who's going to do the announcing then?' she asked, a scowl on her face.

'I'll do it,' said Dexter. 'It's no big deal.' He marched past his fellow performers towards the front of the line. 'Everyone get ready, I'm ringmaster for this rehearsal.'

There were plenty of irritated looks. Being the ringmaster was the easy job. Kratos the giant, who was wearing a light blue romper suit that made him look like a giant toddler, complained on behalf of everyone. 'If Diago isn't bothering to rehearse, then why should the rest of us?'

Dexter stopped in front of Kratos, who was a foot taller than him. 'What happens when we don't rehearse properly?' he asked the giant oaf.

Kratos lowered his head like a sulking child. 'Lack of rehearsal means a visit from Major Cock-up,' he said, repeating a phrase that had been drummed into everyone to express the importance of rehearsals.

'That's right,' said Dexter. 'Now come on. The sooner we get started, the sooner this will be over.'

Hoho the clown, crossed his arms. 'What if I decide not to rehearse?' he said, kicking some sawdust along the ground.

'If you don't rehearse, you'll be fired,' said Dexter. 'And we'll find a new clown to take your place.'

Hoho scoffed. 'Whoever replaces me will have some big shoes to fill!'

There were groans all around. Hoho had done that same joke a million times before. In fact, his threat to quit was only ever made so he could do the "big shoes" joke.

'Idiot!' said Dexter, his irritation clear for everyone to see. He stormed past the clown and headed out to the centre of the arena, twirling an imaginary cane around in his hand, pretending he was Diago. He walked with real purpose in his stride, showing the others the level of commitment expected. He stopped in the centre of the ring and yelled out for the benefit of an imaginary audience of paying punters.

'Ladies and gentlemen, the flying midgets!'

A pair of midgets trotted out of the tunnel and made their way around the outer edge of the ring, waving to the empty seats all around the arena.

Dexter called out again. 'Takemi, the knife-thrower and his lovely assistant, Lyarna!'

Over the course of the next thirty seconds, Dexter called out the names of all the other performers. One by one they walked into the ring and marched around it, waving to the empty seats.

'Okay, one-two-three, *and* back to the tunnel,' Dexter announced eventually. He waved the midgets along, coercing them into leading everyone back into the tunnel.

Dexter stayed in the centre of the ring and waited while his fellow performers embarked on their final lap around the perimeter. The midgets and the knife-throwing act made it to the tunnel that led backstage, but then things took an unexpected turn. An unshaven man in a strange, fuzzy coat just like the invisible one Diago owned, appeared out of thin air, right in front of Dexter.

'What the hell?' Dexter muttered under his breath.

'This is for Flake,' the man said, in a gravelly voice. He reached inside his fuzzy coat, whipped out a big, heavy handgun, and pointed it at Dexter's face.

Dexter never heard the shot that blew his head into a million pieces of bone, brain, blood and goo as it flew off his shoulders and splattered into the face of one of the fire-eaters on the other side of the circus ring.

'WHAT THE FUCK!'

All the circus folk were thinking, *"What the fuck!"* but it was Kratos the giant who actually verbalised it. And it was the cue for all of them to transition into vampires, not by choice but by instinct. It was fight or flight time.

The Bourbon Kid responded by lifting the hood on his coat, vanishing from sight again. It created panic among the vampires. Some froze, some attacked, some attempted to flee.

Takemi the knife-thrower was the first to show some fight. He moved towards the centre of the ring, a throwing-knife in each hand. He swung his knives this way and that, hoping to strike something. But to the horror and bewilderment of his partner, Lyarna, he suddenly stopped and thrust the knives into his own eyes. Forcefully too.

Lyarna screamed. Those knives had done more than just blind her lover. They had gone right through his brain. Takemi slumped to the floor and rolled over onto his side. Lyarna ran to help him, only to see the two knives in his head vanish before she reached him. That was when she realised she was next. Takemi's knives had been hurled at her a million times before without ever piercing her skin, but they were no longer in his hands, they were in the hands of an invisible man, and that made them invisible too. Lyarna knew better than anyone how dangerous knives were, but invisible knives? The threat level was off the scale.

Lyarna attempted to flee, but one of the blades ripped into her back. Her knees buckled and she crumpled onto the floor. Her demise was complete when a second knife was plunged into her heart. She rolled onto her back and gasped her last breath.

Kratos, the big, hairy giant let out an angry roar and charged towards the fallen corpses of his friends, swinging his fists at the air, hoping to hit something.

A loud shotgun blast precipitated the obliteration of his nether regions. The bottom of his blue romper suit fell apart. Blood and bits of dick and scrotum spurted out onto the floor beneath him, He grabbed the squelchy area where his genitals used to be and tried to hold himself together, but his efforts were futile. He tumbled sideways, blood and innards sliding out of the chasm where his crotch once resided.

The remaining circus performers, seeing their giant friend taken down so easily, upped their panic levels. Screams rang out all around the Big Top. Clowns and acrobats were fighting with fire-eaters and midgets to be the first to escape. Some headed for the tunnel. Others tried to be clever, leaping up into the seating areas around the perimeter of the ring.

A trapeze artist was the next to die. He made a run towards the seating area, thinking he was clever by going the opposite way to everyone else. It should have been a good idea, but it wasn't. His head waved goodbye to his shoulders and flew through the air until it came down on one of the male midgets.

From that moment on, it was clear that attacking the invisible foe was a big mistake. Anyone too slow to escape down the tunnel to the backstage area ended up having their legs or head blown off. Some got it from close range. Usually in the face.

A small number of vampires did manage to escape into the night. The final vampires to die in the circus ring were the clowns. Those dumb fucks and their stupid, enormous shoes. They couldn't run anywhere at any kind of speed at the best of times, but in their panic they kept running into each other, falling over, getting up, then running into each other again. Either they were dumb as shit, or they were taking the rehearsal very seriously.

The first clown to die was Hoho. He was sliced in half at the waist by an invisible machete. His buddy, Jimbo had his head sliced off.

When the massacre was over, the Bourbon Kid lowered his hood and looked around at his handiwork. The ringmaster was dead. That was the important thing.

The Kid's only mistake was believing he had killed Diago, when he had actually killed the ringmaster's identical twin brother, Dexter. Diago wasn't even there.

## Seventy-Seven

After arriving at Dinosaur Valley park in the early afternoon, Diago left his colleagues and went into town on a scouting mission with Shattuck, one of the acrobats. Diago had a list of three names given to him by Navan Douglas. The names belonged to three autistic children who lived locally, and were therefore potential targets for the upcoming *Ludus Mortis*. The list consisted of a boy who worked in a sandwich shop, another boy who was sectioned in a mental hospital, and the twelve-year-old daughter of a local gangster named Antonio Rodriguez. Diago and Shattuck scouted the mental hospital first. The place was harder to break into than a prison. Next they checked out the sandwich shop. The boy they were looking for wasn't there, but it looked like an easy place to get in and out of in a hurry if necessary. And finally, they checked on the gangster's daughter. She lived in a huge estate with armed guards all around it.

Having established the locations of their targets, they returned to the circus just after 8 p.m. Shattuck parked their van next to a row of trailers on the grassy area of the park behind the Big Top, and switched off the engine.

'I hope we're not too late for rehearsal,' Shattuck said, disingenuously.

'No point in joining it now,' said Diago. 'Dexter's got it under control. We've got more important things to do, like work out our strategy for snatching these three children. I'm fairly certain we'll have to snatch the girl during daylight hours.'

Shattuck didn't seem to be listening to him. He was staring through the windscreen at the circus tent.

'What did I just say?' Diago snapped at him.

'Can you hear that?' Shattuck replied.

'Hear what?'

'Sounds like fireworks.'

Diago opened his door. Shattuck was right, there was something going on in the Big Top. The two vampires climbed out of the van to get a better look.

Diago sighed. 'I tell you, these idiots can't be left alone. If someone's got the fireworks out again, and that tent goes up in flames, I swear I'll kick someone's head in.'

'Maybe it's just a noisy rehearsal?' Shattuck suggested.

Diago sneered at his much shorter friend. 'Pah! That's not a rehearsal. That's a dancing pig with lipstick on.'

While Shattuck tried to figure out what that meant, Diago marched across the trailer park to the Big Top, his strides long and purposeful. Shattuck gave him a five-second head start then hurried after him.

As Diago neared the back entrance to the Big Top, it became clear that something was amiss. There was a stench of death in the air. Smouldering corpses of vampires were littered around the trailer park. There were screams coming from the Big Top. And gunshots, not fireworks. This was a massacre. And to make matters even more unsettling, there was some creepy music coming from one of the nearby trailers. Diago recognised the tune. It was "Tiptoe Through the Tulips" by Tiny Tim. He walked up to the offending trailer. It belonged to Niko, one of the stage hands. The trailer door was open, so Diago poked his head through and looked around. The trailer was empty, but Niko's old-fashioned ghetto blaster was on, playing its music for no one.

Diago backed out of the trailer and turned around. He nearly jumped out of his skin when he saw Shattuck standing in front of him.

'What the fuck are you doing, creeping up on me?' Diago hissed at him. 'We're under attack, can't you see that?'

'I don't get it,' said Shattuck.

'What's not to get? We've got a gunman on the premises.'

'No, but, *a dancing pig with lipstick on?* I don't get that,' said Shattuck.

'Would you forget about that! Someone is here. Someone serious. Have you a got a gun anywhere?'

'I've got one in my trailer.'

'Well, go get it! NOW!'

Shattuck turned on his heels and headed off to his trailer.

Diago tried to block out the creepy music. He scampered past a few more trailers until he arrived at the rear entrance of the Big Top. There were three smoking corpses lying in the grass nearby as well as several piles of smouldering ash that had once been vampires. Vampire deaths were a curious thing. Some disintegrated into ash and dust, others just dropped dead like regular humans, and occasionally, some vampires just flat-out exploded.

A croaky voice called out Diago's name. He recognised it. It was Yoga. Diago looked around. He was surprised he hadn't realised it before. Yoga was one of the smoking corpses in the grass, except he was still breathing. Diago crept over to him and crouched down beside him. His vampire friend was close to death. Blood was seeping from his chest and a gaping wound in his neck.

'Who did this?' Diago asked him.

Yoga was struggling to breathe. 'The Bourbon Kid is in the Big Top,' he whispered. 'He's killing everyone.'

'He did this to you?'

'No. It was the other…..'

Yoga never finished his sentence. He gasped his last breath and a moment later he burst into flames and disintegrated into dust and ash.

Diago stood up. If the Bourbon Kid was in the Big Top then it was time to make a hasty retreat. The Kid was the baddest vampire killer in the world. Hanging around was not an option. He backed away from the Big Top. After three or four backward steps, he turned around with the intention of fleeing at speed. He was met by the sight of Shattuck trudging towards him with a blank look on his face.

'We've gotta get outta here!' Diago whispered to him. 'It's the Bourbon Kid.'

Shattuck didn't reply. In fact, he looked a bit wobbly on his feet. Diago tip-toed up to him, even though tip-toeing wasn't really necessary. He was on grass after all, not the noisiest of surfaces.

'Didn't you hear me?' he whispered to Shattuck.

Shattuck staggered up to Diago like a drunk. He planted his chin on Diago's shoulder and then drooled down his arm. Diago grabbed him with both hands and tried to keep him on his feet. He was a dead weight.

'What the fuck are you—'

Diago didn't finish the question because the answer revealed itself. Shattuck had a bone-handled knife sticking out of his back. Diago reeled back like he'd been hugged by someone with leprosy. Shattuck collapsed onto the ground with a lively thud. Diago crouched down beside him.

'Who the fuck did this to you?' he whispered.

'I did,' a deep male voice replied from the darkness behind Diago.

The vampire stood up and swivelled around ready to fight whoever had spoken.

SMACK!

A fist hit him in the gut. The force of the blow knocked the wind out of him. He bent over, wheezing and holding his stomach. A curious feeling came over him. His belly rumbled, his ass cheeks twitched. Within seconds of the punch connecting with his stomach, the muscles in his butt lost all control. The contents of his bowels shot into his underpants at high speed. Diago lost his balance and fell backwards onto the ground. His fall was cushioned by a pillow of shit that had just arrived in his underwear. He had a bad case of the sweats coming on too. His forehead was perspiring like he'd been in a sauna for half an hour. He looked up at the man who had inflicted the bizarre discomfort upon him. It was a horrific sight. A dark figure dressed all in black except for a red leather jacket and a ghastly yellow skull mask. Atop the mask was a four-inch high red mohawk.

'Who the fuck are you?' Diago asked over the sound of squelching in his underpants.

'I'm the Red Mohawk,' the masked figure replied. 'Back from the dead to kill the undead.'

The Red Mohawk raised his right leg, giving Diago a good look at the sole of his boot. The boot grew bigger and bigger as it zoomed down towards Diago's face.

CRUNCH!

Everything turned black. The last thing Diago heard was an inquiring voice, gravelly in tone. It said one word.

'Joey?'

*********************************

Joey Conrad, aka the Red Mohawk stepped off Diago and looked around. The Bourbon Kid was approaching him with his Headblaster gun in his hand. He was wearing a translucent coat that looked like it had moving images on it.

'What the fuck are you doing here?' the Kid asked.

'Nice to see you too,' the Mohawk replied. 'God sent me. He thought you might need some help.' He pointed at the smouldering corpses of the vampires he had recently executed. 'I'd say God was right.'

The Kid frowned and pointed at the unconscious vampire by the Mohawk's feet. 'Who is that guy?'

'That's Diago,' the Mohawk replied. 'You killed his twin brother in there.'

'Twin brother?' The Bourbon Kid looked surprised. 'No one told me Diago had a twin.'

'Did you ask anyone if he had a twin?'

'No. Why would I? Who asks a question like that?'

'I would have.'

'Bullshit.' The Kid looked down at Diago again. 'Is he dead?'

'No. I just treated him to a shit-punch.'

'That explains the smell.'

'Yeah. My guess is, this guy's recently had an Indian.'

'Well, now he's gonna die.' The Kid pointed his gun at the unconscious vampire, intending to blow his head to smithereens. But before he could pull the trigger on his gun, the Red Mohawk stepped in front of him and pushed the weapon aside.

'What are you doing?' the Kid asked, confused.

'I spared him because I thought of a really cool way we could kill him. You wanna try it?'

'That depends. What have you got in mind?'

## Seventy-Eight

When Diago eventually regained consciousness, his head was sore, his nose was busted and there was dried blood all around his mouth. His arms were down by his sides. His legs were pressed together too. He could wriggle a bit, but there was something all around him, something stopping him from moving freely. He turned his head one way and then the other. It was dark on all sides. And there was a terrible smell of stale curry and shit loitering in his nostrils. The whole situation was confusing. It didn't take long to work out that he was squeezed into a tight cylindrical object, and he was naked. He twisted his head back as far as the limited space would allow so he could see what was at the end of the cylinder. What he saw was the moon high up in the night sky, shining down upon him.

'Where the fuck am I?' he muttered aloud.

By way of an answer to his question, the hideous, grinning, yellow skull mask appeared in his eye-line, blocking out the moon. 'You're awake,' said the voice behind the mask.

'Who the fuck are you? What's going on?' Diago complained. 'Let me out.'

'I am the Red Mohawk,' the grinning skull face replied. 'My friend is the Bourbon Kid. We will release you when the time is right.'

Diago wriggled his fingers and toes but that was as much as he could manage. He was acutely aware who the Bourbon Kid was. The man had been a menace to vampires for years. As for the Red Mohawk, he'd heard about him on the news. The masked figure had massacred a whole town full of people once, for no particular reason. 'What did I ever do to you?' Diago asked, desperation in his voice.

'Nothing actually,' the Red Mohawk replied.

The face of the Bourbon Kid appeared alongside the Red Mohawk in the hole at the top of the cylinder. Diago had a flashback to the moment earlier in the night when his dying comrade Yoga informed him that the Bourbon Kid was killing everyone in the Big Top.

'How did you get that coat?' Diago raged. 'Did you steal it from my trailer?'

'No. I took it from you the first time I killed you, a few months from now.'

'Huh? What are you talking about? Why are you doing this? I never did anything to you. Let me out!'

'This is for all the children you murdered in the name of entertainment,' said the Bourbon Kid. 'We know what you've been doing for the Atlanteans. And now it's over.'

'Oh.' If Diago had been unaware of how much shit he was in before, he definitely knew it now. Some bluffing was required. 'Er, what? I don't know what you're talking about.'

'I'm talking about your *spin the wheel* game. You know the one, where your fire-eaters chase kids around the circus ring, or you feed them to the lions or the bear.'

Diago could feel his heart rate doubling. These two weirdoes knew everything. 'If you kill me, the most powerful people in the world will come after you,' he warned them. 'I could help you. I can get to them. The three of us could kill them together. The world leaders, they're the ones forcing us to kidnap the children.'

The Kid and the Mohawk stared down the cylinder at him, but offered nothing in return.

'Please, just let me out of here!' Diago pleaded.

'Certainly,' the Red Mohawk replied. 'You know, we came up with a game that you should have included on your wheel of misfortune.'

'What game?'

'Your wheel never had a section on it for shooting people out of a cannon.'

Diago stopped wiggling his toes. 'I'm in the cannon!' he said, finally realising the uncomfortable truth.

'You are,' said the Mohawk, stepping away.

The Bourbon Kid offered Diago one last thing to think about. 'This is for Flake,' he said. 'Happy trails, Diago.'

The cannon began moving. The face of the Bourbon Kid disappeared. The night sky disappeared too. Everything went black. Diago couldn't see anything at all at the end of the cannon.

'What are you doing?' he cried out in desperation, his voice echoing around him. 'I can pay you. I'll give you a million bucks each. Let's do a deal. And who the hell is Flake?'

When the cannon finished moving, Diago was no longer upright and staring at the sky. He was in a horizontal position, staring at darkness. After a short while, a bright light shone on what was ahead of him. The cannon was pointed at a concrete wall ten metres away.

'Oh God. What the fuck is this?' he said, his fearfulness reaching unprecedented levels. 'You're supposed to wear a helmet when you're fired out of a cannon!'

The masked skull-face reappeared at the end of the cannon at a sideways angle. 'We're having a game of squash,' the Red Mohawk said, the horrible teeth on his mask grinning back at Diago.

'Oh, SHIT! PLEASE NO! I'LL GIVE YOU ANYTHING! ANYTHING!'

The skull face vanished.

What followed was an agonising wait. Diago prayed they were bluffing. He begged and pleaded for his life, offering deals he couldn't make, anything to avoid being fired headfirst into a concrete wall.

The sizzle of a burning fuse beneath his feet added to his state of panic. The cannon was lit. The countdown was on. Diago knew how long the fuse took to burn down. He counted down in his head, praying that his tormentors were just teasing him.

They weren't.

Diago was blasted out of the cannon at lightning-speed. His skull connected with the concrete wall, which brought his flight to an abrupt end. The rest of his body kept moving forward, pushing up into his brain, closing him up like an accordion. The flight from the cannon ended when his feet slammed into the back of his skull, leaving him looking like a puddle of bolognese sauce sliding down a wall. His insides had become his outsides.

As the Bourbon Kid and the Red Mohawk watched Diago's remains slide down a drain into the sewer with the rest of the town's filth, the Kid asked his old friend a question.

'Are you back for good?'

'No. God wants me back in Heaven.'

'Will he let you out again in future, if you're needed?'

The Mohawk held up his hands. 'I don't know. I hope so. It's fucking boring up in Heaven. You can't kill anyone. No drinking, no drugs. No TV. No video games. Everyone's depressed and wishing they'd done more with their time on earth. And things got worse a few months ago when half the world got nuked and millions of people showed up on the same day. It's like a refugee crisis up there. I think that's why God was so keen for me to help you out, make sure you killed Diago and got everything back to how it was. And he wants rid of Sanchez. Heaven's not big enough for him and his annoying habits. He's been using God's private toilet and making a horrible mess in there. It's driving the Lord crazy.'

'I can believe that.' JD pulled at the lapel of the invisible coat he was wearing. 'You want this coat back?'

'No. You can hand that one into Jacko. I've already got the one from Diago's trailer. It's in my car.'

'The Mohawk-mobile is here?'

'It is. Hey, did you know God looks like Dalton from Road House?'

JD sighed. 'I had heard, yeah. When you go back there, say hi to Baby for me. I take it you're still speaking to her after she got you killed?'

Joey's mask hid his feelings on the matter. 'I made a choice,' he said. 'Save Baby or save myself. I coulda killed that fuckin' Cyclops thing, but I chose to shoot at a couple of forest creatures that were gonna kill Baby. I got them, saved her, but then had my fuckin' head ripped off by that one-eyed piece of shit!'

'And then Baby got killed half an hour later anyway....'

'Yeah. It sucks. But, given the choice, I'd still do it again.'

'That's true love, man. If it helps, I did kill the Cyclops for you.'

'Yeah, I know.' Joey threw a friendly punch at JD. 'Listen, I gotta go, I can hear God in my conscience telling me to get a fucking move on.'

The two men clasped hands.

'Until next time,' said the Bourbon Kid.

## Seventy-Nine

It was almost nine p.m. on a Saturday night. Doreen and her husband Fred were snuggled up under a blanket on the sofa in readiness for watching *Dancing with the Stars*. It was the only show they both enjoyed. Fred generally preferred shows about gold mining and house building, whereas Doreen loved the soaps. But *Dancing with the Stars* was a show that reminded them both of the days when they went dancing together. Those days were long gone now. Doreen and Fred were both in their early sixties. Dancing was something they watched rather than participated in.

'I fancy a biscuit and a cup of tea,' said Doreen, getting up. 'Do you want anything?'

Fred pondered the offer. 'I'd better not have any more tea,' he said. 'I'll be peeing all night if I do. But I wouldn't mind one of them chocolate digestives.'

'Righto.'

Doreen headed into the kitchen and put the kettle on. This was a race against time. *Dancing With the Stars* was due to start any minute, and Fred had no idea how to pause the television. She grabbed a mug from the cupboard, dropped a tea bag into it, placed it down on the sideboard, then opened the fridge. Chocolate digestives. Second shelf. She grabbed the packet. It was already open. She pulled out two biscuits. Hesitated. One each? Not enough. She grabbed two more, then closed the fridge door and set the biscuits down on a plate. No need for two plates. One will be enough. The kettle was still boiling. Useless thing. She picked up the plate of biscuits and walked back into the lounge.

Her wrist went limp. The biscuits slid off the plate onto the floor. The plate slipped from her grip and followed the biscuits down. She tried to speak, but the only sound to pass her lips was a tiny squeak. What she really wanted to say was, "Who are you?"

Things had changed in the lounge. Fred was not alone. Their home had been infiltrated. A man in a fuzzy black and white coat was standing behind the sofa, leaning over it, holding a knife against Fred's throat. Doreen recognised the knifeman. It was the notorious mass-murderer, the Bourbon Kid.

'Just do as he says,' Fred whispered.

'Are you Doreen?' the Kid asked, his voice gravelly and hostile.

She nodded frantically before blurting out the word, "yes".

'If you want your husband to stay alive, you'll do exactly as I say. Understand?'

The kettle in the kitchen whistled. The hot water was almost at boiling point. Then the intro music for *Dancing With Stars* kicked in. Everything was happening at once.

Doreen took a breath and nodded. 'I understand.'

## Eighty

After terrorising an elderly couple during an episode of *Dancing On Ice*, JD returned to Purgatory to put matters to bed. He returned the invisible coat to Jacko, polished off another bottle of bourbon, caught up on a few hours of sleep, then rose early in the morning and used the portal to take him to Coldworm Abbey. The place held some bad memories so he didn't loiter inside for long. He headed out to the graveyard where he found the final resting place of Beth Lansbury. He stared down at the headstone on her grave. It had the name Ruth Palmer on it, the alias she had used to avoid being detected by the Devil. On either side of Beth's grave were the headstones for her children, Emma and Vincent. *JD's children.*

The rain was pissing down from the sky like it always did when he visited the graveyard. Graveyards had to be getting statistically higher rainfall than anywhere else. But the rain wasn't really a problem. In fact, JD liked the sound of it pitter-pattering on the hood of his long black coat.

He stared at Beth's grave one last time. He said nothing. Words weren't required. Beth could read his thoughts when she was alive, and she could probably read them now too. He was moving on. In fact, he *had* moved on. He'd moved on with Flake, not that Flake would know anything about it. She would be back with Sanchez, unaware of the alternate future she could have had with JD. Only Jacko and Einstein would know what occurred in the alternate future before JD travelled back in time and undid it all. Einstein was now in Heaven, which just left Jacko. The bluesman would never speak about any of it, JD knew that.

The pitter patter of rain was interrupted by JD's phone ringing. He had an incoming call from Alexis Calhoon. He answered it and put the phone to his ear.

'Hey, what's up?' he asked her.

'Hi, JD,' Calhoon's voice came through loud and clear over the rain. 'How's things?'

'Y'know. Same as ever.'

'Well, I've got a job for you, if you're interested?'

'Let me guess, some asshole wants me to drive his daughter to school?'

Calhoon hesitated for a second. 'How did you know that?' she asked, surprise evident in her voice.

'Lucky guess. How much is the pay?'

'Fifty thousand dollars for a week's work.'

'Tell him to make it a hundred.'

Calhoon seemed taken aback. 'Okay. I can do that. The man who wants to hire you is Antonio Rodriguez. Have you ever heard of him?'

'Yeah, gangster, lives in San Antonio.'

'That's right. Well, um, he's been getting anonymous threats from someone who says they're going to kill his daughter, so naturally he's worried. And because he's rich, he wants to hire the best in the world to protect his little girl. You sure you're okay with a job like that?'

'Yep, I'll do it. One week for one hundred grand. But tell him he's got to hire Rex as well.'

'Rex, as well? Okay, I'll pass that on and see what he says. Can you start tomorrow?'

'Sure thing. Text me the details.'

'Will do, thanks.'

JD ended the conversation and immediately made a call to Purgatory. Jacko answered straight away.

'Hey, man,' said Jacko. 'Are you done?'

'I'm done. I'll be at the portal in two minutes.'

'I'll have it ready.'

JD slipped his phone back into his pocket. He took one last look down at the headstone on Ruth Palmer's grave, and then said what he'd come to say.

'Goodbye Beth.'

## Eighty-One

'Where to next then?' Jacko asked as JD re-entered Purgatory via the portal in the men's toilets.

'Tapioca.'

'You sure you're ready for this?'

'No, but it's got to be done sometime.'

Jacko smiled. 'Don't forget to visit.'

JD turned around. The portal was already open. The toilets in the Tapioca were on the other side. He held up his hand as a goodbye signal to Jacko, then walked through the portal back into the real world.

The Tapioca was empty when he entered, so he helped himself to a free bottle of bourbon and a clean(ish) glass from behind the bar. Then he took a seat at a table in one of the Tapioca's many dark corners.

Ten minutes and half a glass of bourbon later, the peace and quiet ended. Rex and Elvis came bounding in through the front doors. They'd been out drinking all night, so everything they did or said was twice as loud as usual, without them even realising it. Elvis's hair was a mess, and Rex's eye-patch was all over the place. Neither of them spotted JD sitting in the corner. Rex headed straight for the bar to grab some bottles of beer.

Elvis sat down at a table not far from JD. He pulled a deck of cards from his top pocket and set them on the table, at which point he finally spotted JD.

'Hey man,' he said. 'How's things?'

'Pretty good.'

'Been up to much?'

'Nah. Been pretty quiet.'

'Amen to that.'

Rex brought the two beers over to Elvis's table. 'Hey, JD,' he said. 'Wanna join us in a game of cards? We just stole a deck from the casino.'

'I'm good, thanks.'

'Suit yourself.'

A painfully slow thirty minutes passed before Flake showed up. JD's heart missed a beat when he saw her coming down the stairs behind the bar. She was wearing a knee-length grey skirt, a white polo-neck sweater and a grey blazer that matched the skirt. And her hair was in a bun. She looked fantastic, to JD anyway. Other folks often missed her discreet good looks.

When she reached the bottom of the stairs she lifted the bar's serving hatch and walked through it into the drinking area.

'Where's Jasmine?' she asked.

'She's not here,' Elvis replied without even looking up. He placed a card down on the table.

'Well, where is she?'

'Don't ask,' said Rex. He didn't look up either. This was a serious game of cards.

'If you two want any more free drinks you're going to have to tell me where she is.'

Rex glanced up. 'She's gone on a date.'

'A date? Who with?' Flake asked.

Elvis placed another card down on the table and swivelled around on his chair so he could face her. 'Remember she had an agreement with God that he'd take her to a basketball game, or something like that?'

Flake's jaw dropped. 'She's gone on a date with God?'

'Yeah,' Elvis replied. 'Any more questions?'

'I'm about to make breakfast. You guys want any?'

Rex replied for both of them. 'We've been to Dirty Marie's.'

'We could do with some more beers though,' Elvis said as he started dealing out the cards for whatever shit game they were playing.

'Help yourself,' Flake replied. 'You know where they are.'

While all this was going on, JD was staring at Flake. He couldn't take his eyes off her. Her pretty face, her great body, her take-no-shit attitude, her casual style, and just her effortless, inner beauty. Neither Elvis nor Rex had even commented on her outfit. Ignorant fuckers. JD waited for her to look his way. She did. They made eye contact. He smiled, even though what he really wanted to do was get up and grab her, pull her in close, like he'd done so many times before on Medicine Island.

'Nice outfit,' he said. 'Suits you.'

'Thank you, Flake replied, a look of relief on her face. 'It's for my meeting with the president on Friday. Can I get you anything? Or have you been to Filthy Marie's too?'

'Dirty Marie's,' Rex said, correcting her, without looking up from the card game.

Flake ignored him and approached JD's table. 'You okay?' she asked him.

He gestured for her to lean in close so the others didn't hear. She moved in and leaned her head down. She smelled great.

'Lose the bun,' JD whispered. 'You look better with your hair down, or in a ponytail.'

'You think?'

'Yeah. The bun just ain't you.'

Flake reached back and untied the bun, then shook her hair to free it down to her shoulders. 'You didn't answer my question,' she said.

'That's much better.'

'Are you okay? You've been kinda quiet lately.'

'I'm fine.'

It was Flake's turn to lower her voice. 'You're thinking about Beth aren't you?'

JD broke off the eye contact and stared down at his glass of bourbon. 'It's not easy losing someone you thought you'd be with forever.'

'She was the luckiest woman in the world,' Flake assured him. 'She knew that. Don't you forget it.'

'Yeah.'

'You know, you probably don't wanna hear this, but there might be someone else out there for you.'

'It wouldn't matter if there was.'

'Why not?'

'Everyone I care about gets killed. That's my curse.'

Flake shoved him playfully on the shoulder, something she had done many, many times during their time together on the island. 'If that was true,' she said, 'everyone here would be dead too.' Then came the smile. A smile from Flake was like a gift from God. 'Now, I know exactly how to cheer you up,' she said. 'I'll make you one of my epic breakfasts. How does a fry-up sound? I've got bacon, eggs, sausages, mushrooms—'

'Thanks, but no.'

'I make the best breakfasts, you know.'

JD smiled. 'There's more to you than just a good breakfast, Flake.'

Flake's smile broadened, and she came close to blushing. JD still knew how to make her a little nervous.

'It's what I do best though,' she said. 'You know, *you* kill people, Jasmine gets naked, Elvis does his Elvis thing, Rex has his magnetic hand, Sanchez is the luckiest man alive, and me, I do the best breakfasts in the world.'

'You surely do. What's on the menu today?'

'I've been working on something new for Sanchez. A special breakfast sandwich. Maybe you'd like to try it first? Take it for a test drive?'

JD couldn't keep the smile off his face. It was so good to be talking with Flake again. 'Go on,' he said. 'I'll be your guinea pig. Don't fuck it up though.'

'When have I ever fucked up a breakfast?'

And then the moment was ruined. Sanchez came thundering down the stairs. When he reached the bottom he stopped and looked around for Flake. He soon spotted her. 'Flake, I want two extra sausages today,' he called over to her. 'And I think I'll have some beans too. My gut's a bit bloated so the beans might help shift a bit of the trapped wind.'

Flake turned away from JD. 'Okay honey,' she called back. 'But I was going to try out my new breakfast sandwich on you today.'

'I don't want a *new* breakfast,' Sanchez replied, recoiling in horror. 'Can you just do the regular please? For fuck's sake! I'm fucking starving.'

'I'll get right on it.' Flake looked back at JD. 'You still want the new sandwich?'

'You bet.'

While Flake headed off to the kitchen to get started, Sanchez strolled over to the table where Rex and Elvis were playing cards.

'What game are you playing?' he asked them.

'You can't play,' said Elvis.

'Why not?'

'Because we're not playing Snap,' said Rex. 'It would take too long to teach you the rules to this game.'

Before Sanchez could grumble about being left out, the door to the ladies washroom opened and Jasmine strolled out. She was wearing a pair of blue cut-off jeans and a white crop top that showed off her silky-smooth brown skin. Her hair was tied back in a ponytail.

'Hi guys,' she beamed. 'Ooh, cards, can I play?'

'They're not playing Snap,' Sanchez informed her.

'Why not?'

'How was your date?' Elvis asked, placing his cards down on the table to signify he'd had enough of the card game.

'We watched a game of basketball in Australia,' Jasmine said. She walked up to Elvis and kissed him on the cheek. 'It was fun.'

'And?'

'And I gave him a handjob.'

Rex spat some beer out onto the table. 'You jerked off God?'

Jasmine slid down onto Elvis's knee and wrapped an arm around his shoulder. A brief discussion took place about whether or not Elvis was okay with the love of his life giving God a handjob. While the debate kept everyone else occupied, JD had his eyes on the kitchen. He could see Flake through the open door. She was laying strips of bacon out on the grill. This was going to be tough, seeing her all the time. Her not knowing they had been living together on a desert island, very much in love. Seeing her with Sanchez was going to be the worst thing about it. There were some rough times on the horizon.

JD's maudlin thoughts came to an abrupt end when he heard Jasmine inform Elvis that to get even with her for jerking off God, he was allowed to sleep with someone else, just once.

Elvis agreed with the deal, and immediately called out to the kitchen. 'Yo, Flake, you up for it?'

'Dream on, loser!' came the reply from within the kitchen.

*"Brilliant,"* JD thought to himself, *"don't ever change, girl."*

Sanchez was less impressed. He put his hands on his hips and glared at Elvis. 'I'm right here you know,' he said.

'I know,' said Elvis. 'I was just keeping you in the loop.'

'Well, stay away from Flake,' Sanchez said in his toughest voice.

'Or what?' said Elvis.

'Or she'll kick you in the nuts.'

Rex sighed. 'Are we playing cards anymore or what?'

'Is it Snap?' Jasmine asked.

'No,' said Rex. 'It ain't Snap.'

'Fine.' Jasmine jumped up from Elvis's knee and headed back to the washroom. Rex picked up the deck of cards and started shuffling them. Before he had a chance to deal any out, a phone buzzed on the table in front of him.

'Hold on a sec,' he said, putting the cards down. 'I've gotta take this.' He answered the call. 'Hello, General, what can I do for you?'

'Is that Calhoon?' Elvis asked.

Rex nodded. For the next thirty seconds he had a discussion with Calhoon about a job. When the call was over he put the phone down on the table and eyed JD suspiciously.

'Calhoon says you insisted on me joining you on a bodyguard job?' he said.

'Uh huh,' JD replied.

'You're lucky it pays well,' said Rex. 'Otherwise I wouldn't be going.'

'You never know, you might like it.'

'What about me?' Elvis asked. 'Am I not needed?'

JD shrugged. 'I thought you'd want to spend some time with Jasmine.'

A commotion in the ladies washroom was followed by Jasmine's reappearance. Only this time, she wasn't alone. She was accompanied by a large brown dog. JD recognised it straight away. It was Goober. The big hound spotted Flake coming back out of the kitchen and immediately charged right at her.

'Holy shit!' said Flake, panicking.

Goober leapt up at her and almost knocked her over. Flake managed to stay upright and stroked the dog's head while he licked her face with great enthusiasm. 'Sheesh!' said Flake, looking around at the others. 'He's friendly.'

Jasmine smiled. 'He loves you.'

JD glanced over at Jasmine. She was smiling at him, a very smug smile.

'Why the fuck have we got a dog in here?' Rex asked.

'I thought JD might like him for company,' Jasmine replied. Then she whistled at Goober, which brought the excited dog back down to earth. He looked round at Jasmine. She pointed at JD. Goober spotted him in the corner and galloped over to him, leaving Flake to wipe a patch of drool off her face. Goober put his paws up on JD's legs and stared at him with his tongue out. The dog had love in his eyes.

'Wow!' said Flake. 'Where did you get him from, Jas?'

'Rescued him,' Jasmine said proudly. 'He got separated from his previous owners. His name is Goober.'

Flake scratched her head. 'And you thought JD would want him?'

'Oh yeah. I know JD better than any of you.'

All eyes turned to JD. Goober was making a major fuss of him, and to the surprise of the others, JD was appreciative of the affection.

After ten seconds of fussing over JD, Goober bounded back to Flake and gazed up at her with adoring eyes, or possibly hungry eyes because the smell of sausages and bacon was floating around.

'I always wanted a dog,' Flake said. 'Are you hungry, boy? He looks hungry. I'll make him some sausages.'

'Fucking hell!' said Sanchez, shaking his head. 'We can't have a dog in here. It'll be pissing and shitting everywhere!'

'Then you and him should get along just fine,' said Elvis.

Sanchez changed the subject. 'Flake, shouldn't you be checking on the breakfast? I don't want my sausages burned again, or licked by a dog for that matter. You know if that dog gets a taste of your amazing cooking we'll never get rid of him.'

Flake walked up to Sanchez, grabbed the sides of his head then pulled him in for a kiss. 'Are you worried he'll love my cooking more than you?' she teased.

'No one will ever love your cooking as much as me,' said Sanchez, slapping Flake across the ass. 'Now get back in that kitchen, you sexy little minx.'

Flake giggled. 'I'll get right on it.' She fussed over Goober some more then looked over at JD. 'Do you mind me feeding your dog?'

JD shook his head. 'He loves your cooking.'

'Does he?'

'Of course he does. He loves you too. I can tell.'

Flake blushed ever-so-slightly. 'Jas, do you want any breakfast' she asked. 'I'm doing a biggie for Sanchez, and my new breakfast sandwich for JD.'

'I haven't really got time for a big breakfast,' said Jasmine. 'But thanks for the offer.'

Flake returned to the kitchen with Goober following close behind. Jasmine strolled over to JD's table and sat down beside him. 'Got a good view of the kitchen from here, haven't you?' she said.

JD smiled at her with his eyes. 'You remember much?'

Jasmine kissed him on the cheek. 'I remember everything,' she said. 'So, next time you're thinking of leaving me stranded on a desert island, just remember, I'm friends with God.'

'Got it.'

'Oh, and one other thing. That Navan Douglas fella, he's not a problem anymore.'

'Navan Douglas? I forgot about that prick. He's gonna give Flake and Sanchez those rings with tracking devices in, isn't he?'

'He *was*,' said Jasmine. 'But I took care of it.' She pulled her phone out of her hip pocket. 'Take a look at this.' She held up the phone so JD could see the screen. It had a naked photo of her on it.

'Why am I looking at this?' he asked.

'Hang on, that's the wrong one. Let me find it.' She flicked through a few more naked photos of herself in various positions before she eventually stopped on the photo she was looking for. It was a picture of Navan Douglas. It being Jasmine's phone, he was naked. It wasn't a pretty sight. He was lying on his side on a King-sized bed with a large pink dildo up his bum. Jasmine swiped onto the next photo where the dildo had been removed from his asshole and shoved into his mouth. She flicked through a few more photos of Douglas in compromising positions. Some of the pictures featured Jasmine doing things to Douglas with the dildo.

'Okay, I've seen enough, thanks,' said JD after the eighth or ninth photo. 'How did you manage this?'

'I was just helping to clean up your mess. Navan resigned this morning because he didn't want his wife seeing these.'

'Hang on a sec,' said JD, rubbing his forehead. 'Who took the photos?'

'Jacko did. He was in the room with us, but he was wearing the invisible coat, so Navan Douglas never saw him. He's quite a good photographer, don't you think?'

'You did good, Jas. I owe you one.'

'You owe me lots. I've got one more trip to make to tie up your loose ends.'

'What loose ends?'

'Well, for starters, the government still wants Zero dead because he filmed the president jerking off.'

'Oh right, that.'

'And of course, killing the elite didn't really work out did it? So I'm going to get them another way.'

Before JD could ask how, Elvis called over to them. 'What are you two talking about?'

'I'm just showing JD some photos of me playing with a dildo.'

'Fair enough.' Elvis laid another card down on the table and resumed his game with Rex.

Jasmine slipped her phone back into her pocket. JD was staring into the kitchen again, watching Flake make the breakfast. Jasmine reached into his top pocket and pulled out his sunglasses. 'You should wear these for a while,' she said, opening them up and then sliding them on over his ears. 'Or everyone will see you what you're staring at.'

JD grabbed Jasmine's hand and squeezed it. 'You're a good friend.'

Jasmine winked at him. 'I'd better go,' she said. 'I've got places to be.' She stood up and walked past Rex and Elvis on her way back to the toilets.

When JD looked over at the kitchen again, he saw Flake by the stove. She was putting a bowl of water down on the floor for Goober. She looked up at JD and smiled. He smiled back. The smile was swiftly interrupted by Sanchez. The tubby bartender walked into the kitchen and started singing the opening verse of his irritating "Do they know it's Breakfast?" song. When he sang the line, "throw your arms around Flake at breakfast time," he snuck up behind her and did just that. They sang the rest of the song together while Flake flipped the food over on the grill and Sanchez squeezed her tightly, like he never wanted to let her go.

## Eighty-Two

For the president of the United States of America, a hot shower on a Sunday morning was one of the best moments of the week. He had time to himself to think about the best ways to stay in power without doing anything to benefit the general public. As he rinsed some shampoo out of what was left of his hair, he contemplated the best way to get more guns into the hands of American teenagers.

He had a fairly quiet day scheduled. It was already 9.15 a.m. and so far no one had phoned to tell him about any mass-shootings anywhere in the country. What a great day to be president. He turned the water temperature on the shower to cold for thirty seconds, before stepping out and drying off with a towel as he admired himself in the bathroom mirror. When he'd finished drying he noticed the bathroom door was closed, which was unusual. He normally kept it open to stop the mirror from steaming up.

He opened the door and walked into the bedroom. He also walked into an ambush. A blur of movement blindsided him, and someone rammed their knee into his balls. That fucking hurt. The president's nut-sack bounced back and forth like a boxer's speed-bag. He dropped to his knees and cupped his balls while he looked up to see who had inflicted the assault on him.

'Good morning, Mister President,' said the lady standing over him. She had creamy brown skin and long dark hair, and she was wearing blue cut-off jeans and a white crop top. The president recognised her immediately from one of his favourite porn clips.

'Holy shit. Lady Sack-punch!'

'Is that what they're calling me these days?' the woman replied.

'It's Jasmine isn't it?' the president said, still wincing at the pain inflicted on him.

'Yes. Your friend Navan Douglas ordered me for you as his resignation present. He said you'd been working hard and I was just what you needed.'

'He did?'

'Yes sir. I'm here to destroy your ring.'

'My what?'

Jasmine reached down and grabbed the president by his arm. He was expecting her to lift him up. But what she actually did was clip a set of handcuffs onto his wrist, then move his arms behind his back and cuff his hands together.

'Woah, this is kinky!' said the president, sensing some great fun on the horizon.

Jasmine dragged him up by his armpits and manoeuvred him over to the King-size bed in the middle of the room. She pushed him down onto it, his face plunging into the soft duvet. He looked up at a set of mirrored closet doors and saw Jasmine standing behind him. She was strapping something onto herself. Something big. What followed was something the president hadn't experienced in weeks. Jasmine treated him to one hell of an ass-pounding with the biggest strap-on dildo he'd ever encountered. She moved him into some pretty serious positions too. He had no idea he was so flexible. Eventually, when she was done with his ass, she moved around to his mouth and treated him to some deep-throat action so he could get an idea what his butt-hole tasted like. For a Sunday morning this was a rare treat. The president made a mental note to send Navan Douglas some Cuban cigars as a thank you present.

Unfortunately, when all the excitement was over, things turned a bit sour for the most powerful man in the world. Jasmine refused to un-cuff him. Instead she plucked a cell phone out of thin air.

'See this?' she said.

'Yes,' said the president, who was lying on his back on the bed with his hands still cuffed behind him.

Jasmine moved around the bed and held the phone up in front of his face. 'This is a photo of the Russian president and one of his bodyguards,' she said. The photo showed the Russian leader in a compromising position with another man and a blow-up sex doll. Both men were naked, but the bodyguard was behind the Russian leader, spooning him and giving him a reach-around.

'How did you get that picture?' the president asked.

'I'm a very resourceful girl.' Jasmine flicked to the next picture, which was of Navan Douglas with a dildo up his ass.

'Wow. You really get around.'

'I do.' She flicked through some more pictures of Navan Douglas getting the same treatment as the president himself had just received. Then she came to some pictures of the pounding she had just given him.

'How did you get those?' he asked, confused.

'I have an invisible friend with me.'

'What?'

'Here's what's going to happen next,' said Jasmine. 'As you probably know by now, your friends at the vampire circus are all dead. And if you and your fellow Atlanteans ever participate in any more kiddy snuff movies with vampires or anyone else, I'll see to it that these photos of you go public. So next time you have a meeting with all your fellow weirdoes, you'd better make it clear to them, the Dead Hunters are onto you, and we can get to anyone at any time. Do you understand?'

The president nodded. 'I do.'

'And I have a friend named Zero who filmed you jerking off to some lion porn. He's handed that footage over to me. Now, if anyone hunts down Zero or any of his friends, I will leak that footage, and bring you down, you and all your Atlantean friends. Get it?'

More frantic nodding. 'Yes, yes, I understand. No more killing kids, and no one touches Zero, I swear.'

'Good, because one slip-up and I'll be back. But next time it won't be a dildo that goes up your butt. It'll be a shotgun.'

To the president's surprise a black man appeared alongside Jasmine. He looked just like Robert Johnson the famous bluesman from the nineteen-thirties. He was wearing the creepy Coat of No Colours.

'What the fuck?'

'I'm Jacko,' the man said. 'And I'm taking this invisible coat with me. No one will ever wear it again, unless you and your friends break any of Jasmine's rules, understand?'

'I do, yes.'

'Good.' Jacko looked at Jasmine. 'Ready to go?'

'Yep.'

'Hey wait,' said the president. 'You haven't uncuffed me.'

Jasmine pulled a small key from the pocket of her cut-offs. 'Okay,' she said in a sweet voice. 'Roll over onto your side, bitch!'

The president hesitated. He glanced down at his penis, which was erect. 'Umm, could you finish me off first?'

Jasmine looked at Jacko to see how he felt about the idea.

Jacko sighed. 'Fine. Make it quick. I'll wait in the bathroom.'

## Eighty-Three

Doreen's drive to work was something she usually enjoyed. She loved her job. And she took great pride in what she did. But the visit from the Bourbon Kid during *Dancing With the Stars* had shaken her up. What he was asking her to do was unprecedented, and weird. Not to mention, unethical. And likely to get her fired. Or reported to the police. But as the Kid had assured her, if she told the truth, the authorities would understand, because she had no choice. If she didn't do it, the Bourbon Kid would come back, and he would kill her husband Fred while she watched. Then he would kill her. Then he would go to their son's house and kill him. The guy was a psychopath.

She spent the early part of the day wondering if she should share her problem with her colleagues. But she was afraid to. The Bourbon Kid could get to her anywhere. He could be hiding in the shadows, listening.

When the moment came for her to carry out the Bourbon Kid's instructions, her hands trembled. She was on a stage in front of an audience of three hundred schoolgirls. Several of her colleagues were sitting behind her, waiting for her to give her weekly speech. They were in for a surprise. That much was certain. Doreen checked her mic was on. It was.

*"Quit stalling,"* she told herself. Just do it.

'Good morning everyone,' she said, addressing the entire hall.

'Good morning Mrs Lampkin,' the girls all replied in their usual sarcastic tone.

She looked down on the innocent faces of the schoolchildren. How were they going to react to this? Not well, probably. She scoured the hall, looking for Paige Rodriguez. The girl with the pudding bowl haircut was standing in a fairly central position in the audience, looking at the floor. Everyone else had their eyes on Doreen Lampkin, their headmistress.

'First up, I have an important announcement to make,' she said. *Here goes nothing.* 'It has been brought to my attention that some of the girls in this assembly have been stealing Paige Rodriguez's lunch, which consists of six tubs of custard and a banana.'

There were some interesting responses to that revelation. A few giggles, plenty of side-eye glances, a few girls looking around for Paige, and then Paige herself looking up at the stage with a furrowed brow.

Doreen took a deep breath. The next part was going to be brutal. She read it directly from the card she was holding in her trembling hand. 'From this day forth, anyone bullying Paige Rodriguez, or stealing her lunch, will be expelled from this school. And if their parents complain, they will be murdered.'

That part was greeted with some gasps, whispers, and a few nervous giggles. It would only get worse.

She carried on. 'Their grandparents will also be murdered.'

One of the teachers sitting behind Doreen, muttered, "What the hell?" It kick-started a whole wave of muttering all around the school hall.

'To summarise what I am saying,' Doreen continued, raising her voice. 'If anyone picks on Paige Rodriguez or steals her lunch, they will get a visit from her friend, the Bourbon Kid. Do you all understand?'

After a short pause, the audience replied in unison, "Yes, Mrs Lampkin".

'Thank you,' said Doreen. 'That will be all.'

## Eighty-Four

Rex drove his van up to the black, arched, iron gates at the front of the Rodriguez estate. Someone must have seen him arrive because the gates opened up for him, enabling him to cruise through without stopping. The estate was enormous. As he drove up to the main house he got a good view of a golf course that was set back from the road, and surrounded by woodland.

He parked the van in a space next to a big black Mercedes. Normally he would have ridden to a place like this on his Harley, but knowing that he could be staying for a week, he'd packed some clothes, and more importantly, enough weapons and ammunition to take out a small army, just in case. He exited the van, pulled open a side door and grabbed his bag. He slung it over his shoulder, locked the van, and headed for a set of gold-rimmed wooden doors at the front of the building. One of the doors opened as he approached.

A handsome, well-tanned man in his fifties walked out and greeted Rex with a big smile that showed off some bright white teeth. The man was in good shape for his age. He was dressed all in white, with the top three buttons of his shirt undone, showing off a smooth bronzed chest. He had thick brown hair, the kind that looked like a wig but probably wasn't.

'Rodeo Rex!' he said, cheerfully. 'Great to meet you.'

'Thanks,' said Rex. 'Would you be Antonio?'

'That's right,' the man replied. 'Did you get the message?'

'What message?'

'Oh,' Antonio grimaced. 'They didn't tell you?'

'Tell me what? Is the job off?'

'Kinda, yes. The people who were threatening to kill my daughter have been eliminated.'

'Seriously? I've driven all this way, and the job is off?'

'Yes, I'm afraid so. I only found out this morning. But, hey, you've travelled all this way, so why not stay for a few days? I'll pay you twenty thousand just for the inconvenience we've caused you.'

Rex groaned. 'Does my buddy the Bourbon Kid know the job has been cancelled?'

'Yes. General Calhoon phoned me an hour ago to say he wasn't coming. He was supposed to call you and tell you not to come.'

Rex was seething. 'Well he didn't. That motherfucker!'

'Come on in,' said Antonio, slapping Rex on the arm. 'Take a shower, use the pool, have some drinks, play some golf. Relax. There's something here for everyone. Give it a chance. I guarantee you, if you take a look around, you'll fall in love with the place. Whadda you say?'

The long drive had left Rex feeling sticky and in need of a shower. He was wearing blue jeans and a black leather waistcoat, and he had a black and gold Harley Davidson bandana wrapped around his head, just to make sure everyone knew that in spite of the van, he was really a proud biker. But even so, he really wasn't interested in spending time with a gangster and his henchmen.

The clip-clop of a horse's hooves filtered into Rex's ears while he was deciding what to do. A woman on horseback approached from the golf course area. It took only one glance to see she was a stunner. She had long dark hair, creamy skin that seemed to glow, brown eyes and a beautiful smile. She was wearing skin-tight black pants, brown ankle boots and a white blouse. At a guess, Rex would have said she was in her mid-twenties.

'That's my wife, Selene,' said Antonio, catching sight of Rex looking at her. 'She's a lazy bitch, but she's great in bed. So, what do you say, stay for a while? You can be my guest of honour. All my henchmen are dying to hear all about your adventures. Come on, eh!'

'I don't think so,' said Rex. 'It's kind of you to offer, but I think I'll head home.'

Antonio looked disappointed. 'Okay, but let me get you your money,' he said. 'Wait here. I'll be right back.'

Rex grabbed Antonio's arm, stopping him from moving. 'Fifty grand just for showing up, wasn't it?' he said.

Antonio grinned. 'You drive a hard bargain, my friend. Fifty it is, just for showing up!'

Rex let go of Antonio's arm. The rich, greasy, gangster-bastard headed back inside his enormous house to find what Rex assumed would be a bag filled with cash.

Instead of waiting around, Rex returned to his van and opened the sliding door on the side. He slung his bag back in, then pulled the door shut again. He turned around in time to see Antonio's wife Selene dismount from her horse. A young stableboy took the horse by its reins and led it away.

Selene wiped some stray hair from her forehead. Then she looked over at Rex and smiled. 'You must be Rodeo Rex?' she said.

'I am. And you are Selene, if I'm not mistaken?'

'That's right.' She walked up to Rex, took off one of her riding gloves and held out her hand. 'Nice to meet you. Should I call you Rex, or Rodeo Rex?'

'Rex will do fine.' He shook her hand gently with his gloved metal hand.

'Oh, goodness,' said Selene. 'That is a firm grip.'

'Metal hand,' said Rex. 'I tried to go easy on you.'

Selene smiled. 'I'm sorry. I was warned. No one said you had an eye patch though. It's none of my business, but what happened there?'

'I had a run-in with some cannibals.'

There was a pause while Selene took the revelation on board. 'Okay, I'm sorry, I shouldn't have asked.'

'It's okay. You're actually the first one.'

'To ask about your eye patch?'

'Yeah. The cannibal thing was quite recent, and no one I've met since it happened has had the guts to ask about it. Congratulations though, I've been waiting.'

Selene smiled again. It made Rex melt a little inside. Her wealthy, gangster husband was a lucky man.

'I see you just put your bag away,' she said, nodding at the van. 'Are you not staying?'

'No,' said Rex. 'The job I came to do has been cancelled.'

'That's too bad. You would have liked it here. You're a biker, is that right?'

'Yeah. Not normally one for driving a van.'

'You ever ridden a horse?'

'Few times, yeah.'

Selene smiled with her eyes. 'Too bad you're leaving then. We could have gone for a morning ride together. The view around here in the morning is stunning.'

'I don't doubt it.'

'It was nice to meet you anyway,' said Selene. 'Have a safe journey home.'

'Nice to meet you too.'

Selene gave Rex one last smile, then walked through the front doors into the house. She bumped into her husband Antonio in the reception hall. He was returning with a brown satchel filled with Rex's money.

'Have a nice ride?' Antonio asked her.

'Yes, thanks.' She looked at the satchel. 'Is that for the biker man?'

'Mind your own fucking business,' he said, slapping her across her backside. 'And do me a favour, make yourself scarce tonight. I've got someone coming over.'

Antonio didn't wait for a response from Selene. He wiped the aggressive look off his face, put on a fake smile, and strolled outside to pay Rex his money. As he set foot on the frontage he saw Rex closing up the sliding door on his van. His sports bag was on the ground. He bent down and picked it up, then walked over to Antonio.

'What's this?' said Antonio. 'You changed your mind? Decided to stay?'

'I sure have,' said Rex. 'I thought about it, and figured what the hell, I could use a vacation.'

'That's great news,' said Antonio, handing him the satchel containing the cash. 'I knew I could convince you to stay. Come, I'll get the housekeeper to show you to your room. You're gonna love it here! Tell me, what made you change your mind?'

'What can I say?' said Rex. 'You were right. I think I'm gonna like it here.'

The End (maybe…)

Printed in Great Britain
by Amazon